BLOOD **DEMANDS** BLOOD.

OTHER BOOKS IN THE
PROJECT W. A. R. TRILOGY

ULTRAXENOPIA

TYPE X

SUBJECT ZERO

COMPANION NARRATIVE

THE RICHTER FILES

SUBJECT ZERO
PROJECT W. A. R. BOOK THREE

M. A. PHIPPS

SHIRE-HILL
PUBLICATIONS

SUBJECT ZERO
PROJECT W.A.R. BOOK THREE

Copyright © 2022 M. A. Phipps
WWW.MAPHIPPS.COM
WWW.BOOKISHDEN.COM

This book is a work of fiction. Names, characters, places, and incidents are either products of the author's imagination or are used fictitiously. Any resemblance to actual persons, living, dead or otherwise, events, or locales is entirely coincidental.

Cover design by Nathalia Suellen
Interior design by We Got You Covered Book Design
WWW.WEGOTYOUCOVEREDBOOKDESIGN.COM

SHIRE-HILL PUBLICATIONS
UNITED KINGDOM

ISBN: 978-1-914483-04-2

For the readers and friends who have stuck with me
to the end of this series. Thank you.

TRIGGER WARNING

Contains dark themes and scenes of violence

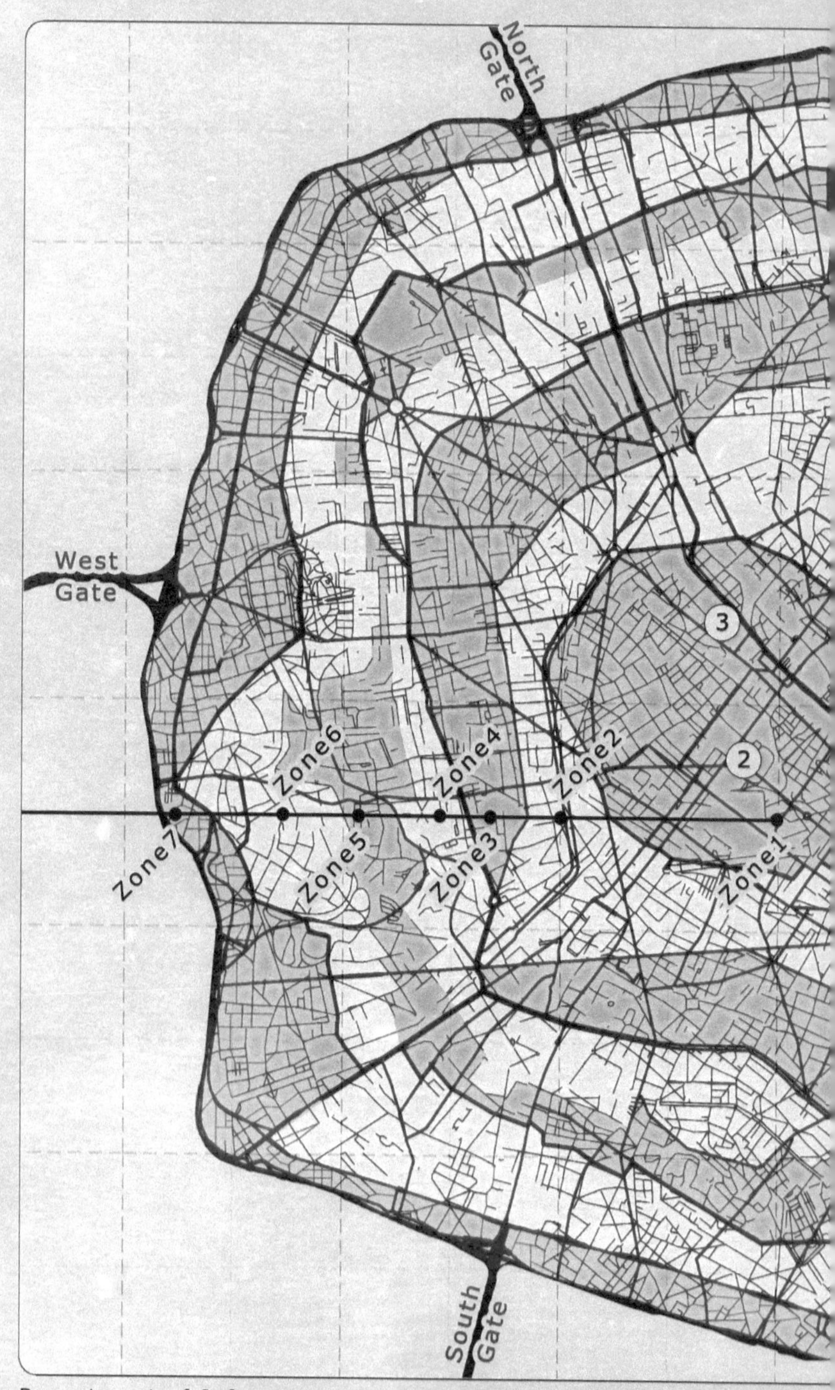

Department of Infrastructure - Document #00425

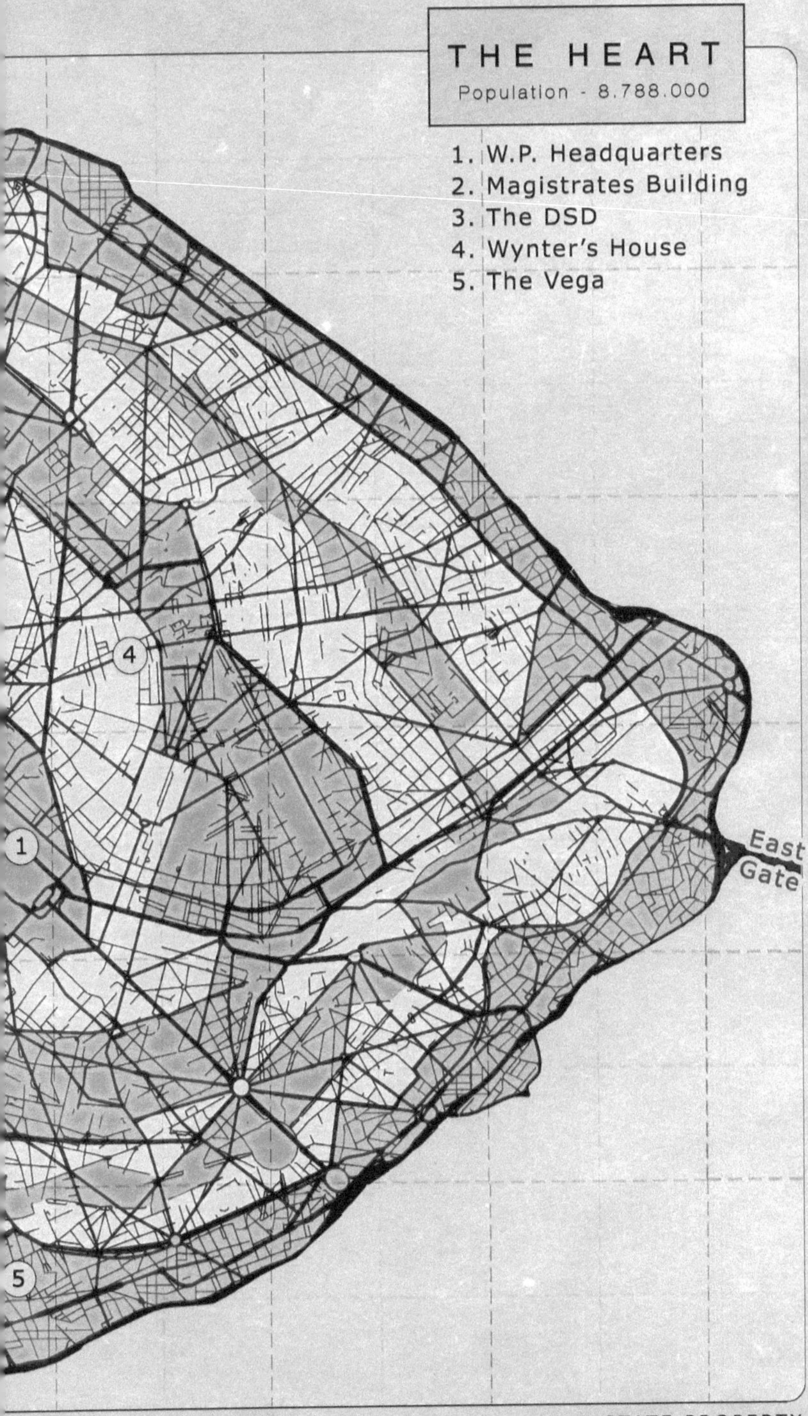

THE HEART
Population - 8.788.000
1. W.P. Headquarters
2. Magistrates Building
3. The DSD
4. Wynter's House
5. The Vega
East
Gate
STATE PROPERTY

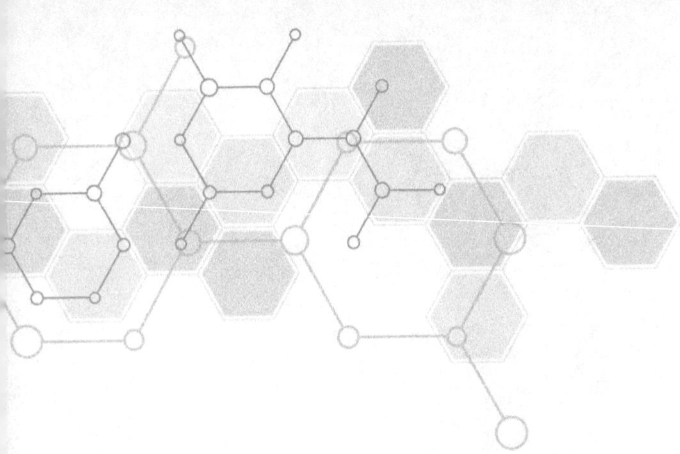

At the pinnacle of war, only sacrifice stands
between destruction and survival.

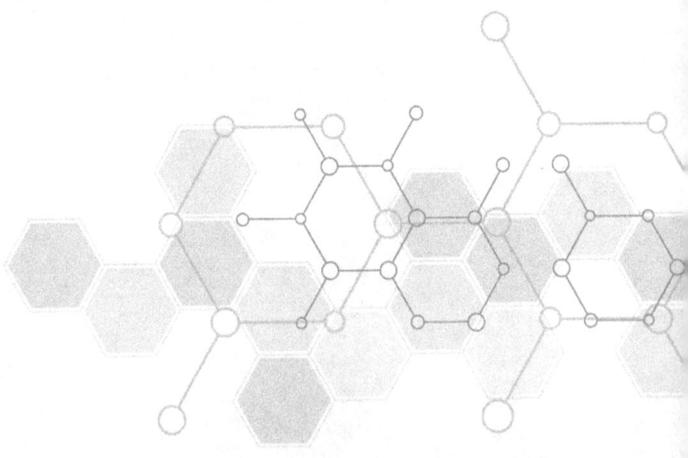

ONE

PAIN, VIOLENT AND MADDENING, TEARS through my body like a rush of heat, boiling my organs and burning every inch of my limbs on its rise to my skin from the inside out. The agony pounding through my head is only interrupted by the clang of metal against tile, the sound of the impact a sharp, grating scratch that draws my blurring gaze to the floor. My breaths reverberate in my ears, and blinking a hazy film of tears from my eyes, I glimpse the outline of my discarded collar.

The one tool keeping my power in check now a hunk of useless metal, destroyed, at my feet.

For the last few years, I wanted nothing more than to be free of this tether to Dr. Richter and to the constant trauma I endured at his hands. But, as the understanding of what losing this link will mean sinks in past the expanding surface of pain, I find myself mourning its loss almost more than I grieved over my father or Rai. Perhaps because, without it, I know there's nothing I can do to save anyone from the monster living and thriving within me—the monster its removal has unleashed on this world.

Without the collar, the few people I have left are dead.

A convulsion barrels through my weakening body, and as the seizure intensifies, my legs buckle, no longer able to support the burden of my weight. What little strength I've been clinging to slips away like heat escaping my skin in the cold.

My lungs constrict as small gasps of air leach from my lungs. I can't breathe. I can't breathe. I can't think. A black mist unfurls across my eyes, and through the expanding fog, I glimpse the exam room floor rushing upward like the jaws of hell opening to swallow me whole.

My kneecaps slam hard into the gleaming white tiles, coaxing a strangled cry from my lips. Although unpleasant, the jarring jolt to my bones is insignificant compared to the fire of pain raging through me. I can feel it—the returning threat of death as it infiltrates my veins like a fast-acting poison, spreading quickly. Burning my insides. The monster has been patient, awaiting this moment, while I've been living on borrowed time, foolishly hoping and, at times, even allowing myself to believe, this day wouldn't come.

Time this disease will now strive to steal back.

Without the collar, the only thing in this world capable of ensuring my survival is gone. There's nothing else in existence that can slow or cure the parasitic plague of my condition. Without the collar to pause the advance of my illness—to keep me in much-needed control—my symptoms will just resume their assault from before the respite of Richter's so-called cure and lead me into the smothering tides of what is sure to be an agonizing death. Now, when all hope is lost, the monster will win. And soon, Wynter Reeves, as I am at this moment…

This side of me will cease to exist.

The unrelenting full extent of Ultraxenopia—finally free of

its cage and running rampant inside me—seems to take on a physical form with its assault, sinking its claws into my flesh without mercy and reclaiming the hold it lost the day Dr. Richter ensnared me in this collar. It grabs me, squeezes me tight in its suffocating embrace, whispers familiar taunts in my ears.

Goosebumps pimple my flesh as it hisses those three weighted words, which have followed me since I was a child.

"I'm sorry, Wynter," the monster says. It speaks in a strange muddled voice, half my father but also half Ezra—a hybrid of the two people I love most in the world, created from my most painful memories and torn straight from the one moment I want to avoid.

The one moment that haunts me now more than ever.

As the mental image of it manifests in my thoughts, the exam room melts away to reveal a warped twin version of myself, the deep pools of her soulless eyes staring back into mine, black, empty, and unblinking. Around us, ash and dirt hang heavy in the air like smog, the taste of death and decay thick on my tongue.

The silence between us is unnerving, but when I part my lips to break it, the ground quakes, signaling the impending end of all life, as if that one unspoken word is the catalyst for the future I've been trying to run from. A moan rips through the desolate landscape, vibrating through the musty air and under my feet, and on all sides, the buildings of the Heart tremble for a moment before caving inward. Surrendering to their fate, they collapse, crumbling into jagged mountains of rock and glass.

"I'm afraid!" the other me shrieks, her voice clear despite the thunderous rumbling all around us. My gaze darts back to hers, my heart racing. But, to my bemusement, her lips don't move and her face is composed—a mask of stone. Unmoving. Unfeeling.

Resigned.

I furrow my brow, staring into her eyes where I see myself reflected in their inky depths. Like her, I've lost what little semblance of humanity I had retained in my appearance. Now, I look inhuman.

Like the angel of death Richter and the State shaped me into.

As my black-eyed twin continues airing her woes, her lips eerily still despite her cries, it registers that the ranting I'm hearing isn't coming from her—from this manifestation of the monster I'm becoming. It's coming from me. *My* fears. *My* emotions, long bottled up.

All of it, every word…

I'm the one saying it.

Tears slip down my cheeks at this realization and gather on my lower lip, filling my mouth with the tang of salt when I speak.

"I don't want to kill anyone else. I don't want to do this. I don't want to die!"

Nodding, the monster extends her hand and touches her fingertips to my right cheek, as if to ease my fear with her touch. But the relief I anticipate doesn't come.

Instead, I feel only terror when her skin grazes mine, my stomach turning as the contact between us triggers the world to tilt on its axis, throwing my center of gravity off balance. Darkness seeps in at the edges of my vision, smudging her face and the surrounding apocalyptic wasteland, both fading into black as I tip to the side, falling…falling…

Falling.

A searing pain spreads through my left shoulder and arm as I collide with the floor, the chill of the ceramic sinking into my bodysuit like a rush of ice water. I'm cold, so cold, and my lids are heavy, but I fight against the temptation of sleep, forcing my eyes to stay open.

Slowly, as I cling to waking, the features of the exam room slide back into focus, and I concentrate on each detail before me in turn, a shaky breath parting my lips. The dim blue light. Rai's body stretched out on the bed. Ezra, Jenner, and Quinn… all motionless on the floor. And *him*.

The man behind this chaos.

Dr. Richter leans over me with a smug smile, squatting down to the floor, his elbows perched on his knees. "Shh…" he croons, brushing the sweat-matted hair from my eyes. "Everything is going to be all right. Soon, this will all be over."

Holding my gaze, he reaches inside his coat, his hand emerging a few seconds later from the interior chest pocket, fingers clamped around a syringe. With a quiet laugh, he flattens his palm, presenting the capped needle like a trophy. I suppose, to him, it is. A symbol of his power and control over me.

Dread turns my stomach. There's nothing I can do. He'll inject me with the syringe's contents and I won't be able to fight back or stop him, every inch of me held down by debilitating pain. I'm helpless. No…worse than that.

I'm powerless.

More tears track down the sides of my face. This is like the collar all over again—another way for him to show he owns me and can do whatever he wants with my body, my own desires and wishes be damned. Just as he's proven time and again throughout the years we've known each other, I can never outsmart him.

Dr. Richter will always win.

I glance down at the shimmery silver liquid inside the

transparent barrel, which glistens in the minimal light illuminating the room. It would be beautiful if the threat of it wasn't so obvious.

Pinching the syringe between his fingers, Dr. Richter removes the plastic cap with his teeth, spitting the clear shell back out on the floor. With his other hand, he grabs me by the back of my neck, raising my rigid body upright.

I whimper, my pulse throbbing deep in my ears. "What... is...that?" I wheeze, glaring down at his hand.

"Shh..." he says again, his grip on me tightening.

His nails dig into my neck, and I wince as the needle punctures the skin at my throat. The liquid is bitterly cold when it enters my body, and I shiver as it passes through me, spreading along the underside of my skin. The sensation—a freezing prickle followed by fire—sends all my nerve endings into a frenzy, igniting the pain receptors in my brain until I feel the frigid burn everywhere.

A rising sense of panic swells deep in my chest, but when I try to scream, the hoarse cry that rips from my throat is a broken sob barely louder than a breath. Every second is drawn out by the agony swelling inside me. I can't take it.

I just want it to stop.

Another seizure strikes without warning, the tremors tearing through me more violent this time. Discarding the syringe, Dr. Richter smooths a hand over my forehead, considering me with a spine-chilling fondness. As his fingers move down the side of my face, caressing my wet cheek, my limbs jerk uncontrollably and bile surges up from my stomach.

It's only now, as the pain sinks deeper and death creeps closer, that I realize my plan has failed. I can't turn myself over to the people attacking the Heart and end this war I'm responsible for...because I'm going to die before I can even attempt to. I'm going to die before I can change a damn thing, and Richter will watch, smiling, as the world dies, too.

My teeth chatter, threatening to bite off the tip of my tongue, when the convulsions intensify, each spasm—along with Dr. Richter's hands—pinning my hips and legs to the floor. My tormentor cocks his head to one side, his eyes tapering behind his silver glasses, appraising my twisted expression with glee.

"Even when you fight against me, you're still the perfect obedient pet, always doing precisely what I expect. And now, thanks to the accelerant taking root in your veins, it won't be long until you fulfill your purpose on this planet." Shifting, he eases my shoulders and head onto the floor, then straightens, his smiling face cast in shadow. Although I try to move, the spasms rocking my limbs and the stabs cutting into my brain hold me down.

As Dr. Richter looms over me, drinking in the spectacle of my pain, the gentle glow from the emergency lights reflects across the lenses of his glasses, obscuring his eyes behind a blue flash. His grin widens, revealing his teeth, and with that one gesture, he looks less like a human and more like something out of the fairy tales my father would read to me when I was young. Like something not of this world, but like something else entirely.

Something truly, unspeakably evil.

Grimacing, I force my gaze to the side, glancing at the three immobile figures spread out across the floor at different points in the exam room—on Ezra, Jenner, and Quinn, who have all been caught in the middle of this warped game between me and Richter. I never wanted this. I never wanted to involve any of them with this part of my life. I only wanted to keep Ezra and Jenner safe. I only wanted to protect them from certain death and destruction.

I only ever wanted to protect them from me.

Guilt constricts my chest, but my nagging thoughts of self-reproach are fleeting, my brain unable to focus for long on anything beyond the crippling pain in my head. Another turbulent fit rocks my body as my eyes shudder open and closed, then wrench open again, my pulse skyrocketing at the sight of the wicked smirk twisting Richter's lips.

He claps his hands together with a low, mocking chuckle. "Everything has fallen into place just as I envisioned. All that's left to do is wake Ezra so he can witness the finale to this grand production. He did, after all, help us get to this point. We wouldn't want him to miss a second of it, now would we?"

"There's only one problem with that—"

My eyes jerk wide, and the same surprise overwhelming my senses flickers across Richter's face as he spins around, putting his back to me. I follow his startled movements as much as my increasingly sluggish vision allows, my heart racing a mile a minute with recognition, anticipation, and fear.

That voice—

My heart constricts when I see him, my brain only managing one coherent thought.

I didn't kill him.

Ezra's name springs free of my throat in a gasp, but he doesn't spare me a glance. Blood is matted in his unkempt hair—dripping down his already bruised cheek from a wound on his scalp I can't see—but instead of worry, all I'm aware of is the relief coursing through me just knowing he's okay. And alive.

I choke out a breath, desperate to coax those hazel eyes in my direction, but I lack the strength to speak. I silently beg him to look at me, but if he's aware of me here on the floor, he doesn't show it, his attention fixed on his brother.

A smirk hooks up one edge of his lips. "I'm already awake."

Ezra thrusts his arms upward, slamming a large, flat object into the side of Richter's skull with such force that, for a moment, I allow myself the gleeful belief that my tormentor might be dead. The collision makes a tinny, metallic sound that results in a wobbling echo.

On impact, Richter's head snaps to the left, his glasses knocked to the floor, the frames bent and broken, the lenses cracked. For a few seconds, he teeters on his feet before crumpling, his gray eyes rolling back in their sockets.

Exhaling, Ezra drops his weapon, the medical tray clanging loudly against the white tiles. His chest heaves as he lets out a breath, and after checking with a nudge of his foot that Richter is unconscious, he finally looks in my direction.

"Wynter?" he rasps. Even in my disoriented state, I'm aware of his panic as he races forward, sliding to his knees at my side. His hands are cold as they press to my face. "Wynter, can you hear me?"

Although I try to stay awake, my eyelids droop, and the exam room melts into an indistinct smear of shades as the finer details fade.

"I'm sorry," I breathe as darkness rises to claim me. "I didn't… mean to…"

"Hey. Hey! Wake up. Stay with me." Ezra grabs me by the shoulders and shakes me gently until I pry my eyes wide. "I got you," he murmurs, wrapping his arms around my torso and pulling me close to his chest. His fingers graze my aching skin through my bodysuit. "Everything is going to be okay."

I manage a weak nod, feigning belief, even though his words are a lie. I know all too well what's coming for us.

Everything is far from okay.

Tears carve lines down his cheeks but he wipes them away, setting me back down on the floor. Ripping off his jacket, he bundles the fabric and places it under my head like a pillow. If I have another seizure, the material should at least protect my skull from any direct impact with the tiles. Not that it really matters.

Seizure or not, I'm already dead.

Jaw straining, Ezra wipes a rogue tear from his chin. "We never should've come back. We should've left—" He falters, and the column of his throat shifts when he swallows, the sound audible in the hush of the room. Clenching his teeth, he mutters, "We should've left when we had the chance."

Mere hours ago, after saving our lives, Quinn offered us the chance to escape, saying he'd take us to a safe place outside the Heart. But we didn't go, we didn't flee, because I encouraged Ezra and Jenner to fight—to hold PHOENIX accountable—and because we were all adamant about saving Rai, even though I think part of me always knew she couldn't be saved. But also, because I knew running wasn't an option.

And, deep down, I had already accepted this war would only end with my death.

Tremors ripple over my arms as I reach for Ezra's hand, my movements lethargic and clumsy. He meets my near lifeless grip and squeezes, his brows tugging together when I guide his fingers to the naked skin at my throat.

His eyes drift down to my neck, then to my discarded collar

on the floor, understanding forming in his gaze. Realizing what I'm trying to tell him, he scowls. "We're going to get out of here," he promises, "and we're going to figure something out. I refuse to lose you, too. I won't."

A traitorous tear dashes from my left eye. Blinking it away, I turn my gaze from Ezra and take in the scene of ruin I've wrought upon the people who were only trying to help—to protect me, even though I don't deserve it. Two bodies lie on opposite sides of the room, one on his back in the far left corner and the other prostrate in a pool of blood not far from the right side of Rai's bed.

Quinn.

"Alive…?" I wheeze, my voice breaking.

Ezra blinks, his face pale with shock, but at the sound of my voice, he snaps out of his stupor and jumps to his feet, stumbling across the exam room. He shakes Jenner by the shoulder, who rouses with a groan and sits up, disoriented but unharmed. Ezra then scrambles over to Quinn, carefully flipping him onto his back.

As Ezra examines him, my vision fades in and out, the clarity of the room changing every few seconds like the ebb and flow of a tide. I squint, watching as he checks for Quinn's pulse before rifling through the ex-Enforcer's pockets, retrieving the very same shackles our former enemy removed from my wrists after saving us from execution. That moment seems like it happened in another lifetime rather than only a handful of hours ago.

So much has changed so quickly. That thought turns my stomach, and as the blood collects beneath Quinn's body, it occurs to me that I never thanked him.

I make a mental note to do just that if he survives.

Exhaling, I press my cheek to the cold floor when another wave of pain slams into the walls of my skull. Through the darkness swelling over my vision, I can just make out Ezra's expression as he jumps to his feet and stalks toward his motionless brother. Rage burns in his eyes as he hoists Richter upright and props him into a sitting position against the metal table on the left side of the room—the same table I was examined on every single day for over two years in this hell.

Nostrils flaring, Ezra binds Richter's wrists in the shackles, his attention flicking between his brother's limp hands and his white DSD-issue coat. Once the restraints are secure, he crouches, removing two objects from the deep pockets—the remote control for my now defunct collar and the pistol Richter used to shoot Quinn.

And possibly Rai, I consider, shuddering.

For a moment, Ezra stares at the remote, understanding darkening his gaze as his eyes drift from the black device in his hand to me. He must know I would never attack him or Jenner. Not willingly.

Not unless I was forced to.

"I didn't mean…to," I whisper again, pushing the words out with effort.

Ezra's face loses the last of its color as his eyes blow wide, returning to his hand. As the realization forms in his gaze, his lower lip quivers, peeling back in disgust.

Raising his hand, he growls, just loudly enough for me to hear, "That piece of shit."

With a shout of frustration, Ezra smashes the remote control against the floor, his chest heaving as the device explodes into several pieces, scattering across the white tile. Rising, he shoves

Richter's gun in his belt—replacing the pistol he stole from one of Nolan's lackeys, which seems to have gotten lost in the chaos—before fixing me with the full force of his gaze.

"He will *never* control you again," Ezra vows, voice hard and hazel eyes silvered with tears.

Then, in the time it takes for me to blink, he's on the move again, dropping to his knees beside Quinn and clamping his hands firmly against the right side of his torso. Blood seeps up through his fingers, gushing over his hands.

"Jenner, a little help?" he pleads.

Jenner, whose face is awash with confusion, turns slowly, locking eyes with Ezra. "What the hell happened?" he asks, sounding dazed.

Ezra sneers. "My asshole brother happened."

A loud cough punctures the silence, followed by a few breathy grunts as Quinn jerks into waking, his obsidian eyes bulging in confusion and terror. When he tries to sit up, Jenner jumps into action, scooping his gun off the floor—which was torn from his grasp when Richter forced me to attack him—returning it to his belt before racing across the room to help Ezra by forcing Quinn back down again. As he restrains the ex-Enforcer against the floor with his forearm, Jenner grabs a spare sheet from under Rai's bed with his other hand, pressing it down on his wound.

"Hey, man, don't move! You're really hurt."

Quinn's only response is a croak as his head lolls to the side, his tongue darting out to wet his dry lips. Although ashen from blood loss, he's awake and alert and makes repeated attempts to move despite Ezra and Jenner insisting he needs to keep still. Ignoring them, he fans his arm out to the side, his hand curling into a fist, except for one finger…which points directly at me.

All three sets of eyes fix on my face as my body contorts, my limbs locking and back arching unnaturally, foam spitting from the sides of my mouth. Ezra calls out to me, but his voice seems so far away, like time and space are separating us, placing us on different fields of existence. Still, he reaches out, crossing that distance, although it feels so impossibly far.

His arms wrap around my back, holding me tight, as a strong, metallic stench fills my nose and a warm, sticky wetness seeps from between my lips, tasting of copper and something acidic. Ezra wipes his hand over my mouth, and although he tries to hide it from me, I glimpse the smudge of red staining his fingers.

Blood, I realize, aghast.

My blood.

Just like I feared, now that the clock on my disease has resumed, the time I have left is being siphoned away as payment for the extra years I survived. Thanks to Dr. Richter, how long do I have?

When is my time going to finally run out?

Ezra shifts position and draws my head into his lap, gently stroking my face. As the seizure subsides, I search for his eyes through the expansive fog of pain weighing on my senses, making me groggy. The hazel depths gazing at me will me to speak.

Despite my exhaustion, I muster the only words I can think of—those at the core of our connection to each other.

Words that always make my past and future collide.

"I'm…sorry…"

His mouth fights a grimace as his face contorts with resurfacing rage. Taking care not to jostle me too much, he props my head on his jacket again, then returns to his feet, yanking Richter's gun free from his belt. The fire in his gaze continues to burn as his finger folds around the trigger.

I force myself to stay awake, focusing on Ezra's retreating back as he storms toward where Richter is slumped, shackled to the table. Leaning down, Ezra slaps him hard, then grabs him by the neck of the shirt, shaking him.

"Wake up!" he shouts, venom lacing his tone.

As Richter comes to, his gray eyes flicker from his younger brother's face to mine.

Ezra releases his grip on his shirt and shoves him hard into the table leg. "Help her." He glances at me, his hand shaking as he repositions his grasp on the gun.

A wry, gloating smile shapes Richter's lips. "I'm sorry to disappoint you," he says, slurring the words, "but I can't do that."

"What do you mean you *can't*?" Ezra barks. He backtracks, reappearing at my side just long enough to pluck the collar off the floor before rounding on Richter again, tossing the thick metal ring in his lap. "You're the one who did this to her, so fix it!"

A nefarious laugh reverberates through the room and ricochets through every inch of my body. As the horrible, calculating echo of it beats in my ears, a rising terror swallows my sanity whole.

"Surely, you're aware by now that collar was the only thing keeping her alive?" Richter asks. "Without it, she's doomed. There is no other cure for her condition."

Ezra cocks the gun, reaffirming the threat in his hand. "Put the collar back on, then," he snarls.

Richter glances between us, his expression triumphant

despite the fact that he's the one handcuffed on the floor. Squaring his shoulders, he rests the back of his head against the leg of the table.

"That collar is a sophisticated piece of technology, the sole of its kind created with the singular focus of protecting and preserving the security of the State. It was designed to cease all functionality should it ever be removed or tampered with. So, you see, Little Brother…" His grin widens, his face splitting into a demented smile. "It cannot be fixed."

During the two and a half years I served as, first, the DSD's guinea pig, and then, the State's weapon, there wasn't a day that went by when Dr. Richter didn't assess the collar for faults. To ensure it was doing its job. He never took it off. He never spoke of upgrading it or altering the model. He only made certain the leash that kept me chained to him and in control was working.

I knew the collar was valuable—possibly even more so than I was—but I always assumed that was because we went hand in hand. Without one, the other was useless.

Except, now, I realize it was more than that. The collar was valuable because it was unique, the sole of its kind…just like me. And since Dr. Richter had no other patients to subjugate, no other victims to turn into weapons since his other attempts to create more had failed, the State had no reason to produce other collars. That technology my control is reliant upon…

It can't be fixed or replaced.

"So, make a new one," Ezra demands, losing patience. "I'm sure you know how."

Richter scoffs. "That one collar took years of development to create and an entire team of qualified engineers to manufacture.

Somehow, I doubt all the needed components survived the explosion…"

I lie still, a silent witness to this conversation, picking up what words I can in my lethargic state. At the mention of the bombing, my eyes drift to Quinn. I recall our conversation outside the DSD, before our confrontation with Richter. At the time, I didn't think much of it—of Quinn's suggestion that someone was working with the enemy from within the State, giving them the intel to target this place. Now that I allow the thought to sink in, I can't help wondering if maybe he was right. Perhaps the enemy isn't really an enemy at all and just wanted to erase what the State had created before it could be used to hurt anyone else.

Before *I* could be used to hurt anyone else.

What little hope had stirred within me at Ezra's words—at the notion of the possibility of a new collar—promptly dies at the amusement in Richter's voice. "Even if, by some miracle, the required parts were all intact, it would still take months to construct a new one. Something tells me she doesn't have that much time."

Lunging forward, Ezra jams the muzzle of the pistol against his brother's forehead. Richter doesn't even flinch.

Instead, a derisive snort pierces the silence between them.

"Are you going to kill me?" Richter asks.

"Tempting," Ezra considers, drawing back the barrel, "but no. As much as I want to pull this trigger, Wynter should be the one to kill you, not me."

Richter chuckles. "She's had the opportunity to end my life countless times, and yet, here I am. Alive. Why do you think that is?"

A lump swells in my throat at his confession. In all the time Dr. Richter held me captive, I had several chances to kill him; there were so many moments when we were alone and I could've ended his miserable life without lifting a finger. But I never attempted to out of fear. Fear of what would happen to me if he wasn't around to guarantee my control. Fear of why I was allowing myself to do his bidding.

Fear of what I was forcing myself to forget.

But now, I remember everything and, unlike before, Richter no longer has the threat of my collar to use against me. He's severed those strings from my body, ending my unwilling stint as his puppet. The control I've been clinging to is gone, along with any reason to keep him alive.

No reason other than Rai, I remember.

Drawing in a tremulous breath, I cut my eyes to the bed in the corner. As much as it breaks me to admit it, she's dead, broken beyond any hope of repair. Her heart might be pumping blood through her veins, but the hard truth—the truth I now have to face—is we lost her that night at the magistrates building.

And for that, Richter doesn't deserve to live.

In my peripheral vision, I glimpse Ezra shrug. "I really couldn't say, but I have a feeling you might've just changed her mind."

Richter responds with a sharp, biting cackle. "You think you know her so well, but the only person who truly understands her is me. She is death incarnate. *Mors vincit omnia.* 'Death conquers all,'" he translates. "Have you seen her kill before, Brother? You think I'm a monster and yet you defend someone who has decimated entire armies—"

"Stop talking," Ezra warns.

"Or what?" Richter goads. "You don't have the stomach to kill me."

Ezra tilts his head to one side and taps the barrel of the pistol to his lips, as if contemplating the idea. "Yeah," he agrees with a tentative nod, "but I never promised not to shoot you."

An ear-splitting bang rattles the remains of the building, which threatens to cave in and crush us to death, entombing our bodies in a grave of sterile surfaces and glowing blue emergency lights. Black spots emerge in front of my eyes, and my ears ring from the gunshot, making the pounding in my head unbearable.

My eyes slam shut, as if doing so will help fight the pain. I'm so tired. I just want to sleep—to slip away from this madness and escape into dreaming, even if where I end up is a nightmare.

A memory jerks me awake, and with fear, I remember something from before I returned to the DSD two years ago. The days spent before the mission to Zone 1. Days I spent in a comatose state.

If I go to sleep now, who knows when I'll wake up? I can't afford to lose any more time.

Not when the clock is already ticking.

Blinking away the shadows from my eyes, I peer at Ezra and at the gun at his side before turning my drowsy gaze to his brother. Richter clutches his leg, his face draining of color as his teeth grit together, biting back what I hope is a scream. As he grunts, blood oozes from a hole in his pant leg situated just above his left knee. His restrained fingers claw at the wound to no avail, only making the blood bubble faster.

As if sensing my joy at his suffering, his wild eyes dart to mine—the hue of his irises nearly identical now to his complexion, his skin growing whiter by the second. Sweat beads along his hairline as he bares his teeth and lets loose an animalistic snarl, spit flying from between his chalky lips.

As the pool of blood building beneath Richter's leg expands across the tiled floor, the room begins to spin, making me nauseous. Dizzy, I close my eyes to settle my stomach only to be assaulted by images I'd rather not see. The one nightmare I can never escape projects onto the backs of my eyelids and in every thought until I see it all over again, just as I did the first time.

Darkness.

Destruction.

Death.

Every aspect of my vision is exactly the same. No matter what I do, no matter which path I take or who dies along the way, the future never veers from its intended destination. It always ends with me...

And with the desolation of our world.

A scream cranks open my lips, ripping free of my throat, as the images fade and yet another wave of convulsions rise to take their place. Leaping up from where he kneels at Quinn's side, Jenner crosses the distance to my thrashing body, tugging my back against his chest and holding me upright and still through my seizure. But he can't protect me from the wrath of this disease.

No one can anymore.

Ezra's eyes find mine as Jenner shouts out his name, but I can't tell if they belong to the Ezra of the present or the Ezra I always see in my vision—the one who's sorry and who I'll have to watch die because I failed to find a way to save him and Jenner from that terrible future. From me.

Whichever version it is, I hang onto his voice as the world around me is engulfed by darkness, his every word the only anchor between me and unconsciousness.

"If she dies, so do you!"

"Don't you understand yet?" Although weak from his wound, Richter laughs again—a cruel, malicious sound that cuts through me like a knife to my chest.

His voice is the last thing I hear before the darkness finally pulls me under.

"We're already dead."

TWO

OVER THE YEARS, I'VE LOST track of how many times I've been forced to return to this moment. Regardless of what I do in the real world, regardless of the choices I make, the future awaiting me is always the same. The same destruction. The same outcome.

The same deaths...over and over again.

I turn in place, my eyes trailing across the rubble and skeletal buildings, emaciated frames of steel and broken glass, that are soon to be all that remain of my home. Maybe the world was always doomed to end this way. Maybe every step I've taken since the day this disease first awoke only took us closer to our pre-destined demise. Whether through the assault on our city or through my own increasingly unstable powers, maybe the violent eradication of mankind was always inevitable.

I let out a tear-soaked breath and wait for Ezra, fearing his appearance more than ever now that I know this vision's eventual re-enactment in reality is certain. At any moment, he'll manifest, muttering the same three words that have plagued me for years. He'll apologize, although I still don't know what for.

Now that I no longer have my collar, I suppose it won't be

long until I find out.

My eyes dart side to side, scanning my surroundings for movement. Aside from the occasional flicker warping the dusty air like static distorting a picture, everything looks the same as it has since unconsciousness dragged me back to this hellscape only moments ago.

An uneasy confusion sends my already erratic pulse racing. The last time this vision took an unforeseen turn, I had to watch Ezra and Jenner both die, a helpless spectator to their gruesome deaths. I don't want to relive that again. My fragile sanity can't take it.

My breath hitches at the soft crunch of footsteps in dirt, and I throw a panicked glance over my shoulder, expecting, dreading, *hoping* it's him. Hoping the vision hasn't changed for the worse.

If anything can be worse than death.

Ezra's name hangs on the tip of my tongue, but I swallow it, stopping short, my chest tightening at the sight of the familiar brown eyes staring at me.

I blink, choking out a single word.

"Rai?"

She fixes me with that maternal gaze that was once so warm and full of life but is now dull and empty by comparison. She takes a step toward me, dragging her feet, while I stumble back, bringing a hand to my mouth.

She's wearing the same clothes she was the last time we saw her—the night we thought she died in Zone 1. Blood has saturated the top half of her long-sleeved gray shirt and pools around her pronounced collar bone, an endless flow of red streaming down the side of her face from the small circular wound near her temple.

"Wynter…" Her voice penetrates the shell of shock freezing me, once again opening the door to my grief. A door I've been trying so hard to close. Great, heaving cries rack my lungs as tears leave thick scalding lines down my cheeks.

"I'm sorry," I gasp, fighting for breath. "I tried. I-I tried to save you—"

She extends a hand toward me, a gentle smile curving her lips. As her fingers cup my face, I close my eyes, trying to remember her touch, her warmth…but no matter how hard I try to recall even the smallest detail, I feel nothing. As much as I want to believe this is real, as much as I wish she was here with me, the truth is I'm alone and Rai is still comatose in the bed Richter fettered her to, forever trapped somewhere between life and death. And this, our bittersweet reunion… It isn't a vision at all but a dream.

A nightmare born of my guilt to torment me.

Steadying myself, I open my eyes and force myself to look at her. The bullet hole at the right side of her forehead has healed, leaving a pockmarked scar in its place, and the clothes she was wearing have been substituted for the minuscule rectangle of surgical paper covering her sleeping body in the real world.

Now, instead of the Rai we remember, she looks like the lifeless doll belonging to Richter.

Her smile transforms, dipping into a frown. "You were never going to be able to save me, you know that." She lowers her hand from my cheek, then drops her voice to a whisper. "But there's still time."

I shake my head, blinking the tears from my eyes. "Time for what?"

As if precipitated by my words, an alarm blares in the distance, the whooping scream of it faint but shrill. I take stock of my surroundings, trying to locate the source, but the air is a thickening whirlwind of dirt and ash, obstructing my sense of direction.

Two voices swirl around me in a vortex, carried by the raging wind. They echo in time with the screeching alarm.

"What is that?"

"Sounds like our not-so-friendly reminder to get the hell out of here."

"Ezra. Jenner." As their names leave my lips, a shudder turns my skin ice-cold and I remember where they still are at this moment. When I remember the danger I've led them both into.

My heart hammers against my ribcage when I look back at Rai.

"Time for what?" I ask again, my voice breaking.

A sheet of dust blows between us, blurring her face. Through the debris, I can just make out her eyes—two deep glistening pools of burnt umber that, despite their warmth, chill me down to the bone.

She stares at me, her gaze pleading. "To save them."

As these words permeate the air between us, the ground caves in beneath my feet and I fall, plunging into the depths of the earth, as a blanket of black blots out the world. Above me, Rai watches, her expression unmoved, looking down at me as I fall…fall…

Fall.

Her voice is all I cling to in the deepening shadows as the echoes of her warning-like plea flood my ears. I hear it, over and over again, telling me what I have to do. But how? How can I possibly hope to change anything or save anyone now that I've been stripped of control?

A few moments pass before I realize I'm no longer free-falling and the darkness around me is lifting, pulling me back into the cruelty of consciousness. The soft blue haze of the emergency lights seeps in at the edges of my sharpening vision, revealing the details of Exam Room B.

My own personal purgatory.

The repetitive wail of an alarm attacks my eardrums, but the sound is muted by the thick gray walls, as if it's been confined to the hallway. Although distant, the racket is more than enough to awaken the throbbing pain in my head, thrusting me the rest of the way into waking.

The arms wrapped around my torso flinch when I rouse, and I glance up to find Jenner leaning over me, his face upside down, those bright blue eyes teeming with worry.

Wrinkling my nose, I part my lips on a moan. "What's that awful sound?"

His warm breath tickles my cheeks when he laughs, his chest spasming against my back with a tearful sigh. He shakes his head at me, his cheeks twitching in an aborted smile. "You had us all worried there for a minute."

"I'm fine," I assure him.

Testing the strength in my limbs, I cautiously push myself into a sitting position. Jenner rises beside me and helps me up onto my feet, keeping one hand on my arm and the other on my back to steady me, should I need it. Every inch of my body screams in protest, but it's far easier to stand than I thought it would be given whatever Richter injected me with.

An accelerant, he called it. I frown at the thought. My brief paralysis might've elapsed but I'm sure such reactions will only become more frequent as the episodes continue and my condition worsens, chipping away at what little still remains of me, Wynter Reeves, before revealing the monster beneath. Before the collar, a single episode could cripple me for days, sometimes longer. How long before I return to that point, especially with Richter's unknown drug in my veins to push me closer to that edge?

How long before this disease destroys everything?

"Just had a minor relapse, that's all." I try to give Jenner a reassuring smile but fail, only managing a grimace.

"Minor?" a voice behind me shouts.

My stomach clenches as I turn and find myself face to face with a furious Ezra. A scowl pinches his brow, his arms stiff at his sides. The anger in his eyes smolders in the hazel depths like embers threatening to spark into full flames.

"You call that *minor*?" he asks, his voice raised over the persistent howl of the alarm. He holds my gaze for a moment before letting out a breath. Then, stepping toward me, he grips my upper arms, dropping his forehead down onto my shoulder. "I..." He trails off, shaking his head, brushing my neck and collarbone with his hair. "I thought that was it."

His voice is barely audible, but I hear it, pressed up close to my ear. I hear it as clearly as I sense his fear.

My arms tremble as they snake around his back. "You don't have to worry." I speak loudly enough so he can hear me but low enough so no one else will. "I've seen it. That's not how I'm going to die."

I'll die surrounded by ash and dirt—the remnants of a world I've destroyed.

Ezra snaps his head up and pulls away just enough to look

me in the eye. Placing his hands on either side of my face, he says, "We're going to make our own future, you hear me? Don't let my brother get in your head." His gruff words are a tender kiss on my lips, but as comforting as they are in this moment, they're powerless to change my fate.

Or the future.

Beside us, Jenner clears his throat. "As much as I hate to break up this lovefest, we really need to get out of here. Whatever that alarm is, it can't be anything good."

Ezra lowers his hands from my cheeks, and I follow his forlorn gaze to Rai, the sorrow on his face beyond any comprehensible words. Quinn sits propped upright against the plastic and metal frame of her bed, eyes closed and dusky brunette hair askew, with the bed sheet Jenner was using to staunch his bleeding now tied around his midsection like a tourniquet. The pallid hue of his complexion is worrying. The only indicators that he's even alive are the gentle rise and fall of his chest and the wheezing breaths occasionally seeping through his lips.

"What about..." But Ezra doesn't finish the sentence.

I reach out, taking his hand, and behind me, Jenner touches my shoulder, forming a chain of support. In our mutual silence, I know we're all thinking the same thing.

The sole point of returning to the DSD was to rescue Rai from Dr. Richter, and now, that decision might have cost us the one ally—although begrudging—who was willing to help us. While I had suspected from my vision that something was wrong, I didn't grasp the full extent of Rai's injuries until I saw her with the clarity of reality and realized exactly what Richter had done.

When it became evident that she wasn't going to ever wake up, I knew then that our mission had failed. Rai wasn't leaving the DSD. She can't, not when the array of necessary machines connected to her body make any notion of escaping impossible.

As for Quinn, who knows how long he has? I never saw him in any of my visions. For all I know, he'll die here, right next to Rai.

I take in her face, perfectly still in eternal sleep. Comatose. Vegetative.

"You were never going to be able to save me, you know that."

Tears prick my eyes at the memory of what she said in my dream. Real or not, she was right. I wrote her off as dead over two years ago, and our quest to save her from Dr. Richter was nothing more than a misguided attempt to assuage the guilt I was struggling to rid myself of. Part of me always knew she was already gone.

"But there's still time," her voice says again in my head.

Is there? I desperately wish I could ask her. How do I know that for sure when it wasn't even really her I was talking to? Machines might be keeping her body alive, but Rai—the Rai we knew—is lost and has been for a while now. I know that. Ezra and Jenner know that, even if some of us aren't ready to admit it.

Just as we all know you can't talk to the dead.

I'm about to tell Ezra that Jenner is right, that staying won't do anyone here any good, when he pulls his hand from mine and storms across the room to the bed in the corner. Even in the shadows, the denial is as clear on his face as the shimmer of tears coating his eyes.

"We just need more time! If we can figure out a way to transport her, maybe we can find someone else to help. To bring her back. And Quinn"—he gestures to the unconscious ex-Enforcer—"he might be an ass, but he saved our lives. He doesn't deserve to die like this, and neither does she."

"Like who?" Jenner asks, exasperation bleeding into his tone. "Do you know any doctors? Because the closest thing we had in our sect was Rai, and even she only knew enough to get us all by." He tightens his hand around my shoulder, his fingertips trembling against my skin. "No one is going to help us, Ez. Not your brother. Not the State. Not even PHOENIX." He pauses, drawing in a shaking breath before letting it out through his nose. "This is a lost cause, you know that."

Laughter rings out beside us, drowning out the alarm.

"Raina isn't going anywhere. None of you are," Richter crows.

Ezra peers back at his brother and scoffs. "And who's going to stop us? You?"

Richter's lips curl into a smile. "I don't need to. The second that alarm began to go off, every door on this floor locked from the outside. We're all stuck in this room until someone comes to investigate, and I have a feeling whoever that is will be on my side, not yours."

Ezra, Jenner, and I all exchange panicked looks before throwing nervous glances back at the closed door, the apprehension hanging in the air so thick and pervasive I can practically taste it.

Steeling myself, I limp across the room until my hand is within reach of the door, shivering when the cool metal grazes my fingertips. I pause for a moment, holding my breath, silently praying that Richter is lying...but knowing in the darkest depths of my own corrupted black soul that he isn't.

I reach for the keypad and enter the unlocking code branded into my memory.

As expected, the door doesn't budge.

"It's locked," I try to say, but my mouth is a desert and the words come out garbled.

I take a step back, assessing our options. I could break the door down like I did to the one in my cell in the PHOENIX bunker outside the Heart, but when I try to summon the energy to do so, I don't even manage a dent. My body is spent, and my head feels like a cracked egg, the pain lingering far too close to the surface.

I glance back at Ezra, and whatever he sees on my face must tell him everything he needs to know about what I'm capable of at this moment…and what I'm not. He holds my gaze for only a moment before pulling the gun free of his belt and aiming it at Richter, his finger hovering over the trigger.

"Shut it down!" he shouts, spitting the words, crossing the exam room until the end of the pistol is less than an inch away from his brother's forehead. "Get that door open or, I swear, I'll shoot you again."

Dr. Richter huffs, his face deathly pale. "And how would you like me to do that?" He jerks his chin toward his restrained wrists. "In case you failed to notice, I wasn't the one who set it off."

"I was."

My heartbeat drums in my ears as my focus shifts to where Quinn sits hunched on the floor, his black eyes locked intently on mine. In answer to my silent question, he lifts one hand, his fingers wrapped around a black device not that dissimilar to the remote Richter used to overpower me through my collar.

"This"—he grimaces, his other hand pressed flat to his side, holding the bloody sheet in place as he pushes off the tile and up onto his feet—"was given to me in the event you ended up back here again."

Dropping the mechanism next to Rai's foot, he grabs onto the side of her bed for support, wincing at the effort of holding himself upright. Beads of perspiration dot his upper lip, glistening in the low light of the room.

"What the hell is that?" Jenner asks, his voice trembling.

"RF transmitter," Ezra answers, his back stiffening like hackles on a growling dog. "They shoot radio frequencies between two points and can be used to remotely trigger alarms. We used them once or twice when I first joined PHOENIX, but they're unreliable since..." He trails off, a wary look crossing his face.

A shudder creeps up my spine. "Since what?"

His eyes narrow on Quinn. "Since most alarms these days are protected against outside interference. For it to work, the security system would have to be either extremely vulnerable or pre-programmed to accept that specific frequency. Which means..." He hesitates, his mouth a thin line. "Whoever gave you that transmitter has access to this facility."

I bristle, gaping at the ex-Enforcer. Why would Quinn have a transmitter capable of prompting the DSD's alarms? And what did he mean it was given to him in the event I ended up back here?

Given to him by who?

Dr. Richter bursts out laughing, cackling like a madman, his expression deranged. Euphoric, even. "Once an Enforcer, always an Enforcer." With a contented sigh, he leans forward until his skull nudges the muzzle of the gun in Ezra's hand. A malevolent smile contorts his lips. "Betrayal stings...doesn't it, Brother?"

"I knew it," Ezra breathes, staggering back a few steps, his arm dropping but his grip on the gun never easing. "I knew you couldn't be trusted—"

"You're a real bastard, you know that?" Jenner seethes, his hands balling into tight fists at his sides, his knuckles turning white from the pressure. "So much for helping us. I should've let you bleed out on the fu—"

He advances on Quinn, but I pitch forward and grab his arm, pushing myself between them. Jenner gapes at me, stunned by my intervention.

Ignoring him, I round on Quinn, my body aching as what little strength I've managed to conjure up seems to leave me in the space of a heartbeat. Quinn doesn't look to be in a much better state. Sweat lines the curve of his hairline and the sides of his neck, drenching the collar of his black shirt, and the white sheet around his torso is stained red, sodden with blood.

Wound aside, he seems so exhausted, so weary. Like someone who's tired of running. Of hiding. The question is…what is it Quinn's running from? Has he always had this hunted look in his eyes and I just never noticed it?

Or am I to blame for that, too?

I shuffle closer. "I don't understand. You saved our lives. Why do that just to turn on us here?"

His jaw strains and he groans, catching himself on the edge of Rai's mattress when his knees buckle, weakened from blood loss. Nostrils flaring, he shoots me a knowing look, hissing, "You don't get it. This *is* me saving your life—"

As suddenly as it appeared, the alarm cuts off, and that's when we hear it—the rumble of booted footsteps outside in the hallway. I recognize that sound, remembering it all too clearly from that night in Zone 1 and from all the months I spent fighting in the State's pointless war. Those tromping, heavy footsteps, a telltale sign of approaching death…

They belong to Enforcers.

Ezra and Jenner both whip around to face the incoming threat while my own gaze turns toward Dr. Richter, who smiles at the apprehension rolling through me. I know he can sense it, just as I can practically hear his snide voice in my ear whispering, *"I'd like to see how well you perform without your precious control to help you."*

The imagined taunt is quickly drowned out by the memory of what he said in those final few seconds before removing my collar. *"Show it to me,"* he had murmured, his breath hot on my skin. *"Show me the destruction you and my mother both saw."*

I swallow as a tingle like static electricity passes over my skin, raising the hairs on my arms. Maybe what I'm feeling is my unrestrained power creeping back to the surface, preparing to finally force me to yield. Or maybe my dread and fear have taken on a tangible form, wrapping around my lungs and choking my airway like a hand gripping my throat.

Whichever it is, I try to breathe past the sensation, hoping my panic won't show as Ezra and Jenner stand side by side, forming a shield between me and the door, even though we all know they'll do little against a team of Enforcers. Our only real hope in this dire situation is me, except…I don't have my collar and I'm too weak and tired to fight.

But I have to. Like I told Ezra before, I don't die here. Neither does he. And Jenner won't either. I won't let him.

I shake my head, shoving all doubt aside. I was in control of this disease for two years. Collar or not, I know how to summon my power. I can do this.

I can find the strength to protect us.

The footsteps cease just outside the door, and everyone in the room goes quiet and still. Ezra peers over his shoulder, meeting my gaze, and I nod, consoled by the thought that this—getting gunned down here in my tormentor's lair—isn't what I saw in either of our futures. Whatever happens here, whatever comes in the next few moments, we'll survive it. I have to believe that.

Otherwise, my terror might actually crush me.

A dull sequence of beeps hums through the closed door, singing out from the keypad outside in the corridor. The metal panel separating us from yet another danger then slides open with an ominous *whish*, and I suck in a sharp breath, tamping down my nerves. Closing my eyes, I beckon my power, just as I have a thousand other times before. Just as I used to when I had my collar.

That familiar pressure begins to build in my chest but far more slowly than I would like, my hold on it shaky. I inhale again, pushing myself, but a hand grabs my shoulder, warning me to stop.

I recoil, glancing back at Quinn, ready to kill him myself for putting us in this position…then pause, taken aback by the look on his face. He retracts his hand, his fingers sticky with blood, and stares at me the same way Rai did in my dream—like they both know something I don't. He opens his mouth, soundlessly muttering a single word, confusing me even further.

Wait.

Before I can ask him why, the click-clack of high heels draws my attention back to the door, my senses alert. A tall woman stands at the threshold to the exam room, wearing a white blouse and dark gray knee-length skirt, framed by a long DSD-issue coat identical to Dr. Richter's. Her light blonde hair is pinned back in a bun and bright, intelligent cobalt eyes sweep across the scene before her, vaguely amused.

"Well, well, well," she croons. "What do we have here?" She signals with a crook of her pointer finger to the group of Enforcers in the hallway behind her. Brushing past her into the room, the soldiers take position around us.

Ezra steps back and pulls me close to his side as Dr. Richter lets out a devious, albeit weak, laugh.

"Fancy meeting you here, Dr. Adler. Your timing is impeccable, as always."

"Adler?" Jenner's tone straddles the line between afraid and incredulous, his cheeks draining of color, as if he's just seen a ghost.

I watch him for a moment, unnerved by his reaction to the woman standing in the doorway. A reaction he only had once he heard her name.

Just who is this Dr. Adler?

Reading my mind, Ezra whispers in my ear, "Evelyn Adler. She's in charge of Termination."

I want to ask him how he knows that, but the words fail to form as I take a closer look at the newcomer—at this woman Jenner seems so afraid of. As the features of her face sharpen before my drug and fatigue addled gaze, I realize that I've seen her before. But not here. Not at the DSD where I spent nearly three years of my life being tortured and experimented on.

No, I know her from somewhere else. It just took me a minute to recognize her and to see past the disguise of her blonde hair and clothes. She looks so different—not at all like the woman I remember from what might as well be a different life. A life where she was someone else.

Someone I once thought I could trust.

It can't be.

I step out of Ezra's arms as my memories of her slide to the front of my brain, unbidden. As the name I used to call her unfurls on my tongue, moisture drips down my cheeks and gathers in a pool on my lips, the taste of each bitter tear triggering the recollection of one of her lies. Of what I now recognize as deceit.

And betrayal.

"Mother?"

THREE

"HELLO, WYNTER," MY MOTHER SAYS from the doorway, her voice steady and placid, as if we're discussing the weather. A reluctant, forced smile hooks up the corners of her lips. "I'm sorry we had to meet again like this."

I jerk my head in disbelief, my mouth opening and closing several times, trying and failing to form the words, *any* words, that will help me make sense of what I'm seeing—of this impossible reality where my mother is not only standing before me after not seeing her for nearly three years but that she's... wearing a DSD-issue coat?

The irony is almost enough to make me laugh. Didn't Ezra once falsely claim my mother worked here as an alibi to cover up my escape from this place? The recollection of his calculated lie flits through my mind, and I wonder if he's remembering that moment now, too. If I could move, if I could just break through the shock of this moment and look at him, I'm sure I would find him wearing the same disturbed expression slapped across my own face.

Never in a million years did either of us ever think he would be right.

I swallow, and the sound is gratingly loud in the silence. No matter which angle I look at it from, the woman looming at the threshold to the room—the woman I once called my mother—is unrecognizable to me. And, in this moment, I realize she's just another lie I've been force-fed my whole life by the State.

No, this woman isn't my mother at all. She's a stranger, just like any other I would pass on the street. Evandra Reeves, if she ever existed at all, is a ghost.

Dead to this world, just like my father.

I eye her carefully, tasting the name Ezra referred to her by just moments ago on my tongue. Evelyn Adler. *Dr. Adler, Richter called her.*

Sneering, I push that thought away. If this is all true—if this isn't just another twisted nightmare intent on unhinging me—then that means the woman who raised me is a torturer.

A murderer.

This time, I can't help the choked-off laugh that escapes. *Like mother, like daughter,* a voice says in my head.

I might be personally responsible for the genocide of thousands of people, maybe more, but I always acted under duress. Can my mother say the same? How many lives has she taken? How many people has she killed all for the sake of keeping our country shackled with fear? After all, that's what Termination does.

They're exterminators and the people living in the Heart are the bugs.

I shake my head again, the threat of madness teasing the edge of every thought. How did I not know? How did my father not know?

A sudden queasiness clenches my stomach, and I let out a stilted breath when an epiphany floods my head. Maybe my father *did* know. They were married for years before he was executed, years during which he was still active with PHOENIX. Years where she must've known, or at least suspected, what he was up to before something made her decide to turn him in to the authorities. Upon learning of my father's involvement with PHOENIX, I had assumed she only reported his crimes because he exposed me—their child—to the danger of his affiliations. But what if I was wrong? What if she turned on him for a different reason altogether?

What if she killed him because he found out the truth?

Pain tears across my forehead again, and my legs wobble as a wave of vertigo disorients my senses, leaving me unsteady on my feet. My lungs constrict with the effort of trying to breathe, as if something is blocking my airway, suffocating my every inhalation.

Confusion and denial both crawl up my throat.

"How?" I gasp. It's the only word I manage to force out.

My mother takes a step into the room, and as the glow of the faint emergency lights reflects off her face, I notice the skin beside her eyes is creased and the corners of her mouth are downturned now. It's the same expression she used to wear whenever she'd scold me for not abiding by one of her rules. Rules she always claimed were for my survival and safety. I never quite understood that look, the way the fear invaded her otherwise severe gaze. But now, I realize what it was she was afraid of—what she didn't want me to know and always tried to hide behind a cold, aloof mask. Now, I realize why she was so desperate for me to remain invisible, unseen from the very government I've fallen victim to. Because if I didn't, I would've found out about her…

And she would have had to deal with me the same way she dealt with my father.

Is that why she's here? I wipe the tears streaming down my cheeks away with the heel of my hand.

Did my mother come here to kill us?

"Wynter—" she begins, her voice careful and low.

Behind me, a scratchy laugh cuts her off.

"It isn't possible."

I pivot, glancing back at Dr. Richter where he sits propped up against the leg of the examination table, his complexion pasty and putrid. The left corner of his mouth twitches every few seconds into a warped expression that's somewhere between a laugh and a grimace.

My brow furrows at the doubt in his voice. Surely, he had to have known who she was, unlike me, who lived her entire life with a liar, her deception beyond comprehensible limits.

Richter swallows, the lump in his throat bobbing, and his lips part, but no other words come out. Like me, this revelation seems to have rendered him silent.

Realization grips me like claws sinking into my skin. Is it possible he really didn't know who she was—of our connection to each other?

Just how many people has my mother fooled?

I peer back at her, bemused, and the lines beside her eyes ease, smoothing out, as she turns her attention to Richter. With that blank expression, she's suddenly that poised stranger again—the one I barely recognize.

The evil monster in charge of Termination rather than the

woman I once called my mother.

Keeping her unblinking gaze locked on his, she proceeds deeper into the room with a calm assuredness to her steps that twists my stomach in knots and prods at the barely restrained anger inside me. I push back against it, suppressing that anger, afraid that—if I cave to it for even a second—I'll snap and kill every single person in this room. It doesn't matter how tired I am, how weak. The threat of my power thrums under my skin as if in direct response to my rage.

When my mother struts toward me, Ezra places a hand on my arm to pull me back out of the way, but I shrug him off and step forward to meet her, hardened by my growing outrage. I'm done with being subjugated by people who think they can control me, with being a tool and always cowering out of fear of what monstrous people like Richter might do to me or to someone I love if I refuse to obey. After all, there's nothing anyone can do to me now that's worse than what Dr. Richter has already done.

Not even my mother has that kind of power.

As the distance between us diminishes and her emotionless gaze shifts from Richter to me—the depths the same blue as my own right eye—I ready myself to unleash everything I've wanted to say to her since she abandoned me the day of my placement exam. My mouth opens once more, my lower lip quivering with the weight of every word.

Words that falter on my tongue when she brushes past me as if I don't even exist.

"I assure you it is," she says, her tone biting.

It takes me a few seconds to collect myself—to grasp that she isn't speaking to me but to Richter. She stands beside him now, her back tall and arms crossed.

Although I can't see her face, I can easily envision the expression she's wearing. I picture it all too clearly in my mind from the day my father was taken away and, again, when she surrendered my life to the State. When she handed me over to be tortured as if I meant absolutely nothing to her. That cold, detached look like he is beneath her, like he is a nuisance…

Like my father and I must've been.

Dr. Richter gapes at her, his skin dewy with sweat. "We've been working together for over ten years. How could I not have known about this?" His eyes flit around the room, agitated in their movements, but they settle on nothing, almost like he's watching the frantic nature of his thoughts unfolding before him.

For the first time, I really glimpse the madness lurking in the monochromatic pools of his gaze. I suppose it was always there; I just failed to see it through his near constant insistence that someone else was always to blame for all the terrible things he's done.

The mother who saw what he would become.

The brother who stole the one person he loved.

Even me, the broken girl who would become his obsession.

"No," he breathes, shaking his head. "The girl's mother relinquished her custodial rights *in person* here nearly three years ago. The woman I met then wasn't you. And Hastings— he was there at her house. He saw her mother's face."

Hastings?

Understanding dawns, and I realize Richter is referring to the DSD attendant who was present when I was apprehended following my placement exam. The one who jammed a needle into my neck and drugged me.

Begrudgingly, I accept that Richter has a point. That man saw my mother's face—

"Hastings works for me." My mother's tone is callous, and she waves a dismissive hand. "You're a clever man, Austin. But you're young, and I've been playing this game a lot longer."

I can sense Ezra's eyes burning into my face, but I avoid his gaze and keep watching my mother, mesmerized by every word out of her mouth…and unsure what to make of any of this.

The heels of her shoes click against the white floor—the once gleaming tiles spoiled by Richter's blood, leaving a trail of red smears in her wake—as she turns around and backtracks toward me. This time, her hooded eyes take me in as if I'm the only other person in the room.

She reaches out a hand to touch my left cheek, but her fingers freeze when I flinch away. Her eyes brim with hurt as they sweep over my face, but behind that surface sheen of pain, there's something else there in the way she looks at me. Understanding, perhaps.

Or regret.

Dropping her arm, she directs her gaze over my shoulder and nods, smiling slightly. "Thank you for bringing Wynter to me. You've upheld your end of the deal and I will see to it that I uphold mine."

Deal?

Acid sloshes against the walls of my stomach and my heart drops into my feet when I turn, following her line of sight to the unapologetic sable eyes watching me.

A breath catches in my throat. Was this what Quinn meant when he said he was saving my life? By making a deal to return me to my mother? But how would they even know one another?

He says nothing as I stare at him, his face increasingly pale, his breathing ragged. Any sympathy I felt for being the reason he got shot has evaporated like water in dry heat. Of course, he never really wanted to help us. He never cared about us finding Rai or preventing the war against the Heart that he helped to ignite by being Nolan's lackey and keeping me out of the State's hands. By keeping me captive. The whole time he's been playing both sides. The whole time he's been playing *me*, moving me around like a chess piece across a board I wasn't even aware I was on.

Positioning the pawn everyone sees me as exactly where my mother wants me.

But why?

I glare at him, silently demanding answers, but his expression is blank despite the probing heat of his gaze. I wanted to trust him. I wanted to believe he really did oppose this war and had turned to our side, but it was idiotic of me to hope that anyone who once worked for the State might have some sort of conscience.

I bite down hard on the inside of my cheek, suppressing a scream of frustration. A million questions make a home in my skull. How did they meet? How long have they been working together? How did Quinn manage to get in so tight with Nolan so soon after leaving the State? Obviously, that had to have been part of the plan. Otherwise, he couldn't have intervened the way he did when we were about to be executed.

Some rescue, I think to myself, laughing under my breath.

As if sensing my unraveling sanity, Ezra grabs my hand, his palm sweaty and hot as his fingers weave around mine, clenching tightly. I stagger toward him, pressing my back to his chest—the only safe place I know as the lies once again build up around me, threatening to bury me alive.

"Can someone explain what the hell is going on?" he barks, his voice loud in my ear.

"All in good time," my mother answers, barely taking the time to spare Ezra a glance. Instead, her blue eyes lock on mine. "We will discuss everything once we're out of here. But first… there's something you should see."

Jenner, who has been silent throughout this exchange, seems to break out of whatever trance had ensnared him upon my mother's arrival and rushes forward, shoving himself between us.

"We aren't going anywhere with *you*." He yanks his gun free of his belt and trains it on her face, his shoulders shaking with a fury I've never seen from him before—not even when he thought Ezra and Rai had been lying to him.

Around us, the Enforcers react to the threat, weapons raised and aimed on Jenner—my terror forming a rancid taste in my mouth as his life flashes before my eyes. Observing me out of the corner of her eye, my mother raises a hand, signaling for the soldiers to stand down.

My heart races a mile a minute, and my pulse only settles when the Enforcers all lower their guns—some holding pistols, others rifles—and return to their at ease positions. I reach out to Jenner, tugging on his shirt to yank him back toward me. But he doesn't budge, and when he finally looks back at me, his eyes are almost feral in their intensity.

Startled by his reaction, I replay the moment of my mother's unexpected appearance in my head, trying to figure out what about her triggered this hostility in him. When Dr. Richter greeted my mother, Jenner had whispered her name with an unnerving familiarity—a familiarity that was explained when Ezra revealed her full alias.

No, not her alias, I realize. *Her identity.*

Her *true* identity.

I wish I could scrub the revelation from my mind. At the time, I didn't have a chance to examine Jenner's shock any deeper, assuming it merely aligned with my own—born from the sheer horror of realizing my mother's position here at the DSD. But now, as I glance between his face and hers, I recall what he told me on the train earlier about the events that led him to join PHOENIX.

About his family.

My stomach sours. If Jenner recognized her name, that must mean my mother was the acting Head of Termination when his parents and sister were killed. If that's the case, then Jenner has good reason to believe she was not only involved with the death of his family…but directly responsible for it.

Vomit rises in my throat, and I glare at her. "Why?" I rasp through tears. "Why should we trust you after everything you've done?" My voice breaks on that last word, and I can see in the way her eyes widen that she knows what I'm asking. How can I possibly trust her after what she did to my father?

After what she did to me.

She huffs out a breath through her nose, as if this conversation is beginning to bore her. "I understand there's some distrust and hurt feelings between us—" Jenner scoffs, earning him a cutting glare from her as she raises her voice, continuing over him. "But I am your one chance to get out of this city alive."

As she says this, she peers at the bed, and the uncertain look

I find on her face makes my body go rigid.

"Who says we *want* to leave?" Ezra counters.

Lifting her chin, my mother averts her eyes from Rai, meeting my gaze again. "Then, you will die. Staying in the Heart is suicide at this point." She allows a moment for her words to sink in before speaking again. "I'm offering you and your friends help, Wynter. Are you going to accept it or not?" When I don't say anything, she gestures toward the Enforcers. "If I was interested in harming any of you, I would've given them the order to start shooting already."

Everyone in the room seems to watch me, waiting, as I consider her offer. I know I won't be leaving the Heart alive—if my vision comes true, none of us will—but I don't want to close that door or the potential for a fresh start elsewhere on Ezra and Jenner, especially if there's no hope of ending this attack or preventing the downfall of our home. I might have told them to stand up to PHOENIX, but we've been back in the city for only a few hours and we're already in way over our heads. Even if we try to intervene, it won't matter if PHOENIX doesn't win this war.

And that's assuming I can find a way to prevent the future I saw. Otherwise, anything we do now is futile.

"There's still time," Rai reminds me, her voice a soothing croon in my ear. Maybe this is how I protect the people I love moving forward. By ensuring there's an exit in place for them, even if there isn't one for me.

I glance at each of the Enforcers around us and then at Quinn, who looks down at the floor, his hand clamped to his still bleeding side, his upper lip curled back, exposing his teeth. With a groan, he eases himself back down to the floor, propping his head against the side of Rai's bed. Although his face is crumpled in pain, he looks almost relieved, his eyes sliding shut—as if he's done what he came here to do and now, can finally rest.

Frowning, I take in the Enforcers again. Quinn might not be much of a threat at the moment, but the soldiers surrounding us are a whole other story. Would they let us leave if we refused to go with them?

Where would we even go if we do?

Jenner's fingers tighten around the grip of his pistol—the barrel still aimed at my mother's face—making me swallow the bitter taste of my fear and come to a decision, as much as I don't like it. Although she's a liar, I can sense that she's telling the truth when she says they're not here to harm us. And while I detest the thought of spending even a second longer with the imposter wearing the face of my mother, given the revelations the last few minutes have exposed, I know accepting her offer will give Ezra and Jenner the best chance of survival—especially if she's telling the truth about having an escape route out of the city. If we don't go with her, we're on our own, surrounded on all sides by enemies who would kill us without hesitation.

My life might be forfeit to this disease, but that doesn't mean theirs have to be.

Plus, in the event I'm wrong and the future is more malleable than I've been led to believe, I don't want my stubbornness to be the reason we all die in this place or by the hand of the Enforcers guaranteed to swarm the building if we turn down her offer.

With a deflated sigh, I release Ezra's hand and step forward until I'm shoulder to shoulder with Jenner, my fingers carefully folding around his wrist as I push down his arm, forcing his gun away from my mother. His face burns red as he shoots an accusatory glare at me, his bright eyes wordlessly asking how I could possibly side with her over him. I'm not—far from it—but I doubt anything I say at this moment could ever make him believe that.

Straining my jaw, I stare down my mother. "I have questions and you have answers. *Both* of you." My gaze slides to Quinn, who pries one eye open, sensing the weight of my attention. When he peeks up at me, I grind out through clenched teeth, "That's the only reason I'm agreeing to this."

My mother purses her lips and nods. Quinn looks like he's about to be sick but does the same, wincing with the effort, before letting his eye slip closed once again. Behind me, Ezra and Jenner say nothing.

My mother tugs back her coat sleeve, peering between her silver watch and the door. "Well, if there's nothing anyone else has to say on the matter—"

"We're not leaving. Not without Rai," Ezra protests.

Confusion flashes across my mother's cold face, followed quickly by comprehension as she once again glances past us toward the bed in the corner. "There's not much that can be done about *that*," she says tersely.

"The only reason we're even here at all is because of Rai," I interject.

For a moment, my mother just looks at me, her face pinched, the wheels of deliberation turning behind those familiar eyes. Finally, with a sigh, she relents. "It's unlikely I'll be able to help her, but I'll try. *After* you come with me."

"What about him?" Jenner asks, jerking his chin toward Richter, who is still staring up at my mother with a baffled look on his face, his eyes glazed over and wide with derangement.

If the blood loss doesn't kill him, the shock might, I note.

She shrugs one delicate shoulder, as if the thought of his fate hadn't even occurred to her. "Oh, he's coming with us. We have unfinished business." The menacing edge to her voice makes me shiver.

I stiffen. "Coming with us?"

Coming with us where?

My mother rolls her eyes. "Don't worry. He won't leave this building alive."

Snapping her fingers, she signals to the two nearest Enforcers, who step forward and grab Richter by the neck of his coat, hoisting him up off the floor. As he's pulled upright, the broken collar falls from his lap and strikes the tiles with an ominous *thunk*.

A strangled cry escapes Richter's lips and he reaches for his injured leg as much as his restrained hands allow.

"We were partners!" he shrieks, finding his voice again through the pain, his expression crazed as his eyes find my mother's. "We were on the same side!"

"Stop." At her clipped command, the Enforcers wrestling Richter toward the door cease mid-step.

Clearing her throat, she stalks toward my captor, her steps balanced and steady despite the tiles underfoot being slick with his blood. Once beside him, she grabs his chin with one hand, tugging until their faces are only inches apart. With the other, as she holds his gaze, she sticks a manicured finger in the bullet hole above his left knee.

When he screams, she forcibly closes his mouth, gripping his jaw so tightly her nails dig into the skin, drawing blood. She then leans in even closer to him, her voice a low and guttural whisper.

"I stopped being on your side the second you took my daughter."

She spits in his face before releasing his chin, and as she steps back, her eyes flick to the floor where my collar sits undisturbed on the tile behind him. She waves at the Enforcers restraining Richter's arms, gesturing for them to take him into the hallway, then brushes past as they make for the door, plucking the device up in her nimble fingers and immediately shoving it in her pocket. Part of me wants to ask why she's grabbed the collar, while another part would rather not know. Whatever the reason, it's useless now.

As my mother turns to exit the room, she beckons to the remaining Enforcers, who instantly abandon their posts at her command.

"What about Quinn?" Ezra calls after her. "You aren't just going to leave him here, are you?"

His words draw my attention back to the ex-Enforcer, and I feel the tiniest twinge of guilt at the wan, near colorless hue of his skin. Surely, dying from a gunshot wound wasn't the outcome he was meant to see from the deal he made with my mother.

"You don't get it. This is me saving your life—" he had said. Whatever his motivations were, Quinn also thought he was helping me, someone he openly considered a monster. Regardless of why he did all this, he still saved our lives.

And for that, he doesn't deserve to die.

My mother pauses in the doorway, throwing an impatient look over her shoulder. The Enforcers tailing her mimic her movements, coming to an abrupt halt behind her.

"How bad is it?" she asks, peering at the bloody sheet wrapped around Quinn's mid-section, one imperious brow raised.

"The bullet went clean through," he mutters. "A few stitches and I'll be fine."

Nodding, she cuts her stern gaze to Ezra. "There you have it. We'll come back for him and your friend once we've dealt with the more pressing matter at hand." She raises her chin, side-eying the door where Richter waits just outside in the hallway.

Deal with it how? I wonder before deciding it's probably best not to ask.

Steeling myself, I step forward to follow when my mother and the Enforcers leave the room, but a hand grabs my upper arm before I can get far, roughly yanking me back.

"Are we really doing this? Are we really *trusting* her?" Jenner asks.

As I turn, my eyes drift between him and Ezra, who lets out a strained breath through his nose.

"Even if she is your mother, she still works for the DSD," he says. "She can't be trusted, you know that."

I hesitate, forcing myself to pause and consider the situation from their perspective. They only know Evelyn Adler as the enemy whereas I've always known her on a different, more intimate level—as the woman who tried to protect me and shield me from danger the first eighteen years of my life. As much as I hate her for her duplicity, I have to believe she won't actually hurt me. And, regardless of the risks, I need answers.

Answers I don't think she'll give me unless we cooperate.

In the silence, Ezra and Jenner mimic my stillness like shadows made of flesh and bone.

Uncomfortable, I clear my throat. "I'm not sure we really have much of a choice. It's not like we have any other options."

Jenner blanches. "She murdered my family," he counters.

"Do you know that for sure?" For some reason, I feel defensive, like I'm somehow an extension of my mother's crimes. Maybe I'm in denial. Maybe I just don't want to believe the woman I relied on for so many years is capable of something so heartless.

At his wounded expression, shame punches the air from my lungs.

"I mean…was it actually her who did it?" I amend.

Jenner runs a shaking hand through his hair, pushing the thick black strands off his forehead. "After my family was taken to the DSD, I begged Rai to hack into the citizen registry database and see if she could find out what happened to them. I had hoped, if we could determine where exactly they were being held, then maybe we could get them out. But we acted too late; all Rai found was their death certificates, signed by none other than a Dr. Evelyn Adler, complete with her smiling mugshot, like the bitch was gloating about what she had done." Nostrils flaring, he glares at the doorway where my mother stands just outside in the corridor. "It took me a second to make the connection, but it's her. I'd know that face anywhere."

Anguish swells in my chest, and I wipe at the tears streaking my cheeks, the residue leaving my skin sticky and raw. I can envision that picture too easily—I can see the subtle smirk shaping her lips just like the one always worn by Dr. Richter. Who knows, maybe being a psychopath is a job requirement to work in this place.

"I understand why you don't trust her—" When he snorts, I lower my voice to a fierce whisper, growling, "Remember, the same woman who murdered your family also sentenced *my* father to death. We've both lost something because of her." Jenner averts his eyes, and I swallow, pushing out my next words with effort. "But, right now, that's secondary to me, to *knowing* I was held captive in this place for nearly three years and she was here the whole time, just watching it happen. She was *here* and never once did she try to help me." I pause, my throat thick, only daring to speak again once I'm sure my voice won't betray me. "I need to know what she wants from me and why she waited until now to come get it."

Jenner might not understand, but, for my sanity, I have to at least try to get answers.

Extending my arm, I touch his hand, tentatively interlacing our fingers. "Plus, we need help, and I think we all know that no one else is going to offer us that."

We came back into the Heart on a whim, without a plan as to what we would do once we got here or an exit in place to ensure we'd actually get out again if we had to. We didn't have the time or information to formulate a strategy, emotions were running high, and we were all only thinking about one thing: saving Rai. But now, things are different. Now, there's a clock ticking over our heads, with every second hurtling us all toward certain doom.

"There's still time," Rai says yet again.

Maybe, I muse, hoping she's right.

And maybe trusting my mother is how I get it.

A pained expression darkens Jenner's gaze, but he doesn't protest my reasoning.

"Fine," he grumbles, yanking his hand free of mine and shoving his gun back in his belt. "But don't expect me to be happy about it."

As Jenner trudges away, Ezra touches my shoulder. "He won't stay mad forever."

Forever.

A lump rises in my throat.

The problem is, I don't have forever.

"Are you sure about that? At what point will I be unredeemable to the two of you?" My chest tightens. "Maybe this crossed the line for him."

A curt laugh fills the space between us. "He blew up a transport helicopter while he was still on it just to save your life. He'd go to the ends of the earth for you. We both would." Planting a swift kiss on my forehead, he whispers, "We're with you. We're always with you, even if we don't like it."

My mother clears her throat from the doorway, and when I look in her direction, she taps her foot impatiently against the floor, beckoning us to hurry. With a sigh, I glance up at Ezra again, but his gaze has shifted, his attention on Rai.

"We'll come back for her," I whisper, but I don't dare utter the other thoughts in my head. The ones that force me to acknowledge that I know she won't be leaving this place.

Unable to bring myself to look at her sleeping face for a moment longer, I peer at Quinn, tugging on Ezra's sleeve. "Do you think he'll really be okay?"

"I can hear you, you know." Quinn groans, lifting one lid to look at me. "And like I said before, I'll be fine. It's really little more than a flesh wound."

The blood still seeping through your fingers says otherwise.

"I meant it when I said I want answers," I say, my tone clipped. "So, try not to die while we're gone."

He lets out a low chuckle, which turns into a wracking cough, his face scrunching as he cringes at the pain. "Don't worry. You'll get them. Just not here. Not now."

"Soon then?" I press.

He exhales through his nose as his eye falls closed again. "Soon," he promises.

FOUR

WHEN EZRA AND I JOIN the others in the hallway, my gaze catches on my mother's face, her lips pursed and eyes lowered, locked on our entwined fingers. I straighten, standing tall under her scrutiny, her disapproval only encouraging me to grip Ezra's hand even harder.

With a *humph*, she falls into step beside me, and without saying a word, we progress down the darkened corridor—the lights still flickering at random intervals, exacerbating the apprehension writhing in my gut. Jenner walks a few paces in front of us, hands thrust in his pockets and shoulders slumped slightly, but the way he keeps looking back tells me he's listening, hanging onto every impending word in the silence.

"What are you going to do to him?" I finally ask, glancing between my mother and Richter, who is sandwiched between two Enforcers at the front of our group. They drag him, ignoring his pained whimpers, just like the orderlies used to do to me when I was a patient here, leaving a staggered line of blood behind them. It streams steadily from Richter's pant leg, marking the tiled floor like a trail of breadcrumbs. "What unfinished business were you talking about?"

"Why?" She crosses her arms, frowning at me. Her irises flash like a cat's in the shadows. "Do you want him to live? After everything he's done to you, do you think he deserves to?"

I gape at her, the sharp edges of a retort poking at the inside of my lips. Even if she wasn't directly involved with the torment I experienced the last few years, even if she didn't have a hand in what Dr. Richter put me through in this place, she still allowed it to happen. She didn't fight for me the day of my exam—the day the Enforcers came to take me away—when, as Head of Termination, she had power. Power that might have changed everything.

Instead, she hid behind her false life and simply let the chips fall where they may, abandoning me to my fate as if I was nothing to her. As if I *meant* nothing. She let me go…the same way she let go of my father.

And because of that, I will never forgive her.

"And whose fault is that?" I bite back. "Remind me who it was who abandoned me to suffer through that tortur—"

She stops walking, and the white coat representing who she really is swishes around her knees as she rounds on me, clutching my left arm hard enough to make me hiss.

"This is neither the time nor the place for this discussion. He needs to be dealt with. *Now*." She gives me a quick once-over, and her eyes narrow, as if she doesn't recognize this person, this *thing*, I've become. Clicking her tongue, she adds, "I wouldn't have thought you'd be foolish enough to extend mercy to such a monster."

A cruel laugh escapes, springing up from my throat. "Haven't you heard? The real monster here is me." I tug my arm back, throwing her off, challenging her judgmental gaze with my own. My upper lip curls back in a sneer. "And I never said I don't want him to die."

If anything, I don't want you to steal that from me.

Ezra stands close to me on my other side, his grasp on my hand tightening. Out of the corner of my eye, I notice Jenner has stopped walking as well, his body turned sideways, his fingers hovering over the gun at his belt as if it's the only thing he can trust.

My heart clenches at the sight of them, always ready to intervene on my behalf and protect me, even when I don't need it. I feel weary, exhausted right down to my bones, from all the fighting and all the lying and pain that's consumed my life in recent years. But, in so many ways, they've had it worse, and I can only imagine how they must be feeling—what they must be thinking—given what they've both been through.

Ezra, whose brother has embraced his madness and who now sits on the brink of death, too dangerous to keep alive. And Jenner…whose family was executed by mine.

I'm overcome by the urge to reach out to him, to console him, but it doesn't feel right. Not here. Not in this place, surrounded by the ghosts of his family. Not when I'd only be seeking to comfort him as a way of easing my own pangs of conscience.

My chest tightens, and I wonder how we cross the canyon of guilt that seems to keep growing between us. How do I release them from the unending shadow my existence always casts over their lives when they're too far lost in the darkness to even remember the light?

I swallow, fighting back resurfacing tears…because I already know the answer.

Soon, I vow, keeping my eyes on my mother so as not to

expose the heartache in my gaze to them. *Soon you'll be free of me and this will be over.*

My mother's brows dip into a vee, and her lips press into a tight, thin line, her hawkish eyes assessing me closely. Whatever suspicion I glimpse in her gaze is fleeting as she lifts her chin, seemingly content with my reaction.

"Hm." She pivots and carries on walking, stroking a contemplative finger along the line of her jaw. "If you feel that way now, I can only imagine what you'll have to say once you see what I have to show you."

My stomach dips at her cryptic words, but I can't bring myself to press her on the matter or ask her where she's taking us.

Because—

"Where are we going?" Even wrapped up in the warmth of Ezra's voice, this question is a sledgehammer to my skull, smashing a hole in my composure.

"One of the sublevels." My mother's face darkens. "There's a…warehouse, of sorts, down there."

"That's only slightly ominous," Jenner grumbles.

She shoots a scathing look at his back. "Yes, well, you'll want to prepare yourselves. I promise you, what's down there isn't pleasant."

Because I know—

"So, then, why are we going at all?" Ezra presses. "Let's just grab Rai and Quinn and get out of here. You said—"

"Not until I've destroyed it!" she snaps. Her scathing response echoes down the length of the hallway, and when her gaze cuts to mine, my blood seems to freeze in my veins. "I can't allow that research to survive. The attack should have—" Her mouth snaps shut, as if she didn't intend to say those words. As if they forced their way out on their own.

As I gape at her, I'm reminded of what Quinn said just before we came back to the DSD. When we were standing outside the ruined entrance, remarking on the damage the building took from the bombing.

"It's as if they knew where to hit," I had said.

And then Quinn answered, with words that resurface as the realization sinks in, *"Maybe they did."*

"It was you," I breathe. My feet drift to a stop, and the others all stop walking as well, as if our movements are linked by some invisible force. I drag in a shaking breath, then more forcefully add, "You were feeding intel to the people who bombed us."

"Someone on the inside," Jenner mutters, echoing his own earlier words.

"Why the hell would you do that?" Ezra steps toward her, releasing my hand. "Why the *hell* would you attack your own people?"

"I did no such thing," my mother counters. "Not directly, at least. There was an agreement made, and we…" She hesitates, her expression pensive, as if she's looking for the right way to phrase it. "We supplied them with the coordinates to destroy this place, that's all. But the damn bombs didn't hit deep enough."

"We?" Jenner presses, but she ignores him, brushing a hand over her face, which suddenly appears a decade older than it did only seconds ago. Does she mean her and Quinn?

Or is there someone else my mother has been working with?

With a sigh, she sweeps back a loose strand of hair. "Yet another spectacular failure. Maybe this is karmic justice at work."

Slowly, the disjointed pieces before me connect until the picture forming begins to make sense. My mother's appearance here. Her unfinished business with Dr. Richter. Her desire to eradicate his research…

She wants to destroy this place for the same reason I'm terrified of seeing what she has to show me.

Because I know what's waiting, I realize.

Bending forward, I plant my hands on my knees as the rancid taste of bile floods my mouth. My legs tremble as the revelations tally up, building one on top of another until I can barely keep hold of my rising emotions as each betrayal, each discovery, stacks up before me. Pressure grows in my chest, but I beat it back. If I'm not careful, my power will slip through the cracks in my mind and unleash who-knows-what kind of devastation.

Except, I do know because I've seen it before. And now that my control is gone, there is nothing to hold back what I'm truly capable of.

Sweat trickles down the sides of my neck, and a wave of vertigo swirls through my head as a black fog encroaches, disorienting my senses. I gasp, fighting to keep myself conscious.

My vision blurs as I think of Rai in that bed, her body still, her serene face frozen in sleep. A metallic stench fills my nose as she once again whispers those warning words from my dream.

"There's still time," I whisper under my breath, wiping the back of my hand across my nostrils. When I pull it away, blood stains my pale skin.

Just stay on your feet, I chide myself, shaking my head to clear the haze and hopefully stop the hallway from spinning. My gaze drops to the floor, but the red streaks of blood across the tiles swirl into a nauseating pattern that makes my light-headedness worse.

I squeeze my eyes shut to escape the vertigo, to escape the

images haunting me, but the memory of the blood and future destruction is already there, branded into the backs of my eyelids, always ready to greet me. To tell me there's nowhere to hide. That it's coming.

To remind me of the monster I am.

"Wynter?" A warm hand wraps around my shoulder and presses gently, steadying me. I know without having to look that it's Ezra. "What is it?" he asks, bringing his mouth close to my ear.

I gulp, trying to force out the words, quickly wiping my bloody hand on my bodysuit. I open my eyes to find Ezra staring at me, visibly concerned, but I avoid his questioning gaze, instead glaring at my mother.

"They're still here…aren't they?" I ask.

My pulse quickens when I glimpse the answer reflected in the piercing storm of her eyes.

"So, you know."

I nod, turning my head to observe the Enforcers holding Richter's sagging body upright between them. Although his eyes are closed, I suspect he's awake. That he knows exactly where we're going and what we'll find once we get there.

"Know what?" There's a wariness to Jenner's tone that I don't want to fuel, but I can't control my lips. They move of their own accord, even as the lump in my throat threatens to choke me.

As I speak, I'm brought back to that tiny cell under the farmhouse where Nolan kept me confined after PHOENIX extracted me from the State. Even now, I can envision him sitting in front of me. I can hear his gruff voice in my ears.

"Nolan…told me what Richter was attempting to do with my blood," I say, breathless. Although my mouth is dry, the words keep coming. "How he was injecting it into other people with Ultraxenopia, trying…to create an army of soldiers."

Once again, my focus settles on Richter, and before I can talk myself out of it, I'm stumbling toward the heartless man who abused me for years. Ezra and my mother both call after me, while Jenner tries to grab my arm, but I don't stop, evading his grasp.

"That's what you meant, right?" I shriek, the accusation like a hot brand on my tongue. "Before, when you said you spent the last two years trying to create more of me. You were making—" Soldiers.

Weapons.

I grimace, suppressing the overwhelming urge to scream. "And they're here, aren't they?"

They're still here.

Dr. Richter's eyes glide open, the skin around them mottled with shades of brown and purple, the sockets darker than normal, concave from the pain of his wound and blood loss. A bruise forming across the left side of his jaw tells me one of the Enforcers must've struck him at some point—probably to stop him from struggling when they dragged him out of the exam room.

He grins at me, revealing teeth stained with red. He deserves far worse than he's already gotten.

You deserve to die.

The sly smile contorting his lips stretches wide. "Would you like to meet your brothers and sisters? Would you like to see why your blood is so special?"

I blanch at his words, unable to speak, as the guilt I've tried so hard to press back washes over me in a devastating wave with a singular purpose—to crush me. My chest constricts, and I can't breathe. I can't breathe. *I can't breathe.* I don't want to see them. I don't.

Not when, at the heart of it all, I know I'm the one who's at fault for their deaths.

"Shut him up."

My mother's heels snick against the tiled floor as she approaches from behind my right shoulder, the harsh growl of her voice a hammer against the walls of my paralyzing panic. I glance at her when she stops beside me and rests a hand on my upper back, breaking me free of its hold.

At her pointed look, one of the Enforcers shoves a gag into Richter's mouth before swinging his arm back and bringing it forward again without restraint, punching my tormentor hard in the stomach. A muffled groan leaches out around the gag, sending an odd surge of satisfaction racing through me.

My mother shifts her hands onto my shoulders and carefully spins me around to face her. "I wouldn't speak to him anymore if I were you," she warns. "He's smart, but he's desperate. He knows he's been cornered, and he'll be looking for a way out at every turn. He'll use that against you if he can." Although she lowers her hands, there's a moment where I sense real motherly concern coming from her, but as soon as it appears, it's gone. The blue eyes staring down at me—so much like my own right eye—are reproachful now, holding all the warmth of ice. "He'll only try to get inside your head."

I let out a deflated breath, a wry smile pulling at my lips.

Too late.

I lift a hand to the back of my neck, my fingernail grazing the knobbly flesh where the tracking chip Richter implanted in me remains, lodged in the top of my spine. A cackle of laughter swells in my chest, expanding in my lungs, the sound unhinged, the madness finally leaking through.

"He's already there," I mutter, certain that, as I speak, I'm donning the soulless black eyes of the monster I always wear in my visions. "He has been since you let the DSD have me."

My mother's gaze holds me in place for a moment, her face an unreadable mask. Distant. Perhaps that's how she shields herself.

How she keeps her own guilt at bay.

Sidestepping me, she grinds out, "Let's go," before resuming her onward march. The Enforcers follow her lead as if they have no will of their own, the two at the front towing a barely conscious Richter toward the one place in the entire world I don't want to see. The one place I know I *have* to see if my mother is going to give us her help—whatever that entails.

The one place where what remains of my sanity will surely shatter into a million, irreparable pieces.

We continue the rest of the way in silence, my mother trudging several paces ahead with the Enforcers while Ezra and Jenner bring up the rear, lingering close to me at all times. I'm not sure how long it's been since we left the exam room— five minutes? Ten minutes? Fifteen? It all feels the same.

"How much farther?" Ezra asks, echoing my own silent thoughts.

My mother doesn't respond. It's possible she doesn't hear him but it's far more likely she can't be bothered to answer, which wouldn't be at all surprising considering her intolerance for questions during my childhood.

I frown at the memory of the naive little girl I used to be…and clearly still am, even now, after everything I've endured. How did I not know or ever suspect who my mother really was? Was she simply that good at hiding the truth? Or did she have me so well-trained to just accept what I saw, to never question anything around me, that I wouldn't think to question her?

Bitterness prickles my skin, and I shudder against it, once again swathed in the understanding that everything I once thought I knew was a lie. And here I am, about to face the worst one of all: the lie I keep telling myself. That I'm a good person at heart. That I never wanted to be a monster.

Even though the blood coursing through my veins and the horror awaiting us say otherwise.

My mother leads us around several corners, then down a flight of stairs to a dead-end passage, bringing our procession to a grinding halt in front of an elevator I've never seen before. A small scanner on the wall positioned at eye level blinks to life when the sensor registers movement.

"Open it."

The Enforcers restraining Richter shove him forward at my mother's command, one pinning his arms behind his waist while the other tugs his head back by his hair, the fingers of the soldier's black gloves intertwining around the auburn brown strands and squeezing. Shifting Richter in front of the sensor, the Enforcers hold him still while the device scans his face, the blue glow emanating from the panel making his skin look sallow in the minimal light.

"Facial recognition scan complete," an automated voice intones from the device. *"Commencing retinal confirmation."*

Richter doesn't fight the scan, his back heaving, no doubt laughing around the gag—thrilled by the notion of me finally coming face to face with what a monster I am. With what he and the DSD turned me into.

"My own little angel of death."

I press a hand to my mouth at the recollection of his voice in my ear, holding back a scream or a sob. Honestly, I'm not sure which. Maybe both.

I don't want to see this.

I have to see this.

I don't want to know.

I have to know.

My thoughts vacillate back and forth until—

"Retinal scan complete. Welcome back, Dr. Richter," the scanner bleats in greeting.

The steel doors slide apart with a hiss, granting us access and beckoning us on board, ready to take us down into the bowels of what will surely be hell.

A crippling fear overwhelms me, and my body goes rigid, my boot soles glued to the floor. I wish the ground would open up and swallow me—anything to stop me from having to step foot on that elevator.

I don't want to see this, I think again, trembling.

I could leave right now and never turn back. I could walk out of this place, pretending what Dr. Richter said is a lie, just like his promise of a cure.

You could, my conscience says, *but you won't.*

"No," I say in a near inaudible breath. "I won't."

Because to do that—to run—would mean rejecting my own culpability.

Bristling, I push forward one step at a time, inching into the cramped metal box, the air inside somehow both hot and cold and smelling strongly of sterilizer. It's claustrophobic, and with the others gathered around me, the walls seem to shrink, pressing in on all sides, the matte metal surface warping our reflections.

"Do you really think an elevator is the safest place to be after the building's *just* been bombed?" Jenner asks. His tone is snide, his skepticism thick behind every word.

Annoyance creases my mother's brow, and she glares at him, her upper lip curling slightly. "It's the only way down. Don't like it? Get off. Otherwise, kindly do us all a favor and shut up."

I try to focus my thoughts elsewhere. To shut them out. To shut *everything* out. But I can't. All I can see in my head is the very real horror I'm responsible for. Not just the deaths I'm destined to cause when this world comes to a violent and catastrophic end, but the countless fatalities that already stain my conscience.

The doors sweep shut, and the air leaves my lungs, my panic an intense living thing that gnaws at my insides, trying to rip me apart from within.

"Hey," Ezra says, his voice soft in my ear, his soothing tenor instantly calming me. "I'll be with you the whole time, okay? You aren't alone."

I shudder as his arms wrap around me from behind, and although I don't deserve his kindness or his sympathy, I lean into it. Because I want it. I crave it.

I *need* it to not lose my flimsy hold on what little sanity I still manage to cling to.

"No matter what?" I breathe, my voice breaking.

No matter what we find?

Even if I'm the cause of it?

As the elevator begins its descent, Ezra's hold on me tightens, his fingers a comforting cage around mine. His nose brushes the back of my neck when he nods.

"No matter what."

F I V E

JENNER SULKS IN THE CORNER closest to me, on my left, chewing on his bottom lip, the entire ride down to Sublevel B—our destination according to the automated voice projecting around us in the overcrowded elevator. The monotone words are distorted by the occasional crinkle of static, likely a result of the damage to the building caused by the bombings on the city.

Bombings my mother helped orchestrate.

The voice announces our arrival at the same moment the doors ping open, letting in a rush of cold air. At first, all I can see is a gloom so thick and foreboding my first instinct is to cower and hide. A chill rolls over my skin as I stare into the darkness—my feet rooted to the spot and legs stiff—unable to bring myself to move forward even as everyone else steps off the platform into the shadows.

Nausea hits me like a brick wall as I drag in a breath, the sour undertone of a noxious odor in the stale underground air potent enough to make me retch. Cupping a hand over my mouth, I recoil, shrinking deeper into the elevator until my back collides with the hard metal.

Crinkling his nose, Ezra stops at the threshold and sniffs, but the revulsion contorting his face dissipates, replaced by a familiar concern when he looks back and sees me flattened against the far wall.

"Hey," he says, closing the distance between us again. "Just say the word and we'll go."

No. I have to see this. I have to know.

"I'm fine," I lie, dropping my arm and finally forcing myself to take a step forward. "Let's just get this over with."

I exit the elevator, pushing ahead into the dim glow of the emergency lights, which burn red on this level. As my eyes adjust to the darkness, I note that the floor is an uninterrupted slab of gray concrete, plain and unassuming compared to the sterile tiles that are so prominent throughout the rest of the building. The smooth surface stretches forward in a broad, half-moon shape, and along the curved edge, the floor collides with a wide pane of glass that stretches the full breadth of the space. The glass slants upward at a forty-five degree angle until it connects with the ceiling, forming an observation deck overlooking another much larger room.

My mother stands in front of the window, looking down at the space below, while the Enforcers accompanying us have separated into three pairs. One duad lingers near the elevator with another waiting beside a door off to the left, which I can only assume leads through to whatever nightmare awaits on the other side of the glass. The remaining pair stands at attention on the right side of the observation deck with Richter wedged upright between them.

Ignoring them all, I press on toward the glass, holding my breath as that stale odor grazes my nostrils, my lips, my tongue, my throat. Trepidation grabs at my skin, trying to find purchase and pull me back away from the window, but I brush the sensation off and tell myself to just keep moving. Even if I don't want to see what's beyond those glass panes.

Even if I know seeing it will be what breaks me.

The cavernous space just past the window is massive, at least fifty times greater in scale than any other room at the DSD—at least, of the ones I've been in or seen. The warehouse spans the height of two levels, and above, industrial fans pattern the ceiling, their constant whirring thunderous, even through the barrier of thick glass.

I watch the blades spin, focusing on the droning hum of each lethal rotation as the fans circulate oxygen, picturing myself standing under their currents. When I imagine the brush of that cool air on my skin, an involuntary shudder rips through me and my mind conjures images of what it is the fans are being used for.

What it is they need to keep cold.

Sinking my teeth into the inside of my lower lip, I press a hand to the glass and lower my gaze to the room below, wholly unprepared for what I know I'll find but unable to delay facing it any longer. If I don't look now, I never will. And by refusing to look, I'd only be denying the cruelty that went on in this place.

Cruelty that I unknowingly contributed to.

Hundreds of metal tables are laid out on the floor, lined up in perfect rows, the mid-section of each covered in a single white sheet—clinical and frigid, just like the rest of this place. At a glance, they remind me of the table I was tortured on in Dr. Richter's laboratory or of the table in Exam Room B, where I endured countless inspections during my time as his unwilling pet. It's only when I look closer that I notice the difference.

It's only when I look closer that I notice the faces.

"What the hell…" Ezra breathes beside me.

Although I already knew what I'd find here—knew in my bones what my blood is responsible for—my eyes still widen in abject horror, locked on this barbaric disregard for human life displayed in the room below like some kind of spectacle.

The acid in my stomach roils as I wonder how many others have stood in this exact same spot, watching as Richter committed his crimes. Why else have this window here? Why else make it so people could see what's occurring downstairs if Richter didn't expect spectators to his torture?

Bile burns my throat. *I'm going to be sick.* But I can't look away no matter how hard I try to. I can't bring myself to tear my eyes from the bodies.

Like Rai, each of Richter's victims is naked, their dignity only protected by the thin, white sheets draped over their torsos, pelvises, and the top half of their legs, offering far more modesty than my friend has been afforded. And yet, unlike Rai, the pallid hue of their unmoving faces tells me they lack the one thing she still possesses, even if she's otherwise dead to the world.

A pulse.

My quickening breaths leave patches of fog on the glass as my fingers tighten into a fist, my knuckles trembling against the broad pane. The power inside me rears to life, vibrating along the underside of my skin, a hum in my blood that threatens to shatter this window.

Gulping down the lump in my throat, I sweep my blurring vision across the organized grid of bodies. These people… They're just like me. Or they were before Dr. Richter got hold of them.

Before my blood was forced into their veins.

A tear cuts a line down my face, and as I wipe it away with the back of my hand, I pivot, shooting an accusatory glare at my mother. She stands a few feet to my left in funereal silence, staring down her nose at the grotesque sight below. A flicker of disgust burns in her eyes.

"You knew about this," I hiss. "You knew what he was doing here."

The biting edge to my voice makes her flinch, as if she had somehow forgotten I was here in the few seconds she's spent looking upon Richter's den of death. Her lips part—probably to excuse her role in this massacre—but Jenner cuts in before she can speak.

"*Of course*, she knew." His face is hard as he sidles up beside me, crossing his arms. "Killing people is what she does."

"Were you in on it?" My whispered words feel pointless because I already know what she's going to say. After all the senseless killing I did on behalf of the State, and then seeing what's happening now in the Heart, I know all too well what sort of evil can be born from ambition.

Richter, Bilken, and Nolan—all three have gone to extreme lengths for their twisted aspirations or to gain or maintain a position of power, so I can only imagine what my mother had to do, what crimes she had to commit, to get to where she is.

To become the Head of Termination, feared and revered by all in the Heart.

Fresh tears flood my eyes. Although the logical part of my brain has already accepted the truth, there's another part—the ignorant child buried deep inside me, screaming out—that still clings to the pipe dream that my mother is good. That my own flesh and blood isn't capable of such monstrosities. That my evil wasn't inherent but made. Because if she really did help Richter do this, then that means half of me—the half of me I got from her—was always a monster, even before he set that side of me loose. And if that's the case, then Richter was right.

I really am an angel of death, born to be a scourge on this planet.

"Not so much recently but yes," she admits and, exhaling through her nose, shifts her body to face me. "Richter and I met ten years ago, at which time I helped him procure his test subjects. He was just a junior researcher then, and he lacked the authorization needed to carry out his experiments. Had he tried, there would have been consequences. So,"—she lifts her chin, shrugging one shoulder—"I helped him be…discreet… and offered my support and backing for his eventual promotion with the proviso I get partial credit for his findings."

Jenner snorts. "And the benefits that came with it, no doubt."

Her eyes dart to his, then back to mine, her lips pursed in annoyance, but she doesn't deny it.

"I stepped back two years ago," she says defensively. "When he moved all his research down here and built *this*." She gestures to the room beyond the glass, her upper lip peeling back into a revolted sneer.

"What about before then?" I manage, my voice a rough whisper.

Were you involved when I was here the first time?

She shakes her head. "I haven't had a direct hand in the experiments themselves for some time, not since Richter was elevated to department Head nearly seven years ago. Once he had the State's full support and internal obstruction was no longer an issue, my active participation became unnecessary. Frankly, there were other people more suited to the type of hands-on assistance he required in the lab, and my specialty was always more…behind the scenes. Like I said, I worked in procurement. Besides, I had my own department to run. So, I observed, I offered my input when he asked it of me, and I continued to provide test subjects for his experiments as and when he needed them.

"The first time you were here, I kept a close eye on you. I knew the only way to avoid suspicion of our familial connection and to stay fully apprised of your situation was to monitor everything, as Richter had come to expect of me. I knew about every experiment, down to the smallest detail…and I knew of their outcomes. The second time, when you came back and Richter's relentless experimentation resumed, I knew I couldn't carry on watching you day in and day out and pretend not to know you any longer. And this…" She casts a sad glance through the glass. "It got so far out of hand."

Her eyes drift to mine, her gaze pleading, as if this confession is somehow supposed to make me feel better. As if she didn't just admit to handing innocent people over to be tested on and killed, all in the name of Richter's research. As if she didn't just come out and say it's because of her support that he reached a position of power that allowed him to commit these atrocities.

My arms shake at my sides, but my building outrage and resentment don't seem to discourage her. She continues, even though I wish she would stop.

"At this point, thanks to his success with both you and that collar, Richter had limitless resources at his disposal and entire teams dedicated to subject retrieval, so it wasn't as if he needed my help. In truth, there was little I could do that wasn't already being done by somebody else. So, I stepped back in all regards except one."

"Which was?" Ezra presses.

My mother flashes a wicked grin. "Despite the endless array of tools at his disposal, there was still one thing I could give Richter that no one else could. You see, over the last decade, I have proven myself to be an indispensable confidant. A valuable ally he could trust. And now, I'm using that trust to destroy him."

My mouth and throat are a desert, arid to the point of pain, as I drag my gaze back toward the window and, once again, peer down at the bodies below. Forgotten. Discarded. Useless.

"How did you do it? Where did you…" My jaw clenches.

Where did you get his test subjects?

Her smile fades. "Termination," she murmurs, and when my head snaps up in response, she makes it a point to avoid my gaze.

I can practically feel the blood drain from my face. I always knew criminals and anyone determined to be unredeemable in the eyes of the State—those sent to Termination for the ultimate punishment of death—were often tested on first, used as guinea pigs in human experimentation, like I was, or tortured for information they likely never had. The goings-on at the DSD have always been common knowledge, and yet, knowing my mother was the one who handed these people over to suffer the kind of horrors I experienced at the hand of Dr. Richter—

Vomit rises in my throat, and it takes everything in me to swallow it down.

"Why?" I blink hot tears from my eyes. "Why would you do this? Why would you help him?"

She raises a skeptical eyebrow but still refuses to look at me. "The only true security in this country is power. Believe it or not, everything I've ever done was for you. To keep *you* safe. I just never imagined—"

"What?" I scoff. "That I would become a weapon?"

I glower at her when she doesn't answer, clicking my tongue in disgust.

"I want to see them," I say after a moment, and when she still doesn't speak, I grab her hard by the wrist. "Isn't that why you brought me here? So I could see this for myself? To show me what a monster he is?" Releasing her, I thrust a finger at Richter.

To show me I don't really know you at all?

Rather than answer, she looks past me at Richter, who now sits slumped on the floor, his face ashen and head nodding forward as if he's falling asleep. When she struts toward him, he jerks awake at the ominous clicking of her heels on the concrete.

She extends her hand, palm up. "Hand it over. I know you have it on you."

He lets out a wheezy laugh, his eyes shuttering closed again.

Crouching to the floor, my mother grabs a handful of his sweat-matted hair and yanks his head back. "We can do this the easy way, or I can have one of my friends here blow out your other kneecap. Which will it be?"

Dr. Richter hesitates for only a second before reaching inside his coat's interior chest pocket and pulling out a plastic keycard clenched between his bloodstained fingers. As he holds it out for my mother to take, his eyes slide to mine and his lips curve into a venomous smile.

That smug expression—that damned, gloating grin I've seen more times than I care to recount—triggers something inside me, a surge of anger I can't contain. In this moment, I want nothing more than to wipe that smile clean off his face and make him regret ever messing with me.

As the rage consumes me, I seem to become an invader in my own body, trapped inside it but helpless to act, watching the scene unfold as a spectator. In my place, the monster uses its newfound freedom to slink to the surface and seize control, just like it did before I had my collar to act as a needed leash on my power—like that night in Bilken's office when I butchered those Enforcers, who, despite working for Dr. Richter, didn't deserve to die. Like then, the monster uses the far-reaching grasp of my mind, ripping the plastic from my tormentor's fingers like it turned those Enforcers' guns back on their owners.

The card whips past my mother's hand before she can touch it. She follows its trajectory with startled eyes as it zips across the observation deck toward my outstretched arm, which the monster raises, pulling my strings like I'm a marionette. An abrupt shock passes through me like a jolt to the heart when the flat side of the plastic collides with my palm.

Disoriented, I peer down at the keycard, confused, the last few moments lost in fog. One second, it was in Dr. Richter's hand; the next, it was in mine. I didn't even actively try to use my power to obtain it. It just happened.

Completely beyond my control.

Oxygen evades me as I draw in a steadying breath, my head dizzy as that familiar metallic odor fills my nostrils and sits on the back of my tongue, tasting strongly of copper pennies. Pain stabs behind my eyes, my surroundings going dark at the edges of my vision, and for a moment, I think I might pass out. The vertigo is too powerful, the stench of my blood too overwhelming. But then my fingertips tighten around the card in my hand, reminding me what I have to do, and that resolution gives me all the strength I need to find my balance again. To cling to consciousness until this is over.

Ignoring the heat of everyone's bewildered—and frightened—stares on my face, I turn on my heel and make for the door at the left side of the platform, glaring at the two Enforcers positioned in front of it, who step aside without a word at my approach. As they shift out of the way, I lift my hand to swipe the keycard through the black sensor box on the wall beside the door, then freeze, my fingers an inch from the wall, suddenly uncertain if I want anyone else to witness what awaits beyond this point any closer.

That same terror and shame that shook me at the magistrates building when Ezra saw my file and witnessed the depth of the treatment I received under his brother's care grips me again now, the trauma of what I've been through like a hand around my throat, squeezing tightly until I can't breathe. I didn't want him to see that then, and I don't want him or Jenner to see this now. I don't want them to look at me like I'm broken. Or worse.

Like I'm the monster everyone else thinks I am.

"On second thought, maybe I should do this alone," I announce.

Ezra comes up behind me and touches my shoulders, turning me around to face him, before leaning in close until the tip of his nose brushes mine. "I've gone through hell to get you back," he says, his voice low, his breath hot on my lips. "I'm not leaving you now. Besides, remember what I told you?" He cups one hand around the back of my neck and trails the other along my right cheek. "We're always with you, no matter what."

I glance behind me at the closed door, wondering who it really is I'm trying to protect by choosing to face this nightmare alone. Is it Ezra and Jenner? Or is it me? Am I just running away like I promised I wouldn't?

"Promise me, you won't run away this time."

The promise I made to Ezra... It seems like I said it so long ago now—like it happened in another lifetime to an entirely different person rather than only two days ago. But it didn't. It happened to me, and if I push him away here when he's offering much-needed support, I would be doing exactly what I promised I wouldn't. Running away. And despite everything I've done, despite my guilt, I'm so tired of running and trying to face my problems on my own, even if, in the end, I have to. For now, I want him and Jenner to stay by my side, to ground me, to soothe me, for just a bit longer. For them to keep fighting for me until the time comes when fighting is no longer an option.

Until we need to say goodbye.

As Ezra's hand skims down the length of my arm, I find myself nodding absentmindedly at his touch. "Okay," I concede with a sigh, meeting his gaze again.

But as these words leave my lips, something doesn't feel right. As much as I want him to stick with me until the bitter end, there's a part of me festering in the darkest depths of my soul that hopes this will be the moment his love for me dies. Maybe, by seeing the crimes I've contributed to with his own two eyes, he'll finally decide I'm not worth fighting for and let me go...the way he should have when we were last at these crossroads two and a half years ago.

"Ready?" he asks, nodding toward the closed door behind me, and I nod back despite my growing apprehension, clutching his hand even tighter.

I peer past Ezra's shoulder at Jenner, who stands nearby with his hands thrust in his pockets, his gaze purposely avoiding the glass. The warmth I'm so accustomed to seeing in his expression is missing, and my fingers ache with the urge to reach out and grasp at the essence of what makes him *him* and somehow draw it back out again. The coldness I find instead makes me shiver.

At my questioning gaze, he shakes his head. "I'm going to stay up here. Someone trustworthy needs to keep an eye on this asshole." He jerks a thumb over his shoulder toward Richter.

Unease swells in my gut as my eyes shift from my mother to Jenner, and then to each of the Enforcers standing like sentinels on the outskirts of the deck. I don't know how I feel about leaving Jenner up here alone with them. While my mother hasn't made any move to harm us, I can't be sure that amity will extend to Jenner if I'm not in the immediate vicinity to ensure his well-being and safety. Especially since he's not exactly looking to play nice with the woman he blames for the death of his family.

The mental image of her touching even one single hair on his head is almost enough to make me lash out.

"If any of you so much as look at him the wrong way, I'll kill you," I warn, speaking loudly enough so each of the Enforcers can hear the threat in my voice. My gaze hardens on my mother. "That goes for you, too."

She rolls her eyes, waving a flippant hand in disregard. "I'm coming with you. So, rest assured, your friend will be safe from my judgmental glaring. For now, at least."

I arch a brow. "Why? Looking to repent?"

She blinks slowly, unfazed by my withering tone. "I've learned to live with the weight of my sins long ago. I'm not looking for forgiveness."

Not even for what you did to Father?

"Good," I retort, letting the acid eating away at my insides bleed out in that single word. "Because you won't get it from me."

Scowling, I turn back toward the locked door behind me with Dr. Richter's keycard clenched between my fingers. Beside me, Ezra clasps my hand, and I nod.

"Let's go." I swipe the rectangle of plastic through the dip in the black pad on the wall, skimming the strip where Richter's security clearance has been embedded across the sensors. It only takes a moment, the light at the top of the panel switching from red to green almost instantly.

When the door slides open, my body goes rigid as the fans waft the warehouse smells onto the observation platform, the putrid stench of death even stronger without the airtight barrier to block it.

I bristle, glancing at Ezra, who squeezes my hand for reassurance.

"Just breathe through your mouth," he murmurs.

I part my lips, ignoring the foul taste that assaults my taste buds, and breathing in, I urge myself to move forward. To take just one single step over the threshold.

"Wynter, wait."

The panic in Jenner's voice halts me dead in my tracks, and pulse quickening, I glance over my shoulder as he crosses the deck, his blue eyes round, their depths gleaming with fear.

Stopping directly in front of me, he says, almost breathlessly,

"I get it. I get why you need to see this and why you're doing what you're doing, just—" He brings himself closer until our noses are nearly touching, lowering his voice. "Don't let this mess with your head, okay? The real monster here isn't you, no matter what you keep telling yourself."

I resist the urge to scream—to shake some needed sense into him, and into everyone else who keeps trying to help me. His words don't bring me comfort; if anything, they only make me realize how difficult it will be to get him and Ezra to stop fighting for me. To finally see me as I am. After all, how can they still believe I'm worth saving when the proof of my monstrosity is right here on the other side of that glass?

I can't bring myself to agree with him. I can't even manage a half-hearted nod because doing so would make me a liar, just like my mother. Jenner, seeming to sense my internal struggle, offers me the barest glimpse of that lopsided smile I love—that light, that forgiveness I desperately crave, emerging from behind the more prominent dreariness in his expression, making him seem like himself again, even if only for just a moment.

With as much of an answering smile as I can manage, I turn my back to him and proceed through the doorway, my eyes locking on the steep metal staircase on the other side, which will take me down into Richter's lair of torment.

Ezra and my mother follow me through the door, which slides shut, locking again behind us once we're clear of the threshold. Together, our hands glued palm to palm, Ezra and I take the unlit stairs one grated metal step at a time, proceeding with caution, my mother trailing behind us and mimicking our every move like a shadow. The rancid odor I first noticed on the elevator only gets stronger as we descend. The frigid temperature might be slowing the corpses' decomposition, but not enough to avoid the inevitable smells that accompany death.

Breathing through my mouth like Ezra suggested, I set my gaze on the vast space, which only seems to grow larger as we near the bottom. I shiver, the air touching my skin getting gradually colder, escaping my lips in small puffs resembling smoke. When we step off the stairs into the hangar-like warehouse, I notice the bodies we viewed from the observation deck are even more disturbing to look upon than they had seemed from above. Up close, I can see their skin—grayish blue and chalky—is riddled with boils and scabbed-over sores, and their mouths—all slightly parted, as if caught in a scream—are stained at the edges with dried, flaking blood.

My lower lip wobbles as I release Ezra's hand and inch toward the table closest to me, risking a terrified glance at the disfigured body obscured by the white sheet. It looks so small, and upon further inspection, I discover the face belongs to a boy, probably no older than nine or ten years old. Even stretched out at full length, he doesn't come close to covering the surface. The cold steel seems to swallow him, as if to demonstrate how tiny and fragile he is.

Was. Unfettered rage boils my blood at the thought. *The bastard killed a child.*

Was this what my mother meant by the experiments getting out of hand?

Was murdering children where she drew her moral line in the sand?

Pressing a hand over my mouth to stifle a sob, I shift my gaze away from the boy's face, unable to bear the sight of the pain and fear frozen permanently in his youthful features for even a second longer. As I take a step back, my eyes catch on his arm, the slender limb hanging lifelessly off the table, peeking out from under that crisp white sheet. To my revulsion, the crook of his elbow is riddled with needle marks identical to mine.

Vomit rises in my throat as I stumble back, my eyes flitting around the warehouse. *No, not a warehouse,* I correct myself. *A morgue.*

This place is a morgue.

Tablets are placed at the end of each table, positioned between the subjects' feet, the screens black aside from a subtle, pulsing blue light situated in the corner of each—so faint it was indiscernible from up on the deck.

Needing to see the full scale of the experiments that occurred here for myself, I skirt around the table beside me and tap my fingertip against the screen placed by the boy. As his medical records illuminate the dark space, I'm instantly brought back to that night in Zone 1. The night we thought we lost Rai.

The night I discovered exactly what the State was planning for me.

My heart races, drumming in my ears, as I flip through the file, skimming every note and detail regarding the boy's brief imprisonment, comparing it to my own time here. If what Nolan said about Richter using my blood is true, then everything I went through was just a precursor to what this poor boy had to suffer. His death, along with the deaths of the others around us… Every last one is on me.

Regardless of what Ezra thinks, or of what Jenner says to try to convince me otherwise, this… What happened here…

This genocide…

This is my fault.

My finger stills as two lines of text flash across the screen, and a tear slips down my cheek as I read them.

**Cause of Death: Cardiac Arrest Following Transfusion
Days Completed in the Type X Trial: <1**

"Type X," I breathe. A strangled laugh erupts from my chest, and despite the cold, despite the fog of mist that forms whenever I exhale, sweat coats my upper lip.

Nolan was telling the truth, after all.

Dr. Richter really was attempting to weaponize my blood.

One day, I digest, reading that second line again, the words fuzzy and nearly indistinct through my tears. This boy lasted less than one day with my blood in his veins.

Looking up from the screen, I swing my eyes to the other tables around me, from body to body. Corpse to corpse. And as I take in each one, my hysteria grows. If this boy only survived one day after being exposed to my blood, how long did the others last? Was their misery drawn out for days? Weeks? It couldn't have been that long if Richter never pushed for production of other collars.

But that thought brings me zero comfort when I think of what they still had to go through. When the end finally came, were they in agony? Or did their deaths come quickly?

Were they at least granted that one small mercy?

Tears curve over my cheekbones as I divert my gaze back to the boy's stony face. Reading about what happened to him here isn't enough; I need to see it for myself. I need to witness what Richter put him through.

I need to witness what *I* put him through.

Tremors roll over my hand as I reach out and brush my fingertips against his limp leg, and as I graze his chilled skin, I draw in a breath through my nose despite the terrible smell. My stomach turns, but I push all thought of my own discomfort away and focus only on calling on my power—on triggering a vision, just like I've done so many times in the past. Control or no control, I remember how to do this.

As easy as breathing, I once told myself.

My lungs deflate, a wavering breath breaching my lips, as my thoughts encompass the bodies around me. Other victims to this dreadful disease. When I was first brought to the DSD, Dr. Richter told me the condition was rare. But if that's true, where did he manage to find so many people with Ultraxenopia to serve as his test subjects? Were all these people in the Heart this whole time, all of us unaware of each other?

Or is something far more sinister at play?

A light sparks in the corners of my eyes, bleary at first, then sharpening as it spreads in front of me, filling my full range of vision. Unlike the other times I've done this, what I experience now is a jumbled mess of distorted images rather than the clarity I grew accustomed to with my collar. Sweat beads across my forehead, suctioning my bangs to my skin, as I fight to control the racing images, which fly through my thoughts in a blur.

As I feel my hold on the images strengthen, the vision finally steadies, revealing itself. Time seems to slow as I'm taken back through the battles I participated in on behalf of the State, but I'm not glimpsing my role in the destruction nor an impending retaliatory attack. Now, I'm seeing the aftermath.

Of what my involvement in the State's sieges allowed.

Enforcers roam the war-torn streets, pulling civilians from their homes and shining small flashlights into their eyes, searching for—

Heterochromia, I realize with a start, remembering what Richter said when we first met.

"Like the people in these documents, you have a rare genetic defect known as Heterochromia. To put it in simple terms, your eyes are two different colors. Although the disorder itself is harmless, we are beginning to link it to a more serious condition. A phrenoextratic disease called Ultraxenopia."

My blood curdles as the truth sinks in and I grasp what it is I helped Richter achieve. I helped him pillage countless cities, and the Enforcers… They were never there to support me but to ravage what remained afterward. To search for any survivors with even the slightest sign of having heterochromia, all on the DSD's orders.

In country after country, the men, women, and children who survived the attacks were all herded into transporters like sheep; I see it happen all over again in my head. And I recognize with increasing dismay that I was not only directly involved with their eventual deaths but personally responsible for their enslavement.

I did this to them.

No wonder the State always sent me in first to neutralize the threat. Minimal damage meant fewer casualties and more potential candidates for Richter's research.

The picture in my head warps, transforming, until a room almost identical to the Research laboratory manifests around me. Fear and anticipation prickle my skin, but instead of reliving my own torture, each of Dr. Richter's other victims flash through my head. I watch as they're strapped down to a metal table identical to the one from my own nightmares and then injected with my blood, their screams shredding what remains of my sanity. By the fifth one, I can no longer bear to watch.

I let out a gasp when the images fade, darkness swathing my eyes and taking the shape of the graveyard that is Sublevel B. Dazed, I step back, my fingers slipping away from the boy's leg, and as the contact between us ends, my knees buckle.

Ezra rushes to my side when I collapse, catching me just before I hit the floor, his arms acting as a safety net, drawing me close. The familiar wetness of blood drips from my nose to my lips, and my head throbs, slices of agonizing pain cutting into my temples, making it difficult to focus on anything other than the burden of my guilt. It's crushing me, but I don't fight it. I can't.

I can't…

"My blood did this," I breathe, my voice cracking. "I did this."

Ezra sweeps my sweaty hair back from my forehead and wipes the blood off my quivering lips with the sleeve of his shirt.

"No, you didn't," he says fervently. "You were just…"

The pawn. The murder weapon.

Fresh tears slide down my cheeks, singeing my skin with their heat, as Ezra pulls me against his chest, hooking his chin over the top of my head. "I know it's hard to see otherwise, to *believe* otherwise, but none of this is your fault," he whispers.

I want to believe that, but how can I?

After everything he's seen me do, how can he?

My gaze drifts up to the observation deck window where I envision Dr. Richter just on the other side of that glass. I never wanted this. I never chose to become this tool, this weapon.

I never wanted to hurt anyone.

Every single thing I've done since finding out I have this disease has been forced upon me. I might not be blameless in what happened here, but I didn't choose for it to happen either.

Whether or not my blood was the underlying cause of these deaths, I never consented for it to be used this way, and I certainly never had a say in what I became or in how my powers were used by the State. I didn't want this—I would *never* want this—but like these people, I wasn't given a choice. My path was dictated for me from the start.

Like them, Dr. Richter also made me a victim.

"You're right," I agree, pushing myself upright, swaying at first but finding my feet.

My jaw clenches as the guilt in my chest relents, surrendering to a much stronger emotion.

I glare up at the glass. "It isn't."

SIX

THE PAIN IN MY BODY is secondary—an afterthought—as I push away from Ezra and stumble back toward the stairs, my fingers gripping the handrail so hard the metal squeals and bends beneath my touch, distorted by the pressure and rage pouring out of my body in an invisible wave. In my peripheral vision, I glimpse my mother, her expression resigned, perhaps even contrite, almost as if she knew this would happen.

Hell, maybe she intended it to.

"Wynter, where are you going?" Ezra asks, his tone panicked.

He races after me, hot on my heels, as I bolt up the shadowed stairs, retracing my steps toward the observation deck up above. For so long, I've been blaming myself for so many things that were beyond my control. But this disease didn't turn me into a killer—my fear of the State and the DSD did. I didn't *want* to go to war. I didn't *want* to murder countless innocent people.

Just as I wasn't the one who pumped my blood into the bodies around me.

No, Dr. Richter did that. All the suffering I've witnessed the last three years, and the pain and the guilt that have nearly consumed me—it's all been because of one person. Him. And Rai, whose death has haunted me for years...

Jenner was right. I repeat this sentiment in my head several times until I believe it. *The real monster here isn't me.*

It's Richter.

"Wynter?" Ezra grabs my wrist, and I stop halfway up the stairs to the deck.

Slowly, I turn, looking over my shoulder. "If my blood did this to people like me," I muse, my voice devoid of emotion as my eyes skim over the bodies below, "I wonder what it will do to someone who isn't."

Without meeting his gaze, I rip my arm from his grasp and continue up the stairs, too hell-bent on revenge to care about his reaction to the implication behind my words or the way his steps falter behind me. If this is what ultimately flips the switch and makes me the monster in Ezra's eyes, then so be it.

One way or another, Dr. Richter will pay.

As I near the top of the stairs, I slide the door open with a single look, forgetting the keycard and crumpling the metal before me as if it were paper. The lock panel protests my forced entry, the automated voice dropping an octave, its tone wavering in pitch as it moans its refusal before shorting out, going silent.

A searing pain threatens to melt my brain as the pressure building inside me expands, spreading along every inch of my skin in an uncomfortable, electrifying tingle that radiates through me right down to my bones. Fighting through it, I step over the threshold.

The Enforcers stationed on the outskirts of the observation deck all jump back in alarm, raising their guns as I tear through the door. Their fear and uncertainty as they regard me is as potent as the stink of death in the air, but they aren't my targets. They aren't who I'm here for. Still, they hesitate, peering past me at my mother, who emerges from the warped doorway behind me.

"Stand down," she commands.

The Enforcers exchange unsettled glances, their confusion apparent, even as they lower their weapons. Jenner seems to share in their bafflement, his black brows furrowed and pupils dilated in fear, but I ignore him, focusing on Dr. Richter, who smiles up at me from his place on the floor.

"Do you believe me now?" he coos. "About how remarkable you are?" He raises an arm, gesturing toward the glass, then drops it back to his side in exhaustion. "Just look at what we've achieved together."

Together.

My loathing ignites a fire inside me, the flames burning in my chest savage and hungry, driving me berserk. They guide my movements, and as I storm forward, blind in my rage, I recall all those times on the battlefield when I surrendered myself willingly to my power. Unlike then, the power coursing through me now is unstable, and every second of use is paired with the worst kind of pain imaginable. But I can't help it, the pressure needs a release.

And I need to make my tormentor pay.

Blood streams from my nose, coating my lips, as I thrust out an arm and lift Richter off the floor without even touching him. The Enforcers standing nearby duck out of the way as I throw him to the side, slamming his back flat to the window. As I pin him to the slanted surface, a spiderweb of cracks branch out across the glass beneath him.

"There is *nothing* remarkable about what I just saw." I clench my fingers as if squeezing his windpipe. His eyes bulge, and he paws at his neck, trying and failing to pull away the invisible touch of my hand on his throat.

Gritting his teeth, he chokes out, "You are…Subject Zero. You lived…while they died…because…you are special. It's a pity… you can't…appreciate…what evolution has…gifted you."

"Gifted?" I scoff, sneering at the notion. "This disease is a *curse*. Seeing this"—I wave a frantic hand at the glass—"has only opened my eyes to just how dangerous you are."

I tighten my hold on his throat, and his washed-out complexion blooms with color, turning red first before darkening into shades of purple, then blue. When his eyes roll back into his head, it occurs to me that letting him die this way would be easy. Too easy. And unsatisfying.

No. I can't allow that. He deserves to suffer the same way all those innocent people downstairs had to suffer at his hands. He deserves to suffer the same way *I* had to suffer. And like hell do I plan on making it quick. Death by asphyxiation would be too merciful an end for someone like him.

My fingers slacken, relaxing my death grip, before I release my mental hold fully, dropping Richter back to the floor. A mewling sound escapes him on impact, and he curls into a ball on his side as he greedily drinks in gulps of fetid air until the normal color returns to his face. Tears shimmer across his pasty cheeks.

The second I release him, that build-up of pressure flows out of my body and my strength slips away just enough that I momentarily lose my balance. From behind me and to my right, I sense Ezra and Jenner stepping forward to help me, but

I hold out a hand, shooing them back.

"What do you say we do one more experiment?" My voice is an ominous drawl as I fix my blurring gaze on Richter's face. "We've seen what my blood can do to someone like me. Now, why don't we see what it can do to you."

He blanches at the threat, his deranged mask cracking. For the first time in the few years I've known him, the man responsible for the downward spiral of my life actually looks afraid. The thought gives me a twisted sense of pleasure I didn't know I was capable of feeling.

I look back at my mother to find a complacent grin on her lips.

"This is what you wanted, isn't it?" I ask. "Why you brought me here? You want to destroy him."

"Not just him," she amends, her stare hard and calculating. "All of it."

All of it. His research. The bodies of his victims.

Destroy it all so it can't happen again.

"Good." My eyes flash to the two nearest Enforcers before snapping to Dr. Richter's trembling body. "Take him downstairs."

When they don't move, my mother says, "You heard her. Escort him downstairs immediately."

"W-Wait!" Richter protests when the Enforcers return to his side and yank him up off the floor. "You can't do this! You *need* me! No one else understands your disease! No one else can help you control it!"

As he kicks and fights against the two Enforcers, I hold out an arm, blocking their path.

"You're wrong," I growl, clenching my hands into fists. "I don't need you. I've *never* needed you."

And you already stole that control from me, just like you stole everything else.

Baring his teeth, he lets out a low chuckle. "Without me, you will die. You know this."

I fight back a laugh. Richter doesn't care if I die. Hell, I don't even think he cares if *he* dies. His only concerns are his own sadistic ambitions and living long enough to see them to fruition.

"I don't wish to save this world. I wish to see it burn."

That was what he said to me in the moment right before removing my collar. Blinded by his obsession with this disease, he wants to witness the destruction I've seen in my vision, to see the full extent of the power I'm capable of with his own two eyes, even if that means decimating an entire planet and killing billions of people in the process.

As I challenge his gaze, I can feel the fire of disdain burning inside me, although I hide it behind a detached facade. The mask sliding into place is one I've worn so many times. The mask of the unfeeling weapon *he* created.

"I'd rather die and deprive you of the one thing you want than let you live for a second longer. It's what you deserve."

My mother places a firm hand on my shoulder, and at her touch, I lower my arm. She nods at the Enforcers restraining Richter, who shoots me one final terrified glance as he's hauled across the observation deck toward the door.

Dr. Richter shouts obscenities at me, but his cries become dulled as he's led down the darkened stairway into the warehouse below. My mother's hand disappears from my shoulder as she follows behind the Enforcers, her heels ticking on the metal steps, beckoning me to join her. But I can't seem to bring myself to move.

My eyes shift to the glass, and I stare blankly up at the fans, entranced by their rotations. I don't know why I'm hesitating. It's not as if I haven't killed before. I've taken innumerable lives in cold blood. But then, those deaths were meaningless to me whereas *this*, what I'm about to do, is different. Killing Dr. Richter will sever a toxic, abusive bond that has kept me captive for years.

Killing Dr. Richter will set me free.

"Wynter."

At the sound of Jenner's voice, I avert my eyes from the window to find him and Ezra standing beside me.

"You don't have to do this," he says, his tone pleading. "I know what he is, but you don't have to sink to his level."

"We should just shoot him and be done with it." Ezra looks down at the floor as he speaks, refusing to look me in the eye.

My heart trips at the possibility that what I'm planning will hurt him, even if any love or affection he once held for his brother is gone. As I consider this, I decide that whatever happens in the moments to follow can't just be about me. I'm not the only one Richter has hurt. Ezra deserves a say in his sentence. This decision can't be mine alone.

And yet, I can't bear the thought of leaving this place with Richter's heart still beating.

"I..." Raw emotion strangles my voice. "I know I'm a monster. I've accepted that." I hold up a hand before Jenner can protest, giving him a look that tells him I'm not finished. "But *he* was the one who made me this way. And Rai..." I shake my head, unable to say it. To put what Richter did to her into words. "Someone who would do that doesn't deserve to live. Not if he's only going to do more of this."

I wave toward the window, gesturing weakly to the mortuary

reeking of death just below. Ezra's gaze follows my hand, his expression unreadable, while Jenner's hard stare remains locked on my face.

"This isn't the same," he insists. "This is the first time you would be killing another person by *choice*. Your mother has been back in your life for five seconds and she's already manipulating you into doing her dirty work. Don't let her turn you into something you're not."

Compassion soothes the jagged edges of my heart. I understand why Jenner has reservations—why he's worried what influence my mother might have on me when I'm already so close to the edge. But this isn't about her. Or even about me.

This is about making Richter pay for his crimes.

Before I can argue and tell him he's being short-sighted, Ezra breaks the silence. Every word that escapes resonates with the same vitriolic hatred I feel.

"Austin signed his own death sentence the moment he *chose* to shoot Rai."

Jenner glances between us in shock. "I can't believe what I'm hearing. Murdering an unarmed hostage isn't right, regardless of if they deserve it. You know that," he says, his eyes cutting to Ezra. "That mercy is part of why I agreed to join PHOENIX."

"And look what PHOENIX has become," Ezra scoffs. "The world will be a safer place once he's gone."

"This isn't the only option—"

"What else do you suggest, then?" Ezra asks, his tone bitter. "Who, exactly, will punish him if we let him go free? Nolan, when he creates the new State?"

Jenner doesn't argue further; he must know there's no logical argument to counter the brutal, honest facts before us. Besides, he wants Richter dead as much as we do—I can see that written all over his face. He's just worried for me, as he always is. About what price I'll pay for taking this life.

About what cost it will have on my sanity and what little flicker of humanity I'm still holding onto.

"I feel trapped," I whisper, glancing at Jenner, whose eyes soften at the hardship behind those three words. "And, so long as he's alive, I will be tethered to him and he will always find a way to drag me back. You must know that or else you wouldn't have killed all those Enforcers to get me away from him. So, please," I beg, "don't think less of me for needing this. For needing to finally set myself free."

I watch the shift in his throat when he swallows, his eyes gleaming with tears as he steps forward and tugs me into a suffocating embrace. His voice is rough in my ear.

"I'll always stand with you, no matter what. Hell, I'll pull the trigger myself if that's what you need. Just…make sure it's your choice, not hers."

My choice…

As he pulls away, putting space between us again, I realize everything he said just now was a test—a chance for me to back out if I needed it. He doesn't want the burden of guilt that comes with taking a life to crush me, despite the fact that I've already taken so many and the guilt is a tidal wave I will never escape. An inescapable ocean in which I am drowning.

Luckily for us both, this is one death I'll never regret.

"It is my choice," I promise.

Jenner exhales, then rolls his shoulder in a slow circle, cracking the joint. "Okay. If you're sure, then let's go kill this prick."

"No. Go back to Rai and check on Quinn. The code to the

room is 84912. I'll meet you there as soon as I'm done here."

Ezra cocks a brow at my words, and even Jenner looks at me as if he doesn't understand what I'm saying. "We're going with you," he argues.

I shake my head. "No. Not this time."

My chest aches at the nonplussed look in their eyes. Even when they don't agree with my choices, they would still walk to the ends of the earth by my side rather than let me face any kind of danger or pain alone, even the kind I inflict on myself.

But I can't let them do that this time.

Meeting Ezra's wounded gaze, I whisper, "You don't need to see this."

Just because he deserved a say in what befalls his brother doesn't mean he needs to witness the outcome.

Before either of them can change my mind or object, I brush past them, crossing the deck to the stairs, unbending the squashed remains of the door to block the path behind me, even though the effort is exhausting.

Ezra's eyes follow me through the observation deck window, and I can only hope that he'll realize what I'm trying to do— that I'm trying to protect him from the images and regret that will torment him should he have a hand in his own brother's death. I'm protecting him the same way he and Jenner have always gone out of their way to shelter me, even when we were little more than strangers.

And with that protective instinct at the front of my mind, I descend into the chilly darkness of the warehouse.

When my feet touch down on the sublevel floor, I scan the empty, cold space for my mother. At the far end of the vast room, past the rows of my dead brethren, I glimpse a faint light outlining a doorway I didn't notice the last time I was down here.

As I near it, weaving through the maze of tables—ignoring that several I pass display children—I notice the door is slightly ajar, and through the crack, I see Dr. Richter propped up in a chair. Shackles bind his wrists and ankles to the metal arms and legs, and he's surrounded by machines and instruments that eerily resemble the laboratory upstairs I was tortured in.

I push the door open the rest of the way but waver at the threshold as recognition pummels my senses. Images of the barbarity I glimpsed when I touched that poor boy's leg flash through my head again.

This is where he tested on them, I realize.

"Are you ready?"

My mother appears before me, and nodding, I shuffle into the laboratory after her, my decision to do this now fully cemented. The echo of her heels clicking against the concrete is bitingly loud in the silence as she leads me over to a silver cart where a syringe is already prepared.

"This won't be pretty," she warns me.

My jaw tenses. "It can't be any worse than what he's done to me."

To encourage her, I push up the left sleeve of my bodysuit and hold out my arm, exposing my vein, which seems to pulse in anticipation, giving her permission to draw my blood. Her mouth purses when she spots the dozens of track marks littered across the crook of my elbow.

Fingers trailing over my wrist, she sweeps an antibacterial wipe across my clammy skin, her touch surprisingly gentle. She doesn't warn me in advance of the pinch that follows from the needle pushing into my vein. She doesn't need to. I already know what to expect.

Silence swells like heat between us, the seconds ticking by at a near stagnate pace, as we both watch my blood—blood that's to blame for so much needless tragedy—fill the attached plastic vial. When my mother finally frees the needle from my skin, she offers me a small square of gauze to staunch the bleeding, which I refuse with a terse shake of my head. Pulling down my sleeve, I turn to face Dr. Richter.

His gray eyes—eyes that once filled me with fear—now stare at me with the same trepidation. "You don't know what you're doing," he says, the words hurried. "If you go through with this, your life and the lives of everyone you care about are over. But, if you stop this, I *will* fix your collar. I'll give you your control back, I promise!"

A laugh churns deep in my chest. "We both know that's a lie. Besides, what was it you once said to me?"

Stepping forward, I jerk his head back, cranking open his mouth with one hand while grabbing fistfuls of his auburn brown hair with the other. Sweat bubbles up on my skin as I focus my thoughts on the pile of gauze layered on the silver cart behind me. Square after square floats through the air toward us and straight into Dr. Richter's mouth, gagging him.

A smile hitches up the corners of my lips. "Sacrifices must always be made for the advancement of science."

The scent of his terror is palpable and almost cloying in my nostrils, strong enough to overwhelm the stink of death emanating from the adjacent room. His eyes widen, flicking between me and my mother, who appears beside me, holding the syringe in her hand.

Offering it to me, she points to a vein on his neck. "Inject it here. The results will be more immediate." I shift the needle toward Richter's neck as instructed, but before I can pierce his skin, my mother grabs my hand, stopping me. "You need to be sure you'll be able to live with this. What we're about to do will haunt you for the rest of your life."

Precisely what I wanted to spare Ezra from.

The smile fades from my lips. "Good thing I won't be around that much longer, then, isn't it?"

Dr. Richter mutters something, his words unintelligible past the wad of gauze in his mouth. I meet his gaze—his eyes gleaming with fear—and to my surprise, I feel strangely calm.

The smile returns as I prick the needle into his neck.

"Don't worry," I murmur. "You'll only feel a minor discomfort at most."

SEVEN

I STARE DOWN AT DR. Richter's slumped form in the chair, his posture slack, his heart and lungs still. His face is shriveled like a grape that's been left out in the sun, and his complexion is stained with varying unsettling shades of brown and black, the skin riddled with multi-colored contusions. Although he's only been dead for a matter of minutes, it's as if the flesh on his bones is already rotting.

Beside me, my mother whispers, "Are you all right?"

My lips pinch into a disgruntled frown. I'm not sure what to say. Am I all right? I thought watching Richter die—I thought being the one to kill him after everything he's done—would somehow make what I went through here worth it. But now, as I graze my eyes over what remains of the person who made me what I am, I don't know what I should be feeling. There's no sense of relief or anger or any of the emotions I anticipated.

Instead, I feel nothing, as if what just happened was meaningless.

My eyes shutter closed, and I watch the vivid memory of his death replay in my mind. I see myself plunging the needle into the side of his neck, injecting him with the same blood he used to kill so many others like me.

As it entered his body, I observed the outcome without remorse, my pulse a steady, satisfied tempo. I didn't startle when his breaths became labored or when his eyes flashed up to mine, terror-stricken. If anything, his pain was a drug and I was an addict fixing for more.

Within seconds of my blood penetrating his body, Richter's skin jaundiced, his ivory complexion turning yellow. Sweat bubbled along the sides of his face, which was breaking out in purple bruises that extended down past the neck of his shirt. As his chest heaved, his lungs constricting—fighting for breath—blood dripped from his nose and the vessels in his eyes all popped, turning the whites a bleak red. His irises rolled back into his skull, then his jaw unlocked and a scream unlike anything I'd ever heard before unleashed from his throat as if his soul was being torn from his body.

When the room fell silent again, he was dead.

The echo of his agony lingers in my ears, the shrill, grating resonance worse than what I remember of my own screams in this place. Worse even than the screams of the young boy, which linger still in my memory.

Why don't I feel better? The man responsible for the suffering of so many—of *my* torment and pain—is dead. He's finished. His experiments are finally over.

Except…they aren't. Not really. Not while there are plenty of others just like him out in the world, ready to rise up and take his place and start this cycle all over again so long as they have access to the right subject. Nolan was just the tip of the iceberg and I have no doubt in my mind that others impacted by the State's war have considered how I could be used to their own advantage, like Nolan stole me away from Richter for his. For all I know that's what the bombings on the Heart are about and the attack on the DSD was a smokescreen. I can't be sure of anything anymore.

Not when I've seen how quickly power corrupts.

And even if I don't live long enough for that to happen—to become someone else's unwilling stooge—Dr. Richter still wins in the end. The destruction and death he wants to inflict on the world will come to pass, no matter what I do.

No, the horror isn't over at all.

So long as I'm alive, it will never be over.

As I open my eyes, it takes all the willpower I possess not to fall to my knees and weep. Not out of regret for what I've done—my hatred for Richter like a red-hot poker burning into my skin, branding me permanently—but because the reality of my situation is closing around my neck like a new collar. One I can't remove.

I've understood for a while now how dangerous my existence is to the well-being of this world, but this is the first time I truly grasp just how much of a threat I really am. Apocalyptic visions aside, the greed of mankind is an enemy I will never be able to defeat. Because even if I found a way to overcome this disease and prevent the decimation awaiting us...

Someone, somewhere, will always attempt to leash me, just as Richter did.

I startle at the touch of my mother's hand on my forearm, and jerking away, I put a few steps between us. When I meet her gaze after a moment, her brow is drawn and she's staring at me with an odd look in her eyes, as if she somehow knows what I'm thinking.

"Let's go," I mutter, cutting her off before she can comment.

I don't look back as I storm out of the laboratory and back into the large open warehouse where the sharp, tangy smell of disinfectant gives way to the stomach-churning stink of decaying flesh. The fans spinning overhead waft cold air over me, chilling me down to my bones, and goosebumps raise all over my body, as if the death in the room is a tangible presence caressing my skin. Around me, the corpses of Richter's victims tempt my gaze, but I keep my eyes on the floor. I can't face them again, not after witnessing what they went through here.

Not when I know it could have all been avoided if I'd never gone back to the DSD in the first place.

If you hadn't, they would still be dead, my conscience reminds me. *And so would you. So would everyone.*

I grit my teeth. Would they? Is it certain the destruction I saw would have occurred any sooner had I never left PHOENIX? And even if it is, why are the only options before me always death or more death?

As I near the stairs, I pause, glancing back at my mother, who follows a few steps behind, keeping her distance. She meets my gaze with those inquisitive blue eyes that are so familiar and yet, make her seem like a stranger.

"This…" I trail off, my tongue suddenly too big for my mouth. Tears disfigure what I can see of her face in the restricted light as I bite out the only words I can manage. "How will you destroy it?"

She considers me for a moment, her expression wary. Does she think, because my eyes are wet with tears, I want to preserve this place? Does she think I want any evidence of what Richter has done here?

Of what my blood can do?

Finally, she says, "By finishing what the bombs started."

Holding her gaze, I swallow around the lump in my throat and nod before resuming my march up the stairs, trudging one leaden step at a time. My movements only seem to get heavier and more sluggish as I climb, as if the darkness below is trying to pull me back into its depths and keep me here amid the death and decay where I belong. I can almost hear the screams of the dead—of my brothers and sisters in this disease. Of my blood in their veins calling out to me, begging me not to abandon them here. Their cries of blame are like nails digging into my skin, regardless of how many times I tell myself I'm not the one who did this.

The heels of my mother's shoes clang on the steps behind me like the unchanging beat of a metronome, the rhythm only fluctuating in the moment it takes for me to peel back the door at the top of the stairs. As the rumpled metal yields before me, the pain I've been staving off fills the remaining space in my head like water seeping through cracks, flooding my pounding skull like a bowl.

A silent scream forms on my tongue as a warm, sticky wetness drips from my nose onto my lips, but I clench my jaw and power through, wiping the blood—both fresh and old— from my face. Stumbling onto the observation deck, I search for Ezra and Jenner, but they're nowhere to be seen. I can only hope their absence means they went upstairs to wait with Rai and Quinn like I asked.

My mother's entourage of Enforcers remain, standing by to accompany us back up to the ground level. I ignore them, crossing the platform toward the elevator, the steel doors hanging wide like open arms eager to embrace me. Out of the corner of my eye, I glimpse the streak of blood staining the floor where Dr. Richter sat, awaiting my judgment, only minutes ago, and I falter mid-step, wondering if he suffered enough—if I shouldn't have drawn his death out longer as punishment for everything he inflicted upon this world.

Upon me.

Shivering, I wrap my arms around my torso and shrink into the back corner of the elevator, trying to escape the thoughts stirring inside me. Thoughts that threaten to plunge me into a dangerous state of mind I might not be able to escape. My fingers rake through my hair, clutching my aching head, as I sink into a crouch on the floor.

Outside, on the observation deck, my mother pauses before the broad window, staring down at the horrific scene below in quiet contemplation. Without looking up, she simply says, "Burn it."

There's an edge to her tone that speaks to something inside me. That makes me wonder if destroying this place is as much about revenge for her as it is about closure and justice for me.

I consider that idea of vengeance as the Enforcers all reach for their belts at my mother's command, each retrieving one of several transparent tubes of carmine-colored powder I only now notice affixed to their uniforms. Without needing any further instruction, they proceed in a single-file line down the stairs, pouring the contents on the floor in a trail starting from the deck and continuing all the way down into the warehouse.

My mother lingers in front of the glass, hands clasped behind her back, watching them work. They return to our level a few minutes later, and as the last Enforcer steps onto the platform, he wavers by the crushed remains of the door, pulling a silver cylinder from his pocket. Twisting the top, he tosses the device down the stairs and quickly steps away from the threshold.

At the clink of the triggering device striking concrete, flames ignite throughout the mortuary, casting everything in a fiery haze. The glow of the fire sends orange and yellow flickers of light through the slanted glass, which dance across the walls in celebration of the impending destruction.

The soldiers don't hang around to witness the blaze, quickly crowding around me in the elevator. When black puffs of smoke cloud the windows—the flames reaching up from below, licking the glass—my mother joins us, swiftly pressing the button to ascend, leaving the warehouse behind to burn. She doesn't look at me once, not even as the doors close.

I can feel the heat of the fast-spreading flames beneath our feet as the cramped metal box carries us in silence back up to the ground floor, but still, my mother doesn't spare me a glance. She doesn't even speak until the doors open.

"The sublevel will keep the fire contained, but another attack could be imminent. I'll see to your friend, as promised, but we need to be quick."

Despite her warning, my steps are lethargic as we make our way back to Exam Room B where Ezra and Jenner are waiting for us. The Enforcers shadow my every move—so much like my personal bodyguards when I was a ward here—while my mother walks a few feet to my left, her steps hurried and clipped, more quiet than she was before.

When I can no longer bear the discomfort of her silence, I murmur, "Did you know?"

"Know what?" she asks, tone tentative.

"That I would be exactly what Richter was looking for." My eyes cut to her face as she lifts her chin, but still, she doesn't look at me. "You said it yourself, you were the one who got him his subjects. You had to have known I would fit the criteria."

She finally meets my gaze, her face a pitiless mask, wearing the same expression she always reserved in my childhood for the rare moments when I was being a nuisance. The ice in her gaze reminds me far too much of the man she just helped me murder.

"For eighteen years, Richter was ignorant of you, and I made sure he stayed that way. He didn't search for subjects himself; he relied on me to find them for him. If I hadn't gotten involved, if it had been someone else doing his dirty work—" The muscle in her jaw clicks when she snaps her mouth shut, as if physically restraining herself from even entertaining that thought. After a moment—and a steadying breath—she continues. "Like I said, everything I did was for *you*. To keep *you* safe. Even when they took you…" She shakes her head. "I wouldn't have let them if I didn't know that I would be able to watch over you after."

A dubious laugh more like a gasp parts my lips, and I slow to a stop, glaring at her. "Watch over me? You call what you've been doing *watching over me*? Where were you when I was trapped in a cell for days on end? Or when I was trying to kill myself by throwing up everything I ate? Where were you when Dr. Richter started torturing me? Do you even know what he made me do?"

"Of *course*, I know." Her tone is sharp, but when she opens her mouth to say something else, she hesitates, seeming to think better of it. Pinching the bridge of her nose between her thumb and forefinger, she lets out a long, weary breath. This time, when she speaks, her tone is more gentle. "Why else do you think I intervened?"

Intervened?

"What, you mean earlier with Richter? *After* he removed my collar and shot Quinn?" I snort. "You were a bit late helping anyone there, don't you think?"

"I'm not talking about today," she says vaguely.

My brow furrows, and I blink at her, confused. "What—"

She holds up a hand. "I promise to tell you everything as soon as we get somewhere safe. But not here. Not right now. It's far too long a story and we don't have that kind of time." Her eyes flash back in the direction we came from, reminding me of our current predicament.

We walk the rest of the way to Exam Room B without another word between us. When we arrive, I pause at the threshold, my eyes sweeping over Ezra where he sits at the edge of Rai's bed, his back hunched and hands splayed through his hair, his fingers mussing the strands in his frustration. Jenner, who had been pacing the room, goes still the instant he sees me in the doorway. Ezra looks up a few seconds later, his eyes finding mine like two magnets drawn together.

I glance between their unnerved faces and shove my hands behind my back. Although clean, they feel dirty with Richter's death, as if his blood is a permanent stain on my skin. If they see my hands, they'll see what I've done, and then, they'll finally see me for the monster I am. And while they should, while part of me wishes they would, my heart can't bear the thought of either of them looking at me the way I looked at Richter.

The lump returns to my throat as I force myself to acknowledge Ezra's questioning gaze. He stares at me, those hazel eyes swimming with tears, asking the one thing his lips seem unable to voice.

As the answer pushes at the boundary of my lips, the sharp, stabbing pain of anguish cuts through my heart, and it dawns on me there's one death I've been ignoring. The only death I will never come back from—that I caused when I *chose* to kill Dr. Richter. Regardless of all the lives I've taken, *that* was the defining moment when I truly decided to become the monster instead of fighting it. Because, for the first time, I didn't just have to kill.

I wanted to.

"It's done," I gasp, pressing a hand to my chest, balking under the sudden hollow feeling inside me.

For so long, I viewed my humanity as the switch to my emotions; that I could abandon them if I just shut it off. But now, I realize it's something else—the only thing standing between who I was before this disease and the monster hovering at the edge of every thought, waiting for me to relinquish myself to its whims. Without that wall separating the two, there's nothing to stop me from losing myself, and nothing to help me come back again should that happen.

Without that small thread, however small, tying me to who I used to be, who will I become in the time I have left?

As this question nags at me, gnawing at the last of my composure, I surrender myself to the barrage of emotions building up in my chest. And in this moment, despite everything I've done, despite all the lives that have been lost and that I've personally ripped from this world…

Despite knowing that I don't deserve to be saved…

The death of my humanity hits me the hardest.

E I G H T

THE TENSION IS PALPABLE, LIKE a thick morning fog, as we stand congregated around the narrow bed, waiting for my mother to deliver a verdict on Rai's condition. Her prognosis. I hold Rai's right hand clenched between both of mine while Ezra clings to her left, as if his own life depends on it, his knuckles white as his fingers squeeze tightly. Jenner sits perched on the foot of the mattress, staring over at her sleeping face in silence.

Our escort of Enforcers all wait in the hallway with the exception of Quinn, who has been moved to the examination table that marked so many of my days here. Propped upright against the wall with his legs stretched out across the full length of the metal surface, he's bloody still but bandaged properly now, the bed sheet replaced with a large patch taped to his side that I glimpse through the ragged remains of his shirt, which my mother cut through to get to the wound. She also gave him some pills, I assume for the pain, and got his bleeding staunched enough that his face is steadily regaining color, stealing away any threat of death.

As for my mother, she stands behind us, tapping and swiping

at the screen of Richter's tablet, scrolling through the notes he left behind about Rai and whatever it is he did to her, her face pinched in concentration.

She sighs, her eyes glowing in the light of the screen. "I'm surprised he managed to keep her here without anyone finding out about it. I can only assume he had your friend somewhere else in the building and then relocated her to this exam room after the attack." Frowning, she places the tablet down on the mattress, meeting my gaze across the bed. "The man was always good at hiding his secrets."

"He wasn't the only one," I comment.

My mother refuses to wilt under the heat of my glare, staring back at me for a long moment. She only looks away when Ezra clears his throat.

"Can anything be done to help her?" he asks.

We hold a collective breath in anticipation of her answer, although the dread pooling in my stomach tells me I already know what she's going to say. Rai told me herself.

"You were never going to be able to save me, you know that."

I've known since the moment I saw her in this bed. There's nothing we can do for her. She's gone.

She's *been* gone since Richter shot her.

"No." My mother's voice is flat. "The damage to her cerebrum is too significant. Although her vital functions are still in working order, there's no evidence here to suggest she will ever wake up. Going off this data, I'm afraid her vegetative state isn't reversible. Whether or not Richter intended that, I can't say. But if there is a way to rouse her, I'm afraid I don't know it."

"So, that's it?" Jenner whispers, his eyes haunted. "All this was for nothing."

His face twists with outrage and anguish, which I can't help feeling responsible for. Even though Richter was really to blame for what happened to Rai, I can't ignore the facts. Both times we fell into Richter's traps because of me—because of my decisions—and both times, we lost her as a result. If it wasn't for me, none of this would've happened.

If it wasn't for me, Rai might still be alive.

I recall the soothing words she spoke in my dream, once again hearing the lie she so easily spun that there was nothing I could have done to prevent this. The lie I know was really just my own brain trying to ease the burden of responsibility crushing me. But it can't be true that we were helpless in this. I can't believe that. I *won't*. Because if I did—if I were to allow myself to follow that line of thought for even a second—that would mean there really is nothing I can do to prevent the future I saw in my vision.

From losing everyone else I love the same way I lost Rai.

My mother's frown deepens, and she offers me a pitying look. "I'm sorry, but we can't take her with us. Now is the time to say your goodbyes."

Panic flashes across Ezra's face followed by a stricken acceptance that dulls his warm eyes, cutting me deep. Swallowing, he squats beside the bed and touches his forehead to the back of Rai's hand.

"Where is it we're even going?" Jenner asks, his voice rough with a suspicion I find myself sharing.

"And why are you taking us there?" I add, my own tone edged with doubt.

Despite what I said earlier about going with her, the truth is, I don't trust my mother. I'm not sure I ever can after all the betrayals that have tarnished our family with tragedy. She might have helped me put an end to Dr. Richter's reign of terror, but that doesn't make us allies.

And it certainly doesn't make her good.

"A safe house," she answers, frustratingly vague again. "Everything else will be explained once we're there."

"Whose side are you on?"

My eyes bolt to Ezra, who glares at my mother, skepticism creasing his face, as if he's not sure what to think of her. As if he's not sure he should believe what she says.

With a forceful breath through her nose, she mutters, "I'm on no one's side. As far as I'm concerned, the State and PHOENIX can battle this out on their own." Her expression hardens, and she crosses her arms. "All I care about is keeping my daughter alive and, from what I've heard, that's what you both want, too."

She's not wrong. All Ezra and Jenner have done since we met is try to keep me safe—to protect me, even when I didn't need protecting. But how does she know that?

What else has Quinn told her?

I examine the details of her prim face, trying to see past the mask of cold detachment she keeps in place like armor. Her tightly pursed lips give nothing away.

"Ma'am." One of the Enforcers appears in the doorway, saluting my mother, who gestures for him to speak. "Rogers has reported an increase in blockades across the zones. If we're to have any hope of reaching the rendezvous point, we need to leave soon."

Nodding, she swings her eyes back to mine. "Whatever you're going to do, decide now."

With one final glance at Rai, she turns on her heel and makes her way to the door. To my surprise, she pauses beside the examination table mid-route, extending her hand to help Quinn up instead of calling for an Enforcer to do it. He scoots forward at her beckoning, grunting as he slides off the metal, landing unsteadily on his feet, and I watch as she snakes an arm around his back when he stumbles, taking the brunt of his weight. It's the first time I've ever seen her do anything at the expense of herself, and I stare, mesmerized, as she leads him out into the dim light of the hallway.

As the door glides shut behind them, I peer down at Rai's limp hand still clutched in my own. Her skin is soft and cold against mine.

"She's right. Rai is gone. I might not have known her well, but I don't..." My throat constricts around the words. "I don't think she would want us to stay here. She'd want us to go."

Ezra raises his head, and he and Jenner both look at me, the same unspoken question burning in each of their eyes. When I say nothing, comprehension darkens their gazes. They know I've seen something, but I can't find the strength to explain it to them. Not now.

Maybe not ever.

"If there was a way, I wouldn't leave," is the only explanation I can offer, my voice a barely-there whisper.

"You were never going to be able to save me."

These words seem to live in my ears, in my skin, in the very essence of who I am—an unpleasant reminder of a truth I will never escape. But they also remind me of something else.

Something that gives me hope.

Although I failed Rai, I have to believe what she said in my dream is possible. That, even though she's beyond helping, there is at least still time to save Ezra and Jenner. To change their fates the way I couldn't change hers.

Releasing her hand, I trail my fingertips across the pitted scar on her forehead, then through her hair, brushing the strands over the skin to hide the evidence of the gunshot that stole her from us. With it covered, she looks perfect—like she could be sleeping. Reality buries its claws deep in my heart.

Leaning forward, I press my lips to her right cheek, no longer able to hold back the tears. They pour out of me, collecting on her skin like dew drops, before dripping down her neck and pooling in the dip at the apex of her collarbone.

As my gaze follows their downward descent, I glimpse a thin silver chain I never noticed her wearing before. Curious, I lift it away from her throat, noting the subtle weight tugging down on it.

Careful not to yank it too hard, I spin the chain around until a small silver locket emerges from the sleek mane of her hair. It's round and thin, easily mistaken for a simple pendant if not for the hinges, and etched into its surface are beautiful ornate swirls that come together to form some sort of pointed flower or star.

A trickle of unease creeps over my skin, and I shiver at the realization that Dr. Richter must've been the one to give her this necklace. Otherwise, I'm sure he would've discarded it.

Exhaling a shaky breath, I touch my fingertips to the engraved metal, and upon contact, an image explodes inside my head, nearly knocking me back off my feet. A bright, white flash fills my range of vision as a stabbing pain cuts into my temples, threatening to rip a scream from my throat. When the light finally fades and the details of my surroundings return, it dawns on me that I'm not in Exam Room B anymore, nor anywhere at the DSD.

This, I realize with growing horror, staring aghast at the long hallway forming before me.

This is the magistrates building.

The corridor is dark, almost pitch-black, and empty, just like that night two and a half years ago. I turn in place, my eyes swinging left and right, unsure what I'm meant to be seeing, when the echo of a female voice slips through the crack of a door standing open to my left. Her muffled words beckon me forward.

My heart races as I follow the sound, my feet stumbling forward as if my body is being pulled by some invisible force I have no control over. When I approach the room, the door swings wide, revealing an office identical to Bilken's. Rai sits at the glass desk within, staring blankly out the large window—forming a mirror image of Dr. Richter and how he looked in the vision I saw of them meeting. In her extended hand, the silver locket lies open against her flattened palm. A blue light shines up from its depths, reminding me of the glow of a hologram.

"If you're watching this," she begins, her voice low. Hesitating, she seems to reconsider her words, and shaking her head, she lets out a sigh. "Okay, let's be honest. If you're watching this, I'm dead. I'd be lying if I said I didn't expect it. I only wish I had enough time and words to tell you just how sorry I am."

I hold my breath as I cross the room toward her, hypnotized by her words—by how real she feels to me in this moment. If I reach out my hand, I can touch her again; I can feel the warmth of her skin. I can remember what she was like when she was alive instead of the shell Richter turned her into.

But then I remember that she isn't real—not like this, not

anymore—and my chest hitches with a sob when I comprehend what this vision is trying to tell me. When it hits me what event this moment is preceding. She knew what would happen.

She knew by approaching Richter, she would die.

"I know you're going to blame yourself, but this isn't your fault, Ezra," she says. "No matter what he thinks, no matter what I'm sure you've wondered yourself countless times, you didn't make me leave. It was *my* choice to join PHOENIX, no one else's. Just as this…facing him again… It's my choice. I didn't tell you what I was planning because I knew you would try to stop me, and I love you for that—for caring about me in this messed-up world where love is so fragile and fleeting. But, the truth is, I'm tired of running from everything we left behind. The past haunts me, and I owe it to myself and to Austin to finally put all this to rest. Put *us* to rest. I need you both to let me go."

A smile spreads across her lips as she spins in the chair, her dark eyes flicking upward to look at the ceiling. I'm amazed by how calm she seems despite her impending death looming over her head.

Not calm, it occurs to me the longer I watch her. *At peace.*

"You and I have been through so much together, and every step of the way, you've always trusted my advice and guidance. Okay, maybe not *always*, but most of the time. So, let me impart some final words of wisdom, all right?" She kicks out a leg, halting the chair's rotations, and, once still, peers down at the locket with the stern expression of an older sister. "Look after Wynter. I know you wouldn't hear it before, but she's important. I can *feel* it. And not just because of what she's capable of…but because of what I know she could be to you."

My feet freeze beneath me as I suck in a breath, and triggered by her words, my memory drifts back to this same night, focusing on our trek through the tunnels as we made our way into Zone 1. I recall, verbatim, my conversation with Ezra and how he said he felt compelled to protect me. On some level, I've always wondered if his feelings for me boiled down to obligation because of his mother. But now, hearing this, I feel reassured that I didn't imagine it when I sensed something between us from the very beginning, even when I wasn't sure what that was. Knowing that Rai could see it—what we were destined to become to each other—fills me with the best kind of joy and the worst sort of fear. Because Ezra has to let me go.

And now, more than ever, I'm terrified that he won't.

"You've shut yourself off for so long that you probably don't even realize it yet," she muses. "I guess it's my own experience that allows me to see what you're trying so hard to fight. You're curious about her. And maybe that doesn't seem like much now, but I can see what it could turn into." She leans back in the chair, a slight smile forming on her lips. "Take it from someone who's made this mistake and doesn't want to see you make it, too. Embrace it. Take a chance. Allow yourself to experience something *real* for once. Something other than the fear and hatred we've all blindly surrendered ourselves to. This life is far too short, and the seclusion we suffer prevents us from having what you've been fortunate enough to have dropped in your lap. So, look after her. Find a way to help her survive. Oh, and Ez?" She cocks a disgruntled brow. "Try not to be too stubborn about it, okay? If you wait too long, Jenner might beat you to it!"

Rai throws a quick, alarmed glance toward the door before

looking down into the blue light again. It's only now, as she crouches over the desk and the glow of the hologram recording illuminates her face, that I notice the tears in her eyes.

"It's time for me to go now," she whispers. "I know the odds of you ever seeing this message are slim, but I couldn't allow myself to die without saying this. I'm only sorry I didn't say any of it to your face when I still had the chance. If I get lucky and you *do* see this, just know that you have the power to create great change. So, go out there and do it. Don't spend your life searching for vengeance. Regardless of what Austin does to me, stay focused on what really matters. And remember..."

The room around me darkens, and, all too quickly, Rai's features fade into the shadow of memory. Panic gives me the strength to lunge forward, and as I scream for her not to go— not to leave us again—I reach out a hand. But she slips from my grasp, now nothing more than a ghost.

In the thickening gloom, as the darkness envelops me, I can just make out the bright warmth of her smile.

"I love you and I will always believe in you."

Stabs cut through my skull in quick succession, and my lungs burn with a scream that seems to set my soul on fire. My legs give out beneath the weight of my pain, my knees slamming hard into the floor. Through my blurring vision, blue smudges at the edge of my eyes tell me the vision is over.

I'm back at the DSD.

Ezra and Jenner both yell out my name, but their voices are dull behind a shrill ringing beating against my left eardrum. The familiar taste of blood fills my mouth and nose—the one commonality I've come to expect from these episodes—and yet, something is different about the effects this time, as if I can sense myself moving one step closer to death. It hangs over me like a constant shadow.

"Wynter—"

Ezra and Jenner come at me from both sides, arms outstretched to offer their help and support, but I brush them off with a strained "Don't," clutching at the side of the bed. Ignoring the agony slicing my brain to ribbons, I carefully pull myself upright until I'm on my feet again.

Fingers shaking, I reach out and grab the locket, which now rests against the top of Rai's chest. My heart pounds in my throat as I pry the latch open with my thumbnail, and inside, I find a small picture—the same photograph Ezra was staring at the night we lost Rai at the magistrates building. The picture of them as children with Richter.

Gritting my teeth, I peel the picture away, searching for the recording device hidden underneath. Rai must've planted it there before we left for Zone 1 with the intent of leaving Ezra a message, even knowing he might never see it.

A sob grips me at the thought, and I bite my lower lip hard to hold back the pain in my chest as I unclip the chain from her neck and extend my trembling hand toward Ezra. Cautiously, he takes the locket from my grasp, confusion alight in his eyes.

Two words break free of the cage of my throat before the tears and grief consume me.

"From Rai."

NINE

I PRESS MY BACK AGAINST the cold wall and tilt my head toward the door, listening for any trace of sound inside the silent exam room. It's been several minutes since I handed Rai's locket to Ezra and left him to listen to her message alone. Everyone else had the decency to follow my lead and give him the privacy needed to process our friend's final words, even though every moment we spend here only increases our chances of being discovered by Enforcers not on the DSD's payroll—assuming that's who the soldiers accompanying us work for—or, worse, falling victim to another attack. Even my mother, who has the authority to talk us out of trouble with any passing patrols, should it come to that, is visibly perturbed by how long we've spent here.

I peek at her out of the corner of my eye where she leans against the wall on the other side of the doorway, standing opposite me. Although her expression is drawn, she keeps checking her watch. It's strange to see her fidget when she used to scold me for that same habit when I was a child, but I don't blame her for being antsy or feeling on edge. My own nerves are shot, and the hush that's engulfed the building since

I stepped out of the exam room has been stifling. Even Jenner is unnervingly quiet.

My mother huffs, peering at her watch for at least the twentieth time in half as many minutes. "We can't afford to waste any more time. If we don't leave now, we'll miss our window."

"Window?" Jenner asks from where he stands on the other side of the corridor, his voice strained with unshed tears.

She tugs on the crisp lapels of her coat, her severe eyes cutting to mine. "The patrols in this area aren't the only ones we have to worry about."

It takes me only a moment to grasp her meaning.

"The safe house," I breathe.

Her brows draw into a vee as she nods. "We only have a brief stretch of time in which we can get to it unnoticed, assuming a blockade isn't already obstructing our path. That window gets smaller the longer we linger. We've already been here"—she glances at her watch again, that solemn frown deepening—"nearly an hour. We can't afford to dally much longer."

Pushing off from the wall, I let out a breath and drag a hand across my face, brushing the hair from my eyes, which burn uncomfortably, aching with exhaustion.

When was the last time I slept?

"I know." I hesitate, casting a remorseful glance at the door. "I'll tell him. Just…give us a minute, okay?"

The dread that keeps biting at my insides resurfaces, and my stomach turns at the thought of walking back into this room…and what it will mean when I come out. Even though I've already been through this loss and suffered this pain once before, the thought of never seeing Rai again is somehow so much worse this time. Maybe because it's real now and we actually have to say goodbye to her—a chance we were robbed of when Richter shot her.

Now, any hope we had of reuniting is lost.

And that's largely because of me, because I didn't see her fate soon enough to prevent it. So, how can I face her again, even in death?

How can I face Ezra when so much of this is my fault?

"Wait." My mother grabs my hand and, turning it over, presses something hard against my palm. My eyes dart downward, narrowing on a syringe not that unlike the one we used to kill Dr. Richter.

"What—" I begin, but she cuts me off.

"I've been holding onto this just in case anyone ever caught on to what I was up to. I figured a quick death was preferable to torture, and I didn't want—" She breaks off mid-sentence, as if the words are too painful to say, then clears her throat, straightening. "Well, it doesn't matter now. Use it on your friend. You'll need it to end her life humanely."

"She's already dead," I whisper, my voice breaking.

"Her brain might be, but her heart isn't," my mother murmurs in a strangely consoling tone. "Leave her in peace. Better you do it than abandon her as she is for someone else to find. At least, this way, she can go surrounded by people who love her."

Abandon. That word cuts thro`ugh me like glass. Isn't that exactly what we did the night Richter shot her? If we hadn't fled the magistrates building—if we had stayed and fought to bring Rai home or, at least, gotten her back to the tunnels—then she could've died peacefully among her friends, her found family, the way she should have. The way she would have wanted.

Then, she wouldn't have been turned into a living representation of Dr. Richter's twisted obsessions. Then, we wouldn't be faced with the terrible decision placed before us now.

A decision which isn't really a decision at all.

My fingers close around the syringe.

I won't make the same mistake twice.

Resolved, I turn to face the door, my fingers trembling as I enter the unlocking code into the keypad. As the barrier yields, sliding open to welcome me, a hand brushes my upper back and I startle.

I glance up at the sudden warmth at my side, meeting Jenner's gaze, the blue depths the same icy shade of water or the hottest burning fire—a combination of cold and heat. My heart swells when a gentle smile forms along the edges of his lips. There's no joy in it, only sadness.

But it's a sadness we share.

"I'll go with you," he says, taking my hand. "This isn't something you should do alone, and I—" He grimaces, closing his eyes for a moment. "I want to say goodbye, too."

Alone... I don't know any other way to survive. Ever since Ezra and Jenner came into my life, I have always tried to shoulder the burden, always tried to prepare myself for the inevitability that I would lose them or that they would be taken from me. Because that's what my life has always been—a never-ending cycle of solitude and loss. Our final impending moments with Rai only confirm that.

Inside the exam room, we find Ezra in the same place where we left him, except now, he's kneeling beside Rai's bed, his forehead on his hands, gripping hers. There's a vulnerability to this pose I haven't seen from him before—not even when he was weeping over the photograph of him and Rai as children the night we first thought she died. The night that also marked the first time we ever kissed.

My heart breaks at the sight of his pain.

"Ezra."

He lifts his head at the sound of my voice, and his eyes—the whites red and raw from crying—shift to meet mine, his expression dazed. Drawing in a shaking breath through his nose, he clambers to his feet.

"It's time to go…isn't it."

A lump blocks my throat, and the syringe in my hand suddenly seems to weigh several tons, threatening to drag me down to the floor along with the regret and remorse of what I know is the right thing to do. It takes all the strength I possess—that I've *ever* possessed—to force myself to nod.

Jenner and I make our way to the other side of the bed, giving Ezra some space. As one, we all look down at Rai.

This is it.

It's time to say goodbye.

And yet, none of us seem able to do it, the silence consuming every word and breath before we're even able to make them. I never thought I'd mourn someone as much as I've grieved for my father, but as my eyes dance over Rai's comatose face, it strikes me just how much I miss her. I barely even knew her and my heart still aches for the hole in our lives created by her loss, the pain of that emptiness crippling. I didn't even know it was possible to feel anguish this deep and unrelenting.

Jenner squeezes my hand, drawing my watery gaze, and once again offers me that same timid smile he gave me only a few moments ago. The smile that tells me I will never be alone in my pain...even though I know he's wrong.

When what I saw in my vision finally transpires, I will be alone in the darkness I've cocooned around myself—darkness born out of guilt for the part I've played in the deaths and tragedy I only wanted to prevent. Even if everyone in the world dies alongside me, in the end—in the moments before I destroy the world, when everyone realizes what's about to befall them—*I* will be the person they blame. Because Richter didn't give me this disease. I was born with it. Fate dictated I would be the real villain in this tale. And if Richter's death has taught me anything...

It's that villains deserve to die alone.

Jenner's whispered voice shakes me out of my thoughts, and I blink, staring at him as he looks down at Rai.

"I never thanked you." Tears streak his cheeks. "Not just for saving me that day but for convincing me to live. To hold on. I promise you, I'll keep living...and I'll keep fighting. Until there's nothing left to fight for."

As he speaks, I'm reminded of something he said long ago. In the tunnels under the Heart, Jenner told me what PHOENIX stood for and why those joined under its banner would fight for the cause until their dying breaths. A message that corruption warped over the years.

Now, those words are a promise to Rai, a vow to keep fighting for the better world she wanted. A world she'll never see.

A world I'm destined to raze.

Jenner swallows, the sound audible in the hush, then gives me a small, encouraging nod, and I realize it's my turn to impart whatever farewell I want to leave her with. I wish I knew the perfect thing to say—something that would close the door on this pain. But what *is* there to say?

What *can* I say that could possibly ever erase these feelings of self-condemnation?

I draw in a breath, letting it out with a whimper, before muttering the only words I can think of. The one truth I can manage in my grief. "I wish I'd had more time to know you."

Leaning forward, I brush my lips across her soft cheek again, and as I pull away, I lament the inevitable goodbye that I'll have to say to Ezra and Jenner. My throat thickens with tears, the thought taking hold like barbs in my skin, piercing my lungs. My heart.

I wish I'd had more time to know them all.

Biting back a sob, I watch as Ezra bends down and plants a careful kiss on Rai's forehead, avoiding the spot where Richter shot her. His lips linger for a moment, his breath a kiss of its own as he whispers, so softly I barely hear it, "Message received."

Our tear-filled gazes meet across the bed, and I lift my hand to show him the syringe. It sits unmoving against my palm.

"For Rai," I breathe, and my voice breaks on her name.

I turn toward the metal infusion stand, which remains situated, undisturbed, near Rai's head, and carefully collect the transparent tubing trailing down into her right arm between my fingers. A tremor rolls through me as I try and fail to insert the needle into the injection port beneath the IV bag.

I hear footsteps behind me, then a familiar hand touches my shoulder before moving to my wrist, steadying my grip.

"Together," Ezra murmurs.

Guiding the needle, he presses my shaking thumb down on the plunger, then takes me into his arms as we watch the silver liquid travel through the length of the tube.

It takes less than ten seconds for the poison to enter Rai's body. When it reaches her heart, the monitor tracking her vitals beeps erratically, screaming in protest like the alarm we heard earlier. Unlike the alarm, it dies quickly, settling into one continuous tone.

As the tears roll fat and hot down my cheeks, the flatline rings around us like a death knell.

TEN

A CHILL HANGS HEAVY IN the air, pressing down on my lungs and constricting my breaths a bit more with each step I take away from Exam Room B and the nightmare of the time I spent trapped in this hell. Even now, the imprint of my trauma remains like a brand only I can see and feel, its presence a constant weight on my shoulders. I had thought, with Richter gone, that weight would lift, but it lingers, like a new sort of tether attempting to keep me tied to this place. Even in death, Richter haunts my every waking moment.

Even in death, I can't fully escape him.

No one utters a word as we file out of the back entrance of the building into the smoke and ash polluted air, stepping past the broken door and emerging into the empty courtyard—the night silent aside from the occasional thump in the distance or resounding shot of gunfire. The resulting echo of triggers pulled without remorse sends a jarring shiver over my skin. I can only imagine how much innocent blood has been shed in the wake of the attack of the Heart, not only from the bombs but from the Enforcers, who now gun down their own people without mercy.

"The State will not support those who cannot contribute. You know our orders."

I shiver again at the memory of that callous voice and the murder of the poor woman that followed, the thought of which tugs my attention to Quinn. He stands propped up between two of the soldiers in my mother's employ, his skin still on the paler side but less clammy than it was twenty minutes ago. Whatever medication my mother gave him to fend off infection and pain seems to be working quickly.

Sensing my gaze, he looks over at me, and as our eyes meet, I wonder if he would be out in the streets tonight, murdering the blameless victims of the attack on our city had he remained an Enforcer and not defected to PHOENIX. Or to work for my mother, or whatever the hell he is now. Doubt about his intentions troubles me, and yet, behind that uncertainty, I can't help remembering what he said after saving our lives.

"I can't live with it. I didn't sign up to be a killer, and I'd rather help you than be part of the problem."

Did he mean that? Or were those impassioned words a lie—a ploy to gain my trust and sell his role in my mother's scheme to have me returned to her, like lost property?

"This way." My mother's sharp tone draws my focus.

I glance in the direction she struts in, her gait purposeful and determined, if not a little too fast to seem completely natural. She walks like someone who can't get away fast enough, her discomfort apparent in her quickening pace and the way her hands clench and unclench at her sides.

The rest of us follow her lead without protest, but as she makes for the motorized gate at the far side of the courtyard, skittering toward it like a bug fleeing death, I find a small measure of peace in knowing that even the Head of Termination isn't immune to fear.

Especially now, when I'm so close to drowning in it.

With every step, I sense the towering presence of the DSD behind me like a living, breathing thing—a malevolent entity that will reach out and claim me again if I don't get away quickly. Matching my mother's stride, I push ahead without looking back, eager to get beyond the extensive reach of its shadow.

The large gate buzzes open as we approach—although I can't see who opened it—and as the steel rack glides along the wheels, I squint into the darkness, unnerved by the thought of what might be waiting on the other side.

It takes my eyes a moment to spot it, the black metal blending into the unlit surroundings. Where the property line of the DSD intersects the street, I can just make out an armored truck facing us, the rumble of its engine a deep purr in the night, its headlights shut off. Behind it, a short distance away, I glimpse a second identical truck.

The sight of the two vehicles gives me pause. How many of these very same trucks were I transported in over the last year, always surrounded by soldiers and treated like a dangerous convict who needed constant surveillance?

How many times did these same trucks carry me to a war I never asked to be part of?

My mother continues, undeterred, and as I pass through the open gate behind her, I can't shake the growing apprehension that I've made a mistake in deciding to go with her—that we've escaped one trap just to fall in another. At my sides, Ezra and Jenner inch closer to me, seeming to share my concern.

My mother looks back at us briefly before nodding to

the Enforcer walking beside her, who—on her unspoken command—trots ahead and circles around to the rear of the truck nearest us. The squeal of metal hinges is thunderous in the night as he pries open the doors.

As for my mother, she stops beside the cab.

"All aboard," she says, sweeping her gaze to the back of the vehicle before pivoting to face us. The Enforcer there mimics her instruction with a silent gesture for us to get in.

Ezra, Jenner, and I all waver, our eyes straying from the propped open back doors to the driver seat where yet another Enforcer sits as still as a statue, awaiting his orders. Although his head is turned in our direction, his face is hidden beneath the opaque shield of his helmet.

At our hesitation, my mother crosses her arms. "You can trust him. He's under my employ."

I peer over my shoulder, noting the other soldiers spread out around the courtyard. Including the driver, that makes seven Enforcers working for my mother. Eight if I count Quinn. Nine if there's a driver in the second truck.

How? I wonder, flummoxed by their involvement.

How did she buy their loyalty?

Jenner snorts. "Like that means anything."

She glares at him, her stern brow creasing, and lifts her chin with a disparaging sniff.

The dignified air she swathes herself in as she scoffs at our reluctance is familiar. How many times did she look at me with this same exasperation when I was a child? How many times did I brush it off as normal?

But normal people—the average inhabitants of the State not in positions of power and authority—don't behave this way in our society. They don't command respect. Or demand it, as my mother always has. Like the day my father was charged with treason when she boldly told an Enforcer to remove me from the room. I always assumed she said it to try to shield me from that trauma—from the distress of seeing my father get beaten—but now, as her words from that day stir in my memory, I realize it wasn't a request at all.

It was an order.

I grew up believing my mother worked in the Financial sector, that she was a law-abiding, run-of-the-mill citizen, so why did I never question it when she dared to order around an Enforcer? And why did her past behavior never stand out to me until now? I suppose I didn't want to see the truth, even though it was right there in front of me from the time I was young.

The truth that she was always a traitor.

My breathing stutters at the thought of my father, but the pain in my chest reminds me why I agreed to do this. Why I'm going with her.

Answers, I say to myself, finding my courage again. *Go along with this until you get answers.*

"Come on." I grab Ezra's hand and step forward, then look over at Jenner, his cheeks smeared with streaks of gray from the ash. Glancing between them, I incline my head toward the truck.

Ezra follows me without question, his face drawn with the distraction of his grief over Rai, but Jenner hangs back, gaping at us as if we've both lost our minds.

"Wait," he hisses, his bright eyes flashing to my mother. "This doesn't strike you as a *really* bad idea? Going with them is one thing. Being trapped in the back of a locked, armored truck is another. Who knows where she could be taking us."

Although I'm sympathetic and understanding of Jenner's distrust, I've reached the limit of what I can take in terms of pushback and second-guessing. I know he's only concerned about me and doing his part to point out any potential pitfalls—to be the voice of reason and sense while Ezra and I both spiral, barely hanging on by a thread—but we're running out of time. *I'm* running out of time. And every second we stall only brings the terrible future I've seen that much closer.

If we're going to do this, we need to go now.

While there's still time to save you, like Rai said.

A tired sigh parts my lips, but Ezra breaks his silence before I can speak. "We'll just have to trust she meant it when she said she wanted to help us."

"*And,*" I add in a harsh whisper when Jenner begins to protest, "if, at any point, we suspect she's leading us into a trap, I'll kill her myself. Sound good?"

As these words escape me, I realize I mean them. To protect Ezra and Jenner, I would slaughter anyone who even *thinks* about harming them. Even if that person is my own mother, the woman who brought me into this cruel, unforgiving world.

Jenner stares at me for a moment, then snaps his mouth shut with an audible click. Grumbling under his breath, he storms past us and makes for the rear of the vehicle, purposely knocking into my mother's shoulder in passing. Sneering, she clears her throat and straightens her jacket, shifting her focus to me.

Ezra shoots me a questioning look, and I nod, urging him to give us a minute. Words need to be said, and I'd rather tackle the subject without an audience.

With a warning glance at my mother, he releases my hand and follows after Jenner, casting one final look over his shoulder before climbing into the back of the truck.

Once we're alone—or alone as we can be with her nearby team of Enforcers—my mother arches a judgmental eyebrow. "Interesting friends you've made."

Baring my teeth, I lunge forward and grab her by the coat, shoving her into the side of the cab. "They aren't just my friends, they're my *family*," I spit, relishing her reaction to my choice of words. She flinches, as if every last one has cut her.

"Wynter," she starts to say, but I interrupt her.

"I love these people, and I swear on my life—on *your* life— that if you hurt them, if this is a trap—"

She huffs, attempting to push me off, but I don't relinquish my hold. If anything, her resistance makes my fingers grip tighter.

Nostrils flaring, she rolls her eyes. "I wouldn't waste time herding you into a vehicle if my intention was to kill you. I could've done that job three times over already."

Although she's right—although I've told myself this very same thing at least twice in the last hour—I scowl, unconvinced.

My fingers clench, the knuckles bone white, and I pull her closer until we're nose to nose. "Just don't delude yourself into thinking the fact that you're my mother will stop me from ending your life."

As I watch her process the threat, her lips trembling slightly, I relax my hand. I then take a step back, putting much-needed distance between us.

It's only when I turn my back to her that I acknowledge how fast my heart races or the burning in my eyes that can only be tears. I draw in one deep breath, then another, until the danger of my emotions fades, refusing to give her any reason to doubt me.

If I'm going to protect Ezra and Jenner from her—the way I

wish I could've protected my father—then I need her to believe that I would kill her if the choice came down to them or her. If I'm going to ensure they survive, that they have a future without me after I'm gone, then I need her to *want* to honor my wishes. And not just because I'm her daughter…

But because she's afraid of what I'll do if she doesn't.

I don't spare her a second glance as I skirt around the side of the truck to the open back, mentally preparing myself for whatever unknown danger awaits us from here. Ezra and Jenner stare out from the hold, looking equally nervous as I climb in and settle on the empty bench seat beside them.

Even with the doors hanging open, exposing us to the night air, the interior of the truck is a claustrophobic box. Like in the elevator to the sublevel, the metal walls press in on all sides until each breath is a struggle and the persistent ache behind my eyes makes me dizzy. Part of me can't help wondering if my reaction is all in my head—if the heat burning across my skin is real or imagined, born from the reminder of the many times I was forced into a vehicle just like this one.

Muffled voices outside draw my attention, and I listen, trying to hear what my mother is saying. If she really expects to take us to a safe house where we won't be discovered, I doubt she'd risk detection by bringing her small hoard of Enforcers with us. Despite that, I'm relieved when two masked figures appear at the doors and help Quinn up into the truck. As angry as I am with him for his deceit, he promised me answers and I intend to get them. And, as loath as I am to admit it, I still feel an inkling of gratitude toward him for saving our lives, even if he only acted because my mother ordered him to.

"I'm glad to see you haven't died on us," I say flatly as the two

Enforcers plop him down onto the bench seat across from me.

To my surprise, he chuckles. "Not yet. But I suppose there's still time."

"There's still time."

Stiffening at his mimicry of Rai's warning, I part my lips to shoot back a scathing remark, but the words die on my tongue when the Enforcers disembark and my mother appears between the open doors in their place, her eyes sharp and intent. She looks at me but says nothing before exchanging a meaningful glance with Quinn. As if in answer to some unspoken question, he nods, and then, my mother slams the doors shut, drenching the hold in impenetrable darkness.

An hour seems to pass in the space of mere seconds as the front door to the cab opens and shuts and the engine roars as the truck is thrust into drive, sending a rumbling vibration through the interior that causes the metal floor plates to quake under my feet. The shadows are too thick for my vision to adjust, and despite the seat under me, I feel like I'm floating, the pressure building in my chest like a balloon.

I reach for Ezra's hand, needing his presence to ground me, and as I interlace our fingers, he squeezes, although he's in far more need of consoling at the moment than I am. Whispering just loudly enough for me to hear, he croons, "It'll be all right. I'm here."

The crunching of tires over broken glass and debris agitates every last one of my nerves as the truck rears forward, leaving the DSD far behind. I don't hear the rumble of the second truck trailing us—which I assume was for the Enforcers—and it's hard to tell how much time passes in the darkness. While I attempt to keep track of the direction the vehicle moves in to have some idea where we're going, I give up after the fifth or so turn. The sensory overload of being temporarily blind makes it too hard to focus on anything other than the reassuring sensation of Ezra's hand in mine. Wherever we're going, we'll be together.

At least, until my time runs out.

The thought sobers me, and I close my eyes, trying to steady my breathing, which grows more uneven with every bump we cross in the road. My mind drifts back to our journey to the DSD only a handful of hours ago and what we witnessed the Enforcers doing to the injured people they found in the streets—the brutality of cold-blooded murder for the sake of maintaining a society built on our usefulness.

My stomach churns at the vivid recollection of what we might be driving over.

A bright light abruptly fills the sweltering hold, and I wince, glaring across the small space at Quinn, who stares down at the communicator clutched in his hand. Frowning, he looks up at me after a moment, his obsidian eyes hooded in the shadows. "We're coming up on a checkpoint. Don't make a sound."

My own eyes flash to Ezra and Jenner—desperate for a momentary glimpse of their faces when, any second now, the situation could take a turn for the worse and we may be separated for good. But Quinn shuts off the communicator, extinguishing the light before I can see them, throwing us all back into the stifling gloom.

Beneath us, the large tires roll to a stop. As the engine cuts off—engulfing us in silence—each thud of my pounding heart is so loud I'm certain the others can hear it.

I strain my ears, noting raised voices coming from outside near the cab, and as the growing tension crushes my lungs, I can feel Quinn's eyes on my face even though I can't see him, his steely features washed in shadow. Part of me wonders if, with our dooms so close at hand, he once again resembles that frightened young Enforcer I encountered a few months ago. It's still so hard for me to reconcile the two—the terrified soldier charging into his first battle and the hardened double agent, whose real motivations remain a mystery to me.

In the darkness, with no one to see him—when he can be his real self—which one is he?

A sharp knock against glass snaps me out of my thoughts, and I listen intently, catching the motorized hum of a window being lowered.

"ID," a gruff voice demands. Even obscured by the thick walls around us, the hostility in his tone is clear.

I hold my breath. There's a shuffling sound and then, for a torturous moment, nothing.

"Evelyn Adler," the Enforcer managing the checkpoint drawls in a bored monotone. "Where are you coming from, Doc?" A sudden pounding on the side of the truck sends my heart jumping up into my throat. "What's in the back?"

"Medical equipment," my mother responds coolly. Her alibi is convincing, even to me, as she adds, "The DSD was hit during the strike and I thought it best to salvage as much of the equipment as possible—"

"Who gave you clearance to do that?"

Goosebumps rise on my flesh at the suspicion behind the soldier's question, and that bubble of pressure in my chest grows larger, my power expanding under my skin like heat. I swallow, trying to tamp it down. If I don't keep my emotions, my terror, contained, then an outburst isn't only likely. It's unavoidable.

And without my collar, everyone in this truck and outside of it will die.

"I am the Head of Termination," my mother snaps, her authoritative tone bordering on malicious. "I don't need clearance to protect my work." There's another pause, and in the momentary hush, I envision her face. The irritation I imagine printed into her features is present in every word she growls. "Don't you have better things to do than hold us up over ridiculous formalities? Like searching for survivors, perhaps? Or evacuating the areas affected by the attack?"

The Enforcer mutters something I can't quite make out and is answered after a few seconds by a garbled voice projecting from a communicator. I can only understand one or two words past the frequent bursts of static.

"Roger," he huffs before clearing his throat. Then, he reluctantly says, "You can go."

Sweat breaks out across my forehead and hairline when the truck finally jerks forward again. Beside me, I can feel the others keeping perfectly still, as if waiting to see if we'll be followed or if the Enforcer guarding the checkpoint will change his mind and stop us again out of spite.

The unease permeating the air is like a perfume I can taste on my tongue, and I hold my breath, counting the seconds as we drive away. But no matter how many pass, I still don't feel safe. No length of time or distance is enough.

I stifle a breath of surprise as a light floods the interior again, illuminating Quinn's face. His brow is puckered as he stares down at the communicator clutched in his hand.

"We're all-clear," he breathes.

No one dares speak another word for the remainder of our

journey. As we pass through the city, heading who knows where, I focus on the noises beyond the truck, searching for anything to distract myself from the recollection of the past few hours and the untold horrors which may still come to pass. A faint siren rings in the distance, but other than that, the Heart is eerily silent, as if the bombings have somehow robbed the world of all sound. It's a sobering reminder of the fate awaiting us all if I don't succeed in preventing my vision.

The tires slow their rotations, rolling to a gradual stop, and the engine cuts off, eliminating the constant reverberations beneath my feet. I bristle in anticipation, but when no questioning voices greet us and the doors to the cab creak open and slam shut again, I let out a sigh of relief.

It seems we've reached our destination.

Bracing myself, I stare hard at the back of the truck as the repetitive clicking of high heels on concrete signals my mother's approach. Her face is just visible, her body a black silhouette, as she pulls the doors open, letting in a rush of night air.

"We're here. You can get out now," she says. Her eyes sweep from side to side as she steps away from the truck, searching the shadows for movement.

Quinn descends first, wincing as he eases himself onto the pavement, followed closely by me, then Ezra, then Jenner. Once we're all free of the stuffy hold, I turn in place, taking stock of our new surroundings. We're alone inside an empty parking structure, encased on all sides by broad concrete walls with only small slips of open stretches that let me see out into the city beyond. Smoke from the explosions seeps in through the gaps like rays of sunlight determined to burn, stinging my nostrils and throat, and although it's summer and the air is warm, there's an undeniable chill to the night. Almost as if the world itself is shivering in fear of what's coming.

Despite the fluorescent strip bulbs overhead, the lights in the structure are off, drenching the vast space in darkness. But I'm not sure if that's to mask our presence or because of the power outages across the Heart.

Completing my rotation, I note that the second truck is nowhere to be seen. Curious, I meet my mother's probing gaze, her eyes reflecting the minimal light.

"Where are your other lap dogs?" I ask, jerking my chin toward the sole Enforcer beside her—the driver—who stands at silent attention.

Her lips twitch. "Scouting the area and keeping a watchful eye on our route out of the city."

"So, you really *do* know how to get out of the Heart?" Ezra asks, surprised.

I've been wondering the same thing. After what we saw on our way to the DSD, it's hard to imagine escape of any kind being possible.

Jenner scoffs. "I hope you aren't planning on using the tunnels. Your little pet Enforcer here already told us they're a no go."

Quinn's upper lip curls back into a sneer, but my mother holds up her hand, cutting him off with a pointed look before he can get a word out.

Scowling at us each in turn, she says, "Being in a position of power has its perks. So does being universally feared. It affords me the connections to make the impossible possible. So, no," she adds, glaring at Jenner, "We will *not* be using the tunnels. But this is not the place for this discussion. We need to get inside. Then I will answer your questions."

My eyes drift along the concrete walls, noting there isn't a single entry in sight.

Get inside where?

At my confused look, she turns, waving for us to follow.

We trail after her without further question, Ezra and Jenner sticking close to my sides, while Quinn limps along behind us with the help of the other Enforcer. His grunts of pain stoke the embers of my guilt again, fanning the sparks into an inferno. He didn't betray us, not really. If anything, he saved our lives not once but twice by working with my mother. Who knows what might have happened at the DSD if she hadn't shown up. If he hadn't been there to lead her to us.

Knowing that, I struggle to cling to my anger. Haven't I done questionable things to protect Ezra and Jenner? Besides omitting the truth, what has Quinn done that can remotely measure up to my own countless crimes?

Haven't we all done things we're not proud of to survive?

My attention shifts back to my mother, and I stare at her back, deliberating over what possible motives inspired her actions over the years. Did she become what she is to protect someone else?

Or to protect herself?

She doesn't lead us very far, guiding our group into a narrow corridor less than twenty yards from the truck that I failed to notice from where we stood before, the entrance obscured by one of many flat protrusions of concrete that I had mistaken for a design feature rather than what it actually is. A nook for masking a secret passage. At first glance, the space beyond appears to be a dead end—a short hallway of concrete and pipework that, under any other circumstances, I would disregard as little more than a utility closet.

"This way." My mother signals to a minuscule gap in the pipes to our left barely wide enough for one person to slip through.

The passage we enter is cramped. The gloom thickens as we progress down a flight of slippery stairs, then down another, our trek continuing until the air grows damp and cool, just like every other time I've found myself in the underbelly of the city. My hand skims the wall in the blackness, the glow of my mother's communicator the only light guiding us forward.

Underground again, I note, shivering at the thought.

"This isn't creepy at all," Jenner mutters behind me, echoing what I'm thinking. Directly in front of me, Ezra says nothing, but I can sense his apprehension in the uncertain grip of his fingers.

"What zone are we in?" I ask with a sidelong glance at the walls, which seem to draw closer together the deeper we descend.

"Three," my mother answers.

Three? I stare at the back of her faint silhouette. That seems like an odd choice of location for a safe house, but then, I suppose that's the point. No one would think to look for us here.

At the base of the stairs, my mother turns right into what looks like another utility area, except, unlike the dead end upstairs, this corridor contains a single door. Proceeding toward it, she presses the palm of her hand to the small black screen above the handle.

"*Access granted,*" an automated voice bellows before the door swings inward, flooding the chilly hallway with light.

I shield my eyes as my mother puts her hand on my shoulder, pulling me over the threshold into a large open-planned living area, which reminds me in some ways of my home in Zone 2. The design—white walls and sparse gray furniture—is almost identical to that of the quarters I shared with her for the better part of ten years.

"Please, make yourselves comfortable," she urges.

Ezra, Jenner, and I all stand frozen, gawking at our surroundings, while the Enforcer plods past us, helping Quinn over to the large L-shaped sofa, which is positioned to border a white marble table that seems to serve as the centerpiece of the space. The back of the longer side of the couch is facing out into the room, toward the door we came in by, while the shorter side is pressed up flat against the wall to my right. The only other furnishings are two glass tables at each end of the sofa and a television screen mounted on the wall opposite the seating. Aside from that, the room is bare.

I spin slowly, taking in the clean decor. "Where are we, exactly?"

We all turn to face my mother as she closes the door behind us, her expression carefully blank.

"A safe house, like I promised."

Beside me, Ezra stiffens. "I've been wondering, what would the Head of Termination need a safe house for?"

The unease and doubt in his voice set me on edge, and I glare at my mother as all the many reasons I had not to trust her pop into my head again.

Her lips curl almost imperceptibly at the corners. "It's not mine," she clarifies.

My blood runs cold at the scuffle of footsteps behind me, and wheeling around, I choke back the murderous instincts of my power as I come face to face with our true host.

Wren Bilken meets my gaze with a glower. "Hello again, Miss Reeves."

ELEVEN

THE LAST TIME I WAS in the same room as Wren Bilken, my hands were wrapped around his throat, my thumbs gouging into his windpipe with a single pressing intent: to kill. Was it really only yesterday we had that altercation? It feels like it happened so much longer ago. Then again, the chaotic events of the last twenty-four hours have completely skewed my perception of time, making it seem like the past few days have spanned weeks. I don't even remember when I last properly slept. If the heaviness in my bones is any indication, it's been a while. Too long, maybe. And just like this disease—or perhaps even because of it—my exhaustion seems to be taking its toll.

Legs suddenly weak, I stumble forward, reaching toward the back of the sofa to steady myself, the room spinning around me. The resurfacing pain in my temples coaxes a fresh dew of sweat to bead along my forehead, the heat flushing along the underside of my skin making me nauseous. Ezra rushes forward to support me, his hands firm on my waist, but I wave him off, assuring him I'm okay. When he steps back, I clench my jaw and snap my eyes between my mother and Bilken as a dozen different emotions go to war in my chest, my heart the battlefield where they collide. I don't know what I should be thinking or feeling, or what game these two think they're playing with us. Hell, I don't even know which side they're on.

"At least your mother had the sense to know which side to choose." That was what Bilken said right after I nearly killed him for insulting my father. Was this what he meant? This… collaboration between them, or whatever this is I'm witnessing. At the time, I thought he had been referring to my mother's decision to surrender my father to the State for being a traitor in the unforgiving eyes of the law. But now, I can't help wondering if he meant something else entirely.

Bilken's callous expression relaxes into a smirk that makes me want to choke him all over again. "I'm glad to see you've all arrived in one piece."

Ezra scoffs, the sound abrasive, like the unsharpened edge of a knife against metal. "Why am I not surprised you're the one behind this? You always were a two-faced snake. What, tired of working for Nolan already?"

"Nolan is a power-hungry fool," Bilken growls, his momentary amusement gone.

"What happened to playing for the winning side?" The words are grainy as they roll off my dry tongue.

Bilken's responding look is scathing. "There is no winning side if everyone's dead. Surely, you've seen enough to know that by now."

His gaze is shrewd, and I wonder just how much he knows about what I've seen, both while as a weapon for the State—witnessing the resulting carnage of war with my own two eyes—and in my visions. Nolan might've used me for information to make his move when the Heart was defenseless—information Bilken was privy to—but Richter was the only one aside from Jenner who knew the full breadth of what I've seen. Who knew about the havoc I'm destined to wreak. I never even worked up the nerve to tell Ezra the truth, though I'm sure he's well aware of it by now. That's a secret I doubt Jenner would've kept to himself once he and Ezra realized I'd fallen for Richter's lie about a cure and gone back to the DSD.

I can only assume Bilken doesn't know the truth about what the future holds for the world, otherwise why is he helping us—helping *me*, the monster destined to inflict it? What's his angle here?

My eyes snap to Jenner's, and the suspicion I glimpse in their blazing blue depths gives me the impression he's wondering the same thing I am.

"So, you had a falling out with Nolan and since you can't exactly go back to the State after jumping *that* sinking ship, you're helping us. Why, out of the goodness of your heart?" He snorts. "Funny how you didn't care about our well-being when Nolan had this asshole put a gun to our heads."

Jenner shoots a scornful look at Quinn, which the ex-Enforcer returns from where he sits, reclined, on the sofa.

"Who do you think it was who told me to get close to Nolan?" Quinn asks. "If it wasn't for me, you would all be dead."

My eyes widen as that word fills every available space in my head.

Dead.

A lash of pain cracks through my skull like a lightning bolt, and I clamp a hand over my mouth, suppressing the violent urge to throw up. I can't make sense of any of this. Quinn was working for Bilken? I thought he was working for my mother?

How does one tie into the other?

"At least your mother had the sense to know which side to choose," I hear Bilken say again in my head.

Sides... Maybe I'm focusing on the wrong thing, too busy scrutinizing Quinn's part in all this and not looking closely enough at my mother's. Who Quinn is working for is irrelevant, but he *is* the common denominator. The link connecting the two pieces I have yet to put together, forming a picture I can't comprehend.

As it stands, only one thing is clear. My mother and Bilken are working together and possibly have been for a while, if what Quinn said about getting close to Nolan is true. But why? To what end?

What am I missing?

I recount everything that's transpired since the day Jenner blew up the transport helicopter. What he had said after, about an inside man helping them to accomplish the job...

Well, now that my initial shock and anger have both worn off from when Nolan revealed their informant was Bilken, I'm not surprised by the latter's decision to leave the State to join PHOENIX. Such betrayal is in line with his character, abandoning one side to join another if he has reason to believe it will keep him alive and, more importantly, in a position of influence. He told me as much himself, and by helping Nolan secure the State's precious weapon, he would've had the new life he desired at his fingertips. A just reward for a worthy prize.

But this? This I don't understand. Why throw it all away? What could he possibly hope to gain by having Quinn intervene in our executions? By turning on Nolan?

And what does any of this have to do with my mother?

Someone says something, but I can't pinpoint who, their voice dull behind the high-pitched ringing now filling my ears, penetrating deep. I can feel the reverberations in the roots of my teeth, as if I've just bitten an exposed wire. My fingers weakly reach for my ears to claw the sound out, but it only gets louder and more shrill, as if reacting to the protesting voices assaulting me from all sides.

My eyes search for Ezra, my vision blurring as his mouth forms words I have no way to hear, a plea for help lost in the cage of my own throat, impeded by the pain. It's unbearable, growing worse with each passing second, and I need it to stop. I need it to—

"Stop," I beg in a thready whisper. The clanging in my head is deafening, igniting another, stronger wave of pain, which drags an inhuman scream from my lips. "Stop!" I shriek.

The voices buzzing around me go silent at the same moment the world seems to tilt on its axis. My hands flail, reaching for the sofa, but miss as my eyes roll upward, my gaze skimming across the smooth ceiling. The rows of circular embedded lights burn fuzzy dark spots across my failing vision.

"Wynter!"

Muscular arms catch my body when I collapse, supporting my limp neck and head, and the shadows swathing the room clear just enough for me to make out Jenner's face, those kind eyes shining with concern. Ezra rushes to his side, leaning over me, but falters as he begins to say my name, his worried gaze catching on my mouth. Frowning, he presses a hand to my face, his thumb gently grazing my upper lip. I know without having to ask what he's seeing. I *feel* the warmth of it on my skin as clearly as I can smell its metallic stench, like rusty coins shoved up my nostrils.

A fearful look passes between him and Jenner, and Ezra's skin pales as he pulls back his hand. At the sight of the blood on his fingertips, another agonizing pain rips through my skull, stabbing behind my eyes, blinding me.

"My head," I gasp, writhing in Jenner's firm grip. Tears cut hot lines down my cheeks. "It's...killing me."

"Move." My mother's face appears in front of me now, her expression distant and detached like always, filling my field of vision like a storm cloud overtaking the sky. Cold fingertips brush my wrist. "Her pulse is weak. She needs to rest and recover her strength—"

"Recover her strength?" Ezra spits through gritted teeth before letting out a harsh, barking laugh. "She's *dying* because of what you assholes have done!"

Dying...

From the beginning, ever since our paths crossed, Ezra has known that's what this disease would amount to—that its parasitic hold on my life would always inevitably result in my death. He never shied away from that knowledge, and sometimes, I think it's that outcome—knowing that our time together is limited—that's coaxed him to fight as hard for me as he has. In a world where so much has been beyond his control, he wants to challenge fate.

And finally overcome it.

But now, hearing that word—*"dying"*—escape his lips so easily makes my fate all the more real...and that much more terrifying. I had accepted my impending death. On some level, I've even welcomed it. And yet, the strain in Ezra's voice as he mutters that single tragic word threatens to undo me.

My mother's sharp riposte jerks me out of my thoughts despite the darkness creeping in at the edges of my eyes. "I didn't do this to her. Your bastard brother did. And *you* did. She's in this condition because of *you*."

Because of Ezra?

I blink slowly, clinging to consciousness, searching for Ezra's dimming face through the haze. He recoils at her words, his confusion apparent in the vee of his brow.

"*Me*?" There's a defensive edge to his tone.

"Oh, yes, I know exactly who you are, Mr. Laramie." My mother glances down at me, and for the first time in my life, I notice what looks like a hint of regret in her gaze. When she next speaks, I'm not sure who she's talking to. Ezra…or me? Maybe both. "The question is," she mutters, "do you?"

What are you talking about? I try to push these words through my lips, but any remaining strength I had slips away and the darkness takes hold before I can speak. Pain, all-consuming and unrelenting, returns to wrap me in the cocoon of unconsciousness.

As my eyelids slide closed, Ezra's face is the last thing I see, the sorrow in his expression reminding me so clearly of another moment in time. A moment we haven't lived yet.

A moment I know is unavoidable.

And when that end comes—with me and him alone at the end of the world, my power raging out of control and a gun gripped in his hand—I can't help wondering if he really will pull that trigger. Or if he'll fail me as badly as I've failed him…

And let that gun fall, unused, to the ground.

TWELVE

THE WORLD IS FROZEN. ASH and dust hang in the air like suspended snowflakes, and I push them aside with my hands as I progress through the wasteland that's become as familiar to me now as the reality I live in. Perhaps this vision—this unavoidable outcome—is even more real to me by this point. More real than Ezra or Jenner. More real even than the trauma I've endured at the hands of the one person who was a bigger monster than I am.

Because this destruction, this chaos, is certain. Whereas everything else—Ezra and Jenner and the lives of all those residing on this doomed planet...

Those fates still hang in the balance, dependent on what I do moving forward.

The gravel and debris crunch beneath my steps as I traipse this desolate landscape alone. The wreckage stretches as far as the eye can see, but for once, I'm not afraid of it or of the knowledge that I am the one who will bring this hell upon us.

Finally, acceptance has sunk in, settling over my skin like drops of water I can't brush away. And as that rain pummels into my flesh, spreading over me, I know I would do anything to avoid the horrific consequence of my disease destined to follow this destruction. Anything to avoid creating further casualties to my unwanted power.

No one else should have to suffer because of me. Because of what I've become.

This is one burden I should bear alone.

Quiet laughter tugs my gaze over my shoulder, and turning, I glimpse the distant shape of three young children chasing each other. Two boys—one taller than the other—and a girl with a shining curtain of glossy brown hair that hangs down to her waist. Their giggles, although stifled behind tiny hands clamped over their mouths, are genuine and infectious, and I find myself stumbling toward them, needing to see their faces more clearly, even though I know in my heart who they are.

As I draw closer to where the children play, the ruination of the Heart ripples like a mirage, the details around me changing. Now, instead of standing among the craterous remains of the city, I'm in a small, confined courtyard surrounded by blocks of lower-income apartments from a time long before the attack. Smog puffs in a thick, black cloud overhead, dragging my gaze toward the looming crematorium—just visible through a gap in the buildings.

This is Zone 4, I realize as I pivot in a slow circle, observing the scene before finally looking back at the children, my eyes settling on one in particular.

The beautiful boy with golden hair and a smile that breaks my aching heart.

This must be where Ezra grew up.

I watch the children play their game, taking in each of their faces in turn. Ezra, so carefree, his smile so bright. So unlike the man I know, the weight of the world always pressing down on his shoulders. Rai, youthful and full of vigor. Unlike now…our lives robbed of her light. Then there's Richter, the oldest of the three, and serious even at such a young age. He's no older than ten or so in this memory, but there's a glint to his eyes as he assesses his brother and Rai, as if he's mirroring their actions, wearing the mask that's expected of him in this moment. As if he's only *pretending* to enjoy himself to appease the other two children.

And yet, I can see a hint of fondness slipping past his carefully poised expression each time he looks at them. He cared for them. He *loved* them.

Until he thought they betrayed him.

Rai trips and falls hard in the dirt, and I gasp, rushing forward to help but stopping dead in my tracks when Richter sprints toward her at the sound of her cry, which she dampens by biting down on her lip. As he tends to her scraped knee, she wipes the tears from her eyes and nods to something he says to her, the words beyond my range of hearing. Grinning, he pats her on the head.

Once he's finished, he helps her back onto her feet, but as he resumes their game, she pauses, glancing down at her leg, head cocked to one side like a curious puppy. The expression on her face strikes me as familiar, and I find myself thinking back on my feverish recollection of how she cared for me when I first sought out PHOENIX after escaping the DSD. How she kept me on this side of death in the days after I cut out my tracking chip. Now, as I stare at the childlike incarnation of her, the irony hits me. The medical training Rai had, however minimal…did she learn it from Richter?

Was the heartless man responsible for so much suffering—*my* suffering—the one who taught Rai what she needed to know to save me?

A sob catches in my throat, and I turn, averting my gaze, no longer wanting to see this. To see how many lives have been torn apart and changed for the worse. By our country's oppressive ways. By rebellion.

By me.

If I had never existed, Ezra's mother wouldn't have told him to find me and maybe Richter wouldn't have grown to become obsessed with my disease. Maybe then, he would've turned out differently, *become* a different person than the madman I knew. And maybe, if I had never existed, these three children would've been able to share a happy life together, free from the moral differences that tore them apart.

Or, at least, as happy as anyone can be in the State.

If I had never existed, Ezra would be safe. And Rai... Sweet, kind Rai...

She would still be alive.

The sound of nearby footsteps has me looking to the right side of the courtyard, and I gape, wide-eyed, at the beautiful but tired-looking woman standing there, dressed in a tattered white hospital gown. At first, I think she's part of the vision— out of place, but part of it. Until, I realize her gaze isn't following the playing children but locked intently on me.

Her skin crinkles beside her pale eyes when she smiles. "Hello, Wynter."

I startle at the sound of my name on her lips, spoken so easily, as if we're acquaintances. I blink, unsure if I heard her correctly, but there's no mistaking what she said. She said my name. She *knows* me. She's *speaking* to me.

But how?

Before I can ask, she holds up a hand. "Don't be afraid. I just want to talk. You have no idea how happy I am that I'm finally able to reach you."

"Who—" The word comes out broken and raspy, and I clear my throat, ignoring the shiver of fear sweeping over my skin. "Who are you?"

The woman clasps her hands loosely in front of her waist. "My name is Alivia Laramie. I'm like you."

Laramie…

My eyes widen. "You—" The words stick to my tongue in protest, as if they can't believe what I'm seeing or hearing. "You're Ezra's mother," I finally mutter after a moment.

She pushes out a relieved breath through her nose and dips her chin, bowing her head in acknowledgment. When she looks up again, her eyes—an usual combination of honey and pewter—are sad. "I'm so glad he managed to find you. And so terribly sorry for everything you've had to endure."

I shake my head, stumbling backward a step. "How is this possible? How are we communicating right now? You—"

You're dead.

I stare at her, my thoughts jumbled. Death aside, Ezra's mother was institutionalized, her mind fractured in the months, or maybe even years, leading up to her death. But this woman, she seems sane, for lack of a better word, her words and eyes focused and clear.

I think back over what Ezra told me—how his mother would say the same thing to him whenever she saw him, repeating it like a chant. *"One green, one blue. Look for Wynter."*

Did she only say these words so he would pay attention… or was that all she was able to say? If so, does that mean I'm seeing Ezra's mother before her inevitable breakdown? Or is this just another frustrating outcome of this disease?

Will I eventually lose the ability to communicate, too, except for with the visions I see in my head?

At the confusion on my face, Alivia smiles. "You and me…" She looks away, gazing fondly at the children running back and forth between us, their laughter now a distant hum despite them being so close, as if the volume on the memory has been turned down so as not to overwhelm this conversation. "We are the epitome of what shouldn't be possible, and yet, here we both are. I'm looking ahead at you. You're looking back at my children and their darling friend, Raina." Her expression darkens. "That poor, poor girl."

She closes her eyes for a moment and draws in a steadying breath, the silence between us morose. When she meets my gaze again, she shrugs.

"I'm no expert, but I suppose we could say it's like our wires are crossing."

My heart jumps up into my throat at her words. She knows about Rai? But then… How much has she seen?

How much does she know?

"This is a dream," I whisper, shaking my head again. "This isn't real. It can't be—"

"And so what if it is?" Alivia asks me. "Dream or not, who's to say what's real and what isn't? You and I have both seen enough to know what we can do shouldn't be possible. If this is a dream, it's a dream. Let's not lose ourselves to semantics and what ifs."

"But…" I trail off, unsure what to say. I don't know what to think. I don't even know why I'm seeing this.

I don't know what she wants with me.

As if reading my mind, she cocks a thin, auburn brow—her wavy hair so much like Richter's in color. "You're running out of time. You know that, right? The moment you've been dreading is fast approaching." She lets out a long-suffering sigh and gestures around us with a wave of one hand. While the children remain, our surroundings have reverted to what they were before.

Once again, we're encompassed by the destruction and death I will inflict on this world.

"It's inescapable…as it has always been," she says.

I lurch forward a step, my jaw clenched, my hands drawn into tight fists. "How much have you seen?"

I narrow my eyes, glaring at her drawn face, her skin pallid and aged beyond her years from the disease wreaking undeniable chaos on her body. If she really has witnessed as much as I fear, then how long did she live with Ultraxenopia before it finally took its toll? The visions she saw and her descent into madness… Is that what I would have experienced if Richter hadn't intervened and escalated my own condition?

My evolution. A spiteful laugh catches in my throat at the thought.

"How much have you seen?" I ask again when she doesn't answer, my tone bordering on hysterical.

As these words leave my lips, I remember what Richter said before removing my collar. *"Have you worked out the reason she saw you yet?"*

A shiver of terror crosses my skin, and the sadness in her

eyes tells me everything I need to know.

"Enough," Alivia whispers before glancing at the children again. I follow her gaze only to find they have ceased their playing and now lie dead on the ground at my feet.

A hand flies to my mouth and I scramble backward, nearly tripping as I flinch away from the small, eerily still bodies in the dirt. A strained cry escapes me.

"So, that's it?" I shout, tears streaming down my cheeks. "There's no way to avoid it?"

Her eyes snap to mine. "There is one way."

I shake my head. "I know what you're thinking and I can't," I protest. "Not until I know Ezra and Jenner are safe from what's happening in the Heart."

Alivia's expression changes and she gives me a look I recognize all too well. I've seen that disappointment enough times on my mother.

"They will never be safe so long as you are alive. You know this—"

Anger, hot and fierce, rips through me, exploding like a burst of fire off my tongue. "Of course, I know that! You think I don't? I—" The rage leaves me suddenly, and I deflate, beaten down by the memories of everything that's occurred since the fateful day of my placement exam. "I've tried to change it," I breathe, my voice shaky. "But every time, I only end up making things worse."

No matter what I do, I always put the people I care about in danger. I want to protect them, not just from this world but from me. And to do that, I know, better than anyone else…

There's only one option left.

"Why did you tell Ezra to find me? He would've been safer

if we'd never met."

Alivia turns in place, taking in our surroundings. Holding out one hand, she collects the ash and dust hanging stagnant in the air on her fingertips. "Would he? His fate has always been tied to yours. As has Austin's." She inhales deeply, then looks up at the sky and says, as if reciting a poem, "Two brothers—one, the creator of a terrible weapon. The other…destined to destroy it."

I balk, my skin going cold. "Destroy…" I go still, the realization gripping my chest. I swallow, my voice breaking. "You mean kill."

Ever since I had that first vision of Ezra, his solemn words have haunted me. Gun in hand, tears streaming down his cheeks, he said, *"I'm sorry, Wynter."* Always those same three words. I never knew what he meant or what he would do that would warrant such a distressed apology. But now…

Now, I think I do.

"Have you worked out the reason she saw you yet?"

Richter knew. Or he deduced enough from what I told him and from that initial vision at the DSD—the first time I saw Ezra—to come to his own conclusion. Which means my mother, his trusted confidant, who admitted to knowing the details and outcome of every experiment he put me through…

She figured out Ezra's role in my vision, too.

"I'm sorry, Wynter."

I shake my head again. No. He dropped his gun. He wouldn't—

Alivia frowns, as if reading my thoughts. "That has always been Ezra's purpose—"

"No," I say, out loud this time. "If that's true, then fate is cruel for letting me—letting *us*—" I snap my mouth shut, unable to bring myself to say anymore. Instead, I close my eyes, tears slipping through, as I imagine every moment I've ever shared with Ezra. His anger. His distrust. His affection.

His love.

I remember it all. I *feel* it all.

And for the first time, I realize how unfair this world is.

Alivia gives me a pitying look. "Fate may lead us to a destination, but the path we take to get there is entirely up to us. We each carve our own path."

"Do we?" I ask, wiping away the sticky residue of tears on my skin. "Because nothing I've been through has felt like my choice."

She nods, then steps forward, crouching down beside the innocent child version of Richter lying on the ground between us. Trying and failing to brush the hair from his face, she says, "I understand that frustration, more than anyone possibly can." Her eyes—such a peculiar combination of the person I love most and the man I hate with every fiber of my being, even now, after his death—lock onto me, hawkish and demanding. "But you need to be strong, Wynter. I—" Her voice breaks. "I don't want to lose another son."

"But—" I bite my tongue, hesitating. She's so worried about what *I* need to do, but does she know what fate awaits *her*? Given what she's seen, surely, she knows this, too. Finally, I force myself to say, "But you're already dead."

She offers me another doleful smile. "But Ezra isn't."

A sudden unbearable shame washes over me. By only mentioning Ezra, it dawns on me that she must also know that Richter is dead. And more so, that I'm the one who killed him.

And yet, there's no trace of blame in her words. Just a matter-of-fact undertone I can't ignore.

"There's still time to change the course of your path," she

continues. "To ensure he lives."

As she says this, I hear the echo of Rai's words from my dream. Like Alivia, she had said there's still time, and when I had pressed her for what, she had answered with three simple words that even now torment me. Three words that shape my every moment.

"To save them."

How? I want to scream. *How can I change it?*

What if I only end up making things worse?

But I don't give voice to these thoughts because I know they're only excuses for the terror that threatens to cripple me. If I do nothing, Ezra and Jenner will die. Saving them is simple. All it would take is one sacrifice.

One sacrifice I know I'm capable of, and yet, according to Ezra's mother, I'm not the one meant to enforce it.

He is.

I bite down hard on my lip. "He won't do it. Not after everything he went through to get me back."

"He will," Alivia counters, "because it's what needs to be done. No one else can do it but him."

"Why?" I press. "Why does it *have* to be him?"

Why is fate so set on hurting us? And if it does have to be this way, why can't I just do it myself or hand myself over to someone actually willing? There are plenty of people out there who would happily kill me.

Why does Ezra have to do it?

Rising, she closes the distance between us and presses a clammy hand to my cheek. I startle at her touch, but she smiles…the way I always imagined a mother would.

"Because you will ask him to," she murmurs, "and because,

at the end of all this, he is the only one you won't try to stop from pulling the trigger. This disease likes to protect itself. It's like a parasite and we are the unwilling hosts, used until our bodies are depleted. You heard what Austin said. He called it the next stage of human evolution." She scoffs. "Who knows for sure what it is. But, I can tell you, it won't let you do what you're thinking while it still has a use for you. And anyone else who tries will be killed. You know I'm right...even if you don't want to admit it."

Images of the many battles I was forced to take part in on behalf of the State rush into my mind all at once, assaulting me with the guilt of the lives I've taken and of all the times I gave myself over to the monster living inside me, even though I knew all along it was gaining control. Even now, with the monster unleashed, I'm still here—still present—but it's gradually taking over, consuming me slowly as if to taunt my weakness.

And, in the end, it will win.

"And if he doesn't do it?" Or worse, if I lose all sense of myself and murder him for trying?

"You will still die," Alivia says, her tone sober. "But so will he. And so will everyone else on this planet."

Her eyes glisten with unshed tears, and in that sadness, I hear the words she left unspoken. The words we both know to be true.

No matter the outcome, you will die.

She wraps her arms around her torso, shivering against the bite of the wind, even though it's a barely-there caress against my own skin. "You and Ezra... Neither of you deserve what's coming, but it doesn't change the fact that it is still your future. We both know it can only end one way." She nods then, as if she senses what I'm feeling. As if she knows those emotions all too well herself. "It's okay to be afraid. Just don't let it stop you from doing what's right."

Suddenly, the ground rumbles beneath our feet, and Alivia falters, thrown off balance, shock and dismay etched into her features. Her face blurs and turns slightly translucent, like a radio frequency losing signal.

I stare at her, alarmed. "What's happening?"

With a watery smile, she meets my gaze one final time. "It seems fate has finally caught up with me."

She doesn't seem afraid so much as resigned. Still, I'm overcome by the urge to help her, even though we both know I can't. Her destiny is already written. She will die. Richter will become a monster. And Ezra will set out on a journey during which he'll unknowingly honor his deceased mother's wishes.

As Ezra's face fills my thoughts, Alivia grips my hand. "Wynter?" Her tone is pleading and as she vanishes into the landscape, her words sink into my skin alongside those raindrops of acceptance, branding themselves into my flesh.

Every last one burns me with a pain I deserve.

"Tell my son I love him."

I collapse to my knees as her hand fades from my grasp until, once again, I'm alone with only the destruction I will cause as my sole companion. I stare at the emptiness around me, and, in this moment, as wracking sobs reverberate deep in my chest...

I know my fate is the one thing in this world I can't run from.

THIRTEEN

I WAKE UP IN A dimly lit room, curled in a ball under a thick blanket, fully naked with a thin layer of drying sweat on my skin. My surroundings are sparsely furnished and bleed together, blurring into a continuous gray and white streak, and the air is cold, as if the room is conditioned. Or as if—

I'm underground.

My head spins as I slowly force myself into a sitting position, trying to figure out where I am. Everything is hazy, and my gaze snaps to my bodysuit where it's crumpled in a heap on the floor—my armor of the last year discarded, leaving me vulnerable and exposed. Fleetingly, I wonder who undressed me but the thought is cast away when I take a closer look at the bodysuit. Even from across the room on the bed, I can spot the dark patch soaked into the collar.

I wipe a trembling hand across my nostrils and mouth, and when I glance down at my fingers, I grimace at the flakes of old blood spotting my skin like freckles.

Bilken's safe house, I remember abruptly, my eyes narrowing on the door as the broken recollections of the events that led me here begin to slowly piece back together. The DSD. Richter. Rai. My mother. Our trek to this hidden, clandestine apartment. I remember it all.

Even my dream.

Alivia Laramie's face is a stain on my mind, as clear to me in waking as it was in my vision. As much as it scares me to think that I spoke to Ezra's dead mother, I can't ignore the twisting sensation in my gut that keeps telling me she was real. Everything she said was a reflection of the hard truths I've been struggling to accept, and maybe, it was for that reason I was able to connect with her now when it sounded like she'd been trying for some time to reach me. Maybe I needed someone to give me a push, to put into words what I already know. Or maybe none of what I saw was real after all and my subconscious was merely manifesting my fears in a form that would finally force me to listen to reason.

As if to remind me what I stand to lose if I fail—what will happen should I bow to cowardice—another face bursts into shape in my head, pushing all trace of Alivia out. A searing pain stabs my eye sockets like ice picks, and as tears obscure my surroundings, I hear a familiar timbre in my ear. I look behind me, following the trail of the voice, sliding off the bed onto my unsteady feet as the small, frigid room melts away.

Shadows wrap around my eyes like a blindfold, but gradually, the darkness lifts, unveiling a cramped space I've been in before. This place... It's the room where I found Ezra tucked away the night of our mission to Zone 1. The night we thought Rai died. The room where he was mourning her loss and I dared to kiss him for the first time.

Just like that night, he sits hunched on the floor like a

neglected child, his back to the wall and gaze hooded, cast down on the concrete. The only visible light floods in from the hallway, forming a line of yellowish white, which begins at the door and ends just past his feet, only kissing a few inches of his body and face.

The soft echo of steps draws my gaze to the doorway, and I glance at the silhouette standing at the threshold, his tall frame snuffing out the faint pool of light.

Jenner.

Once again, his soothing voice fills my ears, repeating the faint words that pulled me into this vision.

"Wynter's leaving. You have to stop her."

Ezra's eyes crawl upward, his face expressionless. "What do you expect me to do?" he asks.

Jenner steps forward, throwing his hands up in frustration. "Go after her!"

Shoulders slumping, Ezra looks back down at the floor. "What's the point? If she wants to go, then let her."

"You…" Jenner blanches, his voice faltering, as he gapes at the downcast, broken shell of his friend. His hands curl into trembling fists at his sides. "You can't be serious right now."

Ezra's answering silence is deafening.

Sneering, Jenner tilts his chin up, defiant. "Fine. Sit here in the dark and mope"—he all but spits that last word—"but I'm not willing to just let her go—"

"She's dying, Jenner," Ezra says bluntly. Tears flood his eyes when he finally looks up again. "Wynter is *dying*."

Understanding dawns as Jenner's pupils blow wide. "And you think, if she leaves, your brother might actually cure her?" A humorless laugh cuts through the minuscule space. "I'm calling bullshit. You're deflecting, Ez. Why are you so goddamn stubborn and unwilling to actually face the truth?"

Ezra scoffs. "And what truth is that?"

Jenner swallows, and the wounded look on his face nearly brings me to my knees.

"I'm not blind," he mutters, his voice walking the tightrope of a whisper. "You put on a good show, but anyone can see you're half in love with her already. Even when you acted like she was a threat, I saw the way you looked at her. You were constantly watching her, and when she fell into that coma…" He shakes his head. "You barely left her side for *six* days. Hell, since she woke up, this is the first time you've let her out of your sight."

When Ezra doesn't respond, doesn't so much as blink an eye, Jenner sighs.

"I know what you're thinking," he continues. "You're thinking, if she stays, there's nothing to prevent you from losing her just like we lost Rai." His voice catches on her name, and he clears his throat. "It's a risk, sure, but if you don't go after her now, you'll regret it for the rest of your life. You'll always wonder."

Ezra leans forward and, propping his elbows on his knees, runs a shaking hand through his hair. The dirty blond strands stand on end where he touched them. Grimacing, he bites out, "If she's so set on leaving, what makes you think I can change her mind? Clearly, you couldn't convince her."

He smothers his face in his hands, but despite his obvious misery, I find myself looking at Jenner, lured by the sad smile curving along his lips as he squats to the floor beside his friend.

Pain grips my heart as he murmurs gently, "Because I'm not the one she wants to ask her to stay."

As Ezra looks up, realization alight in his gaze, the shadows return, swathing his face in blackness and ripping me out of the vision. When the blindfold lifts for a second time, I open my eyes to the colorless room I woke up in, naked and alone.

An all too familiar coppery scent fills my nose, and I brush away a dribble of blood from my nostrils as the pain in my head fizzles to a dull ache. I swallow the rising bile in my throat, scrubbing a hand quickly over my face as a knock drags my sluggish gaze to the door.

"Wynter?"

Ezra pokes his head into the room as I tug the thick blanket off the bed and wrap it around my shoulders, his watchful eyes like flames licking over my exposed skin. The goosebumps pimpling my flesh soften within moments of the warm fleece cocooning my body, and with one last shiver, I let out a breath, plopping back down onto the edge of the mattress.

Without saying a word, he crosses the room and sits down on the bed beside me. I can feel the concern practically vibrating off him like tremors felt after an earthquake, but thankfully, he doesn't ask me if I'm all right.

After all, we're both smart enough to know that I'm not.

I peer at him out of the corner of my eye. It's strange to look at him now, knowing what I know. That we were always destined to meet for a single purpose. For him to kill me. I think I've always known as much, I just didn't have the strength to admit it.

The elements in our lives have always been too closely aligned to brush off as coincidence. And yet, accepting it now doesn't change how I feel. If anything, it only makes my heart hurt—makes this love feel cruel and unjust, like something beautiful that's been poisoned against me.

A broken laugh forces it way up my throat.

I guess I do know how Richter felt.

A frown pulls at the edges of my lips. There's so much I want to say to Ezra and there's the matter of the message his mother asked me to relay, but how do I even begin to tell him something like that? How do I navigate his emotions when I can barely handle my own?

Tears line my throat, distorting my voice when I speak. "I feel like everything I've ever been told is a lie. I'm not even sure what's real anymore."

Quinn. My mother. Bilken. Ezra. Nothing makes sense to me anymore.

Hell, maybe it never did.

Calloused fingers wrap around mine and squeeze. "I'm real," Ezra says. "*We're* real. And I love you. That isn't a lie. It never was."

I turn into his shoulder, nestling my head under his chin so he won't see the heartbreak on my face.

So, what if you do? I'm tempted to ask. *That won't change what needs to be done. That won't change why fate brought us together.*

A whimper escapes me, and I stifle a sob.

"Hey," he breathes, brushing his knuckles against my cheek and tilting my head back until I'm forced to look up at him. "There's still time. We'll figure this out."

There's still time. Those words seem determined to haunt me—to define my remaining moments on this planet. The trouble is, they aren't true.

What time I do have left is nearly expired.

"You know just as well as I do there isn't." My tongue darts out over my lower lip, tasting the tears now running freely. I shake my head. "I don't want to waste what little time we have left together pretending otherwise."

I stroke Ezra's bruised cheek with my fingers, but he moves away, pushing up to his feet.

"So, you're just going to give up? After everything we've been through?"

"No," I counter. No, this isn't giving up. Because my death won't be the end. "I'll keep fighting until this is all over. For Rai." *For Jenner*, I add silently. *And for you.*

A flicker of hope crosses his face, and he kneels on the floor, taking my hands in his once again. Bringing my fingers to his lips—the skin still battered from the beating he took at the PHOENIX compound outside the Heart but now finally beginning to heal—he says against my skin, "Okay, then let's figure out what to do."

"I already know the answer to that," I assure him with a careful, forced smile, "but, for it to work, I need you to promise me something."

He nods, and all the love he has for me seems to pour out in the single word he exhales. "Anything."

Leaning forward, I slant my mouth over his, and as his lips part to let me in, eager to reciprocate my touch, I remember his mother's words from my vision. With a heavy heart, I whisper, "Promise you'll kill me."

He jerks away as if I've burned him, his eyelids fluttering like a moth's wings. "What?"

Tugging my hands free of his tightening grasp, I cup his face, holding him trapped to my gaze. He knows the truth. He said it himself when he lashed out at my mother.

"She's dying because of what you assholes have done!"

Now, he needs to be reminded of it.

He needs to know there's no happy ending where he and I end up together.

"I'm dying, Ezra. And when this sickness finally reaches its pinnacle, I won't be able to stop what I've seen. I don't want that. I don't want to kill the people I love."

"And you think I do?" he growls. "No. *No*," he says again, more firmly this time. "We'll find a way. We always do. I'm not going to *kill* you when there's still a chance I can save you."

"And if you can't?" I ask. "What then? When we're out of options, what else will you do?"

His cheeks flush red, but he says nothing. Because there's nothing to say. There's no magical solution to our problem.

A stray tear darts from his left eye.

As I brush it away, I kiss him again. This time, his mouth is still against mine.

"There's no other way," I mutter against his lips. "Please. If you really love me...you'll do this." I pull away just enough to look at him, all gentleness gone from my voice. "Please."

Ezra climbs to his feet and leans over me, placing his hands on my upper arms and pushing me back onto the bed, the blanket falling away from my shoulders as he joins me on the mattress. As he hovers over me on all fours, his head bows and tears splash onto my chest, sliding in hot streaks across the curves of my torso.

Lacing my fingers through his disheveled hair, I snake my other arm around him and tug him down until our bodies are flush. As I hold him to me, stroking his back and head, he shakes with silent sobs.

"Please," I whisper again, pleading.

He swallows loudly. Then, nodding against my shoulder, he gives me the only thing I'm asking him for.

"I promise," he says, his voice husky.

My lips find his in the pained hush that follows, but as our fingers interlace, our bodies joining, a flicker of doubt seeps into the cracks in my thoughts. And as that doubt festers, I can't help wondering if, like so many other aspects of my life…

If those words are just another lie.

FOURTEEN

I HAVE NO IDEA WHAT time it is when we finally emerge from the bedroom, out of our little pocket of darkness into a sterile light that seems blinding by comparison. The artificial white glare reminds me too much of the DSD, of Richter and the flashes of memories always sitting too close to the surface, ready to tear my already fragile composure to shreds.

A shudder rolls over my skin, tempting me to slink back into the refuge of that bedroom, where the seconds—which now rush by as if to taunt us—seemed to at least stand still for a moment. Now, out here in the open space of the safe house, reality is something I can no longer avoid or put off.

The future is coming, whether I like it or not.

Ezra squeezes my hand, offering the only physical comfort I have aside from the fresh clothes brushing my skin—the first clean ones I've had the privilege of wearing since PHOENIX extracted me from the State. The black pants, short-sleeved shirt, and jacket are soft and less restrictive than my bodysuit was, allowing me to breathe for what seems like the first time in years. Although, I imagine that has less to do with the fabric and more to do with what my previous attire represented. Now, instead of a weapon of mass destruction and war, I'm just me. Just Wynter. Now, the physical representation of Richter's hold over me is gone, discarded like trash.

I glance at the others, who sit perched on the sofa, their postures awkward and tense, drawing attention to the intentional gaps between them, as if they're all afraid to exist too close to each other. The only ones who sit side by side are my mother and Bilken, who—for reasons I have yet to discern—seem to have no issue sharing the same space.

A grimace twists my lips as I narrow my eyes at them, wondering what the nature of their relationship is. Are they just colleagues in their master plan, or are they something more?

Where does her betrayal to my father end?

They stare back at me, although neither one says a word, instead waiting for me to break the silence. My mother cocks a delicate eyebrow, urging me to speak.

I exhale through my nose before crossing the room and plopping down with a grunt onto the empty cushion beside Jenner. He grabs my hand as Ezra looms behind us, standing over me like a protective bodyguard. His fingertips touch my shoulder for reassurance.

As I sit, my gaze never strays from my mother. "You promised me answers. So, talk."

Her face is a stone mask, irritatingly blank and unreadable. A skill no doubt mastered at the DSD.

"Where would you like me to begin?" she asks.

"My father," I bite back.

She begins to recoil but catches herself, as if determined not to show any weakness. Straightening, she clears her throat.

"You might not believe it, but I loved your father—"

I scoff. "Handing him over to be executed is an interesting way of showing it."

A scowl mars her lips. "You don't know the whole story."

"Then tell us," Jenner urges.

I glance at him. Although his tone is calm, there's a hardness behind his words that I can't ignore and a hatred in his gaze I understand far too well. I don't blame him for loathing my mother for the tragedy she inflicted on his life.

For the same reasons, I despise her, too.

My mother lets out an indulgent sigh. "Before the State became what it is now, it was an underground political movement, a group of like-minded individuals who were unhappy with how the previous government ran things and were confident—or, I suppose, arrogant—enough to believe they could do better. Not unlike PHOENIX," she adds, her tone frigid.

"I know this already," I snap, glaring at Bilken, whose expression remains frustratingly impassive. "He told me. What's your point?"

She leans back and studies me, crossing her arms. "Did he also tell you I was part of that group?"

Shock strips the heat from my skin. "What?"

Exchanging a brief look with Bilken, she nods. "I didn't grow up in this city, like you. Neither of us did," she says, gesturing to our still silent host. "Together, Wren and I were sent into the Heart in the early stages of the State's rise to power, before it had actually seized control and word of a new government was still merely rumor, to work undercover and weed out any possible rebellion before it could grow. We were each given aliases and false lives, then told to make connections and report back on any treasonous activity we encountered." At my stunned expression, she adds, "It's much easier to smother an ember than it is a flame," as if that justifies what she did.

"So, my father..." I trail off as acid sloshes in my stomach, making me nauseous. She can say what she wants about loving my father; in the grand scheme of things, only one fact matters.

He was a target to her.

"At first, Wren and I had different marks we were each told to watch and report on. We were young, barely adults ourselves, so we could easily move in social circles and public spheres where those most likely to be involved with an insurgency would be present. Several years passed before I actually crossed paths with your father. I met Freston in a bar in Zone 7 that we had heard was frequented by a growing rebel group, which Wren had been cozying up to for years, since shortly after we first came to the Heart."

"The Vega," Ezra mutters at the same time Jenner says, "PHOENIX."

She nods again, looking me square in the eye. "Wren had already secured connections there, which led to our discovery of the group when it was still a fledgling idea more than an actual rebellion. But once it became more established, there were too many marks for him to cover alone. So, I stepped in to help. That was six years before you were born."

"Six *years*?" Disbelief stains my words as I try to line up the events of my past in my brain. I was just shy of turning seven when my father was beaten and dragged out of my house by Enforcers, taken away to the DSD to be executed. What could've possibly made my mother wait over a decade to turn him in to authorities?

My frown deepens as a more pressing question nags at me. How did she hold off the State for that long? Given my own experience with the DSD and Dr. Richter, I find it hard to believe whoever my mother reported to would've been that patient. Thirteen years is a long time to not deliver results.

"Then why—" I begin, but my mother cuts me off, as if she knows what I'm going to say.

"Do you really think I would've waited so long if I actually had any intention of turning him in?" she barks. "I told you," she mutters, her tone softer now. "I loved your father. I protected him for as long as I could."

Leaning forward, I rub my hands over my face. "I don't understand. Why didn't you just turn him in the second you learned he was with PHOENIX? You know he was the one who founded it, right?"

Why marry him only to betray him?

Her expression darkens. "Why else do you think I made it a point to get close to him? Wren worked out fairly early, through sheer proximity, who the ringleaders were in the group, and once I got involved, we agreed I would focus on Freston while Wren would foster his growing association with Nolan, that way we had two shots at infiltrating the insurgents. Sure, we could've named names from the get-go, but we didn't want to be too hasty in case either of us was being fed false information. The State was playing the long game, so the accuracy of our intel was more important than how quickly we got it. And believe me when I say, accuracy was paramount. The State has never been tolerant of misinformation, so with our futures and positions at risk, it was imperative we didn't make presumptions or do anything that might expose our identities, in turn jeopardizing our mission. With that in mind, we agreed to wait, to dig deeper, and only report back to our superiors with information that would prove we were assets and not liabilities. We wanted to make ourselves indispensable."

Jenner snorts. "Even undercover operatives weren't safe from the State, then, I take it."

My mother unleashes a cold laugh. "Far from it. We were promised esteemed positions in the new bureaucracy should we deliver the head of the snake, but were we to fail…" She laughs again. "Well, as you all are aware, the State doesn't take kindly to failure."

"But you didn't fail. You did eventually turn in my father. You got your *esteemed* positions," I spit. My gaze locks on Bilken again, and as I glare at him, picturing him gloating in his tall, glass tower, I remember what he said to me back at the bunker.

"Men like me get into positions of power because we do whatever it takes to survive…"

"There was more to it than that," he rumbles, finally breaking his silence, his voice a low, threatening boom. "You think it was easy for your mother to do what she did? We both had people we cared for. People we didn't want to see suffer."

"But my father did suffer!" I shout. "He died! He died because of *you*." I cut my eyes to my mother, who winces at the accusation in my words. Shaking, I suck in a trembling breath. "Tell me, were you partnered because you actually loved him, or was that just another part of your cover? Of the fake life you used to trick him into trusting you?"

Her lips purse, and she snaps back, her tone defensive, "I had every intention of just going in and doing the job I'd been assigned. But intentions change when you're in love." She scoots forward a few inches, as if to bring herself closer to me. "I didn't partner with him because I had to. I partnered with him because I *chose* to. I couldn't bring myself to betray him."

"So, why did you?" Ezra asks. "Obviously, something changed."

Her face falls. "Just because I didn't want to betray him doesn't mean I had another option. You don't say no to the State." She chews on her bottom lip for a moment, then shrugs. "Wren and I stalled for as long as we could, giving the people we reported to obscure leads and lesser names whenever pressed for information, making excuses about needing more time to build up the required trust to uncover who was really in charge. I'm not proud of it"—she glances at me then looks down at the floor—"but I sacrificed others in your father's place to buy myself time." Her voice drops to a whisper. "To buy *him* time."

Sitting back, she brings a hand to her mouth and bites down on the tip of her thumbnail. For a moment, she's silent, her eyes averted and glassy, as if lost is some distant recollection.

"Eventually," she continues, her voice melancholy, "his views became too outspoken, and I knew it was only a matter of time until his role in PHOENIX would become known to the wrong people. I couldn't think of any other way to protect him than to make myself a threat."

A threat...

The words I read in my father's journal take shape before me, rewriting themselves across my thoughts. I recall the entry he penned, expressing the divide that had formed between him and my mother and how he feared her allegiance to the State. In that same entry, he swore to put PHOENIX aside for the sake of his unborn child.

For me.

But despite stepping back from the organization, he never really put it aside. The siren of rebellion always called to him, and when I was a child, he exposed me to its song, even though doing so would have put me at risk.

It's only now, with my mother sitting before me, that I can see the situation from a different angle. If she hadn't done what she did—if she hadn't positioned herself as a threat to my father— would he have allowed that siren to pull me into the water?

Would he have allowed me to drown alongside him?

Exhaling, my mother shakes her head. "It killed me to put that distance between us, but I could accept his distrust if creating that rift meant he'd live. I had hoped, by making him afraid of me, he'd choose to give up the rebellion—that he'd pass on the torch out of self-preservation. And he did...but only once I told him I was pregnant with you."

Once again, I recall my father's words from his journal. "*I must abandon everything and all that I stand for, and, for the sake of my unborn child, I must stay and wear the mask of a man who conforms.*"

My mother scoffs, as if reading my mind, and when she next speaks, her tone is surprisingly bitter. "I thought we were free. That we'd be able to rebuild our love. But my pregnancy only subdued him. It didn't extinguish the fire he had burning within him, and when I discovered he was exposing you to that danger, that *world*, I knew he hadn't let PHOENIX go. He was simply biding his time, and what was worse, he had every intention of bringing you into the fold." Her voice breaks, and the desperation in her eyes as she meets my gaze is completely alien to me. "He left me no choice, Wynter. If I had let things carry on, I would've ended up losing you both. You were only a child. You were guiltless. I needed to protect you before he drew you in, too. Before there could be no saving you, either."

I hate the feeling expanding in my chest—this fear that my father was so blinded by his love for the past that he failed to see the danger that love put me in. A danger I'm now beginning to realize my mother tried to shield me from, even if, to do that, it meant making me hate her.

"So," she says, wringing her hands in her lap, "I did the only thing I could. I reported him. By this point, the State was no longer interested in eradicating PHOENIX. Instead, it saw the benefit of using the insurgency as a common enemy to unite the people against, amassing further power with the threat of domestic terrorism, which the State itself was actually responsible for. PHOENIX's mission and ideals were warped to create a smokescreen that would align the public under the government's rule."

Beside her, Bilken hooks one leg over the other and laces his fingers around his knees. "All the precautions the rebellion has taken to stay hidden over the decades have been fruitless. Even with the limited intel we provided, the Enforcers could've easily tracked PHOENIX under the city and eliminated the entire movement at any time. Especially once Freston was taken into custody. But the State opted not to do that, instead using PHOENIX to oppress the people and your father's execution as an opportunity to remind everyone of what happens when you act against the State, further cementing the fear it utilizes so expertly to manipulate public perception."

My brow furrows under the weight of my confusion, and although I'm wary of the answer, I ask, "What are you saying?"

Bilken gives me a sympathetic look then says, with a clarity that makes my lungs deflate, "Your father's execution was broadcast."

Vomit rises in my throat, and it takes all the willpower I possess not to spew across the sterile white rug. My father's execution was broadcast? I never knew that, and I certainly didn't see it, which means my mother must've gone to great lengths to ensure I wouldn't have to—an incredible feat considering everyone in the State is required to tune in to public executions.

I don't have to ask how she kept the truth from me. Growing up, no one ever said anything to me about my father being a rebel leader or about his involvement with PHOENIX, and why would they? Fear of suspected association would've tied even the bravest person's tongue. Besides, my mother was the one who reported him. She cemented our devotion to the State with that action. If anything, she made it clear to all those around us just how far she was willing to go for that loyalty.

Beside me, Jenner raises his hand. "Wait a minute. So, when you turned in Wynter's father, no one found it odd you had somehow failed to notice your own husband's involvement in the rebellion?"

"I said what I had to," my mother retorts. "That he covered his tracks. That he would've made a great operative for the State had he not been a traitor." She rehearses the words so convincingly that it's easy to envision her saying them.

"And they bought that? The people you reported to?" Ezra asks. Even without looking at him, I can picture the dubious expression he must be wearing just based on the tone of his voice.

My mother snorts. "What other choice did they have? They

had no proof I knew anything of his connection to PHOENIX. The only other person who knew the truth was Wren, and we were careful with what we documented so as not to incriminate ourselves. But…" She falters, her gaze once more distant. "Just because they didn't have proof doesn't mean they were accepting of my ignorance." Her eyes flick from Ezra, settling back on me. "I was punished for falling victim to what they believed to be your father's duplicity, but I accepted that punishment because it meant that I could stay with you. That you would be protected. *Safe*."

My pulse picks up speed, thrumming under my skin.

"What punishment?" I whisper, breathless.

"Aside from losing my husband, the man I loved, the father of my child?" She huffs, peering up at the ceiling, as if to hide the sheen of tears in her eyes. Sneering, she sniffs and looks down at her hands. "I was given my current job at the DSD."

Behind me, Ezra squeezes my shoulder. "How was being given a position of power at the most feared establishment in the State retribution?" His voice is unnervingly calm, the opposite of how I feel at this moment. Because I already know what she's going to say—I *fear* it—the weight of her unspoken confession hanging heavy in the air between us.

My mother considers Ezra for a moment, and I can sense the way she measures every word before she dares to speak. "The job wasn't the punishment," she finally says. "Killing Freston was."

Ezra's fingers tighten their grip, and next to me, Jenner stiffens, the hand wrapped around mine suddenly sweaty. I can feel the heat of his gaze on my face, as if he expects me to leap off this sofa and strangle my mother for this revelation. But I can't bring myself to move. I'm held still by the resurfacing pain in my chest and by the words that keep spilling from her lips, intent on torturing me with the truth.

"The State is often backhanded with its rewards. Everything must be a lesson—a reminder of where that reward came from and what happens when you bite the hand that feeds you," she says, as if I need further explanation for why she chose to turn on my father.

Her level tone sparks a writhing fury within me that tears at the underside of my skin, but still, I don't move, trapped in place by the small part of my mind that's led by reason and determined to listen to her side of the story. That needs to fully understand what she did.

"I was awarded an elevated position at the DSD for my devotion to the State and for making the ultimate sacrifice by reporting my husband's activities. But of all the jobs they could've assigned me—" Her breath catches, and she swallows, the sound audible in the encompassing hush. "It wasn't enough that I handed him in. The State wanted me to prove my loyalty by ending his life."

Tears scald my eyes, and I bite hard on my tongue to keep my rising sobs at bay. For so long, I've blamed my mother for what happened to my father. First, for not intervening when the Enforcers came to take him away, even though I've always known no one can intervene with the State. Then, once I learned of the full extent of her betrayal, I blamed her for turning him in. For being the one to steal my father from me. I blamed her in every sense of the word for his death, but never once did I think she was the one who killed him, that she was the one who snuffed out his existence like water on a flame.

In my mind, she was responsible for his death but not his

murder, and that disparity mattered. The separation between the two was what allowed me to keep seeing her as a mother—that let me live under the same roof and still love her all those years before my placement exam. Before she inevitably betrayed me, too.

My mother blinks when tears slip down my cheeks, burning raw lines into my skin. She inches forward on the sofa again, the temptation to console me etched plainly across her face, even though she has never been one to show outward affection. But I don't want her comfort.

I don't need it.

Wiping the anger and grief from my face, I growl, "You could've said no. You could've turned the job down."

At my words, the mask of the woman who pulled me away from my father in our final moments together and who handed me over to the DSD to be tortured slides back into place. Any hurt I thought I glimpsed in her gaze dissipates, vanishing behind a wall of ice.

"Do you honestly believe that?" She arches an eyebrow. "Wynter, the job was a test. There was no saying no, or I would've ended up just like your father."

"Okay, so why not just hand you a gun?" Ezra presses. "That doesn't explain why they would give you a job at the DSD. The staff there is all doctors and scientists—"

"As am I," she interrupts, her voice hard. "I had already begun my training in healthcare when I volunteered to infiltrate the rebellion, and it was agreed I would receive a prominent position if I delivered information that would strengthen the State's foothold. As part of my cover, I began working in a small local health center, but when the DSD was established,

I was sent there as a way of protecting my cover and alias, albeit in a junior position. One that wouldn't draw needless attention. At work, I was known by my birth name, Evelyn Adler. But everywhere else, I was Evandra Wright—then later on, Reeves—an insurance broker from Zone 2. Any intersection between my two lives was minimal, if altogether non-existent. And I insisted they stay that way, even when I turned in my husband and they offered me Head of Termination as my reward. A reward that came with a hefty condition."

"That you murder my father," I finish flatly.

She nods. "Don't you see? I never really had a choice in the matter. I was forced to accept the job. If I hadn't, my allegiance would've come under question and I was already being scrutinized at every angle. My options were accept or die." She sighs. "I know what you're thinking, but turning the position down wouldn't have saved your father. Besides, if I hadn't agreed to their terms, if I *had* resisted, what would've happened to you?"

My mouth opens to snipe back a scathing retort, but then closes as understanding sinks in. Everything my mother did back then…she did to protect me. I know all too well how powerless the individual is against the State, and as much as I hate her for betraying my father and for handing me over to be experimented on by Richter, I can empathize with being forced into a position where, no matter which option you chose, you lose. How many times have I been torn between two terrible choices and acted out of a desperate desire to protect someone I love?

How can I condemn her when I'm guilty of the same crimes?

She might not have been an affectionate mother, but she loved me enough to do what she did and to live with the burden of that choice. I'll never forgive her for it, but knowing her loyalty wasn't to the State, as my father had thought, but to her daughter. To *me…*

Well, that has to at least count for something, even if that loyalty has caused us both pain.

"And you?" I ask, shifting my gaze to Bilken. "What was your reward for your role in all this?"

He regards me for a moment, appraising me with those knowing dark eyes, one hand scratching along the scruff of his facial hair.

"Just before your father's untimely death, your mother warned me what she was going to do. So, I gave Rodrick a heads-up. I told him he needed to stay underground and out of the limelight until I gave him the all-clear. He had gone to ground several years earlier, more out of fear of getting caught by Enforcers than out of any real desire to help those who had fled the State's reign, but we were still in contact—"

"Wait," I interrupt, and the air punches from my lungs as I choke out two words. "He knew?"

Nolan knew my father was going to be executed and he did nothing to help him.

"I was sorry to hear about what happened to him." Nolan said that to me. He looked me in the eye and acted as if his own inaction didn't play a part in my father's death.

"You *both* knew," I seethe, fighting back my re-emerging tears. "You both knew and you did nothing."

"And what would you have liked us to do?" Bilken asks. "I wasn't going to act against your mother's wishes, and had Nolan offered your father refuge with PHOENIX, what would have become of you?"

Me?

Had my father survived, had he gone underground as he always intended, what *would* have become of me? I might've gone with him, I might've grown up with a different life than the one I was forced into. Or…

I glance at Jenner, his hand eerily still around mine, that *or* in my thoughts like a tangible presence in the silence between us. When he joined PHOENIX, his family suffered—not because he had become a rebel but because the State needed someone to blame for the two Enforcer deaths that resulted from his actions that night. And it would have been no different for us. My mother would've been punished for not turning my father in—as an operative working for the State, it was her job to be on the lookout for potential insurgents—and I, as her child, would've ended up caught in the crossfire.

Swallowing, I blink the fresh mist from my vision. As much as I want to believe my father would've protected me, the reality is—

"They would've killed us," I whisper.

"Or worse, in your mother's case," Bilken says cryptically, although I know all too well what he means.

Torture, at the hands of the very institution she works for.

Pushing the image of that place from my mind, I press, "What was the plan, then? Other than letting my father die."

I don't look away from Bilken, although, in my peripheral vision, I see my mother flinch at my words. Good. The barb hit its intended mark.

Leaning back, Bilken crosses his arms. "Well, I knew Rodrick would be insulated well enough from the fallout of your father's execution. The trouble was, your mother and

I wouldn't be. Nor, by extension, you. Not unless I came up with a damn good excuse to explain why we had been blind to Freston's involvement with PHOENIX. Something big to soften the blow."

"You needed a scapegoat," I realize.

He nods. "And Rodrick was the perfect fall guy. But I couldn't exactly tell him that he was in danger and to keep out of sight for the foreseeable future without telling him how I came by that information. So, I told him the truth about me—that I was an operative working for the State but that my loyalties had shifted and I wanted to help him. That I believed in his cause."

"And did you?" Jenner asks, his tone snide.

Bilken hesitates, as if considering his next words, then says, "As much as a double agent could, I suppose, although nowhere near to the same extent Rodrick did. He genuinely believed it was his mission—his divine purpose, even—to lead our country into a new age. I, on the other hand, saw PHOENIX for what it was: a back door, should the State eventually fail. Not that Rodrick ever knew I held that mindset. As far as he was concerned, I was a changed man, brought into the light of reason by this grand thing he had helped build.

"Years earlier, prior to Freston leaving PHOENIX and before Rodrick—who had fallen victim to his own paranoia and growing extremism—moved underground to fully devote himself to the cause, they both extended personal invitations for me to join PHOENIX. Up until that point, I toed the line between supporter and friend, always making the same excuse as to why I couldn't properly join the movement. That I had someone I didn't want to leave behind, who I couldn't bring with me had I agreed, a reasoning Freston deeply empathized with."

I blink at him in surprise, wondering if there's any truth to that statement or if it was just a lie to fend off my father and Nolan. It's hard to believe Bilken could care about anyone more than he cares about himself. Considering he's not from the Heart, I doubt he has any family here. Hell, I don't even think he's partnered. I can only assume his *esteemed* position got him out of that requirement.

Unaware of my internal musings, he continues. "But, at that moment, I leaned into that foundation of trust built between us, letting Rodrick believe I was ready and willing to not only turn against the State but to help dismantle it from the inside. I told him what I stood to gain in my career and how that aid could, in turn, eventually bolster the rebellion and elevate it to new heights with the information that would be at my disposal. That he would need that information if he ever wanted to knock the State off its pedestal and install PHOENIX as the new ruling power. All he had to do was lie low for a while and wait for me to contact him."

"And you're saying he happily waited for over *twenty* years?" I ask, incredulous.

My father was executed in the year 2050. That was fourteen years ago, when I was just shy of turning seven years old. From what I read in my father's journal, Nolan had already gone to ground before my mother found out she was pregnant with me. That means he sat by and waited for Bilken to contact him for twenty-two years. *Twenty-two years* spent underground, obsessing over a message that may not ever come.

"That's a hell of a lot longer than a *while*," Jenner mutters under his breath, echoing my own thoughts.

Bilken glares at him. "Rodrick valued the cause more than he cherished his freedom. Or, should I say, he valued the notion of what the cause could become. He was skeptical, of course, when I relayed my intentions to him, but considering I hadn't turned him in to authorities in all the years we'd known one another… Well, he was inclined to believe me."

"So, Nolan made himself scarce and you, what?" I ask. "Gave the State his name?"

"Along with an in-depth report outlining how he had founded PHOENIX alongside Freston Reeves. I gave detailed descriptions of their movements and how they had been clever with who they allowed into their circle, explaining why it had taken so long to get usable intel and uncover the true roots of the organization. I manufactured false leads and presented them as fact, selling the idea that we'd been led astray. *Both* of us," he emphasizes, gesturing to my mother. "But I did it in such a way as to balance our shortcomings against the value of the information we were providing to make our overall mission seem like a success. Remember, the State valued accuracy and we were risking much by admitting fault. That was why I needed to give our superiors something that would overshadow our failures and, in turn, guarantee our safety and preserve the futures we'd been promised. We told whatever lies we had to in order to make the story work, and there wasn't any tangible evidence to refute our claims. Like your mother said, they couldn't question our guilt if there was never any proof that we knew."

My brow hooks upward as I peer between my mother and Bilken. He could've left her to fend off the wolves on her own, to suffer the consequences of her actions, regardless of what they might've been, but he didn't. He secured alibis for them both, even though doing so would have put his own life at risk. If he hadn't acted, if he had stayed silent, what might have happened to her? And why did he care? Why did he emphasize that his report was meant to protect both of them, unless—

"I toed the line between supporter and friend, always making the same excuse as to why I couldn't properly join the movement. That I had someone I didn't want to leave behind, who I couldn't bring with me had I agreed, a reasoning Freston deeply empathized with."

Shock passes through me, rattling me to my core. Was my mother that someone he mentioned? When he said they both had people they cared for, people they didn't want to see suffer…

Was he actually talking about her?

Is she the person he wants to protect above all—like Ezra and Jenner are for me, and I apparently was and maybe still am for my mother?

Bilken's rough tenor steers me away from that thought. "Despite my best efforts to allay their suspicions, your mother's loyalty was called into question. For whatever reason, our superiors didn't feel the same need to test me. I suppose because I wasn't sharing a home with the enemy. And as we were careful not to make it known that our collaboration as field operatives had transcended into friendship, they didn't suspect I would know anything of real consequence about her partnership with Freston. If I had, surely I would've reported her…or so I'm sure they assumed." He casts a sidelong glance at my mother before fixing his perceptive eyes back on mine. "My reward for my dutiful service was my position at W. P. Headquarters."

"Which you would later use to make yourself an asset to PHOENIX, just as you told Nolan you would." Ezra lets out a low, deliberating hum. "Did he know why you wanted him to lie low? That you were planning on selling him out?"

Bilken waves a dismissive hand. "He was already on the Enforcers' watch list as a rebel instigator, much in the same way you are. And as the State had just been given a public face for the rebellion, divulging the true extent of Rodrick's involvement barely put him in any additional danger. He was already in hiding, and he was smart. He knew not to stay put in one place for too long. Besides," he adds, "he wouldn't have left the door open for me to join PHOENIX if he didn't believe I could deliver what I promised."

"Which was to smash the hierarchy!" Jenner says in a jubilant voice, slapping his left fist against the palm of his opposite hand. "Seems strange, though," he comments, tone suddenly languid, "that you'd willingly destroy a system that worked so well to your benefit."

Bilken shrugs. "You forget, I made that promise to help the rebellion before I had any real power, so, at that moment, I was living under the State's thumb just like everyone else, my life governed by constant fear. But even if I had been in a different position at the time, the fact remains. You can only oppress a people for so long before they choose to retaliate. It was always inevitable the State would fail and a new regime would rise to overtake it. I merely saw the warning signs early and wanted an exit strategy in place for when that time came."

"Okay, so if PHOENIX was your exit strategy, your 'back door' as you called it, then why are you here now instead of out there with Nolan?" Jenner points a finger towards the white concrete ceiling. "If he's your friend, why help us when he wants us dead? Surely, by now, he's worked out you betrayed him."

Bilken exhales an indignant laugh. "Rodrick and I are *not*

friends. We were once, but we haven't been for a long time now, not since I told him the truth about who I was. That is, if you can really call yourselves 'friends' when the other person doesn't know the real you." He sighs. "I believe he could have killed me that day. He might have tried had he not seen the value in keeping me on this side of the living." He laughs again, the sound more callous this time. "What we have had since is a mutually beneficial relationship, one that I consider over now that I've gotten what I need from him."

Apprehension settles deep in my bones when his eyes narrow on mine.

"You mean me," I breathe.

Bilken turns his head, looking again at my mother, but this time with a fondness I didn't think the stern man capable of. When she returns his gaze, it dawns on me that it isn't just friendship I glimpse in his face when he looks at her, but something else. Something more. Something that would make him go to the ends of the earth to protect her, like Ezra and Jenner keep doing for me.

He loves her, I realize.

"I have only ever had one real friend, Miss Reeves," Bilken says, his eyes never straying from my mother, "and, long ago, I promised I would do anything to ensure the survival of her daughter."

FIFTEEN

MY HEARTBEAT HAMMERS IN MY ears, and every jagged breath I exhale is deafening in the hush that follows Bilken's admission. Like always, I feel like I'm dangling at the cliff edge of understanding, so close to losing my grip.

"You're confused," Bilken says, cocking a wiry eyebrow.

Jenner blows out a frustrated breath through his nose. "Who isn't?"

Prickles of pain speckle my forehead, and I wince, rubbing my fingertips across my right temple. The influx of information being laid out before me is proving difficult to keep track of, and my head spins as I try to make sense of the tangled web of words my mother and Bilken are weaving.

Her story is too elaborate to be fabricated, and I want to believe her just to put the pain of my past to bed. Besides, what reason would she have to lie at this point?

That's what I keep asking myself, and yet, there's a niggling voice of doubt in the back of my head, ever present and jeering, that keeps drowning out whatever reason I still cling to.

Bilken has been trying to protect me? it repeats on a loop.

I suppress the overwhelming urge to laugh.

Noting the skepticism creasing my brow, Bilken frowns. "Everything your mother has said is true. We were sent into the Heart to infiltrate the rebels as a pair, although we were told to target its members separately, so that should one of us be compromised, the other's cover would remain intact. We were strangers isolated in a unique situation together, and, believe me, leading a double life takes a toll—"

"You would know," Jenner grumbles.

Bilken ignores the interruption. "It was a lonely job that spanned many long years, and throughout that time, Evelyn needed someone to lay her burdens on, just as I, in turn, laid mine on her. Our friendship was one built on secrecy and trust."

A shudder of revulsion creeps up my spine, my shoulders raising like hackles on a hissing cat, and I grimace as something inside me snaps.

The loyalty these two found in their deceit was stronger than anything my mother could have had with my father. Bilken said it himself—can you really be friends, or more in my parents' case, if the other person doesn't truly know who you are? Bilken always knew the truth of who my mother was, whereas my father died thinking she was someone else. If our paths hadn't crossed again at the DSD when she intervened with Richter, I suppose I would have died thinking that, too.

It doesn't seem fair that my mother could create victims of her own family while Bilken got off clean. He never intentionally hurt the people he loved. After all, the only person he clearly loves is my mother. If he did have anyone else he cared for, he wouldn't be here, helping us. Helping *her*.

A sour taste floods my mouth at the thought that he is the

only person who really knows her.

I breathe out, grazing my palm against the sofa cushion, concentrating on the brush of the soft fabric against my skin—focusing on anything other than the resurfacing urge to jump up from my seat and strangle Bilken. I don't want to hear about this. I don't want to hear about the bond he shares with my mother.

I don't want to hear him say how he helped me when, because of him, Rai is dead.

Sensing my distress, Ezra presses his fingertips into the skin just above my collarbone, his hand a comforting weight on my shoulder, grounding me when I need it most. His touch calms the building pressure in my chest.

"That explains your relationship, but what does any of this have to do with Wynter?" he asks.

"It has everything to do with her," Bilken counters. The deep mahogany pools of his eyes lock on mine. "When the DSD apprehended you following your placement exam, your mother came to me. She begged me to find a way to help you, to get you both out of the State. To make you disappear so no one would be able to find you. And because of that friendship between us, I agreed—"

"At the risk of your own life?" I interrupt. "I find that hard to believe." Even knowing that he did so once before—in the events leading up to my father's execution—I struggle to associate that notion of a selfless Bilken with the man I know.

He sneers. "Because you know me so well, Miss Reeves?"

I lurch forward on my seat, but Ezra and Jenner both grab me, restraining me as I shout, "You were the one who told me not to confuse ambition with loyalty! *You* told me you don't stand by alliances that only serve you in the immediate moment!"

"I was baiting you!" he fires back. "Everything you know about me is a carefully constructed facade, a role I tailor to whomever it is I need to manipulate. And, in that moment, I needed to fool you. To *make* you believe I was your enemy."

"Why?" I gasp, sinking back onto the sofa.

He scrubs a hand across his face, his collected composure finally slipping. "To understand, we need to start from the beginning." He draws in a deep breath through his nose. "During your first stay at the DSD, your mother kept tabs on you from within while I worked on a plan to get you both out of the State in one piece. But increasing security over the years has made it difficult to expatriate anyone from the Heart, especially an individual under such heavy surveillance as you were under Richter's guardianship. My options were limited, and I knew the only way I could help my friend, help *you*, was to seek assistance from somewhere else."

"Assistance?" Ezra repeats.

Bilken nods. "After Freston's execution, I kept in contact with Rodrick, mainly to ensure the offer to join PHOENIX still stood, even if I wasn't sure I ever intended to take it. But, over time, it was a risk maintaining that contact. Not in the way you're likely imagining—not out of fear of getting caught, although that's the way I pitched it to him. I told him contact channels were being monitored and that, if we weren't careful, his location would be discovered, once again reiterating how vital it was he remain out of sight, feeding his growing paranoia. In reality, I needed to keep a healthy distance between us so I wouldn't inadvertently encourage him to do anything that might jeopardize my position in the event I ultimately decided against joining PHOENIX. Deniability, Miss Reeves. It is how one stays above the law.

"Still, when your mother came to me, I almost reopened that contact for her sake. The only reason I didn't was because I knew, even as Freston Reeves' daughter, PHOENIX would never willingly involve itself with the DSD. Rescuing you from that fortress would've been a suicide mission for all involved. But then, you escaped and sought PHOENIX out all on your own, solving that little logistics problem for us. All I had to do to guarantee your safe return was make good on the promise I had once made to Rodrick. To remind him of why I was a good friend to have."

"The transmission to Nolan," I breathe. "It really was bait to get me, but not for Richter—"

"No, not for Richter," Bilken echoes, "although, luckily for us, he didn't know that. As far as he was concerned, I had offered my help to retrieve you for *him*. For the State. And it worked. Unfortunately, the rest of our plan didn't go as intended."

A mocking laugh punctures the air beside me. "Which part would you be referring to?" Jenner asks. "The part where you didn't bother to turn up? Or the part where we were ambushed by Enforcers? Oh"—he holds up a finger—"I know. You mean the part where our friend got shot and was turned into a human trophy by that sadistic dick." Clicking his tongue, he rakes a hand through his mop of black hair. "And while you're answering that, I'd love to know why the *hell* Richter would trust you."

Bilken shrugs, unfazed by Jenner's outburst. Like before, he directs his next words at me. "The same reason he trusted your mother. We have a history, a rapport that we were both careful to cultivate. To build trust, you need to sometimes give someone what they want without expecting anything in return. Then, when the time is right, you can turn that trust to your advantage. That's one lesson I learned long ago, thanks to the State—that power on its own is never enough. To be truly safe in this world, you need to have other powerful people in your pocket."

"What do you mean?" Ezra presses. There's an edge to his voice that closely mimics the unease unraveling my insides.

Bilken picks at a loose thread on his shirt cuff. "I gave Richter what he needed to expand his research when the pool from Termination was no longer fruitful, ultimately paving the way for him to claim his position as Head of the Research department. *Access*," he clarifies when none of us utter a word. "Once he knew what prerequisites needed to be met, it was easy to find him new subjects among the general populace of the Heart."

Stunned, I turn the full brunt of my gaze on my mother. Back at the DSD, when we were in Richter's underground morgue, she told me she procured test subjects for him before he became Head of Research. Before the State gave him free rein to inflict his madness on his victims unhindered. And now, I know she didn't do it alone. She and Bilken both fueled my tormentor's ambitions, enabling his research like it was an addiction.

I glance back at Bilken as the apprehension pooling in my stomach turns sour.

"The key to true security—not power, *security*," he emphasizes when I try to interrupt him again, "is to make yourself an asset to those you wish to use. Let them believe they have the upper hand, that they're the ones calling the shots. That way, when you steal from them or depose them, they'll never see your treachery coming. Richter saw me as such an asset, and because of that trust, it took very little convincing on my part to involve myself with your retrieval. I presented the idea to coax PHOENIX with the offer of inside intel and used that transmission as my one opportunity to reach out to Rodrick directly.

"As for your other questions," he drawls with a sharp glance at Jenner, "I was never meant to be there that night, nor was Richter. The plan was to send in a group of Enforcers, who were under orders to detain Wynter and bring her to a secure location, where Richter was told to meet them and aid with transporting her back to the DSD. The part of the plan Richter wasn't aware of was that we planned to intercept his Enforcers with our own team en route to that secure location." His eyes shift back to mine, and the corners of his lips twitch, offering me a frown which borders on sympathetic. "You needn't feel bad about killing them, by the way. The plan was always for those Enforcers to die."

I remember the outcome of that moment so clearly, the way the Enforcers' blood soaked into the white carpet underfoot in Bilken's office. The way the bullets perforated so many priceless artifacts of a time long lost to us.

My stomach churns at the memory, and I grimace at Bilken's brazen disregard for human life.

He snorts. "You judge me, Miss Reeves, but everything that transpired that night was done in an effort to help you—"

"Help me?" A disdainful breath slips through my lips. "Rai *died* because of that mission." I became a weapon because of that mission. If I hadn't gone that night, I wouldn't have encountered Richter again and he wouldn't have swayed me back into his clutches. If I hadn't gone, I would've escaped years of torment and torture and succumbed to my disease surrounded by people I love.

No, you wouldn't have, a small voice lurking in the back of my head has the indecency to remind me. *You would've ended the world and taken everyone with you.*

The unavoidable fate which now awaits us despite everything I've done to alter my path.

"Let me see if I have this right," Jenner says. "Your strategy was to intercept the Enforcers before they could drag Wynter kicking and screaming back to the DSD, but then Richter turned up where he shouldn't have, derailing that plan."

Bilken grunts in confirmation. "I was ignorant of his connection to Mr. Laramie and Miss Dorne, so had no reason to suspect he'd intervene. In hindsight, I should have anticipated that he would do something so…inconvenient."

"Inconvenient?" Ezra parrots, his words dripping with anger.

"The man was a complete narcissist," Bilken drawls. "He needed to believe he was the smartest person in the room. That every move made was by his design."

My teeth roll over my lower lip as I drop my gaze to the floor, staring blankly at the carpet as my mind revisits the tragic events of that night. If I didn't already blame myself for what happened to Rai, I do now that I know the real purpose of the mission that put her back in Richter's path.

Sniffing, I wipe my nose with the back of my hand and glance up again, glaring at Bilken. "Was the transmission a genuine offer? Or was it just another lie to get what you wanted?"

Cocking his head to one side, he says, "It was genuine in as much as I was willing to give Rodrick what he wanted to see you returned."

"Which was what, exactly?" Ezra presses. "You gave him

reason to come after Wynter the moment you handed over her file. If the intent was to get her off everyone's radar, you failed."

"It's called a back-up plan," Bilken retorts. "By the time Rodrick saw the file, Wynter would've been far away from the Heart and out of his and Richter's reach for good. The information would've been useless to him…unless things didn't go as planned, which we are all well aware that they didn't."

Jenner leans forward, exhaling a startled laugh. "You devious bastard. You *intended* to give him a reason to want Wynter for himself, didn't you?"

Bilken squares his shoulders. "Hence why it's called a back-up plan. I needed a reason to get PHOENIX involved in the event our mission to retrieve Wynter failed."

I stare at him in amazement, begrudgingly impressed. And here I thought Richter was a maniacal genius. He never stood a chance against my mother and Bilken.

"And the connection mentioned in the transmission?" I ask. "The person who was supposedly equipped to handle my illness?" Before tonight, I always thought it was Richter—that Bilken's aid was just a ruse to force me back into my tormentor's shackles. But now… Understanding dawns and I glance at my mother. "It wasn't Richter, it was you."

She straightens slightly under my scrutiny. "I'm no expert on your disease, but I did know of the collar Richter had been designing and that it could potentially curtail your symptoms and prolong your life. Maybe even allow you a shot at a normal one."

My brow furrows. "And what, you were going to steal it?"

Once, it would've been impossible for me to imagine my mother stealing from the State—from the very government I was always so convinced she was loyal to.

Now, I'm beginning to see just how shallow that loyalty really is.

"If I had to," she says without hesitation. "But then the mission failed and you went back to the DSD and Richter fitted you with that collar himself. At that point, all we could do was wait and hope Nolan would take the bait Wren had dangled in front of him."

"Which he did," Bilken mutters, grinning smugly. "As expected, your file exposed just how valuable you could be to him. After that, Rodrick merely came to conclusions I had already predisposed him to see."

"How?" Jenner asks.

Bilken's grin widens, unsettling me. "By stoking the flames of his megalomania and forcing him into the background of his own creation. And by making him believe he would need my help if he ever *truly* wanted to take on the State.

"Between the two founders of PHOENIX, Freston was always the realist and Rodrick the fantasist. He was willing to do whatever it took for the pipe dream of power, even if that meant receding into the shadows and waiting for a signal that may not ever come. As I hoped, he saw the transmission as that signal and the file as just the beginning of the goldmine of information I had promised all those years ago. Having bided his time for so long, he was ready to finally take control of PHOENIX and emerge to fight the war he felt destined to lead. And, as I knew he would, he viewed Wynter as the prime tool needed to do that.

"When he contacted me for my help with extracting you,"— Bilken meets my gaze—"I made it a point to only agree to offer my continuing aid under the condition that I could join PHOENIX, like he once asked me to. I wasn't going to make the same mistake I made with the mission to the magistrates building. This time, I would be present to see to your safety myself. And between my ability to pass your friend here"—he nods to Jenner—"off as an Enforcer and the drugs needed to restrain you, which PHOENIX wouldn't have otherwise had access to, he couldn't very well refuse my demands."

The drugs…

I remember the paralyzing effects of whatever I was injected with when I woke up at that bunker. At the time, I didn't remember Rai or what she once told me about PHOENIX's lack of access to medical supplies. Otherwise, I might have suspected a bigger player's involvement.

A swell of laughter fills my throat. "See to my safety…by allowing Nolan to execute me?"

Jenner stiffens at the same moment Ezra's fingers tighten around my shoulder, and I know they're thinking of the same thing I am, the memory of our almost executions vivid in my thoughts even now. It could have gone so much differently. And it would have, if—

"Whose idea do you think that was?" Bilken snaps. He glares between the three of us, staring at each of our faces in turn. "Are any of you dead now? Why do you think that is?"

Because Quinn saved us, that voice in my head whispers.

My attention jumps to the ex-Enforcer, who has been silent this whole conversation, a spectator to the revelations assaulting me. His cheeks are flush with color—a sign the medication my mother gave him must be working—and there's a clarity to his obsidian eyes that wasn't there the last time I looked at him.

His drug-addled haze seems to be wearing off.

"You were working for Bilken the whole time," I murmur. "You were planted there to get close to Nolan."

His eyes flick briefly to my mother and Bilken, as if seeking permission before he answers. "I was planted there to get you out...by any means necessary."

I shake my head. Why would Quinn—or any Enforcer, for that matter—abandon the State when the consequences of that betrayal were significant? What was he getting out of such an arrangement?

And how the hell did he cross paths with my mother?

"Why?" I ask, confused. "Who are you, really?"

"An Enforcer, who could no longer fight for a country that was so quick and willing to commit genocide." Anger burns in his gaze, the black depths like chips of hard onyx. His chest puffs out as he draws in a steadying breath, and pushing it out through his nose, he speaks slowly, as if every word is an effort. "I was drafted into the State's war a year before it began—I wasn't old enough to become an Enforcer yet otherwise—but I joined willingly because of certain privileges the position afforded."

Like getting out of the partnership requirement, I muse, recalling our conversation back at the bunker when he escorted me to meet the Heads of PHOENIX.

"My first time in the field," he continues, "I saw what they had you do, what you were capable of, and what you would *continue* to do until there was no one left to conquer or destroy. After that battle, I knew I couldn't be part of it, and upon returning to the Heart, I abandoned my post, thinking 'to hell with the privileges.' I didn't really have a plan, and I had no desire to join PHOENIX, unlike some other recruits who had fled—"

Nolan's lackeys, I note, remembering the Enforcer-like guards the PHOENIX Head seemed to constantly surround himself with.

"—and, of course, I had no clue how to get out of the city, so it wasn't long before I was caught. They didn't even ask why I ran away. They just branded me a traitor and sent me straight to Termination."

"It's always bad publicity when an Enforcer goes rogue," my mother chimes in. "It sends the wrong message about their authority. Because of that, their executions are never broadcast."

Her focus drifts to the closed safe house door, and as I follow her gaze, I allow the tentacles of my power to unfurl, reaching beyond the thick slab of reinforced steel. Beyond it, I sense a presence—the steady rhythm of a heartbeat belonging to the Enforcer who brought us to this place, ever silent and obedient. Even now, he stands watch, loyal to my mother, although I don't understand why.

My mother's eyes swing back to mine, as if sensing my unspoken question. "I have Enforcers loyal to me because I saw the opportunity they presented. The few I keep close were all spared from execution and, thanks to Wren's extensive reach and connections, given forged identities that allow them to roam the Heart freely and aid me whenever the situation calls for it. For all intents and purposes, each of them died when they were meant to. Including Quinn here." She nods toward the ex-Enforcer slouched on the sofa, who dips his chin in acknowledgment, then repositions himself on the plush cushion, wincing as he pushes himself fully upright.

"In exchange for sparing my life, we made a deal," he explains, picking up where my mother left off, as if the silence is pressing him for his side of the story. "Per our agreement,

Bilken would help me seek asylum with PHOENIX, and he coached me on what to do to gain Nolan's trust. It wasn't particularly hard. AWOL Enforcers make good little soldiers the Heads can shape to be cannon fodder for the cause. Once they're sure we hold no loyalty to the State anymore, that is."

Although his words should surprise me, they don't. My most recent encounter with PHOENIX had all too clearly demonstrated how its priorities have shifted over the last few years. Instead of helpless, terrified refugees, the only members in that bunker were armed muscle for Nolan.

"I was with Nolan for nearly two months prior to your extraction, and in that time, I did everything I could to make myself invaluable to him," Quinn says. "I ran his errands like a good little minion and force-fed him a story about how much I hated and feared you." When I cock an eyebrow, he adds, "I needed to give him a good reason to let me be on the firing squad."

"Oh, so, *that's* why you were such an asshole to us," Jenner scoffs.

Quinn's responding glare is icy. "I couldn't do anything that would make Nolan suspect my allegiance or put my mission at risk. I'm sorry if I hurt your *feelings*," he spits, "but your opinion of me meant absolute shit."

Snorting, Jenner stretches his arms out along the back of the sofa.

"What did you get out of this bargain, other than your life?" Ezra asks. "Surely, there was something more in it for you since you had to have known you couldn't stay with PHOENIX."

The ex-Enforcer crinkles his nose. "Nor did I want to. The plan was to 'execute' Wynter and then reconvene with Dr.

Adler and Bilken at a safe place a mile southeast of the bunker's location where we would all then escape the State together. You two"—he wags a finger, pointing between Ezra and Jenner—"were just excess baggage."

"Excess baggage?" Jenner squawks at the same time I say, "Escape?"

Quinn ignores Jenner, locking eyes with me. "That's what I was promised. The chance to begin again somewhere else. Somewhere far away from the State's ideologies."

"And this fresh start included you two?" I ask, once again peering at my mother and Bilken, who traces the shape of his well-manicured, close-cropped beard with his fingers.

"This country has gone to hell, and we were tired of playing both sides," he admits. "Sometimes, power isn't worth the struggle it takes to hold onto."

His words take me aback, and a long moment passes as I once again try to align this version of Bilken—the man behind the mask—with the cold-hearted coward I assumed him to be.

He and my mother sit silent, waiting for me to speak. In the seconds that follow, I note the traces of exhaustion lining each of their faces. Faint purple smudges ring my mother's eyes, and Bilken's salt and pepper hair is beginning to look more gray than black. All that scheming must be catching up with them.

With a strangled breath, I sink back into the cushion. "Let's say everything you've told us is true, and that everything you've done really has been to help me. Why goad me into attacking you? Why not just tell me the truth?"

Why make me hate you?

"Just another part of the plan, Miss Reeves. You and I were never going to be able to speak freely with Rodrick always watching you. There were cameras everywhere in that bunker. He and his soldiers were aware of every move you made, even when you thought they weren't." He cocks an eyebrow at Ezra and Jenner, and I know he means when they broke me out of my cell. "There was no opening to expose my plan to you, and frankly, the less you were aware of, the better. The way it played out was far more believable than if you or your friends had been in the know." He pauses for a moment, and his lips part again on a sigh. "As for why I provoked you? Simple. It gave me the opportunity to plant a tracker on your person. That way, had you refused Mr. Stohler's offer of refuge, which you did," he grumbles, his eyes swinging to Quinn before returning to me, "your mother and I could have traced your location. Which ended up being a necessity given your...detour."

Inside me, sparks of outrage threaten to burst into flame, and I glower at Bilken, once again repressing the urge to strangle him. He's just like Richter, treating me like some possession that needs keeping track of.

I wince as a sharp pain stabs behind my eyes, the agony chipping away at my brain. This is all too much. I'm drained just trying to unweave this complicated web of endless lies and deception.

Shaking off my growing fatigue, I cut my gaze back to Quinn. "And the RF transmitter? If they were already tracking me, and if you had the means to contact them,"—I nod toward the communicator on his belt—"then what was the point of having that?"

"Because the DSD is the one place the trackers and communicators don't work," my mother says, answering for him. "That place is...*was*," she corrects herself, "a fortress. It was constructed with materials designed to prevent anyone on the outside from accessing the sensitive intel and equipment stored inside, or from anyone already inside from transmitting to an exterior location. That included access to personnel movements." Frustration leaches into her tone as she glances between Ezra and Jenner. "Why do you think PHOENIX never managed to hack the DSD's systems? Because it can only be done from *within* the building. Sure, we were able to track you to the DSD's doors, but beyond that, we were blind to your location. The RF transmitter Quinn used had a short range and only targeted alarms—and, in turn, the locking mechanisms—in the immediate area." Her gaze flicks back to mine, and her expression softens. "That's how I was able to find you so quickly. I was already there, I just needed to know where to look."

I blink, stupefied into silence. They really did think of everything—covered every possible angle and outcome.

And yet, there's still one thing I don't understand.

"If the plan was to escape the State, then why help us get back into the Heart?" I ask Quinn.

He cocks a dark brow at me and snorts. "That ticket out was entirely dependent on delivering you to Dr. Adler. You insisted on going back into the Heart. Would I have been able to stop you?"

He's right. We would've just gone on without him if he hadn't agreed to come with us, and he couldn't exactly tell us the truth. I had just tried to kill Bilken with my bare hands and I never would've believed my mother was working for the DSD, let alone serving as the acting Head of Termination. Not that it would have mattered if he had. Rai was still our priority.

To uphold his end of the bargain he made with my mother,

Quinn had no choice but to return to the one place he was so desperate to leave, to accompany me for as long as it took to fulfill his mission, all in the vain hope that the path to escape would still be there at the end of it.

"What's done is done," my mother says brusquely. "The decision was made and now, we have to work with the hand we've been dealt if we are to get out of this city alive."

"And your plan is...what?" Jenner prompts. "Because I'm assuming you have one."

Sitting forward, Bilken props his elbows on his knees and steeples his hands, touching his fingertips to his lips in contemplation. "You forget, Evelyn and I are not from here, and my position has allowed me a certain degree of, shall we say, freedom and accessibility not afforded to others? All that to say, I have made valuable friends and connections abroad over the years. Connections, who would be willing to harbor fugitives and aid their escape from"—he shrugs, gesturing vaguely with one hand—"an oppressive regime that's currently under attack?"

Surprise ripples through me. "You have a way to contact people outside the Heart?"

He might've provided PHOENIX with the instructions to set up a secure contact channel between them that night at the magistrates building—even if it wasn't entirely necessary, based on what he's since revealed about stoking the flames of Nolan's delusions—but that communication line was still within the boundaries of the State. Whereas, what he's talking about now... He's implying that he's had access to the outside world this whole time—that he's always had the option of freedom, while those of us trapped inside the Heart's borders didn't.

Just how far can one man's reach extend?

"My dear, when you work at the center of something, you familiarize yourself with its loopholes and flaws. You learn to play those weaknesses to your advantage. Take the DSD, for example. These connections of mine wanted to eliminate the threat before it came to them, so I gave them what they wanted—the beating heart at the foundation of the State's war."

As Bilken's eyes hold mine, it sinks in what he's saying. He doesn't just mean the DSD. He means Richter's research and the weapon it created that allowed the State to pursue such ruthless endeavors. And now, with this attack, his *connections* think they've destroyed the threat.

They think they've destroyed me.

Fear is a hand tightening around my windpipe. What will happen when they realize they didn't?

"And my reward for orchestrating an end to the State was a one-way ticket for us out of the Heart," Bilken says, but I barely hear his words past the terror soaking into my thoughts.

"The inside man… It wasn't Adler, it was you," Jenner accuses, sitting upright, his arms slipping down onto the cushions beside him. His tone holds neither question nor surprise. He's simply voicing what I think we all suspected from the moment we arrived at this safe house.

I glance at Quinn, who—given his part in this conspiracy— must have been aware of Bilken's role in the attack despite claiming otherwise. Our conversation outside the DSD replays in my thoughts and, again, I hear Ezra and Jenner theorizing that someone might be working with the enemy from within the State as a double agent. At the time, although he was the one who brought it up, Quinn had shrugged the notion off as a mere possibility rather than a fact.

Can't say for sure, huh?

Bilken lets loose a rough laugh. "Did you not wonder how I would continue to make myself useful to PHOENIX after fleeing the State? I know *you* did," he adds, nodding at me. "I'm not a fool. I know Rodrick would have disposed of me the moment I was no longer working for him from the inside. That was the only worth I held for him. So, I gave him his tool to take on the State and then outlaid what he had to do to use it. It wasn't enough having the DSD's weapon at his disposal. He knew as well as I did you weren't going to attack your own home—"

"But that didn't mean someone else wouldn't," Ezra mutters behind me.

Bilken nods. "The plan, at least as far as Rodrick was concerned, was for me to tip off the 'enemy.' To give them a reason to strike the Heart, offering a potential end to our global conflict by means of an attack, which would provide PHOENIX with the opportunity to broker peace and establish themselves as the new governing power. Once peace was publicly made, military support from outside would sweep through the Heart, allowing the rebellion to supplant the State. I simply made the introduction between him and these friends, at which point, they stated their terms and Rodrick agreed."

"PHOENIX planned this?" Disgust roils in my gut. Now, I know why Nolan was so willing to let millions of people in the Heart suffer. He isn't just some power-hungry opportunist seizing an opening. He *created* the opening with Bilken's help.

He brought this chaos to our doorstep.

Bilken frowns. "Believe it or not, this conflict was inevitable. Had you remained Richter's puppet and continued forging a path of death across the globe, someone would've retaliated—"

"They wouldn't have succeeded," I cut in, but Bilken is already shaking his head.

"They would have found a way," he insists, "just like I found a way to take down your transport helicopter. As for PHOENIX… Well, like Rodrick, many were tired of withering away in the shadows. They would've come to a head with the State at some point."

"Not like this," Jenner whispers, his head jerking side to side in disbelief like the sway of a pendulum.

The weight of Ezra's hand disappears from my shoulder, and he steps around the sofa until he's standing beside me. "All this, a war with millions of lives sacrificed, just to get Wynter back for her mother?" Shock distorts his voice, and his face is unnervingly white, painted pale with the same revulsion I feel ripping a hole in my chest.

As he meets my gaze, I know I made the right choice in acting on his mother's words and asking him to kill me. Ezra would never risk so many lives to save mine. He would choose right. He *will* choose right.

And the right choice isn't me.

"And to secure our escape from the State, although that wasn't the only reason," my mother protests. "You saw for yourselves what Richter was hiding in the DSD. He was attempting to create an army, and I think we all know he would have succeeded eventually. Then, it wouldn't have mattered where we went. We wouldn't have been safe anywhere. That was all the incentive we needed to intervene, casualties be damned."

The mention of the bodies in the sublevel of the DSD churns the minimal contents of my stomach. I wish I could bleach my eyes and scrub the memory of that room from my brain.

The memory of what I am indirectly responsible for.

The memory of what Richter was trying to create with my blood.

A dour laugh presses at the wall of my lips, breaking through. "Let me guess, that was the price for their help. That all the weapons of the State be destroyed."

"The price," my mother clarifies, "was that PHOENIX provide the coordinates to the source of the weapons, where they were being created and stored. But when the blast didn't wipe out the full scope of the DSD as intended, I knew I had to finish the job myself or else risk them reneging on their side of the arrangement where our escape was concerned. And…" She hesitates, wringing her hands in her lap again. "So no one else would ever have to go through what you have. So no one else could continue what Richter had started."

I brush off her forced attempt at reconciliation as a blanket of calm settles over my senses, extinguishing my simmering rage. I've heard enough. I understand why my mother and Bilken did what they did, but their actions change nothing. They offer no way to put an end to this war—only the offer to run away from it like a coward.

But there can be no running away, not for me. Not for any of us.

Not if the future plays out as I know all too well it will.

Slowly, I rise from the sofa, taking a few calculated steps back toward the bedroom before pausing, glancing over my shoulder.

"Everything you did was in vain. The collar is broken— there's no way to control this disease. And you do realize these 'friends' will never let me go once they realize what I am, right? They'll want me dead, just like everyone else with Ultraxenopia."

"We won't let that happen," my mother assures me. "Wren already drafted a new identity for you just in case they learned your name. No one needs to know who you really are or that you're sick. We have options." As if to prove her point, she pulls the remains of my busted collar from her coat pocket, setting it on the marble table before her. Hand shaking, she gestures to it and says, "Once we're out, I'll find a way to fix it. To cure you myself. We have time—"

Even if I believed her—which I don't since there can be no hiding the severity of my illness or fixing a device none of us knows the first thing about, not in the time I actually have—it doesn't change the fact that she would willingly leave everyone else in this city to a fate they don't deserve. What's to stop her from doing the same to Ezra or Jenner if it came down to protecting them or me?

I won't risk it.

"Except, we don't. Because I'm not leaving the Heart. My time is almost up. I'll die in this city." Turning fully, I fix a cold glare on my mother. "And if you keep trying to 'help' me, you'll die, too."

You all will.

SIXTEEN

COLD WATER STRIKES MY FACE, an icy deluge that brings relief for all of five seconds before the nausea rolls through me again. My tongue darts out across my chapped lower lip, and I swallow, pushing down the bile burning the inside of my throat as I raise my gaze to the mirror. Gripping the sides of the polished stone basin, I grimace at the gaunt face staring back at me. Whatever healthy color I had to my skin has faded, resulting in my chalky complexion, and shadows mark the edges of my now protruding cheekbones, the skin around my eye sockets mottled with blistering shades of purple and black. Even my eyes seem to have lost some of their vigor and hue, the irises dull, taking on tones of gray.

I splash water on my face again before peering down into the sink.

"It really is trying to make up for lost time," I mutter, biting back an unhinged chuckle, which quickly fades into a sob. I clamp a hand over my mouth to keep quiet.

This disease really is determined to kill me.

Pain slashes through my skull as if in response to that thought, and I cry out as a searing flash of light explodes behind my eyes, blinding me. The room spins, my surroundings blurring, and my knees buckle, dragging me down to the floor.

As my fingertips graze the tile, searching for a way through the sudden fog obscuring my vision, a voice calls out from the distance, calm and collected.

And, above all, familiar.

I glance in the direction it's coming from, unsurprised when the light fades and I find I'm no longer on the floor in the washroom in Bilken's safe house but in the magistrates building in Zone 1. Standing, as if this disease isn't killing me.

I recognize the office I'm in, and my chest tightens as I peer down at the carpet, the fibers bleached white, erasing the evidence that it was once soaked with the blood of at least a dozen Enforcers. Erasing that Rai was shot in this room.

Resurfacing bile burns my insides like acid as my focus drifts to the broad wall of windows and the looming figure standing before them, looking down at the city below.

Even from behind, I know him.

As if sensing my presence, Nolan turns on his heel, but his pale eyes look past me because I'm not really here. I follow his gaze to the line of still people behind me, awaiting his next words in silence.

"It's time," he says to the other Heads of PHOENIX. Then, clearing his throat, he takes a seat at what was once Bilken's desk.

Folding his hands on top of the glass surface, he straightens as three floating black balls take position a few feet in front of him, buzzing softly in the hush. Spotlights project from the recording drones, illuminating Nolan's face.

"Citizens of the State," he announces, enunciating every word. "I come to you in this dire time to offer you much-needed hope for the future."

Behind him, flames cast an orange and gray smoky haze across the city. I stumble forward, approaching the window, my hands flattening against the panes as I stare out at my home, so much of the immediate area now reduced to rubble and ash.

Tears thicken in my throat as a list of people I blame for this shuffle through my head on a loop. Richter did this. My mother and Bilken did this. Nolan did this.

I did this.

"For so long," Nolan continues, and I pivot to face him again, staring into the cameras, invisible in my grief, "you have all been led to believe that PHOENIX is the enemy. That *we* are the threat. But now,"—he gestures to the ruin beyond the windows—"our borders have been breached by those the State has goaded into a war. So, I ask you…who is the real enemy here?"

"You are," I whisper. "Because you did this." Once again, I rehearse that list of names.

Richter.

My mother.

Bilken.

Nolan.

Me.

"The State does not care about you," Nolan says. "You are cattle with one purpose: to produce. To be productive members of society or perish under the umbrella of uselessness. Now, when outsiders come here to slaughter you, who are the ones offering you shelter and safety? Is it the State? No, it's us—the terrorists the State has conditioned you to fear."

He shakes his head, clicking his tongue in disdain, and as I skirt around the desk again to look at his face, it dawns on me that he isn't acting. The rage and fear in his gaze are both real.

And, despite his scheming and planning, he's afraid.

For all Nolan's faults, he's right—the State doesn't care about us. It never has. We're all just cogs in a machine, oiled just enough to keep us working and discarded without thought the moment we break. But the problem is, regardless of what he says to try to calm the peoples' terror, he isn't any different. And the disheartening truth I'm beginning to realize is…I'm not sure any government can be. We are all part of the machine, and those who are smart enough to be the ones turning the wheels are aware that, if the machine stops working, they lose their hold on power. So, it's inevitable. Once PHOENIX takes control, it will only be a matter of time before the people become victims again, used to serve someone else's greed until someone new steps up who wants to be different.

But Nolan isn't different—he's more of the same. Any words he utters to suggest otherwise are just lies wrapped up in a pretty bow of denial.

"But PHOENIX is not a terrorist organization—"

I grimace. That might have been true once, but he made it one with this attack.

"We are like you," Nolan continues, insistent. "We are also afraid, but we want to cure you of that fear. We desire peace and the freedom to live, just as we desire that freedom for you. The State has kept you all in a prison, which we will liberate you from in return for your trust. Let us lead you down this road, back to the haven of freedom."

What even is freedom? I wonder. Has anyone living ever truly experienced it? Or is it just a dream? More pretty words to use as a weapon of oppression?

"This attack..." He averts his gaze from the cameras. Perhaps to hide the truth from the people watching who are bound to see the guilt in his eyes. "The State has brought this upon itself with its unnatural experimentation and greed. Its greatest interest has always been expanding the cage instead of protecting its lifeblood. Its *people*. I promise you," he persists, shaking his head, "the State will not protect you from this. Even now, it executes you in the streets like sick dogs instead of offering aid when another attack could be imminent." He pauses for a moment before looking back at the drones, and goosebumps pimple my skin, reacting to the sudden change in the air. There's a peculiar weight to this silence.

An expectation.

"And so," he finally says, "I come to you with a proposition. *Join* us. Turn away from the State, let us help you, and together, we can create a new future of peace and prosperity where war is a thing of the past—a distant, terrible memory we tell our children about to warn them away from making the same mistakes we have. Rise up!" He slams his fist on the desk. "Rise up against the Enforcers who seek to enslave us! Help me prove to our attackers that we are not the enemy. We are *not* the State."

I stumble back a step. "No," I breathe, then more forcefully repeat it. So much for wanting to save the people—Nolan wants to turn them into his own personal army. Doesn't he see how that will backfire? Isn't he aware of the Enforcer patrols lined up throughout the Heart? They won't hesitate to shoot; by encouraging a revolt, he's only going to get everyone killed. And if everyone's dead, who then will he lead?

My hands curl into fists, my nails biting half-moons into my palms. I don't know what arrangement Nolan and Bilken made with the people attacking us, but I'm assuming this is all part of their plan—this unspoken assumption that the attacks will stop and they'll swoop in to help him seize control. That's the only explanation that makes any sense. The only reason I can see as to why even he would suggest this madness.

But someone coming to PHOENIX's aid at the eleventh hour isn't what's going to happen—I see that now as Bilken's old office disintegrates and I find myself outside the magistrates building, watching helplessly as Enforcers gun down unarmed citizens as they, in turn, are bombed from above. Corpses litter the ground, while before me, the massive structure—where Nolan and the other Heads wait out the attack—burns like a sacrificial pyre.

My surroundings change again until, once more, I'm back inside Bilken's office where Nolan screeches into a communicator. He coughs into his fist as a cloying gray smoke billows under the door and wafts into the room.

"That wasn't the deal," he rasps between coughs. "You never said you needed physical proof, just that she needed to die!"

My brows draw together as I take a step closer, straining my ears to hear the other side of the call past the mayhem and noise just outside.

"No. *No*, that's not what you said. You *said* to take her out of the picture, which we've done. Not to mention we handed you the DSD on a goddamn silver platter. You have the coordinates and the girl is dead, I swear it. I saw to it myself after I used her to convince the others of the attack—" His eyes widen. "W-What? That's not—"

The hum of an angry voice on the other end of the line

interrupts him.

Indignation paints Nolan's cheeks bright red. "I'm not hiding the girl! She was a stain on this world. I wanted her gone as much as you did." He jerks his head in vehement denial, although there's no one here except me to see it. "Call off the attack as you agreed," he pleads. "Do that and I'll produce her body. I just need a little time to get out of the city to fi—"

He blanches, pulling the communicator away from his ear. He then stares at it for a long moment, his face draining of color when a message lights up the small screen. Inching toward him, I squint at the words which appear in bold letters, reading them over his shoulder.

PROOF OR NO PEACE

A short video clip replaces the words, showing a high-resolution image of my face close-up before panning out, giving me a better idea of when this footage was shot. Between my clothing and the length of my hair, it's clear this video—likely filmed from an enemy drone—was taken several months before when I was still under Dr. Richter's control and engaging in battle on behalf of the State.

My stomach sinks as Nolan throws the device to the floor. I was right. These people do know what I look like.

And just as I feared, Nolan's plan—his hope to establish peace between them—will fail.

"Damn it!" Nolan sinks to his knees, and as he combs his fingers through his ashy hair, he looks as helpless as I feel. But I have no sympathy for him, and a large part of me hopes he burns inside this building.

Like the State, he brought this upon himself.

Around me, the office goes black, my vision blurring as it always does when I'm dragged through time and thrust back into the present—into the grim reality where I belong. The walls of Bilken's washroom rebuild around me brick by brick, stone by stone, the concrete repainting itself snow white as I slump to the ground.

Heaving, I scan my bleary surroundings, and with my target in sight, I fling myself forward, spewing into the toilet as I clench my eyes shut. Pain is a sledgehammer against the inside of my skull, and when I finally pry my eyes open, it takes a few seconds for my horror to penetrate the agonizing pressure in my temples. Blood. There's so much blood. And not just dripping from my nose, but on the ground…and in the toilet bowl, the white porcelain stained with smears of crimson and black. I didn't so much as vomit as hurl my actual insides out of my body, and the sight of it triggers a terror stronger than any fear I've ever known in my life.

I collapse back against the nearest wall, sobbing. And not just because of how close I am now to death—its presence touching my skin like a phantom caress—but because of how pointless this destruction has been. Nolan was never going to get his peace. Even if he did have proof of my death, I'm sure our attackers would still change the terms at the last minute, citing some new stipulation for them to cease their attack on our home.

And I'm certain Bilken knew this would happen. His only concern has been getting us out of the State because that's what my mother asked of him. He's never cared about the damage left in our wake or what casualties would rack up as payment for our survival. He made that clear enough when he sentenced those Enforcers to death at the magistrates building two years ago.

I always thought Richter and Nolan were clever, but Bilken has played us all like fools. He is the real mastermind behind everything, dictating our movements while we carry on, none the wiser. And Nolan…

Nolan was just his latest victim, and behind the scenes, Bilken was whispering in his ear, using decades of desperation and lust for power to his own advantage.

Where does it end? I wonder weakly.

When do we stop manipulating each other?

I cough, and blood speckles the palm I press to my mouth, but I'm too tired to care or move. I can barely even find the strength to lift my eyes when a knock on the door pulls me out of my stupor.

"Wynter?"

Jenner opens the door before I can protest, stepping into the small, single-person washroom. He stops when he spots me in a near lifeless heap on the floor, the confusion creasing his brow immediately giving way to alarm.

"Shit!"

Rushing forward, he drops to his knees beside me, dirtying his pant legs on the blood-smeared tile. Without hesitation, he lifts his arms and bends as if to scoop me up, but then pauses, as if he's not sure he should touch me. I don't blame him. I don't think I've ever looked quite this sick before.

"I—" he begins to say, but I shake my head and he goes silent.

"Nolan," I manage.

He blinks. "What about him?" Then, understanding registers on his face and he says in a softer voice, "What did you see?"

"A broadcast. He..." The dryness in my throat is unbearable, making it too hard to speak. I try to swallow, but every effort is wasted and I only end up gagging, my tongue like sandpaper.

Realizing what I need, Jenner jumps to the sink and cups cool water in his hands. Then, lowering himself beside me again, he brings his fingertips to my lips. As he feeds it to me, the water dribbles from the sides of my mouth, but it satiates me enough to speak.

"He's going to try to stop the attack," I wheeze. "But...but it..."

"Stop it how?" Jenner asks.

"A public call for a ceasefire." I nod to myself, rewatching Nolan's one-sided conversation in my memory. "I think... I think that was...the plan. The way they intended to...establish peace, like Bilken said." I wince as another jagged cough escapes me. "But...it won't work."

Jenner is quiet for a moment as he considers the severity of my words. When he finally speaks, his tone is somber. "So, Bilken's connections go back on their deal?"

I shake my head as much as I'm able to.

"I'm not sure...they ever intended to honor it. At least, not the part of the deal...made with Nolan. They don't trust him. They know he was holding me outside the city, and now, they want proof of my death." *Proof or no peace*, the message to Nolan said. I shiver. "Without it, they won't honor the ceasefire...and they'll continue to bomb us until there's nothing left."

Until the Heart is nothing but ruins, like the desolate future I've seen so many times in my visions.

Jenner's mouth pulls down at the corners, and the misery in his gaze mirrors what I feel so acutely that I can't help wondering if I'm somehow sharing my pain with him.

"So," he mutters, "decimating the DSD was never going to be enough."

I wish it was. I wish this could have all ended with Richter's death.

But, like always, fate has other ideas.

I let out a pained laugh. "They know what I look like. If my mother were to try to smuggle me out, they'd recognize me. A new identity isn't enough. I'd need...a new face." I smile, laughing again under my breath, as if that notion is the funniest thing in the world.

Jenner's frown deepens, causing my smile to slip.

"They think Nolan is hiding me, keeping me in his back pocket. They want proof...or—"

"Let me guess, we all die?"

My silence is answer enough.

With a weary sigh, he runs a hand through his hair, pushing the strands back off his forehead. "What do we do?"

"Regardless of the role the State and Richter had in this war, I can't help...feeling responsible, too. I...want to find a way to stop it." *And to save you and Ezra.*

He shoots me a cautious glance. "Okay," he hedges, "but how do we do that?"

The only way we can.

"I think we need to pay PHOENIX a visit," I murmur.

Jenner's ebony brows shoot upward, making a reach for his hairline. "What? Why?" He holds up a hand as if to stop me. "You *do* realize they'll kill us—"

"They already tried that, remember?" My chest heaves, my lungs aching with the effort of each strenuous breath. Exhaling, I whisper, "They want a ceasefire...and thanks to Bilken, Nolan has a direct line to the enemy…even if they don't trust him. The Heads will hear me out, especially when I tell them about his hand in all this."

Jenner scoffs. "That's assuming they weren't in on it, too."

I offer a barely perceptible shrug, too exhausted to raise my shoulders any higher than the half-inch I manage. "It doesn't matter. The only way to end this attack is to make peace, and I…can offer that to them. I'll give them their proof."

Jenner's pupils blow wide at my words, and he lurches forward, placing his hands on my arms. His nails dig into my skin through my shirt. "If you think for one minute that Ezra or I will let you—"

"It isn't your decision, Jenner."

As this sentiment leaves my lips, a convulsion tears through me, and I gasp for breath as my lungs cough up fresh blood onto the floor. Jenner reaches for me, this time not hesitating to wrap an arm around my back to keep me upright.

"Shit, this is bad. I'm going to get your moth—"

He props me into the corner and moves to stand, but as he rises, I grab his shirt in my fist.

"Don't," I gasp. "Not yet. Please…just stay."

His lower lip wobbles as he crouches beside me. "You're not well. You need medical attention, which I can't give you."

My eyes flutter closed, and I huff out a laugh. "What good will that do at this point? I'm a…lost cause. The sooner you accept that, the better."

His warm fingers cup my cheek, and I lean into his touch, forcing my eyes open again. The swirling blue depths of his gaze in this moment remind me of the sky on the verge of a storm.

When he speaks, his voice is gentle but stern. "That won't

stop Ezra or me from trying to find a way to save you. You're our family." Leaning in, he presses his forehead to mine. "We both love you. You know that, right?"

Family.

My heart clenches as tears burn the corners of my eyes. "I know." My fingers tighten in his shirt, and I peer up at him, pleading. "You won't leave, will you?"

He glances at the ajar washroom door for a moment before settling on the floor beside me, wrapping me in a towel and wiping away the crusting blood from my face. As he snakes an arm around my shoulders, pulling me close, I rest my cheek on his chest, listening to the soothing *thump thump* of his heart.

The consistent sound guides me away from the pain, and as my eyes drift closed, Jenner whispers, "Never."

SEVENTEEN

A COMFORTING WARMTH ENVELOPS MY body, and I wake to find myself back in bed, blanketed under the heat of the duvet. Blinking the sleep from my eyes, I raise a hand to my face and wipe at the skin just under my nose, expecting the dried blood—evidence of my worsening symptoms—to flake off at my touch. But, to my surprise, nothing comes away on my fingers. I'm clean, as if someone washed me while I was sleeping.

The memory of my last waking moments rush back.

Jenner.

I press a hand to my forehead, a dull pain lingering behind my temples. He must've brought me here after I passed out.

Groaning, I push into a sitting position, pausing mid-movement when my gaze snags on the dozing figure in the chair beside the bed. My chest tightens and I instantly relax.

As if attuned to my movements, Ezra snaps his eyes open, and he looks at me for a long moment, trapped in that disoriented stage between sleep and awake. When I offer him a smile, he draws in a breath and leans forward.

"Hi," he murmurs, his deep voice husky.

"Hi," I mutter back, my own croaky.

Rising from the chair, he shifts himself onto the mattress beside me. "How are you feeling?"

I shrug. "Okay, I guess. Did Jenner bring me here?"

A frown tugs at his lips as he nods. "I thought—" The words catch in his throat, and he swallows. "There was a moment there where I thought…"

I press a hand to his cheek when he looks away, turning his face back toward mine. "I'm fine," I whisper. For the moment. "Trust me, you'll know when it's time to worry."

Because you'll be there, holding the gun that will kill me.

But this seems to be the wrong thing to say because he jerks away from me, his lips pulled taut. Swinging his legs over the side of the bed, he stands to leave.

"Ezra—" I begin.

"No." He glares over his shoulder at me for a second, then looks away again. "You keep talking like it's inevitable. Like I'm supposed to just accept that you'll die."

Because it is. Because I will. But I can't bring myself to utter these words.

Exhaling, he lets his arms fall to his sides before slumping down onto the bed beside me again, this time with his back facing me. "I won't let you go. I've already lost too much."

The sorrow in his voice is like a blade edge against my skin, cutting so deeply I'm not sure the wounds will ever close. Biting back tears, I plant my cheek on his shoulder and wrap my arms around his torso, hugging him tightly from behind. His heartbeat drums under my fingers.

"I'm sorry," I gasp, but the apology sounds hollow, even to my own ears.

I wince at the dry ache in my windpipe. There's so much more I want to say, but the words get stuck in my throat and stay there, never reaching the liberation of my lips.

The time we had together might've been brief but at least it was ours.

The tears break through now, soaking the back of his shirt, but still, I don't speak. I can't bring myself to.

Not when there's nothing I can say to undo what we both know is coming.

My breath catches when Ezra pivots in my embrace, turning around to scoop me into his arms. His fingers weave through my hair, pulling my head into the space between his chin and chest.

"I won't give up," he says low in my ear, "even if you already have."

The door swings open and we startle apart, our eyes locking on Jenner, who stands at the threshold. "It's happening," he breathes, his eyes wide.

There's only one "it" he can be talking about. Straightening, I fist my hands in my lap to hide that every inch of my body is trembling. "The broadcast?"

He nods, then gestures for us to follow before turning and vanishing from the doorway.

Ezra and I don't exchange another word as he helps me up from the bed, and he keeps one arm latched around my waist as we exit my temporary quarters, stepping back into the open living space of the safe house. Everyone else is gathered already...or maybe they never left the room? It's growing increasingly difficult to keep track of time, and I can't say for certain how long we've been down here. One day? Two?

Too long, a snide voice says in the back of my head.

A dull ache spreads through my skull, each throb like the tick of a clock, reminding me that every second spent here is draining what little time I have left in this world. At this rate, my disease will kill me long before I get to Nolan. And if that happens…

Well, at that point, any hope of salvation for anyone is lost.

Sliding out of the loop of Ezra's arm, I pause beside the sofa and sink down onto the armrest, training my gaze on the illuminated screen on the wall, watching—as transfixed as the others—as Nolan makes his futile plea for peace. It's always strange to witness an event that's previously played out in one of my visions, like I'm being forced to watch a broadcast I've already seen. Even if I turned it off, the memory of his words would remain. As would the knowledge of their outcome.

"Eerie," Jenner mutters under his breath, shooting me an unsettled look. "You told me it would happen, but it's still weird as all hell actually hearing it."

An amused grins tempts the corners of my lips. "Now, you know what it's like for me."

Knowing the future is a curse disguised as a blessing, an unending nightmare that fuels me with the constant false hope that I can change what I've seen when time has proven, over and over again, that I can't. Even after everything I've been through, even after all the pain and loss I've suffered, part of me still clings to that hope.

Now, so close to the end, it's all I have left.

As Nolan rambles on, I watch without really listening, calm and content in my decision. I'll do whatever needs to be done to put an end to this war, so if that means surrendering myself to PHOENIX so they have their proof, then that's what I'll do. It's no different than what I was initially planning, and at this point, it's all I *can* do.

Before returning to the DSD to save Rai, I had already begun to realize this conflict would only end one way. There's no turning back, no altering the path or decisions that led us to this outcome. But that doesn't mean I'll go down without a fight or let Nolan use my death for his own personal gain. My end might be written in stone, but there's still time to change the future for everyone else.

Or die trying.

"There's still time," Rai whispers in my head in agreement.

When the broadcast concludes a few minutes later, the picture cuts out with a burst of static, then goes black before transitioning to a gray screen with the words PLEASE STAND BY stamped in the middle. In the bottom right corner, the State's insignia looms under the text—a clenched fist bursting out of tree roots; the general populace being the roots the State draws power from—as if to remind us who is really in charge. But the damage of PHOENIX's interference is done. They've exposed a chink in the State's armor by hacking its television servers and making this very public declaration of war, and now, doubt will begin to fester and spread through the Heart. Between the attack and Nolan's announcement, the people's eyes will be opened and they will see how tenuous the State's hold on them really is. They will switch sides, led by the belief they now have the freedom to alter the course of their lives.

Quinn is the first to break the silence, blowing out a loud breath through his nose. "Nolan was convincing, I'll give him that."

"Not to everyone, it would seem." Bilken's baritone draws my attention, and when our eyes meet, he cocks a questioning eyebrow, his stern gaze lingering on my face. I stiffen, challenging his stare for a moment, before it registers that he's talking about me.

Relaxing a little, I shrug. "Because I know it won't work."

"Of course, it will." He shoots me a patronizing look that seems to say I'm too naive to understand such matters. "A ceasefire was always the arrangement—"

"I don't *care* about your damn arrangements, or scheming, or plans," I snap. "Once your connections find out I'm alive, they won't honor any deals you made. Or, at least, not any made with Nolan."

Assuming they ever planned on honoring them at all.

My eyes spring wide at the thought. "You know, I'm starting to think maybe that was intentional. I mean, the only deal you really care about is the one that ensures you two"—I wag a finger back and forth between my mother and Bilken—"survive this whole mess, am I right?"

"And you," my mother protests, but I talk over her, keeping my eyes locked on Bilken.

"Or"—I shrug again—"maybe I'm wrong and you aren't as clever as you think. I mean, if you are, then I'm surprised you weren't prepared for this. That you weren't aware, despite your *extensive connections*, that our attackers would know what I look like." As a weighted silence descends on the room, I click my tongue. "Seems you didn't account for every possibility after all."

My hands curl into fists as I remember the harrowing scene that followed my vision of the broadcast. What I saw while the magistrates building burned. Although I only witnessed one side of the exchange between Nolan and the people attacking our city, it was clear what our assailants were demanding.

My death.

Furious words spill from my lips in a rush. "Did you really

think they'd just take Nolan at his word? Or that they wouldn't change their demands at the last minute?" Bilken is smart enough to know what people are like once they believe they have the upper hand. That notion of power makes us brazen. I saw it enough with Richter to know. "What was the deal you made, anyway?" I press.

Before he can answer, my mother throws her arms in the air with a frustrated huff. "This is ridiculous. Why wouldn't they honor the ceasefire? As far as they're concerned, you're *dead*. We did our part. We gave them the DSD—"

Jenner snorts. "Well, clearly, that wasn't enough. It seems your *friends*"—he hooks his fingers into air quotes—"knew, or at least suspected, that Wynter was being held outside the Heart, and now, they want proof of her rotting corpse. Those are the new terms."

"Proof or no peace," I murmur, repeating the words I saw blazing across Nolan's communicator screen.

My mother flinches, and her eyes are daggers cutting into my soul as her gaze jumps to mine. "You know this?" she asks, and I can hear in her tone how desperately she's hoping I'll say no. When I nod, her frown deepens and she looks down at the floor. "Well, all the more reason for us to leave immediately, then. We need to get out before leaving is no longer an option."

"I'm sorry, did you not hear the part where they'll know who she is?" Jenner leans forward, his expression mutinous. "They're willing to let this entire city burn on a hunch that Wynter is alive, so what makes you think we have a chance in *hell* of getting out of the Heart unnoticed? Or that we'd even want to leave? This is our home. Someone has to fight for it—"

I shake my head. "No, Jenner, she's right." Before he can

protest, I shift my tired gaze to my mother's. "You're right. You *should* go. In fact, you should *all* go…as far away from this place and from me as possible."

Except Ezra, a voice that sounds eerily like Alivia Laramie breathes in my ear. A somber reminder of the role he has yet to play.

Echoing that thought, Ezra says, "That isn't happening." He touches my left cheek, pressing slightly, forcing me to look up at him where he stands resolute on my right. When our eyes meet, he murmurs, "Where you go, I go. Remember?"

Jenner tsks, knocking my shoulder with his. "Seriously, how many times do we have to say it?" When I glance at him, he rolls his eyes. "You know we aren't leaving you alone in all this."

My chest tightens at their words, and I bite the inside of my cheek to hold back the resurfacing threat of tears. I wish they would stop fighting for me. I wish they would just let me go.

After all, we're nearing the point when they'll have to.

Bilken lets out a chastising laugh. "After everything we've done to get you away from the State, you now want to stay behind and burn along with it? Or are you misguided enough to think you can stop this war, Miss Reeves? You are the one who created it."

White hot anger floods my body like heat, and scowling, I push forward onto my feet. "Which is precisely why I'm the only one who can stop it. These people attacking us are only here because of what *I* have done."

And because he gave them incentive to strike.

I step forward, and Bilken recoils a little, like prey caught in the gaze of a predator. His hand flies to his throat on reflex—a trauma response from when I choked him at the bunker—and the apprehension radiating off him as I approach is so palpable I can almost taste it, like a dank odor permeating the room.

I look down at him where he sits next to my mother. "I don't care how valuable you think you are, they wouldn't have made that deal with you unless they viewed me as a threat. And it doesn't matter if Richter and the State were behind all this, I'm still the one who did the killing. I'm still the one who decimated entire armies. This began with me—"

"Wait a minute," Ezra interrupts, his tone wary. "What exactly are you proposing?"

I hesitate for a moment, worrying my lower lip between my teeth before forcing myself to peer over my shoulder at him. Those hazel eyes I've looked into so many times stare me down, their warm honey depths rife with a fear I know all too well from my vision.

Keeping my expression neutral, I glance at Jenner, who slumps back into the sofa cushions, making it a point to evade my gaze. His avoidance is all the confirmation I need.

It seems he didn't tell Ezra about our little bathroom conversation, and I'm not sure how to feel about that. On the one hand, if he already knew what I'm planning, that would take the sting out of what I'm about to say. On the other, it's only fair if he hears it from me.

Breathing in, I force my eyes back to Ezra, and when I speak, my voice is a jagged-edged whisper. "That I give them the proof they want."

Understanding drains the color from his complexion. "No." He stumbles forward, and fury instantly hardens his face. "*No. I won't let you die for this*—"

"What other choice is there?" I ask, and he stops dead in his tracks. Looking around the room at each of the others' silent, staring faces, I growl, "Whether or not any of you want to admit it, I'm running on borrowed time. You might not want to hear it, but I'm going to die. Soon." And leaving this city won't escape what's coming. This war isn't the ticking time bomb, counting down to impending explosion.

I am.

But ending this conflict is the right thing to do, and if handing myself over for execution kills two birds with one stone, then I'll do it. I'd do anything to guarantee Ezra and Jenner survive and to preserve the future for them. Even if I'm not part of it.

"Go or don't go," I mutter, "but I'm staying."

And nothing any of you say will change my mind.

I can't let it.

Rising from the sofa, my mother steps toward me. "Wynter, I didn't do all this for you to stay behind and try to be a hero—"

She raises a hand, but I step back before she can touch me.

"I'm no hero," I counter, "and I didn't ask you to intervene. Every choice you've ever made was done on your own and without my input or consent."

A crazed laugh escapes me at the realization of how much I've changed since the day of my placement exam. Before this disease, I would've never spoken this way to anyone, least of all my mother. But I'm not that frightened little girl anymore. I'm different. Stronger. And I've found my voice.

That thought encourages me to be brave.

"I've had very little say in the events of my life. So, this?" *The last thing I ever do...* "This will be my choice, understand?"

I turn again, locking eyes with Ezra, who grimaces, arms tense and shaking at his sides.

"Do you really expect me to just stand by and watch as you hand yourself over to be *killed*?" His words are a furious growl, and the pain in his heart is reflected on his face, swarming those warm eyes in shadow.

Closing the distance between us, I flatten my hands against his cheeks and rise onto the tips of my toes, gently pressing my lips to his. "No," I whisper, so softly only he can hear. "I expect you to remember your promise."

"Promise you'll kill me."

When I release him, he takes a step back, his gaze distant as his anger fades and he wilts under the weight of my words. Jenner glances between us, his confusion evident in his downturned brow. He looks at me, his intense gaze relaying his unspoken question, but I shake my head.

Silence swallows the room like a black hole sucking all sound from the world, and I stand still, feeling the hot touch of everyone's watchful gazes as exhaustion creeps through me. I can't delay any longer. If I'm going to go, it needs to be now.

"I'll go with you."

With a grunt, Quinn pushes off the sofa and stands, keeping one hand on his injured side. Holding my gaze, he extends the other toward me.

A peace offering.

I blink at him, stunned. "What? You're injured, and last I checked, this arrangement was your ticket out of this city."

"True," he agrees. "But I left the Enforcers because of moral differences. How can I stand here and say I'm any different than the State if I leave this city to burn?" When I still don't take his proffered hand, his lips pinch into an offended glower. "Look, do you want my help or not?"

I consider him for a moment, wondering how much I can trust him before reminding myself of the only fact that matters. Quinn saved our lives. Twice.

And in this world, you can't get much more loyal than that.

"Okay," I breathe, taking his hand. And we shake.

"Although…" Quinn says, trailing off.

"Although what?" I ask, unable to mask the uneasy edge to my tone.

As I retract my hand, he frowns. "Well, it won't be easy getting to Nolan. He's holed up in the magistrates building, and since we can't exactly use the route PHOENIX planned to get there, we'll have to travel topside again, like before. Trouble is, there are at least a dozen checkpoints between where we are right now and there. We'll need transport…and cover."

His eyes swing to the left and mine follow, landing on my mother. Quinn's right. We got lucky before, getting, first, to the DSD and then to the safe house undetected, and now that Nolan has challenged the State's rule, it's all but guaranteed it will respond in force, deploying Enforcers to stop anyone who tries to freely move throughout the city. Hell, we already had a few close calls.

Although I don't want to rely on her any more than I have to, I face my mother, my decision made. "Everything you've done has only gotten people I love killed. I don't *want* your help… but I need it. So, help us. Get me there."

Her cobalt eyes are piercing. "If I do this, I'd be leaving you in this city to die. After everything I've done to get you back, how can you ask me to do that?"

"I'm already dying," I remind her. "Besides, you did it once before." A rueful smile twists my lips, and I shrug. "How hard can it be?"

A pained expression flits across her face, and she lets out a near silent laugh. "You'll never forgive me, will you?" she rasps.

Drawing in a calming breath, I take a tentative step toward her and hold out a hand like Quinn just did to me. Then, looking her square in the eye, I nod.

"I will if you help me end this war."

EIGHTEEN

WE WAIT UNTIL MID-MORNING TO depart Bilken's safe house. While, under normal circumstances, the cover of darkness would have masked our movements, there are too many blockades erected throughout the city now to reach the magistrates building unnoticed. Going at night would've only aroused unwanted suspicion, leaving us with no other option but to proceed during the day and hope no one questions what we're doing or looks too closely at the vehicle we'll be hiding in. If they do, I'll have to act—to create a path for us—which I don't want to do unless I absolutely have to. I'm so tired of killing, and using my power will only push me that much closer to death.

A risk I can't afford until this is over.

We emerge from the obscured path into the empty parking structure above the safe house, the only sound in the morning the cacophony of our footsteps as we approach the truck. The smoke and dust clouding the air have both settled a bit since I was last outside, the ash a thin layer of gray on the pavement, resembling a fresh dusting of snow that shouldn't be possible considering the structure is under cover and any exposure to the elements from here is limited.

My eyes shift to the nearest open stretch in the wall before me, scanning what I can see of the silent city beyond. Despite the returning clarity to the air, my nose wrinkles at the sulphuric stink that seems to cling to every surface around us. I breathe through my mouth to escape the scent, but the taste it leaves on my tongue isn't much better.

Grimacing, I hang to one side of the truck as my mother and Bilken prepare for our departure, conversing in hushed voices with the Enforcer who served as our driver before—then our watchdog while we were all hunkered down in the safe house—and with Quinn and Ezra, who are actively involving themselves with the plan. Although I should be listening, I find myself tuning their voices out on reflex, too mentally drained after the endless chatter of the last two or however many days it's been since we got here to take in any new information.

So, instead, I observe. I observe and I try to force myself to stay calm despite knowing how close I am now to my death.

And to the deaths of everyone if my plan doesn't work.

Shaking the thought from my head, I watch, bemused, as the Enforcer gestures for Quinn to join him in the truck, extending a hand to help him up onto the bed before advising him to strip off his clothes.

As I turn away to give them privacy for whatever it is they're doing, my eyes land on the only member of our party keeping his distance from this congregation. Jenner leans against the wall just beside the concealed entrance leading down to Bilken's safe house, arms crossed and eyes downcast on the floor.

My fingers fidget with the hem of my jacket, my teeth sinking into my bottom lip as I cross the large, empty space, closing the canyon of distance between us. So much has happened in only a few days, with Jenner focusing solely on me and my problems while suffering in silence, shoving his own heartache aside. My chest tightens at the thought of what unspoken emotions he must be bottling up even now, and I fear the resentment that might be growing inside him.

Resentment towards me for forcing him into such close proximity with the woman responsible for his pain.

I gulp, pushing down the rising lump in my throat. I see him, I see his grief, and the last thing I want is for him to think that I don't.

His eyes find mine as I draw closer, his sullen expression easing a little. In typical Jenner fashion, he offers me a lopsided smile.

"I see I'm not the only one who's grown tired of the planning brigade over there."

He arches a brow, peering past me, and with a quiet laugh, I follow his sardonic gaze, looking over my shoulder at the rest of the group. He's not wrong. All they've done since last night is discuss routes, potential pitfalls, and just about anything else we might encounter today.

Sighing, I step forward and turn on my heel, leaning against the smooth concrete wall beside him.

"I'm sorry if I've made you feel like you have to go through with this or tolerate my mother for my sake. I know you don't like accepting her help. Believe me, I don't either," I mutter. Shifting so my back is facing the others, I look him square in the eye, lowering my voice to a whisper. "But we need it. If something goes wrong…" I shake my head. "I can't take out that many Enforcers. Not without the collar." Not unless I want to risk decimating an entire city block and everyone near it. Or triggering the vision I'm in a race to outrun. "We need to at least *try* to get there without bloodshed."

Raising his hand in a fist, Jenner gives me a gentle, playful knock on the chin. "You haven't forced me into anything, Wynter. I am and will always be there for you, no matter what. And no matter who else might be, too. But…" Frowning, he glances over my shoulder, and the silence between us stretches on for a moment too long.

Reaching out, I touch his hand. "But what?"

His frown deepens. "Will you really forgive her after everything she's done? After what she did to your father? Some people don't deserve forgiveness…or to live in peace."

I nod, repositioning my back to the wall. "Maybe not. But if telling her I'll forgive her means keeping you and Ezra alive, then it's worth it to me. They're just words," I mutter, shaking my head again. "If they mean that much to her, she can have them."

The clomp of boots on tarmac draws my attention, and I look to my left, spotting Quinn, who walks toward us dressed in an Enforcer's uniform, tugging at the collar with one hand while the other holds the matching helmet tucked under his arm. His face is set in a scowl and he looks uncomfortable, reminding me of the first time I saw him.

Once we're within earshot, he stops and jerks his head toward the truck. "It's time to go," he says.

"Ready?" I ask with a backward glance at Jenner.

He shrugs, the barest grin touching his lips. "As I'll ever be."

We make our way toward the others without exchanging another word, Quinn proceeding at a clipped pace a few strides ahead. Once we reach the truck, he indicates for us to get in, and upon approaching the open back doors, the first thing I notice is the unfamiliar man standing at attention nearby. He's dressed in black clothes I know I've seen before, the fabric soiled with blood on the side of the torso.

Quinn's clothes, I realize on closer inspection.

Although a fresh outfit was waiting for me—spare garments my mother prepared to replace the DSD-issue clothes I was wearing—Bilken didn't have anything on hand for the others, not even Quinn, who was an active part of their plot. Our pit stop at the safe house was never included in their plan to flee the State and it's possible, even if it had been, he didn't anticipate having so many extra bodies to account for.

Still, given what I know about him, I found this lack of preparation odd, further fueling my assumption that he never intended to ensure the safe escape of anyone other than himself, my mother, and, begrudgingly, me. When I pointed out his poor planning on the matter, he merely scoffed and said arrangements had been made to accommodate us once we fled the city, although who that "us" was referring to, he didn't say. The bitterness in his voice when speaking of these arrangements—arrangements I was purposely rejecting—was enough to dissuade me from asking.

We didn't talk about clothes or leaving the city again after that.

For Ezra and Jenner, the lack of new attire wasn't a pressing issue. They weren't wearing anything branded with insignia or visibly recognizable that might put our identities or mission in jeopardy, unlike me with my military grade bodysuit. But for Quinn, not having that option to change meant remaining in garments stained with his own blood.

My gaze jumps back and forth between him and the Enforcer in my mother's employ, and as I once again observe the regulation uniform on Quinn, I find myself wondering why, exactly, they swapped.

"Planning on rejoining?" I joke, cocking a brow at him.

He doesn't even crack a smile, his tone husky as he says, "It'll be easier to get through this unchallenged if they think I'm one of them. Call it a fail-safe."

"And him?" I press, nodding at the Enforcer, who looks strangely naked without his uniform and helmet. "I take it he's not coming with us?" If I had to guess, the deal my mother made with Quinn wasn't extended to everyone in her employ.

Quinn responding snort is dismissive. "Don't know. Don't care. Ask your mother or Bilken if you want to know so badly."

Wincing, he climbs into the back of the truck, then kneels, releasing a circular spring-loaded plate in the floor with his thumb. The button—no larger than a watch face—pops up with a click, exposing a catch, which Quinn grabs and yanks back to reveal a hidden compartment under the metal sheeting.

Leaning forward, I peer into the dark, empty space, confusion spreading through me like a chill.

"You need to hide," Quinn clarifies when I look up at him.

Hide? My brow furrows as I assess the cramped space. *In there?*

"Another fail-safe?" I ask.

Beside me, Jenner balks. "I know you don't expect me to climb into *that*. Small spaces aren't really my thing." He shudders.

Quinn clambers to his feet and looks over us like a disappointed parent. "Need I remind you, we got lucky last time. There's no way we'll make it through a dozen checkpoints without at least one Enforcer checking back here. They won't suspect me if I'm dressed like one of them. But you?" He scoffs at the thought. "We need to get *there*"—he points in what I assume is the general direction of the magistrates building—"with as little fuss as possible. Unless you'd prefer to just kill everyone in our path?" He narrows his eyes at me.

Jenner and I both shake our heads before silently doing as we've been instructed, climbing up into the truck and exchanging one last dubious look before taking turns to lower ourselves into the hidden compartment, lying flat until we're squished under the floor like a pair of sardines.

A moment later, Ezra appears overhead and climbs in beside us without saying a word. Grunting, we shift as much as we can to make room for all three of us to fit, but it's snug and the space is overwhelmingly warm, already making me sweat.

"This will be cozy," Jenner grumbles under his breath.

On my other side, Ezra's fingers wrap around mine. "You can still change your mind," he whispers. "We can go out the way we came in and all leave this city together."

The strangled hope in his voice draws my gaze.

"And then what?" I counter. "Regardless of where we go, I still…" *Die*, I finish in my head. *Regardless of where we go, I still die.*

Drawing in a shaking breath, I dare to imagine a life outside this city's walls. A life where I am healthy and free. A life where Ezra and Jenner are safe and *stay* safe from the threat of war.

But only one of those things can happen, and I know, without a doubt, which life I choose.

When I swallow, the shifting of my throat is deafening in the confined space.

"I've seen what's coming, and if we abandon the Heart now, the people we leave behind will be slaughtered. If that happens, especially when we had the means to prevent it, then Quinn was right. We are no better than the State. Or PHOENIX. Or the people attacking us. All sides are guilty in this." *Even me.* A tear escapes, sliding down the side of my face. "It needs to end."

"Okay," Jenner says, jumping in before Ezra can speak. He grabs my other hand, and when I look at him in the darkness, he smiles. "Then, let's end it together."

NINETEEN

THE CRAMPED COMPARTMENT IS UNCOMFORTABLE as the truck bounces along the empty streets, the tarmac littered with glass and debris. Even without seeing it, I can envision how badly Zone 1 has been hit by the bombings, the impact devastating, even in the areas beyond our attackers' targets. I can feel every rock, every pop of the broken shards beneath the tires, and the vibrations marking our forward progression flood the metal coffin-like space, whirring in my ears like white noise.

Beyond the low hum of the truck, I can just make out the occasional sprinkle of gunfire, but trapped in the darkness, I'm blind to what's happening outside—what mayhem is raining down over the city. My imagination doesn't help, filling the empty seconds that follow with screams.

I clamp my eyes shut and draw in one deep breath after another to steady my heart, which only grows more frantic in my confinement. My pulse skitters under my skin until I feel the racing tempo everywhere. In my throat. Behind my eyes. I can even hear it in my ears, a low *ba-dum ba-dum* that only escalates my increasing anxiety.

A sheen of sweat coats my skin, and drops of perspiration slide from my forehead down the sides of my face. The space under the floorboards is a hot box cooking me alive.

Hysteria grips me as I squirm against the two bodies pressed close on each side of my own, the proximity making it hard to breathe. Swallowing despite the grating dryness in my throat, I focus on satiating the burning need in my lungs, but no matter how many times I draw in a breath, each inhalation feels like my last. The pressure building in my chest is a crushing weight pinning me down to the floor.

Whatever self-control I had learned with my collar is lost as I succumb to my panic, leaving my fragile mind unguarded to the vision that suddenly strikes in the blackness. Gunfire. Bodies. Flames. One after another, these images enter my thoughts, showing me what I can't see with my eyes.

Just as I knew it would, the Heart has devolved into a state of complete anarchy. Everyone has turned on each other. The Enforcers against the people. The people against each other. Around me, all I see is death. So much loss.

So much needless destruction.

The gunshots I hear beyond the reinforced walls of the truck echo in my head, projecting from the images like I'm in two places at once, the vision mimicking reality. My eyes burn, and I tremble against the hard floor, weeping and wishing for this assault on my senses to stop. But it doesn't. If anything, the vision only strengthens its hold, digging deeper into my consciousness.

Forcing me to see what my existence has led to.

A sticky wetness pools under my nose as pain slashes through my temples, pulling a scream from my throat, which is quickly muffled by a hand over my mouth. A gasp slips through my covered lips, and I startle at the touch of hot breath on my ear. "It will end. You'll get through it, but you need to be quiet. Breathe, Wynter. Just *breathe*."

The tension in my body eases at the soothing sound of Ezra's voice, the violent tide of the visions instantly ebbing. On my other side, warm fingers wrap around mine.

"It's okay," Jenner whispers. "We're right here with you."

Above us, a booted foot stomps down hard on the floor, rattling the metal plating. "We're coming up on the first checkpoint," Quinn warns.

My insides turn liquid, and tears squeeze from my eyes as I bite my lower lip to tamp down my whimpers. As we come up on the checkpoint, Ezra keeps his hand clamped over my mouth.

We make it through the first two checkpoints unscathed. At the first, the Enforcers guarding the blockade granted us passage almost immediately upon learning my mother's identity, satisfied with her story about transporting medical equipment to a safe location. They didn't even consider checking the truck. But at the second, the Enforcers only relented once Bilken intervened, although not before questioning why he and my mother were together—their positions in our society unrelated, rousing suspicion as to why their paths would cross if they weren't partnered. He didn't dignify them with a response, instead—rather haughtily—taking a moment to remind the soldiers who he is. Bilken holds one of the highest positions in the State, and while he isn't personally in charge of our country's military force, he *is* partly responsible for its recruitment. To join the Enforcers, the CEO of W. P. Headquarters must personally approve and sign off on every transfer request. Without him, the State wouldn't even have a military to speak of.

Once the truck is far enough away from the second checkpoint, Quinn stomps his foot on the floor again. "How are you three doing down there?"

Jenner laughs under his breath, then shouts back, "We're having a grand old time, aren't we, guys? Couldn't be more comfortable!"

On my other side, Ezra snorts.

By the time we reach the third checkpoint, the seconds feel more like hours and the minutes more like days until it seems like I'll never get out of this truck. My whimpers have ceased, the pain in my head fading to a dull ache, and Ezra has long since removed his hand from my mouth, although his hand never strays far, his fingers gently stroking my cheek. I turn into his touch, matching my breathing to his, as the tires beneath us roll to a stop.

Like at the last two checkpoints, I can just make out the muted conversation.

"Identification?" a gruff male voice asks. There's something peculiar, something I can't quite pinpoint, about the way he says this word.

There's a brief pause, and I can all too clearly envision my mother presenting her wrist to their scanner along with the look of sheer disdain on her face. If she's nervous or afraid, I highly doubt the soldier would know it.

"Dr. Evelyn Adler..." The Enforcer trails off, but there's a deliberating edge to the way he says her name that triggers goosebumps all over my body, even in the suffocating heat of the underfloor box. I strain my ears, waiting for him to continue, and in the lull, I'm certain I could hear a pin drop.

"You work for the DSD?"

My mother's answering tone is bored. "That's what it says, doesn't it?"

The Enforcer whistles, as if signaling to someone out of earshot, then shouts, "Everyone out of the truck!"

"For what reason?" my mother questions, but the usual authority behind her words wavers a little. "You are interfering with sanctioned—"

I suck in a breath at the sharp click of a gun being cocked.

"Shut your mouth, lady, or I'll shut it for you. Now,"—there's the tinny sound of the driver's side door wrenching open—"get out of the truck." After a short pause, he adds, "You two, check the back."

I note the heavy tromp of boots approaching, the sound all too familiar after all the time I spent accompanied by Enforcers. It grows louder as the weight at the front of the vehicle shifts. My mother and Bilken must've climbed down from their seats and disembarked the truck as instructed.

"I think this is all a misunderstand—" Bilken begins, but his protest is silenced by a blood-curdling *thwack* that sends a ripple of dread racing through every inch of my body. A heavy thud follows, and even with the thick, metal carcass around us, I can hear my mother gasping.

My panic burrows deeper, making the cramped compartment feel even smaller, but I barely have time to process what's befallen my mother and Bilken before the back doors of the truck are forced open.

On each side of me, Ezra and Jenner go still, holding their breath, and I do the same, listening. Above us, Quinn is perfectly quiet.

"Hey, you," a new voice grumbles. "Why are you alone back here? Where's the rest of your unit?"

Like the first Enforcer who spoke, his accent is slightly clipped. Strange. Did the State call in reinforcements from the other eight cities that, along with the Heart, form our country—assuming they haven't also been caught up in the assault? I've never met anyone from outside the capital to know if we all sound the same.

Quinn clears his throat. "I've been reassigned as a temporary escort for Dr. Adler until the crisis is over. I was instructed to stay with her and Mr. Bilken until they're at a safe location."

There's a tremor in Quinn's voice, but I doubt it's from fear—I've seen him in worse situations and he's a far cry from the spooked soldier I met months ago. If anything, it sounds like he's in pain, and I wonder if the medication my mother has been giving him to stave off the discomfort of his injury is wearing off. He was only recently shot, and I'm still amazed he wanted to come with us considering how close to death's door he had seemed that first day, in the hours after it happened. I suppose it says something about his stubborn need to maintain his moral high ground on the issue of our country that he's on this mission at all.

"Get out of the vehicle," the Enforcer barks.

Quinn does as he's told, his boots bearing down on the metal plating in slow, careful steps as he inches toward the open doors and the awaiting Enforcer below on the pavement. The truck shifts again from the displacement of weight when he jumps down into the road.

There's a second of agonizing silence, then the harsh slap of palms against the floor right above us.

"It isn't customary to search one of our own," Quinn grunts. He bites back a groan. The Enforcer must've grazed his wound.

"I'll do a lot worse if you don't shut up."

I frown, staring hard at the ceiling—even though I can't see anything in the darkness of the box—imagining Quinn's hands on the other side. He's right. Why would an Enforcer target another Enforcer? I've never seen that happen, not even in the year I worked closely alongside the State's military.

My frown deepens. Something about this whole thing feels off. There's the faint rustle of clothing as Quinn is patted down and his weapons are confiscated, his muttered cursing just audible through the floor.

My breaths grow increasingly ragged in the enclosed space, my heartbeat thunderous in my ears. But past the building cacophony of my hysteria, I note a near imperceptible click in the panel above my face—my ears acutely aware of every sound in an effort to balance my deprived senses.

"You find it?" the first voice calls out from the front of the truck.

"No," the soldier nearest us answers, yelling back, "She isn't here."

She?

Comprehension is a hand tightening around my lungs. Enforcers are searching the city for me—what other "she" could they possibly mean? But why? Richter is dead and no one in the State has seen me since I boarded the transport helicopter Jenner blew up to extract me. For all I know, everyone I was in contact with during my time at the DSD assumed I perished in the explosion that claimed so many others. Even if they *had* thought I survived, I didn't think anyone other than Richter and Bilken knew I was back in the Heart. I killed all the soldiers guarding the East Gate, and anyone in power still living after the attack would have no reason to believe I'd be in this city, let alone alive.

So, who could've sent them? Are they being directed by someone I'm unaware of? Someone hoping to use me to control the outcome of this war?

What am I missing?

"Where is she?" the first Enforcer shouts, drawing my split attention to the front of the truck.

"Who?" my mother coos with mock innocence.

When the soldier next speaks, his voice is a threatening growl. "Your little monster. You work for the DSD, so you should know. *Where is she?*" he asks again, enunciating each syllable slowly.

"I don't know what you're talking about—"

A sharp slap cuts her off. "Don't lie, bitch!"

My body is a tightening coil springing to snap. I resent my mother. On some level, I hate her. But that doesn't mean I want her to die or to be executed like some helpless animal in the street.

I have to do something.

I have to stop this before anyone else gets killed because of me.

Ezra, sensing the change in me, moves his hand from my mouth to my wrist, his grip tight, bordering on painful. "Don't," he warns, his voice a fierce whisper, but I barely hear him, too preoccupied with the scuffle of footsteps outside the truck.

"Get them down on the ground. And shoot that one. See if it jogs her memory."

Panic writhes within me, and my insides feel slippery, like I'm going to be sick. Who was the Enforcer talking about? Shoot who? Bilken?

Quinn?

The thought of the ex-Enforcer taking another bullet after everything he's done to help not only me but Ezra and Jenner is one step over a line I'm not willing to cross. Driven by my protective instincts, I shoot my hand out, clawing at the panel above me.

"Wynter—"

I ignore Ezra's protest, shaking off his and Jenner's combined attempts to hold me back. The false floor gives way with ease when I push, and as I climb out of the shadows of our hiding place, it occurs to me what that click I heard before was.

Quinn unlocked the compartment, I realize. When he was being searched against the truck bed, he popped the latch in the hidden door, setting us free.

No, not free, I correct myself. Because he didn't intend for us to run.

What he wanted was to set me loose.

The back doors of the truck hang wide on their hinges, offering me a perfect view of Quinn, who faces me on his knees in the road, hands clasped in surrender behind his head. The Enforcer who searched him is standing to his left, aiming a pistol at his right temple—his back turned toward me as he barks orders at another soldier beyond my line of sight.

I step forward, drawing in a steadying breath, and as my feet reach the edge of the truck bed, Quinn's gaze shoots up from the cracked pavement, locking on mine. Inhaling again, I close my eyes.

The power in my mind is like tentacles reaching out, searching for the soldiers' heartbeats and using the draw of each *thump* to pinpoint their positions around us. I sense six in total.

This time, instead of expanding outward, the bubble of pressure in my chest is like a black hole, ready to suck everything in.

To destroy.

I call that destructive force to the surface before the soldiers are even aware of my presence, envisioning the bone structure of their spinal columns as I jerk my own head to the side. The sole Enforcer in my range of vision drops to the ground. To the side of the truck, I note the identical thud of a limp body hitting dirt.

Two down, I muse, stumbling backward. I try to reach out again to the Enforcers at the front of the vehicle—to make sure I got them, too—but the flash of pain cutting into my temples makes it too hard to zero in on them a second time.

I thrust out a hand toward the side of the truck to catch myself when my legs buckle. Chest heaving, I look down at Quinn, who lowers his hands, a harrowed frown on his face. He glances around, his complexion ashen, before calling up to me, but whatever he says is drowned out by the hum in my skull.

Exhaustion drains the strength from my legs, and my knees bend on reflex, giving out and pitching my body forward over the lip of the truck bed. Strong arms catch me mid-fall, tugging me back, and I instantly recognize the warmth and smell that encases me despite the added odor of sweat.

Eyes glassy, I peer over my shoulder at Ezra. "I'm fine," I mutter, finding my feet. "I'm okay."

Holding onto his arms for support, I push myself upright then glance down at Quinn, who is crouched over the body of the Enforcer who held a gun to his head, a puzzled look crossing his face.

"What is it?" I ask as Ezra helps me down from the truck. Jenner follows closely on my other side, brushing the sweat-dampened hair off his forehead.

Quinn glares at us. "These aren't Enforcers. Look."

He rolls the dead man onto his side, propping him up with one hand on his shoulder while pointing with the other to the embroidered crest on the left sleeve of his uniform. The symbol is barely visible against the black fabric.

As if they intended for it not to be seen.

Quinn lets go of the dead soldier, letting his lifeless body flop back to the ground. "The uniform isn't exactly the same but it's close, especially with the helmets. If I had to guess, they took those off the Enforcers who were originally stationed here."

"And who are probably dead now," Jenner mutters.

Quinn nods. "What better way to ambush someone than to pose as one of their own?"

My eyes widen when the answer clicks in my brain. The unusual accents. The strange, black insignia.

"It's them," I whisper. "The people Nolan made his deal with."

In my memory, I glimpse flashes of the magistrate's building burning and of innocent people gunned down in the streets. This invader Bilken brought into our lives—no, that *I* brought into our lives—is only here because of me. Only killing our people because of me. Because of what I have done to countries like theirs, my actions on behalf of the State merciless. And now, because of the fear I've instilled within them, they're inflicting the same kind of slaughter on us, killing without remorse, carving a path through the city while looking for me.

Just as I knew they would.

Ezra snorts. "So much for waiting until peace was established."

I glance at him, suppressing a grimace. He's right. Bilken said the enemy would offer military support to PHOENIX—that they would sweep through the Heart, offering the needed numbers to supplant the State. To remove it from power. But this feels much more covert. Like these soldiers were here on a specific mission.

Not to help establish peace in the city.

A shout drags my attention back toward the front of the truck, and glancing at the others, it dawns on me that our party is short two members. My voice is hoarse, my mouth bone dry, as I force out the words, "Where's my mother?"

Quinn retrieves his weapons from the body of the enemy soldier. Then, nodding to Ezra and Jenner, he skirts around the right side of the truck while they both go around the left, guns drawn and at the ready. I follow closely at Quinn's heels despite the exhaustion pushing at the underside of my skin.

As we come around to the front of the vehicle, sticking close to the cab for cover, I glimpse my mother on the ground less than ten feet away, kneeling beside Bilken, who is on the ground, unconscious. Maybe even dead. Her hands are pressed to his head, blood seeping between her interlaced fingers. Around them lie the prone bodies of three soldiers, their necks bent at unnatural angles. The fake Enforcers I killed only moments before.

That only makes five, I note with unease, and then I see him—the sixth soldier I sensed. The one my power failed to reach.

He's cowering behind the barricade erected across the road, but, unlike the others, he's not wearing an Enforcer's helmet, his pasty, stricken face on full display. Shouting again, he aims his rifle at my mother.

"You're not her! I've seen her face... You're not her!" His cries are incoherent, and his eyes bulge with terror as they dance across the crumpled bodies of the soldiers between them. "What did you do to them?" he screams.

Quinn crouches, aiming his gun, but before he can shoot, I brush past him and walk out into the open street, exposing myself to the soldier. Recognition flashes across his face.

"She didn't do this. I did."

As these words leave my lips, I jerk my head to the side, using my power again despite the excruciating pain that follows. Pressure squeezes my skull, and the tang of blood coats my nostrils and the back of my tongue, but I barely notice either beyond the war occurring in my thoughts. All I can focus on is that soldier.

When he falls, I find myself torn between succumbing to the guilt of all the deaths I keep causing or slinking back into the safety of numbness, far away from where I don't have to feel anything, just like I did when I was the State's weapon. The numbness is tempting, and yet, I know feeling nothing would be giving the monster exactly what it wants.

And I don't want to exit this life as the monster everyone thinks I am.

Clenching my teeth, I choose to embrace the guilt but push it aside for the moment, my blurring gaze tripping on my mother and Bilken, whose face is slack, his eyes closed. His head wound is still bleeding profusely despite my mother's best attempts to stop it.

Stumbling forward, I wipe away the fresh blood from my nose. "Are you okay?" I ask, standing over her. Although I can sense them behind us, Ezra, Jenner, and Quinn all keep their distance, giving us space.

My mother doesn't look up at me. "Yes, but Wren's injured."

"What happened?" I press, although I'm certain I already know the answer.

She shakes her head. "That asshole struck him with the butt of his rifle. I think he might have even cracked his skull. I need to clean the wound and stitch it up before he loses too much blood." Lifting her gaze, she glances past me toward the others. "There's a first aid kit in the truck. Will one of you grab it?"

Ezra yanks open the vehicle's passenger door and climbs inside, emerging a few seconds later with the first aid kit clasped in his hand. When he presents the metal box to my mother, she nods for him to put his hands on Bilken's skull in place of hers, offering the needed pressure to staunch the bleeding while she prepares the supplies to disinfect and close the wound. To my surprise, Ezra does so without question, planting his hands on Bilken's head. He only moves them once my mother is ready to work, handing her gauze and whatever else she needs when she asks for it.

As my mother sets to stitching the broken skin together, I kneel beside her. "You should go," I say point-blank. "Call your Enforcers, take the truck, and go back."

Her fingers pause their movements, and she blinks at me, confused. "What? No, I'm taking you—"

"You don't get it. These soldiers?" I wave a hand toward the broken bodies around us. "They *weren't* Enforcers. Those people Bilken and Nolan made their deals with are here and they're looking for me. Helping me will only get you both killed, especially if they find out you work for the DSD. They'll blame you. For Richter's research. For me. For everything." I add that last part in a soft breath, hoping my words carry the weight to make her understand.

"So, they aren't just attacking while waiting for proof of your death, they're actively looking for it?" Jenner asks.

I roll my lower lip between my teeth, thinking. "It's...more than that. This is retaliation. Even if they had proof of my death, I'm not sure it would be enough to stop the attack."

"Then what's the point?" Ezra snaps, his eyes shooting daggers at me over Bilken's unconscious body. "Why hand yourself over if it won't put an end to all this?"

Annoyance grips my chest, and a fury unlike anything I've ever known washes through me. Ezra's upset—he wants to find justification in agreeing to what I've asked of him—but I'm tired of trying to make them understand.

Of trying to make them see what will come to pass if they don't let me go.

"What do you think will happen when this disease kills me?" My eyes flash to Jenner over my shoulder. "Or have you forgotten?" Although I spit the words, they come out more cruel than I intend, and I find myself averting my gaze, not wanting to see the hurt look on his face.

With a tired sigh, I look back at Ezra. "This war will only end one way. Because I *make* it end. And if the way to do that is to hold the entire world hostage unless they agree to my demands, then so be it. I will gladly let them burn if they refuse."

"Even if it means burning us, too?" Ezra breathes.

The dejected notes in his voice extinguish my rage, and I immediately deflate. We stare at each other for a long moment before I can finally bring myself to answer.

A regretful smile pulls at my lips. "If it comes to that...

nothing I do will save you anyway."

Glowering at me, Ezra jumps to his feet and storms away from us back toward the rear of the truck, raking a bloody hand through his hair. Jenner and I exchange a look, and with a quick nod, he follows after him.

Beside me, my mother is unnaturally still.

"Wynter, I—"

"I forgive you," I say suddenly, and as the words rush out, I realize there's a part of me that means them.

My mother gapes at me, as surprised as I am.

"I understand why you did what you did," I continue before she can utter a word, "and I'm grateful you came back for me and helped us get this far, but…" I hesitate, shaking my head. "But you need to let me go. *I* need to see this through, but you don't." I glance between her and Bilken and at the delicate way her hands cup his head. Before, their closeness infuriated me, but now…

Now, I'm just glad she won't be alone at the end should the future I'm trying to avoid come to pass.

My throat thickens. "You two can still get out. Use Bilken's connections or sneak out some other way if you have to. Just get as far away from here as you can."

My mother's gaze hardens, and she clenches her jaw. "Even if I agreed, how do you expect to get the rest of the way without transport? We're still miles from the magistrates building."

"You got us this far, but going through the remaining checkpoints isn't an option. Not anymore." My eyes drift across the dead soldiers around us. "We'll be better off on foot from here. A truck will draw too much attention."

Leaning toward me, my mother reaches out a tentative hand,

using her thumb to wipe away the bead of sweat building on my forehead. Then, she carefully touches my nose, and when she pulls away, I glimpse the blood on her fingers.

"I didn't want to accept it before, but I see it now. I recognize it from—" Clearing her throat, she drops her hand, as if she can't bring herself to touch me and mention her crimes at the DSD at the same time. Still, although the heat of her hand is gone, her eyes burn me when she says, "Your body is failing, Wynter. At this rate, you'll be dead before you even get there."

A strange calm settles over me, and I nod.

"Then I better make every second count."

TWENTY

MY MOTHER FINISHES BANDAGING UP Bilken's wound, then rouses him with a capsule of smelling salts from the first aid kit, which I catch an unpleasant whiff of from where I kneel beside her. His eyelids snap open, his dark eyes unfocused, and nostrils flaring, he lurches away from the stink of ammonia with an agonized groan.

"Don't," she warns, grabbing his wrist in a pincer-like grip when he lifts a shaking hand to his head.

Bilken's gaze is bleary as she forces his arm down, pinning it to his side with her knee. "Wh—" he begins, his confusion evident in the crease of his brow, but she hushes him.

"*Don't,*" she says again, more forceful this time. "Just be quiet for a minute. I need to examine you before you can move."

Pulling a small flashlight from the box, my mother clicks on the white beam and shines it in Bilken's eyes, watching in silence as his pupils respond to the light. After a moment, a hum of consideration breaches her lips.

"Your pupillary response is slower than I would like. Do you feel nauseous at all?" she asks.

"No," he mutters, then, with a heaving sigh, adds, "I'm sure

I'll live, Evelyn. Can I sit up now?"

With a disgruntled huff through her nose, she glances over at Quinn, who waits by the truck, gun in hand, standing lookout. Frowning, she looks at me. "Do you think you can help me get him up? I'm not sure Quinn is in the best condition for this."

Nodding, I follow her lead, wedging one hand under Bilken's back and placing the other on his shoulder while my mother carefully cradles his neck, slowly easing him into a sitting position.

"Are you dizzy?" my mother presses him. There's an undercurrent of worry in her voice I've never heard before.

"A little," Bilken admits, waving her off. "But, like I said before, I'll be fine."

I snort. "Of course, you will be. You're a human cockroach," I mutter, but my words hold no malice. If anything, I'm beginning to revere Bilken's stubbornness when it comes to his survival, and not just in political situations where he exploits the playing field to his advantage but now from an actual assault that could have easily killed him. Either fate is watching over him or he's incredibly lucky. If it's the latter, then I wish that fortune was contagious, so I could force him to pass it on to Ezra and Jenner.

My mother arches a surprised brow at me, her shock at my caustic tone clear on her face. As I glance at her, I'm certain I know what she's thinking. What does she glimpse when she looks at me? Does she see a stranger much like I do when I look at her? After all, I'm nothing like I was before my placement exam. What happened that day changed me—not just physically but mentally—and although there's so much that's transpired along the way since then that I wish I could have done differently, I'm free in a way I never was when entangled in the restrictive rules of the State. Even with a timer counting down over my head, at least I can approach the end of my life knowing I had the chance to find the real me. The person I lived as for eighteen years, the person my mother must think I still am…

She died that day I escaped the DSD, cut out of me alongside my tracking chip.

Bilken exhales a strangled laugh, drawing my gaze. "Well, I'd rather be a cockroach than dead. So, I'll take it."

Once she's convinced his injury isn't life-threatening, my mother gestures for me to help her lift Bilken and, together, we ease him up onto his feet. Reluctantly, he slings an arm over my shoulders, and although the dead weight of his arm is heavy, it's light in comparison to the invisible burden I already carry.

Soft breaths part my lips as I trudge forward one step and then another, stumbling along beside Bilken as we lead him over to the truck. Quinn, unable to do any heavy lifting in his condition, holds open the passenger door, keeping one hawk-like eye on our surroundings at all times, ever the watchful soldier even when injured.

"Quinn, a word?" my mother says once Bilken is settled in his seat.

The ex-Enforcer's obsidian eyes flash to mine, then he turns, heeding my mother's summons, tailing her away from the truck. I watch their retreating backs for a moment before peering at Bilken, his skin slightly sallow. His breathing is hitched, like every inhale is a struggle.

"How's the head?" I ask, turning my back to the propped-open door.

He groans, sliding his eyes shut for a moment before wrenching them open again with a sigh. "Like a cracked egg. I suppose I should take this as a sign that I'm getting too old to be mixed up in this business."

I press my trembling fingertips into my tired eyes. "I know the feeling." *Well.* "Time for retirement, I guess."

Bilken lets out a low rumbling hum of agreement. "Looks like it." Averting his gaze, he stares out through the windshield at my mother. "For both of us," he adds under his breath.

The fatigue I've been fighting back hits me tenfold at these words, and I slump against the door, my knees wobbling uncertainly beneath me. Silence, as thick as the tears in my throat, hangs between us for an uncomfortable moment, and I follow his distracted line of sight to my mother, watching as she hands something small and indiscernible to Quinn. Even from here, I can see the dazed stupefaction on the ex-Enforcer's face.

There's something about the way she looks back at him that I struggle to put into words. Something so final, like what I envision a goodbye looks like without the spoken sentiment.

Heart clenching at the thought of my own impending goodbyes, I return my focus to Bilken. "You'll take care of my mother?" I murmur, my voice soft.

He begins to nod but stops mid-movement, wincing. "I've been doing my best by her for the last thirty-one years," he mutters on a broken exhale. "I'm not about to abandon her now."

"Good," I whisper. Then I say nothing else, content to let the quiet return.

The scrape and crunch of approaching footsteps draw my sluggish gaze to my mother and Quinn, who walk back toward us now—my mother with a somber frown on her face and Quinn still wearing that same shell-shocked expression from a few moments ago. Ignoring me, he presses on past the cab and continues onward to the back of the truck, while my mother makes a beeline for me, jerking her head once she catches my gaze.

My stomach twists at her unspoken command—at this gesture of beckoning for me to go to her—and as I push away from the door, closing it behind me, I feel strangely nervous. Like waking believing everything was a dream and instead learning the nightmare is actually real.

She lingers several feet away from the truck, pacing and chewing on the tip of her thumbnail. Her agitation surprises me. I don't think I've ever seen my mother look overwrought.

"What's wro—" I begin to say, but before I can finish, she grabs my hand, flipping it over.

"Take this." She places a gun on my outstretched palm, then curls her fingers around mine as if she just gave me the solution to my problems rather than a weapon that will be useless to me.

I blink, staring at the pistol where it touches my skin—the sleek black metal cool against my overheated flesh.

"I don't—"

"Please," she begs, her plea drawing my gaze to hers. Anguish dulls her eyes as she tightens her grip. "I know, just…please. Let me leave here feeling like I've at least done something to protect you."

Her hands relax, and with a stilted breath, she pulls away, quickly retracting her fingers. Her eyes slip from mine, dipping to the ground.

As an awkward hush rises between us, I find myself staring at the spot where she touched me. She's touched me before but never like this. Never with this desperation.

Never like my life has depended on it.

For all the attention I received from my father, I think that might have been the first time my mother has outwardly shown me she cares.

The first—and last—physical affection she will *ever* show me.

"Are you sure I can't get you to change your mind?" she asks, her voice just a step above silent.

Shaking my head, I tuck the gun in my waistband, shivering when the metal brushes up against the small of my back. "Even if that was an option…no. This is the right thing to do."

The *only* thing to do.

She nods. "For what it's worth, I think…" She hesitates, clearing her throat, her eyes shiny, then gifts me with an unexpected smile. It's despondent and screams of regret, but there's also something else behind it. Something almost like pride. "I think this is what your father would've done, too."

With a shuddering breath, she caresses the side of my head, her fingers lingering for just a moment, brushing over my hair. Then, her hand is gone, her touch nothing more than a memory, almost as if I imagined it.

Flicking a tear off her cheek, she turns and struts toward the truck without looking back.

My mother and I don't speak again. She returns to the driver's seat of the cab and, after checking on Bilken, turns over the engine. We don't even make eye contact as she reverses the vehicle, heading back in the direction we came from.

As I watch her drive away, I don't know what to feel. Anger? Sadness? Regret? Relief?

All of the above?

Or, maybe, nothing at all.

"Are you okay?"

I jump at the sound of a gruff voice in my ear, and I look back to find Ezra standing behind my left shoulder, a concern I'm all too familiar with swirling in the warm hazel depths of his eyes. My gaze darts from his, scouring our razed surroundings, searching for Jenner amid the rubble, who I spot across the street, talking to Quinn. I wasn't even aware they were all back yet from wherever it was they stormed off to.

With one final glance down the road, I turn, squaring my shoulders to face Ezra head-on. If he's still upset with me, the drawn expression pinching his lips into an emotionless line doesn't show it. Regardless, I feel the need to say something. To clear the air. To preserve whatever time, however little, we have left together.

Even if it's tainted by the understanding of the roles we both have yet to play.

I draw in a breath, preparing myself, but before I can get a single word out, he closes the distance between us, scooping me into a firm embrace that punches the air from my lungs. My body freezes in his arms as he whispers, "It's okay, you know. To *not* be okay."

I pull away slightly, unsure what he means. He mimics the movement, looking me in the eye in that cryptic way he does, the silence saying so much more than words ever can. Brushing my hair behind my ears, he leans in again, cupping my face in his hands.

"Putting aside what she's done, who she's hurt… At the end of the day, she's still your mother. It's okay for you to be upset by how things have turned out or pissed off or whatever you want to feel. And if that means talking about it or crying or, hell, screaming as loud as you possibly can, then just do it. You have my ear and my shoulder. Whichever one you need is yours."

As he lowers his hands, I push out a slow breath through my nose and bow my head until my cheek rests on the top of his chest. "How do you do it?" I mumble.

His heartbeat is strong and steady, and his voice is a throaty purr as he asks, "Do what?"

Console me when your pain outweighs mine.

Console me when all I've done is hurt you.

I burrow my face against his neck. "You're angry at me, and I don't blame you for that—"

"Stop." Grasping the tops of my arms, he pushes me back a step, forcing space between us again. When I look up at him, confused, he growls, "I know what you're going to say, and you don't need to say it. You don't *ever* need to say it. Because you and I both know I'll always be here for you, Wynter. Even—" He grimaces, choking on some unspoken thought, as if he can't bring himself to vocalize what we both need to hear. Tears shine in his eyes, and he swallows loudly. "Even at the end," he breathes.

I hear the pain in those four words as clearly as I sense the acceptance behind them. Ezra finally understands. Jenner *made* him understand. Or maybe he got there on his own and has merely been wearing his denial as armor.

Whichever it is, I can't help feeling a certain sense of loss, like the embers in a hearth burning out. Those embers were what remained of Ezra's lingering belief that I might actually survive this.

And now, that hope is gone. Extinguished.

As he pulls me in again, holding me close, I'm reminded of the dream-like conversation I had with his mother a few days ago.

"He won't do it. Not after everything he went through to get me back," I had said to her, adamant Ezra would never agree to what I backhandedly made him promise to do.

"He will," she had countered, *"because it's what needs to be done."*

I nod against his shirt, pressing my nose into his collarbone, as tears—fiery and unrelenting—slip down my cheeks.

He will, I think, repeating those words.

He has to.

Behind me, someone clears their throat, and I lift my head, breaking away from Ezra, even though every atom in my body screams for me not to. He keeps a hand on my back as I turn to face Jenner and Quinn, who flings a rifle he must've retrieved from one of the soldier's corpses over his shoulder. Beside him, Jenner flashes me a small doleful smile.

"We'll have to go quite far on foot from here, and the road ahead will be dangerous. I hope you're all prepared," Quinn says, his dark eyes scanning our surroundings.

Ezra's responding breath tickles my ear. "Sure you're okay with this? Your ticket to freedom is driving away as we speak. I'm sure you could still flag them down if you wanted."

We all turn, watching the shrinking form of the truck as it turns a corner at the far end of the road, disappearing from sight. As Quinn stares off into the distance, as silent and stoic as ever, I observe his drawn face, wondering if he regrets his decision to stay. When we reach the end of our current path, will he wish he'd run when he had the chance? Or has he realized what no one else seems to understand, no matter how loudly I shout it?

That if we fail to end this war, we're all as good as dead.

Scowling, Quinn jerks his gaze to mine, as if he somehow

heard my thoughts. "Do you want me to help you get to Nolan or not?"

When I nod, Ezra grabs my hand and interlaces our fingers.

Before leaving the relative safety of the now unmanned blockade, we spend a few minutes discussing our revised plan of action, pouring over a map of the Heart that Bilken gave Quinn just before we departed the safe house—in the event we needed to resort to Plan B—trying to work out which roads we should take from here to avoid any further obstructions. Although the map doesn't reveal the locations of the roadblocks standing in our way, Quinn's past experience as an Enforcer, however brief, lends us knowledge of how the State would enact martial law, including what areas they would prioritize in cutting off access to when locking down the city.

"We're currently in Zone 2, and the magistrates building is on the opposite side of Zone 1 from where we're approaching it from, so we have a bit of a trek ahead of us. We'll likely have to adapt our route as we go, and it won't be the most direct path, but we'll get there," he mutters, tracing a finger along the hologram.

My eyes dip, honing in on the side of Quinn's torso, his wound masked by the thick armor plating of his borrowed uniform. "Think you can manage the journey?" I ask, unable to hide the concern in my voice.

His eyes lock on mine, probing in their intensity. "I could ask you the same question," he murmurs.

"I'm fine," I insist. But as I say this, I catch a glimpse of my reflection in a window to the left of the roadblock, the broken pane visible over Quinn's shoulder. Eyes, mostly black, stare out from the web of cracks in the glass, calling me a liar.

"Well, you have us," Jenner says with a swift glance at Ezra. "We'll make sure you get there in one piece."

No one says another word as we pass the blockade and proceed down the road, the streets in the immediate vicinity silent, as if everyone still alive in the area is holding a collective breath. As we advance, Ezra scouts just ahead while Jenner takes up the rear, leaving Quinn and me in the middle, our steps slow with exhaustion and the aches of wounds both visible and unseen.

I peer at him out of the corner of my eye, watching as he fidgets with something small in his hand before stuffing whatever it is in his pocket.

"Is that what my mother gave you?" I ask, unable to keep the curiosity at bay any longer. Inching closer to him, I press further. "What is it?"

He cocks an inky brow, and I shrug.

"I know it's none of my business," I mutter.

"And yet, you asked anyway," he grumbles.

My face flushes at the admonishment in his tone. "You don't have to tell me—"

"Her gratitude."

At my confused expression, he fishes the object free of his pocket and extends his hand toward me.

"What is this?" Plucking the silver disc up with my fingers, I turn it over on my palm. It's a thin piece of steel carved with an ID number, but, beyond that, I'm not sure what I'm looking at.

As I hand him back the disc, he scoffs. "I 'died' when I quit the Enforcers, remember? As far as the State is concerned, I was executed the day of my arrest. This"—he pinches the minuscule piece of metal between his thumb and forefinger, holding it up to eye level—"is how the government records our deaths. At the end of our lives, this data chip is all that remains, containing every morsel of information the State deems important about us. *That* way our sins can follow us even beyond the grave."

"Our sins?" I echo, my stomach souring.

Quinn snorts. "What the State sees as sins, anyway. I prefer to call it having a conscience."

I give a weak nod. The list of my own sins is extensive, something my conscience often reminds me of. But with so many of my crimes committed on behalf of the State, I can't help wondering... What would my data chip say? Likely something about dying in service of my country, the thought of which makes my skin crawl. Especially when, by comparison, someone like Quinn, who abandoned the Enforcers in protest of mindless killing, would be seen as a criminal.

"Okay, but why keep these records?" I press. "Once a person is dead, their crimes die along with them."

He shrugs. "Not always. Not if there are indications others may have been involved. The records help pinpoint where the State should be watching for any potential...subversion."

"You mean *who* it should be watching," I correct him.

Like Jenner's family, who paid for his crimes. Or my mother and me, who were probably under surveillance because of my father. Just how long did the State watch us after his death before we were no longer considered a threat?

Shaking away that thought, I ask, "Why would my mother give that to you?"

Quinn shifts his hand so the disc is laid out flat on his palm. "Because of this." He pulls a compact device free of his belt— an ID chip scanner identical to the ones I've seen Enforcers carrying a hundred times before—then runs the red light it projects over the ID number engraved in the metal.

"*Record deleted,*" the scanner intones. "*The information stored on this data disc is no longer accessible.*"

My brow furrows. "I don't understand."

Quinn curls his fingers around the data disc, then stuffs it back inside his pocket. "Your mother… She wiped my entire identity, taking it back to a clean slate, so regardless of what happens or who ends up in power here, it'll be as if I never existed. There's no information for anyone to access about me. No pictures to cross-reference, no record of my past. *Nothing.*" As he fixes the scanner back on his belt, a rare smile tugs at his lips. "By doing that, she didn't just make me a ghost. She gave me my life back. I can start over, like I would've done outside the State if I had gone with her and Bilken as planned."

I balk at his words—at this notion that all evidence of his life and deeds are somehow gone, erased from public knowledge like an ocean tide washing away footsteps in sand.

Envy scratches at the underside of my skin.

What he's describing almost sounds like freedom.

"Is that even possible? What about your ID chip? Wouldn't it still—"

He shakes his head. "The servers linked to our mandated chips were all fried by a localized EMP in the initial attack. The State isn't tracking anyone now, not that they even could in my case. PHOENIX disabled mine as soon as I joined."

My feet stumble to an abrupt standstill. "Wait…what? The chips don't work?"

I gape at the ex-Enforcer, my body rigid with shock. This is news to me, and I wonder why my mother and Bilken didn't feel the need to tell us about this—especially when Bilken admitted to putting a tracker on me back at the bunker. Then again, that tracker was discarded when I tossed out my bodysuit, and Ezra, Jenner, and I—and now Quinn—don't have functioning ID chips anymore. The State wasn't tracking us for such news to matter.

The skin at the base of my skull tingles, and I suddenly remember the chip Richter planted there. Well, one person was tracking me, but, thankfully, he's no longer a problem.

"Nope," Quinn answers. "According to your mother, it was part of the plan to cause as much mayhem as possible during the attack and to make it harder for the State to rebuild, should it *actually* win this war."

"You say that like you don't think it will," I note. Although part of me doesn't believe it will either, another part is well aware of just how far the State is willing to go. At this point, it has nothing to lose, which only makes it more dangerous.

I wouldn't count it out of this battle just yet.

A harsh laugh breaches his lips. "Of course, it won't. And when it falls and PHOENIX or whoever the hell takes over, I can rest easy knowing they'll have nothing to link me to the State."

I consider that for a moment, turning the knowledge of everything Quinn has done since abandoning the Enforcers over in my head. Finally, I say, "Won't it be worse for you if they link you to me?"

I'm being hunted down on all sides by every enemy in our path. The State wants to use me. PHOENIX and our attackers both want me dead. If Quinn is found aiding me, surely that will put him in a far worse position than he ever was as a double agent.

A thoughtful expression darkens his face, and he nods, as if coming to some internal decision. "Not if I help you put an end to all this."

I consider him, a frown tugging down on my lips. It didn't occur to me how Ezra, Jenner, and even Quinn might be impacted by their connection to me even after I'm dead. The last thing I want is for them to survive this only to then be punished for my crimes.

One more thing to negotiate with PHOENIX, I muse.

We continue for a few minutes in silence, but with every step, what Quinn said before about my mother eats away at me until I can't stand the question burning through my thoughts any longer. I can't make sense of it—why she would honor her agreement with him if she didn't get what she wanted.

"So, my mother upheld her end of the deal...even though she walked away empty-handed?"

The ex-Enforcer might have delivered me to her as they agreed, but the rest of the plan went to shit, making everything she did over the last few years meaningless. And while none of that is Quinn's fault, my mother has never exactly struck me as the generous type.

Once again, that contemplative expression crosses his face. "Maybe she didn't," he says, then shrugs. "Maybe she got something else she wanted instead."

Something else?

My eyes widen as the realization hits me, and a soft laugh escapes as I resume my forward march, fixing my gaze on the far-stretching road ahead. My mother's actions were never defined by her need to save me from my illness or even from the State but by her desire to ease the burden of guilt on her shoulders—a weight I'm far too familiar with. And all she needed to lighten that load was one thing. The *only* thing I still had in me, even after everything, to give her.

My forgiveness.

TWENTY-ONE

THE TEMPORARY SILENCE THAT ENVELOPED us back where we parted ways with my mother is shattered completely as we progress toward the border to Zone 1. Sprinkles of gunfire pierce the musty air, seeming to come from every direction at once, and explosions light up the horizon with smoke, the black smudges visible as they rise in the sky against the rapidly dwindling daylight.

The stink of sulfur I noticed back in Zone 3 touches my nostrils again, but there's something else behind that smell— something rancid that makes my stomach roil. Although I wish I didn't know that stench, I recognize it from the battles I fought in and from the carnage I helped the State inflict on our unwilling victims.

Grimacing, I flinch away from the smell of burning flesh as if it has physically struck me.

Exhaustion weighs down my movements until every step is a struggle, but I push ahead despite the increasing pain in my skull, determination coursing through my veins like blood. Overhead, the sky shifts as we press forward, the evening light dimming until the city is swallowed by night.

Zone 2—a place I called my home for many long years—is unfamiliar as we navigate the empty streets. Quarters, not unlike the terraced house I lived in with my mother, are now more like empty husks, quiet and dark within, aside from the ones we pass that are burning. The flames, almost white in their fiery rage, eat through them as if they're made of paper.

At the sight of one house in particular—so close in appearance and color to the home I once shared with my father—I stumble, jolting to a standstill. Could it be the same quarters? I was so young when we were relocated that I can't help believing it's possible.

I inch toward the front door, led by a strange, trance-like sensation washing over me. I almost make it when a hand grabs my shoulder, stopping me dead in my tracks.

"Wynter?" Ezra asks.

Disoriented, I blink once, then again, before finally turning and meeting his gaze.

"Are you—" he begins, but he cuts off mid-sentence. His hazel eyes spring wide in horror.

My stomach seems to fold on itself as I stagger backward an unsteady step. "I…don't feel very well," I manage, resisting the sudden urge to throw up.

A trickle of wet heat slides from my eyes down my cheeks, and swaying, I shift my gaze back to the house only to find it ablaze, shining white like a beacon of light.

My brow creases in confusion. The house wasn't burning a moment ago.

"Wh—" But before I can get the full word out, a reel of images explodes inside my head like a single fatal gunshot. My legs shudder and I fall, my knees slamming hard into the asphalt, as a deranged, inhuman scream escapes me.

Around me, the windows of the quarters lining the street implode one after another with a resounding *pop-pop-pop*, the glass cascading down onto the pavement like a rain of knives. A shadowed figure shields me from the torrent, but I can't make out their face through the terrifying crimson haze in my eyes. All I'm aware of is the scream clawing at the inside of my throat, and as my shrill outcry persists, the ground quakes underfoot, fissures sprouting under my hands and knees, as if the planet is reacting to my pain.

Rough fingers clamp over my mouth, dulling my scream, as familiar voices coo my name, but I'm only half-aware of them calling to me through the violence carving a path through my brain.

Like the vision I had at the safe house, I see chaos devouring the Heart, eating through the streets like a ravenous worm, leaving only destruction and death in its wake. Soldiers gun down innocent civilians running for their lives, but the images move too quickly for me to know if the murderers are Enforcers or this new enemy merely posing as them, like the ones we encountered at the barricade earlier. The images flicker, shifting from past to future to present and back again until I'm not sure what's already happened and what atrocities are still yet to come.

"Wynter!" someone calls to me, and I latch onto that voice, using it as a tether to guide me home. The images flashing behind my lids slow in response, instead merging to create a new picture.

My heart drops when a familiar wasteland rises before me, my surroundings barren and still except for the ash and dust stirring in the breeze and the far-off figure standing with their back toward me.

I know, even at a distance, it's Ezra.

As I cross the space between us—momentarily unbound by the crippling confines of reality—he turns, meeting my gaze, his own silvered with tears. When I stop a few feet away from him, there's a split second where I swear I see the ghost of his mother standing just behind his left shoulder. But as suddenly as I thought I saw her, she's gone, and as the two of us face-off, he raises his gun—

"Wynter!" Ezra says again in my ear.

I snap my eyes open to find him leaning over me, holding me in his arms close to his chest, his features and what I can make out of our surroundings dyed red. Before us, the terraced quarters I mistook as my childhood home is no longer burning.

Maybe it never was in the first place.

My back arches against him as I let out a soft whimper. I can feel it—this disease eating away at my brain. I'm beginning to see things that aren't actually there, and it feels like I'm one vision away from exploding and taking an entire city block with me.

Strange, I note.

How I can feel so weak and so capable of total obliteration at the same time.

"I got you," Ezra murmurs, holding me close, his hand sliding away from my mouth. "You're okay—"

"I can feel it," I rasp, my voice hoarse.

"F-Feel what?" he stammers.

I touch a hand to my damp, sticky cheeks, wiping at the skin under my eyes. My fingertips pull away coated in blood.

Biting back a sob, I force out the words, "I'm running out of time. Remember—" I gasp when a sudden pressure squeezes my skull, and a moan rumbles in my chest as sweat beads along my forehead and upper lip. "Remember what you promised."

He shakes his head, his voice taking on a panicked edge. "What if I can't do it? What if I don't?"

A wheeze rattles my lungs and the taste of copper floods my mouth when I cough. "Then we all die," I breathe once the fit passes. "And I don't—" The lump in my throat distorts the words, and I let out a shaky breath before trying again. "I don't want that, Ezra. Please."

A tear dashes from his left eye as he tugs me closer, gripping my body so tightly it hurts. "There's still time," he whispers in my ear.

I swallow, biting back a laugh. Of course, he would utter the very words that keep haunting me. *Is* there still time? I'm starting to think maybe there isn't and the belief that's pushed me this far is wrong.

There's still time, Rai echoes in my head, as if to tell me not to lose hope.

I grit my teeth. *You've made it this far, Wynter.* If I give up now, then everything we've done, all the sacrifices we've endured to get to this point, would be meaningless. I can't give up. Not now.

Not ever.

"Help me up," I beg, gripping Ezra's hand.

He considers me for a few seconds then nods, looping his arm behind my back, and as he climbs to his feet, he brings me up with him, using his weight to support my own. It's only once I'm upright again that I finally notice Jenner and Quinn. Jenner stands close on my other side, ready to step in if needed, while Quinn keeps his distance, fear and uncertainty teeming in the charcoal pits of his eyes.

"I'm okay," I assure them as I wipe my face clean on my sleeve, clearing my gaze. "Let's keep moving."

It takes longer to reach Zone 1 than any of us would like, our advance proceeding at a much slower rate and getting slower by the minute as my symptoms worsen. Ezra and Jenner take turns acting as my crutch and bearing the brunt of my weight, even going so far as to carry me in the moments when I can't carry myself, my vision sporadically clouded by incomprehensible hallucinations of past and future overlaid on our present surroundings, blinding me to our current path.

We stop sparingly and only when needed, although the chaos in Zone 1 makes those pit stops frequent. The anarchy I witnessed playing out in my head is a real stain on the Heart now, painting every street we walk in red. We often find ourselves having to hide from passing patrols to avoid detection—to avoid us ending up just as dead.

The acrid stench of smoke and death is a cloying, almost tangible presence in the air, choking my throat and lungs the closer we get to the center of the city. The devastation seems so final, so irreversible, that part of me worries there isn't anything we can do to change it.

There's still time, Rai reminds me, her voice inescapable, like a beating pulse in my ear.

It takes all the lingering strength I possess to believe that.

The nearer we get to the magistrates building, the harder it is to steer clear of the mayhem, and with every breath, I fear I won't have the strength in me to act—to protect us if it comes to that. Ezra, sensing my exhaustion, corrals our group into an abandoned health center, the glass front doors broken by large chunks of shrapnel, offering us uninhibited entry.

"Let's rest here for a minute," he says, depositing me carefully on the gray waiting room sofa. When I wince on impact, he drops to his knees before me, taking my face in his hands. "Just a bit longer. We're almost there," he says before brushing a chaste kiss across my lips.

Jenner searches the office and adjacent exam room, running back into the lounge after a moment with a few bottles of water, the first of which he extends to me before sinking down onto the sofa. I drink the liquid down greedily as Quinn props the map of the Heart—specifically Zone 1—on the low table between us.

When the hologram manifests, glowing blue in the shadowed room, he points to an intersection of roads not far from our location.

"We're close. Less than two miles, barring any unforeseen obstacles." A pensive scowl warps his face, and his eyes dart to mine. "Once we get there, that's it. You know that, right? No more dodging patrols. No more hiding in side streets. The second they spot us, we'll be seen as the enemy. What's to say they won't think you're there to attack them?"

I shrug, even though the movement makes my skull ache. "That's a chance I'll have to take."

"So, what's the plan?" Jenner asks. "We stroll up to the magistrates building and surrender? Remind me again why we don't just contact Nolan on his communicator and handle this from a safe distance? Also, how do we even know all the Heads will be together? Seems kind of risky for PHOENIX to have all their leaders convened in the middle of a war zone."

"It's not a risk if they think they'll win," I mutter.

Ezra rubs a hand across his chin, blowing out a slow breath through his nose. "This is the first time PHOENIX has initiated an all-out offensive, and to get everyone on board with the plan, the Heads would've needed to display a united front, which would've meant throwing themselves into the fray. If they don't win here, they won't win at all. It was everyone and everything or nothing. As for why we can't just call Nolan, contacting him takes away the element of surprise, and we need the other Heads there when we talk to him so we can expose the part he played in this attack. The easiest way to get in front of both and kill two birds with one stone is to turn up unannounced, even if that means surrendering."

Quinn snorts. "If we surrender, they'll take our guns, and I guarantee someone will put a bullet in our heads before we even get to Nolan."

The thought of that happening ignites an unexpected fire of adrenaline within me. "I won't let that happen," I growl.

My heart races like a hummingbird trapped in my ribcage. Maybe I do still have the strength in me for this, after all.

Ezra's hand grips my shoulder, and I instantly go still, as if his touch has smothered the flames of my rage. "Wynter, you can't fight everyone," he chides. "You can barely even stand."

My eyes snap up to his, determined. "I won't hesitate to protect you. All of you," I add, looking at Jenner and Quinn.

Jenner leans forward, planting his elbows on his knees. "Let's hope it doesn't come to that and that the Heads will hear us out."

We don't drag out our stay at the health center any longer than we need to, only remaining long enough to hydrate, catch our breath, and plot the final part of our path. When we leave, we go out the back entrance of the building and stick to the alleys and side roads, staying as far away from the sounds of gunfire and screaming as we're able to.

It's well into the early morning hours by the time we reach the magistrates building, its silhouette a towering, visible presence even against the black clouds behind it. Unlike the last time we were here when the plaza was empty, this time, the open stretch of cobbled ground is swarmed with people waiting to get into the building.

Citizens seeking shelter from the attack, I realize.

For a while, we loiter out of sight in a narrow backstreet offering an unobscured view of the plaza. Jenner and Quinn hang to one side of the alley while Ezra and I keep close on the other, his arm around my waist at all times to steady me.

"Do we just join the crowd and try to pass ourselves off as refugees?" Jenner whispers.

Quinn sighs, then retorts, "That's unlikely to work and it wouldn't get us anywhere close to the Heads. Besides, it doesn't look like that line is moving quickly, if at all."

I trail my eyes over the maelstrom of bodies, flinching when the pandemonium from the vision I had at the safe house flickers on top of the scene, fading in and out like a mirage. Flames lick across the massive structure before vanishing, as if nothing more than a temporary figment of my imagination.

Shaking my head to clear it, I say, "The fastest way to reach Nolan will be through one of his lackeys. Or by making a big enough scene."

"Option A," Ezra deadpans. "Making a scene might draw attention we don't want."

Slumping back against his chest, I nod, acknowledging that

he's right. If the enemy discovers my location and comes for me, then whatever hope I had of using the Heads to barter an end to this war will be forfeit. We need to get in front of Nolan with as little fanfare and fuss as possible.

And soon.

Quinn wipes a dew of sweat from his brow before pointing to the far end of the plaza, just past the densest part of the crowd. "The soldiers not blocking the entrance to stop these people from overrunning the building will be on rotation, doing patrols around the immediate area." He draws a large circle in the air with his finger, indicating where he means. "We just need to find one of those sentries and hope they don't shoot us."

Ezra lets out a soft laugh that wafts the hair against the back of my neck. "I know just the guy."

Before I'm even aware of what's happening, Ezra is retracting his arm from around me and, after propping me against the wall to ensure I won't fall over, runs off into the night toward a tall figure skirting the edge of the large mob. All I can see clearly about the vague man in the distance is the rifle he carries.

My heart jumps into my throat, pushing a terrified cry from my lips.

"Ezra!" I shout before slapping a hand over my mouth. Fear is a writhing entity inside me as I silently scream for him to come back.

"Where the *hell* is he going?" Quinn snarls from the other side of the alley, looking as conflicted as I feel.

Beside him, Jenner just cocks his head, his bright blue eyes narrowing. "Wait...is that?"

"Duke!" Ezra calls out.

The hulking man pivots at the sound of his name, and

when he turns, his face becomes a degree or two clearer in the minimal light smeared across the plaza. At the sight of the figure running toward him, he raises his gun, but recognition stills his hand.

"Ezra?" Duke lowers his weapon and races forward, meeting Ezra halfway, slowing to a stop less than twenty feet from where I remain in the shadows, exhaustion gluing my weak body to the wall.

To my right, Jenner seems to explode out of the alleyway, and when Duke's gaze tracks the movement, he gasps.

"Holy shit, Jenner." His eyes, almost black in the darkness, dance back and forth between his two friends. "When the transmission cut off, I didn't know what to think," he says, pulling them each in for a hug. "Gotta admit, I panicked. Thought maybe you guys were dead."

"Came close a couple of times," I hear Jenner say, "but we're still kickin'."

"More like lucky, you son of a bitch," Duke retorts with a gruff laugh.

"Who is that?" Quinn hisses at me across the small side road.

I only met Duke once and we didn't exchange a single word at the time, but he was there the night we lost Rai. *Here,* I correct myself with a sullen glance past him at the magistrates building. He shared in the grief we all felt in the tunnels; he *knows* what we went through that night. And he was the one Jenner tried to contact for help from the bunker when we were cornered by Nolan.

He's older than I remember him seeming in the darkness of the tunnels under the city—his mid-thirties, maybe older, weathered by the hardships of underground survival—and while I don't know much else about the man besides his name, there's a kind sincerity radiating from him as he speaks with Ezra and Jenner that lets me believe, lets me *hope*, we can trust him.

"A friend," is all I say in response.

Quinn grunts, either in disapproval or acknowledgment. I'm not quite sure which.

"Listen," Duke mutters to Ezra and Jenner, "it's good to see you both and I'm relieved as shit you're okay, but everyone's on high alert…and we have our orders. Specifically about what we're meant to do if we see you. If they find you here—"

Duke stops short when his gaze catches mine, and he gawks at me, his mouth hanging wide, as if he can't believe what he's seeing.

Clapping him on the shoulder, Jenner steers Duke toward the shadowed recess of the alley. The large man lumbers along obediently, never once tearing his eyes from mine.

"What have you heard about us, exactly?" Jenner asks once we're all crowded in the narrow side road, out of sight of everyone in the plaza and—more importantly—any passing patrols.

Duke doesn't respond at first, too shell-shocked by my presence to speak. Or maybe it's my appearance that has him lost for words, just like he was that night in the tunnels under Zone 1 when he looked at me in a similar manner. If that's what's troubling him, I wouldn't blame him for feeling unnerved. I can only imagine what I must look like right now.

Finally, he shakes his head and grumbles under his breath, "I've heard a lot of shit, man."

"Give us the abridged version," Ezra presses.

Duke white-knuckles his rifle as he peers over his shoulder, probably checking for any sign of the next patrol amid the nearby crowd. After scanning our surroundings for a moment, he turns back to face us. "All right, so word around the rumor mill is *this one*"—he jerks his chin toward me—"went insane and tried to murder Nolan…and that you two then helped her escape." Duke glances between Ezra and Jenner.

"Well, they got it half right," Ezra mutters.

"Everyone's callin' you traitors, sayin' you've been brainwashed by the State or some shit. It's *serious*," Duke growls when Jenner scoffs. "Our instructions are shoot to kill upon sightin'."

Jenner snorts. "Shoot to kill? What are you, Enforcers now?"

"Wait," Ezra says, confusion creasing his brow. "Why has Nolan issued shoot to kill orders if he thinks we're already dead?"

Jenner considers this question, then shrugs. "Maybe he knows we're alive?" Tilting his head in Quinn's direction, he adds, "Which means Nolan's also gonna know you betrayed him."

The ex-Enforcer rolls his eyes. "If he doesn't, I think he'll figure that out the moment we reveal ourselves to him."

Recalling the vision I had of Nolan back at the safe house, I shake my head, interjecting, "He doesn't know we're alive."

Jenner cocks an ebony eyebrow at me. "How do you know?"

"I saw it," I answer simply. "Believe me, he doesn't know." I glance past Duke toward the magistrates building, remembering the flames that consumed it in my vision—or *will* consume it…at some point. Considering the structure isn't currently burning, I can only assume what I witnessed within hasn't happened. "Not yet, anyway," I mutter.

Dread is an icy trickle down my spine. That vision could play out at any moment. The attack I saw could happen the second we step foot in the building with us all trapped inside. I could be leading the only two people I love straight to their deaths if we proceed, and yet…what other choice do I have?

All I can hope now is that we reach Nolan first and finally prove the future can be changed.

Once again, I picture the words I saw light up across Nolan's communicator after he spoke to our attackers, feeling their presence like a weight on my skin.

Proof or no peace.

This is the only way, I remind myself.

"Why would Nolan think you're dead?" Duke asks, peering at each of us, his expression perplexed. His deep voice drags me out of my thoughts.

"Because he ordered our executions," Ezra says bluntly.

"Maybe that's precisely why everyone in PHOENIX still thinks you're alive," Quinn suggests, glancing between us.

I frown at him. "What do you mean?"

The ex-Enforcer gives me a condescending look. "Think about it. Nolan has used this situation to establish himself as some sort of benevolent leader—"

"A savior," I whisper breathlessly, reciting Nolan's words from the broadcast in my head. Once again, I hear how he appealed to the masses with promises of security and peace, offering a better world where the State no longer exists.

"He has always liked to keep his hands clean," Ezra muses. "Better to let someone else do the dirty work so he always seems like the good guy."

Jenner crosses one arm over his chest and drums the fingertips of his other hand against his chin. "Looking at it that way, he must think our executions would somehow tarnish his image."

"And deter people from siding with him," I murmur.

Quinn nods. "Which is exactly what would happen. I mean, would *you* seek shelter with a man who ordered the executions of two of his own and an unarmed hostage?"

Ezra huffs out an incredulous breath. "I'd hardly call Wynter unarmed."

Quinn raises one shoulder, then lets it fall again in a dismissive gesture. "Me neither, but almost no one at that bunker saw her use her power. Come to think of it, few have outside the Enforcer units. And she knew people in PHOENIX before, right? People who saw how sick she was?" An *I'm just saying* look crosses his face. "Remember, it only takes one person to sow a seed of doubt. Besides,"—he lowers his voice—"if word got out he was playing judge and jury, the DSD comparisons would be unavoidable."

"So, he lied and turned us into the bad guys, and now, everyone thinks we're just running amok." Clenching his jaw, Jenner slams the side of his fist against the brick wall to my left. "This is *bullshit*. We aren't brainwashed traitors. Hell, the real traitor here is Nolan. Did you know he planned all this?" Peering at Duke, he waves an arm, gesturing vaguely all around us.

Duke blinks in confusion, attempting to follow Jenner's erratic movements. "What?"

"It's true," Quinn asserts, his tone grave, still not bothering to introduce himself to Duke. "This attack is only happening because of a deal he made to push the State out of power. A deal he used to coerce the other Heads into giving him full control of PHOENIX."

The broad, muscled man slings his rifle over his shoulder before raising his hands, palms out. "Whoa, whoa, wait a minute. Everyone is sayin' this happened because of *you*."

Once again, his wide eyes shift to mine.

"Also true," I admit, drawing everyone's gaze.

With a slow, calming breath, I push away from the wall, and Ezra's hand shoots out, his fingertips pressing against my waist to steady me. Wrapping my hand around his forearm, I look over at the magistrates building and at this chaos I helped to cause.

"This attack is retaliation for everything I was forced to do for the DSD, but that's only half of it," I explain. "The other half is down to the deal Nolan made with these people—"

"Whoever the hell they are," Jenner grumbles under his breath.

I pause only long enough to lick my dried lips. "In return for helping him overthrow the State, Nolan agreed to a set of demands, which included destroying the DSD's weapon. But he trusted the wrong person to do the job, and now, the ceasefire is at jeopardy without proof of my death."

My eyes flash to Quinn, then quickly look away. I don't bother explaining to Duke that the "wrong person" in question is currently standing here with us.

"Okay." Duke runs a hand back and forth over his head, the blond hair there so closely cropped to his skull that, from some angles, he almost looks bald. "Okay," he says again, looking at Ezra now. "Tell me everythin'. Start at the beginnin'."

TWENTY-TWO

"SHIT," IS ALL DUKE CAN manage once Ezra finishes relaying the events that led us here, beginning with my extraction. At that part, he had gaped at Jenner in awe, as if he couldn't quite believe his friend had not only infiltrated a State airfield but that he had managed to bring down one of its helicopters and live to tell the tale.

But his focus on Jenner is fleeting, and as Ezra continues, I often catch Duke's eyes on my face, their depths brimming with an apprehension that makes me wonder if he'll actually help us.

"You know how crazy this all sounds, right?" he asks a minute or two after Ezra falls silent.

My pulse trips at his skeptical tone, but I find myself unsurprised by it. Of course, it sounds crazy. Unfortunately, that doesn't make our story any less true. Or our situation any less dire.

"It's all true," Jenner counters, as if voicing my thoughts, his tone barely above a growl.

"Oh, I don't doubt it," Duke says. "Hell, it actually explains a lot."

Quinn cocks a dubious brow. "Like what?"

Duke scoffs. "Like the fact that all our transmissions have gone completely ignored."

My fingers tighten around Ezra's forearm. "Transmissions?"

Glancing at me again, the burly man nods. "Since the Heads established themselves in the magistrates buildin', they've been puttin' out transmissions every hour to every possible frequency, tryin' to initiate a ceasefire. Between those and Nolan's very public declaration of war on the State, there's no way these assholes attackin' the Heart haven't heard us by now."

"Are we sure the State isn't jamming the signal?" Jenner asks.

Across from me, Quinn shakes his head. "Unlikely." Pulling the palm-sized device from his belt, he turns on the hologram map we used to get here, his hooded eyes following the glowing lines hovering over his hand for a moment before shutting it off again. "If they were, then GPS would be affected as well. It wouldn't be just communicators." He looks at Duke. "I'm assuming PHOENIX hasn't had any issues with theirs?"

Duke, who stands at least half a foot taller than Quinn, meets the ex-Enforcer's questioning gaze. "Nope. Everythin's been working fine. It's more like the bastards just aren't listenin'."

"And they won't," I mutter under my breath. "Not until they know I'm dead."

A fraught silence fills the backstreet at my words—only broken by the ominous murmuring of the crowd—and for a while, no one says anything else, the tension permeating the air speaking for us. I loosen my grip on Ezra's arm, but as I pull away, he grabs my hand, interlacing our fingers. Refusing to let go.

Duke stares at our conjoined hands for all of five seconds before glancing upward, narrowing his muddy brown eyes on my face. "So, your plan is to do what, exactly?" he asks, the slight waver in his voice giving away his unease.

My lips press into a determined scowl, and I say, shoulders tensing, "To make them listen."

Once again, that uncomfortable hush floods the alley, and a long moment passes before anyone dares to break it. Nodding, Duke lets out a loud breath, the husky sound caught somewhere between a sigh and a groan.

"Okay," he murmurs, peering between me and Ezra. "You've convinced me. What can I do to help?"

"We need to speak with the Heads," Jenner answers.

"And with Nolan," I add reluctantly.

While I want to expose his crimes—to tear him apart and make him pay for being willing to sacrifice an entire city—I'm not foolish enough to deny we still need him. Among the Heads, he's the only one who can make direct contact with our attackers and negotiate terms with them that will actually end this merciless assault on the Heart. No number of blind transmissions will sway them, but if Nolan reaches out and says he has me in custody…

That he's willing to trade my life for peace—

Duke exhales again, scratching his chin. "I can take you to Nolan, but after that…" He hesitates, his eyes flitting from my face to Ezra's, then to Jenner's, and finally, to Quinn's. "There won't be anythin' more I can do, especially if the other Heads take his side."

Ezra's palm is sweaty as his fingers clench a little tighter around mine. "We understand. Just get us in front of them."

Unloading the rifle from his shoulder, Duke grips his weapon in both hands and turns his back toward us, facing the plaza and the sea of bodies congregated before the magistrates building. Then, taking a step out of the shadowed alley, he says in a gruff voice, "Follow me."

We all tail Duke's hulking frame without question, my stomach dipping when we walk out into the open despite the increasing cover of night. I've never felt so exposed, and with every step we take across the plaza, I know there can be no turning back.

The faint buzz of frantic voices and weeping grows louder as we approach the dense throng ahead, the sinister din forcing me to cast off any lingering trace of doubt and fear still clinging to me like sweat on skin. There's no room for either anymore, only courage.

And yet, although I've stood against entire armies alone, I feel anything *but* brave as we carve a path through the crowd, balking under the brush of curious eyes observing my every move.

Despite the early hour, no one is asleep, the noise in the city impossible to tune out. Faces dirty with the residue of ash and smoke surround me on every side, like a sea of judgment ready to rise up and drown me. A shudder crawls up my spine, and I'm struck by the overwhelming urge to shy away from those piercing gazes—to bury my face in Ezra's chest and squeeze my eyes shut to hide from their scrutiny. But I don't let myself. Their suffering is my fault. *I* caused this.

And I deserve the weight of every glare focused on me, even if I'm only imagining them.

"All these people…" A lump sits heavy in my throat. Clearing it with a quiet cough, I force out, "Did they come here seeking shelter from the attack?"

Ezra must hear the tremor in my voice because he releases my hand and slides his arm around my hip, pulling me close to his side. "Why haven't they been moved underground yet?" he asks, his words equally soft. "If this building is hit, they'll—"

Duke flashes a warning look over his shoulder, as if to tell Ezra to watch what he says, before slowing his pace until he's barely keeping two steps ahead of us.

"It's madness out there," he murmurs. "Enforcers are prowlin' the streets, people are dying…" He tsks, shaking his head. "We've been evacuatin' as many areas as we can, but honestly, I don't think any of us anticipated it being this bad. We're movin' them underground, it's just been slow-goin'. Every time we relocate a group, another ten times the size shows up on our doorstep. We can't keep up." He gestures to the surrounding horde, proving his point.

"It isn't safe for them here," Ezra breathes.

"No," Duke agrees, "it isn't. But if we tried to tell them that, considerin' what the rest of the Heart is like right now, would they believe it? Are they in any more danger here than they would be elsewhere in the city?" He shrugs. "Are any of the zones even safe anymore?"

My teeth sink into my bottom lip, biting hard enough to draw blood.

Probably not.

Nowhere in the State—or in this world—will be safe until I'm dead.

Snorting, Duke rubs a hand across his shaved head. "It's actually too bad the outer cities aren't real. Then we'd have someplace to escape to."

My chest constricts, and the air rips from my lungs as my eyes flash to the back of his head. "What?"

Disbelief threatens to suffocate me. What does he mean the

outer cities aren't real? That can't be true...

Can it?

All my life, I've been raised to believe there are eight other massive cities just like the Heart—nine total that make up our country, demonstrating the extensive reach of the State. The Heart was always the grandest, the capital, but it was never alone in its power.

Yet, if what Duke is suggesting is true, that means the State is so much smaller than I ever imagined, isolated to just this one city—this walled-in metropolis everyone is forbidden from leaving.

Throughout our years of education, we were always taught that certain high-ranking officials and, sometimes, Enforcers could travel to the other cities with special permission, for purposes we were unaware of. But...have I actually seen that happen?

Before my own involvement in this conflict, did I ever even see a helicopter leave this city?

No, I realize, and my stomach turns as it registers just how much I've been lied to. And not just about the limits of the State's borders but the actual reasoning behind this whole war.

A war the State only started once they had me to use as a weapon.

Because its army isn't as big as it wants people to think.

My alarmed gaze swings upward, locking on Ezra, whose face is unnervingly composed.

"You knew?" I hiss, my tone accusatory. It takes a moment to collect my thoughts enough to frame the rest of my question. "You knew the outer cities aren't real and you never thought to mention it?"

A sheepish look crosses his face, his cheeks pinking a little as his hazel eyes snap to mine. "I didn't mention it because it changed absolutely nothing about our situation. The outer cities were never going to help us, so it wasn't relevant. But yeah," he admits. "We've known for a while now. For over two years, actually," he adds, his words weighted.

Two years?

I gape at Ezra, stunned, trying to discern his meaning when the answer strikes me.

"Bilken," I mutter.

This time, when Ezra speaks, his expression is sullen. "Why else do you think Nolan got it in his head that he can actually overthrow the State?"

I blanch, a staggering nausea hitting me. "Because Bilken told him it's only one city."

Why did my mother fail to mention this when she was disclosing the details of her past to us? Because it wasn't relevant, like Ezra said? Or maybe she didn't see the point since, as members of PHOENIX, he, Jenner, and Quinn were already well aware of the truth. Maybe, she assumed I was, too.

I roll this concept around in my head, going back through everything my mother told us about her life in the early days of the State. When she said she and Bilken weren't from the Heart, she didn't mean they were from one of the other cities in the State... They were from a whole different part of the world. Which also means the people who founded our so-called country weren't merely part of an underground political movement that rose to power...

They were conquerors, and they sealed us in this city as if it was a cage.

Ezra nods. "Whatever this country was before, the State

infiltrated it piece by piece and tore it apart from within until only the Heart was left standing."

My eyes widen as I recall the content of my father's journal entries. The rumors he heard. The reason no one around him seemed to blink an eye when the State seized power…

"The State didn't begin with the Heart," Ezra continues. "It just ended here."

In front of us, Duke lets out a harsh laugh. "Well, that certainly seems to be the case now."

Duke leads us around to the side of the building, and there's a rumble somewhere in the distance behind us as we make our way through the rest of the densely packed crowd. Thunder, maybe. An incoming storm.

Or a sign of what's to come.

I shake off that thought as we pass several heavily guarded doors before approaching what I instantly recognize to be the same entrance we used to gain access to the premises the last time we were here. The night of our mission to meet Bilken, before we knew of his role in all this. The mob is thinner around here—most of the refugees have gathered back by the front of the building—and there's only one guard stationed at the door, with no other wandering patrols in sight.

Not yet, at least, I muse.

As Duke escorts us to the door, his agitation is almost palpable, like a rancid odor in the air. His unease does nothing to ease my own dread, and I find myself leaning in closer to Ezra, whose arm instinctively tightens around me.

"It's okay," he whispers in my ear. "Just a little bit farther."

At our approach, the PHOENIX member stationed at the entrance—a young man, who doesn't look to be much older than me—straightens and repositions his grip on the rifle he's holding. Alarm burns behind his warm ocher eyes, which narrow, locking on Duke in confusion.

Face scrunching in surprise, he calls out, "Aren't you supposed to be on perimeter patrol, Masterson?"

Before my eyes, Duke seems to grow in size—his chest puffing out, as if to block our presence behind him—as he closes the distance to the younger man, his own weapon in hand. "I need to see the Heads," he barks back. "It's urgent."

The guard scoffs, then averts his gaze from Duke, observing the rest of us one at a time, blatantly searching for a threat in our group. "They're in a meeting. Besides, kinda late for a house call, don't you thin—" he says, but then cuts off abruptly, his attention fixed on my face. "Holy shit." He takes an uncertain step back. "Is that...?"

"Like I said..." Duke peers over his shoulder at me, then looks back at the guard and repeats, "It's urgent."

The color drains from the man's face as he fumbles his rifle, nearly dropping the gun to the ground. Catching it, he raises the barrel, taking aim at his intended target. At me. "S-Stay back. Stay right where you are."

Shifting the full breadth of his muscled body in front of me, Duke reaches out and grabs the barrel of the man's gun. "Lower your weapon," he snarls.

I blink at Duke's large back in surprise. He might be friends with Ezra and Jenner, but he doesn't know me. He owes me no loyalty, and I certainly never expected for him to put himself between me and a bullet.

"Don't—" I start to say, but the guard's frantic voice overshadows my own.

"Our orders are shoot to kill!"

"You *really* don't want to do that," Jenner insists, stepping forward until he's nearly shoulder to shoulder with Duke.

No, you don't, I add in my head. *Please, just let us pass.*

Duke shoves the guard's rifle downward until the muzzle is safely pointed toward the ground. "I know what our orders are, but they have information the Heads *need* to hear." Then, in a low voice, he says, "She'll kill you before you can even pull that trigger. Do you want to die for this?"

The man falters back another step, and in the minimal space between Duke and Jenner where they stand side by side, I glimpse him shaking his head.

"W-Weapons," he chokes out after a moment. "You can't go in with your weapons."

Heaving a resigned sigh, Duke surrenders his rifle, handing it to the guard. "Fine." He then gestures for us to do the same. "You'll have to leave them here," he instructs, staring pointedly at Ezra's hand where it hovers over the gun on his belt.

Ezra and I exchange a quick look, and I can see my own worries reflected clearly in his conflicted gaze. Going up against the Heads defenseless is a risk. And if something goes wrong and I can't protect them—

Ezra's sharp retort interrupts my thoughts. "I really hope you know what you're doing," he grumbles, turning over his pistol.

The muscles in my stomach constrict as I watch the gun slip from his fingers before begrudgingly following suit, tugging the farewell present my mother gave me free of my waistband and handing it to the soldier. Although useless in so many ways, that gun was her small sentiment of love and protection when nothing in this world can save me. And now, it's gone, like everything else will be if I don't get to Nolan.

That makes two of us.

Once everyone has relinquished their weapons, the guard steps to the side of the doorway, hesitantly granting us entry into the building. Duke goes in first, leading the way, and although the man doesn't attempt to deter us again when Ezra and I move to follow, his eyes burn their distrust into my face and then my back as I walk past.

Whatever momentary concern I have that the guard will try to shoot me once my back is turned is forgotten as soon as I step over the threshold. I had assumed all the refugees were being kept outside in the plaza for some inane reason, like to keep them separate from the Heads—who, if they're anything like Nolan, likely prioritize their own safety over that of the citizens seeking their help. What I hadn't expected was the grim reality before me.

On both sides of the hallway, survivors line the walls as far as the eye can see, some injured but conscious and others half-dead, if not already all the way there. One woman sits slumped under the sill of a bay window, her dark head of hair flopped forward, the strands hanging limp, obscuring my view of her face. Beside the woman, a young child shakes her by the shoulder, crying for her to wake up.

"Mother," the girl whimpers, tears streaking her filthy cheeks, and in her terrified gaze, I see myself.

"They…" My voice breaks, and I swallow a sob.

"Just keep walking," Ezra breathes against my neck, one hand against my lower back, gently nudging me forward.

"This is…" Jenner whispers behind us, but he doesn't finish the thought, as lost for words as I am.

"We brought in as many of the injured as we could," Duke says, keeping his eyes turned ahead. "But like I said, they just keep comin'."

Just keep coming…

Tears filter in from the edges of my vision, then expand, blurring the path ahead. There are too many people to help and not enough people to help them. Or enough time.

Time. The thought is like a weed taking root in my brain. It grows regardless of what I do, even if I try to starve it.

There isn't enough time.

Sweat breaks out across my skin, and a long moment passes before I realize I've stopped walking. Somewhere, a distant voice calls to me, but I can't see who it belongs to. All I'm aware of is the crowded hallway, which seems to grow longer, extending before me indefinitely, with no visible end in sight.

Static distorts my surroundings as it has so many times before, but in the uninterrupted stretches of stillness, I see the weary faces congesting the corridor. Every last one glares at me—even the ones that were dead, alive again in their hatred—their unblinking eyes declaring that I am to blame for this.

I stagger forward a step as an overwhelming heat flushes through me, perspiration trickling down the sides of my face, neck, and back. The warmth seems to blister my flesh, my body consumed by invisible flames.

Static again. The hallway warps, and in the flickers, I glimpse the future awaiting us. It blankets itself on top of the present, warning of its outcome. Devastating, unavoidable…

And immediate.

A harrowing cry wrenches open my mouth, but the sound breaching my lips is swallowed by the volatile fire now raging around me.

"Wynter?" that faint voice calls again.

Hands grip my shoulders and shake me roughly, yanking me out of the vision like a lifeline pulling me from under a wave. When I blink, my face is turned toward the ceiling, my jaw hanging wide, frozen mid-scream.

A terrified breath escapes me as I lower my head, finally noticing Ezra, who stands before me, his hands on my arms, his fingernails digging into my skin through my jacket. Tears burn lines down the sides of my face, and the metallic taste of blood coats my lips, which I lick to ease the dryness there.

"Wynter?" Ezra says once more, and the uncertainty in his voice mirrors the unrelenting panic racing through me.

Just as I feared…

Trembling, I inch backward out of his grasp, my misted gaze sliding to the nearest window. Although the panes are coated with ash, hiding the city beyond from view, I can sense the incoming danger behind the glass.

My heart sinks. I glance back at Ezra, who stares at me, expectant, a confused fear in his eyes. And as one thought plays through my head in a tortuous loop, my lips hurry to shape another.

We're too late.

"Run."

TWENTY-THREE

SMOKE BURNS MY NOSTRILS AND throat, and I cough on reflex, spitting blood onto the hard wooden floorboards. Jagged glass shards cut into my palms as I push myself upright, my arms shaking under the weight of my aching body, which lies prostrate in the middle of the sweltering corridor. Every inch of me hurts, and the building pressure in my head only adds to my disorientation.

A shrill ringing reverberates deep in my ears, and my vision is cloudy as I lift my head, squinting through the rippling waves of heat and potent smog filling the hallway. I cough again. All I can make out around me are indistinct silhouettes.

The injured refugees, I realize. Some are screaming. Some are attempting to flee. Others no longer move at all.

Panic digs its talons into my fracturing sanity, and I scramble to my feet, my head spinning as I scour my surroundings for Ezra. I barely had time to tell him to run before the explosion hit behind us. The blast projected me several feet forward from where I was standing before, but he was directly in front of me when that happened. He should be here.

Why isn't he here?

I brush the sweaty hair away from my forehead, wincing when my fingertips graze a deep gash near my temple. As I check the extent of the damage, something sharp pokes my thumb. Clenching my teeth, I pull a small piece of glass free of my skin. I glance at the bloodied fragment then drop it to the ground, my eyes shifting to what remains of the windows lining the wall to my left. The panes in every last one are shattered, giving me an unobscured view of the madness outside.

Like in the vision I had at the safe house, Enforcers storm the plaza, gunning down the unarmed civilians whose only crime was seeking shelter with PHOENIX, while gunfire and small-target bombs rain down from above, turning this part of Zone 1 into a battlefield. Enemy aircraft whirr overhead, but I can't see them through the black smoke shrouding the air.

I inch backward, a ragged breath parting my lips as I clamp a shaking hand over my mouth. The attack came out of nowhere, even though I knew it would inevitably come. Death and destruction follow me wherever I go. I was foolish to think we could outrun fate.

And now, everyone here is paying the price.

Once again, I search the hallway for Ezra, desperation igniting a fire in my bloodstream that sets my whole body ablaze.

"Ezra!" I shout, turning in circles.

The hazy corridor blurs, and my stomach lurches as the ringing and pressure in my skull intensify in tandem. Somewhere in the distance, I hear the distinct sound of gunfire, but I don't know if it's coming from outside or approaching from the far end of the hallway.

I stumble forward in the direction we were heading before, staggering a few steps to the left. I squint again. More screaming.

Then gunfire again—closer this time.

My pulse skitters under my skin, and I swallow, sneering at the acrid taste of smoke on my tongue.

"Ezra! Duke!"

No response. I look over my shoulder, searching the path behind me for the others, but the smoke is so thick, it's like a tangible wall.

"Jenner! Quinn!" I cry out, my voice breaking as another hacking cough racks my lungs.

Sweat drips down my face as I look forward again, the hallway painted with orange patches of fire. Everywhere I turn, smoke or flame blocks my path.

I sway, light-headed, and my shoulder collides with the wall, my elbow brushing against the protruding remains of a window, the serrated edge tearing a hole in the arm of my jacket. Wheezing, I grip the broken frame for support, ignoring the searing cut of glass in my palms.

We're all going to die here and it's my fault.

"Jenner," I whimper. "Ezra…"

"Wynter!" a frantic voice shouts from somewhere behind me.

Blinking slowly, I veer my gaze to the left, toward the growing wall of smoke, when the voice shouts again.

"Wynter! Ezra!"

My heart trips as recognition sharpens my senses. "Quinn?"

Pushing away from the window, I trudge through the hallway, going back in the direction we came from, even though every logical part of my brain is telling me to run away from the smoke and flames instead of into them. Pressing my mouth and nose into the crook of my elbow, I push on toward the blaze, my eyes watering from the heat and fumes.

"Quinn!" My voice is hoarse from the tainted air and my sleeve muffles his name. I try again. "Quinn! Where are you?"

"Wynter! Over here!"

A burst of adrenaline surges through my body, and without sparing a second thought for the danger, I charge ahead, sidestepping the flames.

It takes less than ten seconds to find them, the tears clearing from my eyes just enough for me to spot Quinn kneeling in front of a broken ceiling beam, trying to lift its weight off the man pinned to the floor underneath it.

"Where's Jenner?" I ask as I race forward, squatting and planting my hands on the beam, my nails digging into the wood. My stomach clenches when I spare a glance at the injured man on the floor below us, taking in his inky sable hair, his bruised jaw and cheeks blackened with soot, and his wide blue eyes, which lock on me, freezing the blood in my veins.

"Pre...sent," Jenner says, his voice strained.

His name is a petrified breath on my lips.

"Help me!" Quinn pleads as he shifts position, propping his back against the debris. Blood trickles from a cut near his hairline and seeps through the side of his uniform, where he's probably burst his stitches trying to lift the beam on his own. Despite still suffering from his own wound, he puts all his strength into the task, but even with our combined efforts, the wood doesn't budge.

The beam snaps at one end, bringing its full weight down on Jenner's chest, stirring a panic within me that makes me want to rip the flesh from my bones. If I don't do something, he'll die.

"Get out... Go... Leave me...here..." Each word is a struggle as Jenner gasps to breathe.

He's running out of time.

"Move," I command when Quinn lets out a howl of frustration. If he keeps this up, he'll die here, too. "Move!" I bark again, grabbing him by the shoulder and pulling him away from the beam.

He shoots me a wary look but doesn't fight me, slinking to the side of the hallway and looking more frightened than I've ever seen him.

Fear and anger are my driving forces, and I look to them in place of the control I had become so reliant on, using them as fuel to feed my power. I'm weak, and so close to the brink of death, but I know I can do this.

"There's still time," Rai says in my head, as if to say she believes I can, too.

A shiver rolls over my skin despite the broiling heat, and my right eye twitches as I focus every ounce of strength left within me—both mental and physical—on the length of wood. Pain, agonizing and all-consuming, cuts through my head like the shards of glass on the floor and window frame that bit into my hands.

If I had my collar, this would be easy, like lifting a twig, but I'm exhausted. No, not just exhausted, depleted, like an empty tank running only on fumes.

My eyes narrow on the beam, but the harder I push with my mind, the more my grip on the wood seems to slacken. Sensing my struggle, the monster drags its claws along the underside of my skin, reminding me of its inescapable presence now that it's unleashed. I could do it—I could surrender and let it take over if doing so would let me save Jenner. But I'm afraid...*so* afraid...that if I tap into that monster—if I yield to it again for even a moment—that will be it. There will be no coming back from that precipice and any hope I have of changing the future will be lost.

"Move, damn you!" Blood drips from my nose, pooling on my bottom lip, as an inhuman shriek tears from my lungs. My hands thrust out in front of me, as if to strengthen my mental hold on the beam, and when the sound of my scream fills the corridor, I finally feel the power I need rushing through me.

The monster nods its approval as the force of my mind slams into the hunk of debris, blowing it backward off Jenner where it then splinters, crashing into a wall several feet away.

My chest heaves as I watch the pieces land, my concentration wavering. Others could be trapped here, too. Others might need my help, even though I'm not sure I have it in me to help them. Still, I reach out with my senses, searching for anyone who might be alive among the wreckage.

Aside from Quinn's, the only heartbeat I sense in the immediate vicinity is Jenner's.

Staggering forward, I drop to my knees beside him. "Jenner—"

I look him over, searching for broken bones or any other visible damage while trying not to fear the worst—the damage inside his body I won't be able to see. His shirt is torn where the beam struck his chest, and I can already see the black and purple bruises forming on his torso through the slashes in the fabric.

His eyes shutter open and closed a few times. "I'm...okay..." he says between gulps of air.

Curling my hand around the back of his neck, I help him into a sitting position, taking care not to move him too quickly. Before he's even fully upright, he recoils from my touch, his face scrunching in pain.

"Shit." He grimaces, his hand darting to his side. "I think...I might have broken a rib."

Worry envelops me, its grasp suffocating. If his rib *is* broken and it punctures a lung—

"We need to find help," I breathe.

Remembering Quinn, I look over my shoulder, locking eyes with the ex-Enforcer where he sits on the floor, propped up against the wall. My gaze falls to the hand clamped tight to his side.

"Quinn?" I ask. I can't help wondering if he can hear the tremor in my voice.

A shaky breath parts his lips as he nods. "I'm good," he says, even though I know he isn't. Based on the blood seeping through his fingers, he definitely reopened his wound.

Grunting, Quinn rolls over onto his knees, then pushes up to his feet before straightening, only pausing in his movements to cough. He jerks his head, fighting to stay conscious in the encompassing heat, then wobbles toward us, his balance precarious.

As he squats on Jenner's other side, the fire roars—lashing out around us with hungry intent—and more debris falls from the ceiling, the remaining wooden beams overhead cracking, threatening to come down on us at any moment.

"Help me get him up," Quinn barks.

Panting, I fling Jenner's right arm over my shoulder while Quinn does the same with his left. Then, together, we lift him up off the floor, displacing the majority of his weight between us.

"Stay awake," I murmur, and he nods, although the movement is weak.

Jenner is conscious, but his breathing is unstable, and his

eyelids keep fluttering, making me fear sleep—or something much more final—is beckoning him. If only I could tell just how badly he's hurt.

"Where are Ezra and Duke?" Quinn shouts to me over the crack and hiss of the spreading flames.

Shaking my head, I peer at him from under Jenner's arm. "I don't know. I haven't seen them since—"

The crash of falling timber behind us drowns out my voice, and we trip forward when a rush of heat strikes our backs, nearly knocking us all to the floor.

"Damn it," Quinn hisses, regaining his balance as I struggle to do the same. "We need to get out of here."

His obsidian eyes glow orange in the light of the flames as he looks around for an escape route. The way we came from is blocked, desecrated by one of many ongoing explosions if the rumbling quakes intermittently rocking the building are any indication of the hell raining down on us from above.

"This way," Quinn says in a rush, guiding us forward toward the nearest broken window.

When we reach the sill, I stop dead in my tracks. "We can't leave. We need to find Ezra and Duke."

Quinn pauses with one hand on the frame, gaping at me in disbelief. "You hear that?" he asks.

I follow his leery gaze down the hallway—in the direction we were heading in before the attack—noting the sprinkle of gunfire and screaming. So much screaming. Both closer and louder…

So much louder than they were when I last listened for them.

Sneering, Quinn meets my gaze. "They're probably already dead."

"No!" Ezra's face fills my head, and my heart seems to cave

in at the thought of never seeing him again, even though our time together was already close to being over. "He isn't!" I protest, my scream edging on hysterical. "Ezra isn't…"

I sink my teeth into the inside of my cheek. Ezra *has* to be alive. He has a part to play still. I *need* him. He can't be gone, because if he is…

Then there's no one left to stop me.

"He isn't," I say again, softer this time.

"Wynter's right," Jenner murmurs, drawing both our stunned gazes. Lifting his head, he lets out a low, crackling exhalation, and once again, I worry about the state of his lungs. "We can't…leave them behind."

"Damn it," Quinn mutters under his breath. But, to his credit, he doesn't fight us on the matter, instead leading us away from the escape of the window and down the seemingly unending hallway.

Others seem to have had the same idea as Quinn, and as we push ahead, the three of us hobbling as one unit, I watch as refugees climb out through the windows, while others die on the floor, succumbing to the choking smoke and flames.

I cough into my elbow, feeling the smoke's grasp on me growing, my head increasingly dizzy with each step and with every breath drawn into my lungs. Still, I push on, consoled only by knowing that I won't die here in this burning building—that there *is* still time, like Rai keeps saying.

My eyes scan our murky surroundings, searching for any sign of Ezra or Duke's hulking frame among the wave of civilians racing toward us, away from the gunfire, which is so close now I can smell the sulfur in the air.

Panic. Havoc. Both consume the overheated corridor as the

bodies pile up.

"Do you see them?" I bellow, grunting when an elderly man limping past knocks into my shoulder.

The source of the gunfire is visible now, the soldiers forming a black mass in the distance that moves toward us like an unstoppable plague. Even if the guard at the entrance hadn't taken our guns, the reality is, we're vastly outnumbered.

If we keep going, they'll gun us down.

"No!" Quinn answers, quickly followed by, "Wait! Over there!"

He steers us through the frenzied throng, pointing his free hand in the direction of a junction up ahead where the corridors intersect. The pack of Enforcers approaching have cut off the opposite side of the hallway we're in, leaving only three paths open—the way we came from, which is blocked by fire and debris, to the left, which will only lead to certain death at the hands of the chaos outside, or to the right, the only viable option if anyone hopes to get out of this alive.

My heart pounds in my ears as I follow Quinn's outstretched finger, spotting Ezra and Duke, who take cover from the gunfire at each side of the crossing, facing us with their backs to the wall of the passage cutting horizontally through the main hallway. Although faint, given the mayhem around us, I can hear them both shouting—directing the innocent civilians who have been caught in the middle of this war to take that right-hand path and flee.

"Ezra!" I cry out, unable to contain my relief.

His gaze snaps toward us at the sound of my voice, and when our eyes lock through a gap in the crowd, the entire world seems to stand still for a moment.

"Wynter!" he calls back, bolting away from the safety of the wall and sprinting toward us.

He pushes through the mob, closing the distance between us in seconds. "Are you okay?" he asks, roughly taking my face in his hands before glancing at Jenner and Quinn. "You guys hurt?"

"We're coping," Jenner mutters with a wheezy laugh.

Ezra nods, and when his eyes turn back to mine, I notice the dirt and ash on his cheeks, hiding the bruises underneath. The filth on his clothes. His disheveled hair...

Just like he always looks in my vision.

"I couldn't find you," he says, his voice thready. "The blast knocked me out cold, and when I woke up, it was chaos. People trampling each other. I—"

"It's okay," I interrupt, pressing my palm to his cheek, wiping away a rogue tear with my thumb.

He looks over his shoulder when the gunfire draws uncomfortably close, grabbing hold of my hand. "Come on. Follow me."

"No." I dig my heels into the floorboards when he yanks me forward. "We still need to find Nolan."

Quinn scoffs. "If the Heads aren't dead, they will be soon. Just like us, if we don't get out of here."

He's right. I *know* he's right, but we came all this way and the plan is falling apart right in front of my eyes at an alarming rate. I don't know what to do.

I don't know how to fix this.

"Ezra! We have to go! Now!" Duke shouts from the intersection, manically waving us forward.

Ezra's hazel eyes swing to mine, imploring. "We'll come up with another plan."

Another plan.

I frown, my tongue darting out and licking across the blood drying on my lower lip.

We don't have time for another plan.

"Behind you!" Jenner rasps suddenly, throwing the full weight of his body on mine and whirling us around until we've swapped positions.

At the same moment, a deep voice yells out, "Target sighted!"

I barely have time to process the soldier aiming at me through the shattered window when a gunshot cuts through the surrounding commotion like a knife through butter. Jenner shudders against me, and my heart goes still.

"Jenner?"

In my peripheral vision, I'm aware of Ezra launching himself at the enemy soldier, wrenching the pistol free of his grip before turning it on him and pulling the trigger. The man's head snaps back, and he falls away from the window, crumpling to the ground out of sight.

Jenner's arms go slack around my torso, and with a stilted breath, he stumbles backward a step, his face pale under a thick sheen of sweat. "Ou…ch…"

I can barely breathe, time and space slowing around me as Jenner tilts his head, looking down. His eyes are glassy, and terror strangles my throat as I force myself to follow his gaze.

"Jenner?" I whisper again, tears streaking my vision as red expands across the front of his shirt.

The blood is like a blooming flower, unfurling across his chest until almost every inch of the pale fabric is drenched. I can't move. I can't think. I can't breathe. This is just like that vision I had after we met when it dawned on me that I would be responsible for not only the end of the world...but for the deaths of the people I love.

People like Jenner.

"Today...is not...my day," he stammers before collapsing to the floor.

"Jenner!" Ezra and Quinn both rush to his side, but I stand rooted to the spot, the shock racing through me like ice in my veins, freezing me.

I can't move.

I can't think.

I can't breathe.

Inside my head, the monster seethes. *They did this*, it says, and I lift my gaze, my eyes locking on the black mass of approaching Enforcers. Or maybe they aren't Enforcers at all, but this new nameless enemy.

It doesn't matter who they are, I tell myself, and the monster agrees. *They're all the same.*

And every last one of them deserves to die.

"Wynter?" Ezra's voice is distant, like he's speaking to me from behind a glass wall. The ear splitting ringing returns to my head, and my right eye twitches as my hands clench into fists at my sides.

The soldiers have breached the intersection now. The civilians who haven't escaped are shot, and in the back of my mind, I'm aware of Duke running toward us to escape the spray of bullets, even though the path this way is a dead end.

Kill them, the monster croons in my ear as the surfacing pressure in my chest seeks an escape. *Let me help you kill them all.*

Whatever lingering hold I had on my sanity is lost as I cede control to the monster. Power stretches under my skin, and

Ezra screams my name as I break free of the shock binding me, storming ahead with only one goal in mind: to destroy anything that stands in the way of my anger.

I use my rage as both a shield and a weapon, projecting it at everything in my path. The civilians who screamed in terror of the soldiers now run the other way in fear of me, trapped between the two like a mouse caught by two grappling vipers.

"They did this," I mutter to myself, stalking forward, and for a moment, I can't stop the flood of grief washing through me as I'm reminded of all the people I've lost because of the State's obsessive need for power. My father's face fills my thoughts followed by Rai's. Then, I see Jenner.

His face lingers the longest.

"The State did this," I growl, possessed by my fury. It's a fire curling under my skin, stoked by the monster, who wants to see the chaos I can bring to this world.

Just like Dr. Richter, I realize.

"I hate you!" I scream as a wave of energy explodes out of me, shattering the few remaining windows and rendering anyone unfortunate enough to be near me to mere piles of ash. "I hate you all!"

The State did this.

Richter did this.

The soldiers, so close now and aware of the danger I pose, aim their weapons at me, pulling the triggers. The bullets don't get far before I turn them back on their owners, like I did the last time I was here in this building when I murdered the group of Enforcers sent by Richter. Just like then, I watch as they drop, one by one, to the floor like dead flies. And as the light leaves their eyes, I realize I am Death, just like Richter said. But more than that, I am chaos incarnate.

And this is what I was created for.

"Wynter, stop!" someone shouts, grabbing my arm, but I throw them off, refusing to let them stand in my way. They crash to the floor with a grunt, and as I turn to face them, I take in the result of my wrath. Bodies everywhere—some soldiers, most not. Few, if any, are left standing.

I turn, concentrating on the figure bold enough to attack me, ready to eviscerate him like I did the others, when I glimpse the pitiful gun in his hand and the hazel eyes staring at me, pleading for the monster to stop. The pistol shakes in the man's grip, but he doesn't lower the barrel or point it away. His finger hovers over the trigger.

A tear cuts down his cheek. "Please," he begs, and I can see in the furrowed lines of his brow that he doesn't want to do this. He doesn't *want* to shoot me.

But he will.

He'll kill me to put an end to my rampage.

He'll kill me even though he loves me.

That thought is what finally snaps me out of my frenzy, and I gape at Ezra, mortified at how close I came just now to ending his life.

"Ezra—" His name is garbled in my mouth as a spurt of blood breaches my lips, and I gasp, gripping my skull in both hands, as the pain in my head brings me to my knees.

Darkness is a snake slithering over my vision, sheathing my surroundings in black. And like so many times before, I sense the taut leash of unconsciousness, pulling me back into its grasp against my will.

As it rises to take me, I have just enough time to meet Ezra's gaze—to let him know I'm me again. That I don't want to hurt him or anyone else…

But that I'm glad he'll do what needs to be done to stop me when I do.

"I'm sorry," is all I manage to say as the world turns sideways and my head hits the ground.

TWENTY-FOUR

I WAKE WITH A START, a jagged groan splitting my lips as the minimal contents of my stomach threaten to remove themselves from my body. My head feels like it's been cracked in half, the pain like a hammer behind my eyes and temples, each swing chipping away at my skull in time with every beat of my pulse.

When my eyelids wrench open a few seconds later, I flinch away from the gentle light on my face, my retinas oversensitive, even though the room around me is dark. Tears distort my vision, blurring the blue light stretching before me into streaks.

What is that? I wonder.

With another groan, I shift myself upright, feeling the rough fabric of an armchair grazing my fingers. My entire body hurts, like my bones have all been broken and reset wrong.

Wiping the moisture from my eyes, I blink several times, forcing the details of my surroundings into focus. At first, I think I'm back in Bilken's office—back in the setting of so many of my worst nightmares and of one of my most guilt-ridden memories—but the more I take in the encompassing space, the more I notice the differences. Instead of white carpet, the bare floorboards underneath are exposed, and in place of a glass desk, a steel conference room table stands before a windowless wall. Most striking of all, unlike in Bilken's office, there are no extra spaces or adjacent nooks in this room to display possessions paid for with the people's blood.

Breathing in, I squint at the source of the light—a vast depiction of the building projecting from a small device in the middle of the table—and just behind it, I glimpse Duke, Ezra, and Quinn, assessing the schematics while in heated discussion, their faces drenched pale blue in the glow.

As if sensing me watching him, Ezra turns his head, meeting my gaze through the flickering hologram.

"Wynter." He quickly skirts the table, crossing the room to my position in seconds.

Relief and guilt go to war in my chest as he kneels before me, those hazel eyes brimming with a concern I don't deserve. Does he feel the same way? After coming so close to pulling that trigger—although I asked him to do it—can things ever be the same between us?

Or is this almost tangible sadness I feel in the shared air we breathe as permanent and inescapable as our fates?

My mouth is dry, and I can taste the bitterness of regret on my tongue as I force out the words, "How long have I...? Where..." Trailing off, I press the heels of my hands into my aching eyes. "Where are we?"

"Not long," Ezra murmurs. "Only a few minutes. We're in one of the western annex offices, as far from the fires as we could get for the moment."

Trepidation prickles along my skin as I lower my arms. "The exits?" I ask.

I draw in a breath through my nose, noting the stench of smoke isn't quite as potent as it was before when we were caught in the thick of it. Still, the smell of it clings to my nostrils, and I know it's only a matter of time before the flames reach us and force us out of our hiding place.

He averts his gaze, his lips set in a serious line. "All blocked. There's no way out, at least not from this level. The doors are either all inaccessible because of the explosions or pinned down by soldiers shooting anyone who tries to leave the building. I think the fire is what's keeping them at bay, but who knows how long it will be before they send in the next wave."

"Are we sure they were Enforcers?"

When we were ambushed at that roadblock in Zone 3, the soldiers looked just like Enforcers. It wasn't until Quinn pointed out the blacked-out crests on their sleeves that we realized they were this new enemy in disguise. At a glance, it was virtually impossible to tell them apart.

Ezra nods. "We checked a few of the bodies, and the ones you took out in the hallway definitely were. I think, between the number of patrols in the city and Nolan's call for citizens to side with PHOENIX, it's probably safe to assume the soldiers outside all belong to the State."

Not all of them, I muse, but I can't bring myself to utter those words.

"Regardless of the attack, the State was never going to tolerate such outright betrayal and treason," Ezra continues. "Besides, with PHOENIX out in the open and their whereabouts on full display, it makes sense the Enforcers would choose now to strike. Eradicate PHOENIX and you eliminate half the current problem."

Images of the massacre occurring just outside this building's walls stain my mind yet again. "That isn't…"

A tear cuts down my cheek.

"What is it?" Ezra whispers, leaning in.

I shake my head. "It isn't only Enforcers. That soldier you killed…" I swallow, and my throat is unbearably thick. "He wasn't with the State!" I cry out. "He was going to—" Pressure squeezes my chest, and an inconsolable sob breaks free of my lungs. "But Je—" A spasm restricts my diaphragm as my fingers frantically tear at my eyes, trying to rip out the memory branded to the backs of my lids.

That crimson flower of blood blooming across Jenner's chest is a nightmarish image I will never escape.

He shielded me. He put himself in my place and took the bullet intended to end my life, even though all I've wanted to do since the day we met is keep him alive. I didn't ever want him to protect me.

I only wanted to protect him.

Why did you do that? I wish I could ask him. *Why did you sacrifice yourself for me when my life is already over?*

"Jenner," I gasp, weeping into my hands.

A warm hand brushes the hair away from my face. "Hey, it's okay."

No. No, it isn't.

How can Ezra say that when his best friend not only died… but died because of *me*?

My grief is a bottomless ocean, and once again, I find myself drowning in it. This time, I fear I'll never find my way back to the surface.

Maybe I don't want to.

"Wynter, listen to me!" Ezra pleads, grabbing me by the shoulders and shaking me. "It's okay! Jenner's alive!"

Jenner's...alive...?

Those words are a wrecking ball against the walls of my heart as I finally meet Ezra's gaze. His pupils are blown, his own chest heaving.

"Wh-What?" A soft hiccup breaches my lips, and the shock of this revelation calms me enough that I manage to say, "Jenner's...okay?"

He nods, wiping the tears from my cheeks with his thumbs. "I'm so sorry. If I had known that's what you thought—"

I grip the backs of his hands, pulling them away from my face. "That's why..." But I can't find the will to finish the rest of that sentence. To admit what I did to all the refugees trapped out there in the hallway alongside us, whose only crime was trying to escape the terror inflicted on their lives by me.

By being in the same proximity as the people I wanted to blame for my pain.

Fresh tears well in my eyes, but I push them back. "Where is he?"

Understanding and pity both flit across Ezra's face as he helps me up from the chair. When he points out where Jenner is—propped up by cushions on the floor in the corner of the room to keep him upright and take the weight off his lungs—it requires all the self-control I possess not to throw myself at him and hug whatever life he still has out of his body.

As I stumble toward him, his eyes flutter open.

"Hey," he croaks, gifting me with that lopsided smile that always warms my chest. When he looks at me like that, it feels like home.

"How?" I breathe, dropping to my knees beside him, noting the belt tied across his chest right under his armpits. "You… You were shot."

He chuckles, then goes still, his face contorting in pain. "Yeah, I remember. Son of a bitch really hurts, too. But I guess now we know why Quinn was being such a baby," he says between strained breaths.

"I heard that," the ex-Enforcer grumbles from the other side of the room.

I scowl at Jenner. This is no time to be joking. This is serious. He could have *died*.

"But you…" I shake my head. "I saw—"

Jenner taps the belt, then tugs down the neck of his bloodstained shirt, revealing a wad of fabric against his bare chest. It looks like the torn remnants of a shirt, the original gray of the cloth only visible at the edges. The rest is soaked almost entirely red.

I risk a quick glance at the others. Considering no one in this room is short on attire, I'm not sure I want to know where they got it from.

You mean who, my brain corrects me.

Shuddering, I stare at Jenner, wide-eyed, as he says, "The bastard caught me in the shoulder. So, thanks to his shitty aim, I'll live."

I blink, looking closer at the makeshift dressing and tourniquet. He was shot in the shoulder. Not the chest. Not the heart.

His *shoulder*.

"I-I thought…" I stammer, fresh tears spilling over as I raise a trembling hand to my mouth.

"I know," Jenner whispers, playfully poking me in the left

cheek. "And I'm touched you'd go on a murderous rampage to avenge my death."

These words aren't said with any humor but with a morose understanding of just how much he means to me...and of how far gone I am. Of how willing I am to let the world burn for daring to harm one hair on his head.

It would be easy to blame the monster. To plead innocence and shift the guilt of my actions onto this parasitic illness and claim some invisible entity taking over my body made me do it. But the truth is, there is no monster. Only me.

Me grappling with my own inner demons as I lose myself to the madness of this disease.

"I..." The lump in my throat is thick enough now to choke me. When I swallow, it hurts. "What I—" Tears curve over my fingers and lips, tasting strongly of salt and cinders.

Of ash, like all that remains of some of my victims.

"Those people—"

Ezra wraps his arms around me, kneeling directly behind me and pulling me back against his chest before I give into the guilt. Pressing his face into the crook where my neck meets my shoulder, he murmurs, "It doesn't matter now, Wynter. They all would've ended up dead anyway."

There's a pain in his voice that makes me realize he's right. He said it himself—the soldiers outside are shooting anyone who tries to leave the building. That would mean any of the people I didn't kill in my frenzy would've been met with the same end once they fled outside. Just like all the refugees he and Duke tried to help, their act of selfless bravery reduced to nothing.

Ezra's arms squeeze me tighter, and I can sense his anguish in the hot breaths on my neck and the way his fingers dig into my skin. I don't want him to hurt anymore.

I just want this nightmare to end.

Sinking into a chair to my right, Quinn scoffs. "And now, we're all going to die here, too."

Ezra's arms retract from around me, and as he stands, he grinds out through gritted teeth, "Don't be a dick. It isn't helping anyone."

Quinn flops his head against the back of the chair, as if he's lost the will to argue. "I'm only speaking the truth. I stayed behind to help end this conflict. To *fix* things. Not to die like some scared sewer rat in hiding while innocent people are slaughtered." With a disgruntled sigh, he scrubs a hand across his face. "The whole plan's gone to shit."

"No," I breathe, clambering to my feet. "Not yet it hasn't. We can still find Nolan."

I turn into the heat of Ezra's eyes on my face. He stares at me, his expression dejected, and in this moment, it occurs to me that Quinn isn't the only one among us who's lost hope. "Wynter, he might be dead—"

"He's not," I blurt out, my voice jumping an octave. "He's not," I say again, softer this time, the words barely above a breath. "He's alive. I've seen it." I look down at Jenner. "That vision I told you about? Proof or no peace? When I saw him get that message, he was *here*, in this building, in a room that was filling with smoke."

"So, you're saying you think that vision only just happened? Or maybe hasn't even occurred yet at all?"

Meeting Ezra's gaze again, I nod. "They think Nolan's lying about me being dead—that he's hiding me to use against them later. But they've offered him an olive branch. The chance to prove I'm dead and to end this."

"Bombing us doesn't seem like much of an olive branch," Quinn points out, grimacing as he raises his head.

I shrug, conceding his point. "No, but something tells me that's the idea. They want Nolan to know they're serious about not letting up until he gives them what they want. This attack…" The whiplike snaps of crackling flame and the echoes of gunshots resound in my head, and I wince at the memory of the horrors we left beyond this room. "I think it was only a warning."

With a long, low whistle, Duke leans against the side of Quinn's chair. "One hell of a warnin'."

Quinn's black eyes narrow on my face. "Even if he *is* alive, we don't have time to search every damn room in this place hoping to find him—"

"We don't have to," I interrupt, ignoring when he cocks a dubious brow at me. "We can contact him on his communicator, like Jenner suggested earlier."

Ezra, Jenner, Quinn, and Duke all exchange pensive glances, as if considering the validity of my idea.

I look between them, annoyed by their silence. "Is it not possible or something? Surely, one of you knows what frequency band he's on?"

"What happened to the element of surprise?" Jenner asks, repeating Ezra's earlier words. "If we call him, won't that run the risk of the other Heads never finding out what he did?"

I falter, worrying my lower lip between my teeth, unsure what to say to that. He's right. Calling Nolan directly removes what leverage we have over him from the equation. As much as I need him to make a deal with this enemy and help me put a stop to this war, I can't agree to anything until I'm certain my friends, my *family*, will be safe from threat. That includes not only Ezra and Jenner but Duke—who had no real reason to get involved and help me but did anyway—and Quinn, who for all his grumbling isn't quite as surly as he wants us to think. The ex-Enforcer might have a real chip on his shoulder, but we wouldn't have gotten this far without him. I owe him the fresh start my mother promised.

But how can I protect any of them when there's no one left alive I can trust? No one I can be certain will see that my wishes are honored long after I'm dead?

"I can try Jaed," Duke suggests.

My eyes flick to his. "Jaed?" The name sounds familiar, but I can't place where I've heard it before.

"Jaedyn Vance," Duke clarifies. "She's Head of the sect I was transferred to after…" He hesitates, looking first at Ezra, then Jenner, and in that shared glance between them, I know what he isn't saying—what moment he's referring to with his silence.

After I went back to the DSD where, for all they knew, Richter would've tortured me for information about PHOENIX's whereabouts.

I stare at Duke for a long moment, processing Jaedyn's name and searching for her face in my recent recollections— in particular, from when I was forced to recount my vision of the attack on the Heart before the Heads several days earlier at Nolan's request. I remember her now, just as I remember the fear that had swelled in my chest, alongside a begrudging respect. As the only female in a group of ambitious men, she deserved that much from me, even if, at the time, I thought she supported Nolan's plan for the Heart. A thought, which I'm hoping was misguided, if Duke really believes she's someone we can turn to.

Clearing his throat, Duke folds his arms across his broad chest. "The Heads were meetin' when I was bringin' you to see them, so, if she's alive, there's a good chance she's with Nolan right now. She can tell us where they are or, at least, give us a clue where Nolan might be if they aren't together. Then, we can still go directly to them as planned. Or, if we can't, we use her as the go-between, so someone else knows what's goin' on."

Ezra is the one to ask the all-important question. "Can we trust her?"

My heart catches in my throat, and my palms are sweaty as I curl my hands into fists.

More importantly, I add in my head. *Will she help us?*

Duke offers a noncommittal shrug. "I'd like to think so given what I know of her. If any of the Heads are goin' to have a lick of sense, it's Jaed. Plus, she's against this whole operation."

"Against it how?" I press.

She didn't seem against it when all the Heads were nodding their approval regarding the attack. Then again, some did seem more reluctant in their agreement than others.

Duke gives me a look that says the answer is obvious. "Against lettin' thousands of innocent bystanders die. She thinks we should have tried to prevent the attack rather than use it to benefit PHOENIX. Unfortunately, she was in the minority, and, as we all know, majority rules."

A frown tugs at the corners of my lips. "And you know she thinks this...how?" I stifle an exasperated sigh, sincerely hoping this isn't another case of half-truths running wild and becoming rumor. We can't risk the only opportunity left to us on second-hand information.

Duke lowers his eyes to the floor. "She told me."

Quinn snorts. "You're saying the Head of your sect just so happened to confide this very timely and relevant information to you?"

The stocky man flushes to the tips of his ears and swallows so loudly I'm certain everyone in the room can hear it. "Uh… Yes," he says, looking uncomfortable.

"Why?" Quinn asks. I cock my head to one side, appraising Duke and wondering the same thing.

Jenner barks out a laugh that quickly turns into a yelp of pain. Glancing between me and Quinn, he deadpans, "Wow, if you two were any denser, you'd be robots. For clarity, I blame the State for that, not either of you." Then, with a mischievous grin at Duke, he purrs, "Bedding a Head. You sly dog, you."

I didn't think it was possible for Duke to turn any redder, but his skin burns deep crimson at Jenner's teasing words. It takes a second for their meaning to click in my brain. When they do, "Oh," is all I can think to say.

Coming up behind me again, Ezra loops an arm around my waist. "So, there's already a precedent there for her to hear us out. And maybe the other Heads, too, now that the plan hasn't gone the way they hoped."

I peer up at him, nodding my agreement, before turning to Duke once more, steadfast in my commitment to seeing this through. To get to Nolan and end this the way I always intended to.

"Do it," I say, my voice a determined growl. "Make the call."

TWENTY-FIVE

WE EMERGE FROM THE OFFICE ten minutes later, after Duke has made contact with Jaedyn. I could only hear his side of their conversation, which lasted maybe two minutes but seemed to span hours as the rest of us waited with bated breath, hoping whatever information he gleaned from the Head would help us track down Nolan.

The memory of their one-sided exchange plays again in my head as we weave a path through the smoggy, smoke-stained hallways.

"Don't worry about me," Duke said when Jaedyn answered the call. *"I'm fine. Where are you?"*

A pause.

"Is Nolan with you? What about the other Heads?"

A longer pause.

"Tell me how to get to you. We need to talk to Nolan immediately."

Duke hesitated then, his mossy brown eyes finding mine in the darkness of the office.

"The State's weapon," he muttered, staring at me. *"She's here. Along with some others who just want to help."*

Silence again.

"I know what we've been told, but it isn't true. Nolan's lied to us," Duke growled after a moment. Then, softer, he said, *"Jaed... You'll just need to trust me on this. Please."*

The call ended shortly after that plea, at which point, Duke had returned to the schematics of the building's layout hovering over the table. Inserting a location marker into the hologram map, he grabbed the projector and crossed the room, tossing the device to Quinn before squatting to help Jenner up from the floor.

"Seein' as you're hurt, I'll give Jenner a hand and you can lead the way," he had grunted, nodding at the ex-Enforcer in passing as he made his way to the door. "I think *your* hands are already full," he then added with a knowing glance at Ezra.

He wasn't wrong. Since my outburst, I can barely stand on my own, let alone walk anywhere unaided. As we progress through the first floor of the building, avoiding the fire-ravaged paths, Ezra keeps close beside me, never letting me stray too far in my disorientation.

When I do, his fingers draw me back.

"So, where is it we're going, exactly?" he asks, tightening a hand around my waist.

"Jaed said the Heads are hunkered down in a safe room in the basement while they figure out what to do next," Duke answers.

"This place has a safe room?" Jenner slurs, stumbling along beside Duke, his uninjured arm draped across the older man's shoulders.

"Most of the government buildings do," Quinn asserts, calling back to us from where he keeps pace a short distance ahead. "Considering the State's most influential members have offices here, it makes sense they'd have a secure location to evacuate to in the event of an attack."

A humorless laugh parts my lips. "Ironic."

"What is?" Ezra murmurs.

I lift my shoulders in a half-hearted shrug. "That PHOENIX emerges for the first time in decades, and now, it's right back underground where it started."

No one says another word as we traverse the long hallways, searching for the entrance to the basement Jaedyn mentioned to Duke. We find it—an unassuming door hidden in plain sight, surrounded by others just like it, with the only difference being a keypad where the handle should be—back in the eastern side of the building, which seemed to take the brunt of the damage from the explosions. Access to entire passages are blocked off from caved-in ceilings and other varying forms of burning debris, and the fire is still raging, though spreading far more slowly than I would expect.

It's possible the stunted growth of the inferno is a result of the chemical compounds used in the bombs, the slow spread intentional to drive home the warning message behind the attack—to threaten PHOENIX, to maim it, but not to destroy it. Though, it's just as likely due to the lack of flammable objects, or any objects at all, in the corridors. Either way, the flames still find prey to devour, the blackened corpses lining the floor adding the stink of burning charcoal to the air, turning it putrid.

The resurgence of smoke in my lungs is debilitating, and the temperature of the flames scoring the walls nearby is unwelcome against my already overheated skin. Sweat trickles down the sides of my face and the back of my neck as I watch Quinn enter the code Duke recites to him into the keypad. When the last digit is entered, the door unlocks and swings inward on sturdy hydraulic hinges into an unlit passage beyond, blasting us with a rush of unpolluted air.

With a hacking cough into the crook of his elbow, Quinn removes the flashlight from his belt and staggers forward into the darkness. The brilliant beam of light cuts into the shadows, revealing a set of stairs leading down.

"How did the Heads know the code to get down here?" I ask. But as we descend, I note the similarities between this space and the pathway beneath the parking structure in Zone 3 that my mother took us down to get to the safe house.

The words have barely left my lips when I make the connection.

Coming to the same conclusion, Ezra grumbles, "If I had to guess? Bilken."

That would explain why the Heads chose the magistrates building as their base of operations and acting headquarters during the siege. Aside from being in a central location, insider intel about the layout made it an ideal place to go to ground and wait out the attack.

Unless there's no way out, I muse.

In that case, the safe room might as well be a tomb.

At the bottom of the stairs, I glimpse a faint light on our right, then movement, a face taking shape in the murky shadows of the passage.

"Duke?" a hesitant voice calls out.

"It's us," the brawny man says in response.

There's a moment of hesitation, and then Jaedyn Vance steps forward, her features sharpening in the beam of Quinn's flashlight. Her chestnut skin is flushed, her expression caught somewhere between relieved and nervous.

"Are you okay?" she asks Duke. Her eyes find mine, and she

stills, making no move to come any closer.

Duke answers with an affirmative grunt. "You?"

Jaedyn heaves a shuddering sigh. "I will be once this is over." Her eyes hang on mine, and I can sense her silent deliberation. Finally, she nods and says, "Right. Follow me."

Jaedyn leads us along a winding passage, the gloom thick enough to swallow us whole even though glass sconces line the walls, offering—but failing to provide—the solace of light. Come to think of it, the only place I've seen fully operational power since the attack began was at Bilken's safe house. Even the DSD, which has a back-up generator, was limited to the use of emergency energy; the only functional lights on in the entire building were mere strips of ominous blue lining the floors. Is the State's infrastructure really that fragile and crumbling that quickly as a result of the bombings?

Or is it purposely keeping the city in darkness to demonstrate how much control it has over us?

"It's so empty down here," I whisper, a shiver crawling up my spine.

How many of the terrified refugees outside in the plaza could have been saved in this most recent assault if the Heads had diverted the civilians who looked to them for help down here in the interim? Why didn't they take advantage of this sprawling space if they knew it was here?

I can only assume it was because Nolan didn't want to sacrifice the Heads' only access to shelter to the very people he believed expendable in this war.

Jaedyn stiffens, her shoulders raising defensively. "The attack happened so quickly," she says, her voice curt. "There wasn't time..." She shakes her head, then mutters something unintelligible, sweeping a black curl behind her ear before repeating, "There wasn't time. We only just made it down here ourselves and we barely managed that much with our lives." This time, her tone is regretful, and I can't help imagining that she *did* want to save those lives, but something—or someone—stood in her way.

Her reaction to my unspoken accusation is telling, and I realize, maybe Duke was right, after all. Maybe there is one Head of PHOENIX left we can trust.

One who still has a firm grip on their conscience.

"Does Nolan know we're comin'?" Duke asks, falling into step behind Jaedyn as Jenner grunts, working to keep up.

Her large, round eyes cut to his over her shoulder, her lips pursed in a deliberate scowl. "No. Given what *little* you told me, I figured it would be better this way."

"I'm sorry about that," Duke mumbles, and Jaedyn shifts her attention back ahead with a *humph*. "There wasn't time to fill you in on the details."

She falters then, only pausing long enough to look back at me where I linger at the back of our procession. Molten brown eyes gleaming black in the darkness, she says, "Well, I assume we'll all find out the truth soon enough."

We continue the rest of the way to the safe room in silence, the trek taking less than five minutes in total, even with our listless pace, although, mentally, the journey seems never-ending.

While the path we take is similar in style and layout to the one we took to Bilken's safe house, in so many ways, this underground passage reminds me of the tunnels we traveled that night two and a half years ago. The night we first lost Rai and the course of my life was altered, turning me into this monster.

In many ways, this moment mirrors what we went through back then. The difference is that I won't make the same mistakes. I won't be tricked or fooled by the cunning of someone else and their immoral motivations.

This time, the outcome will be decided by me.

The glow of Jaedyn's flashlight illuminates a reinforced bulkhead door at the end of the corridor, which is once again devoured by shadow when she turns to face us.

"Before I open that door..." She hesitates again for the breadth of a heartbeat, then raises her chin, forceful and resilient, unflinching as her glare pins me down. "I don't know what's going on, but I sincerely hope you came here with a solution. Not to create more problems for us."

I can feel the weight of the others' stares on my face. This is it—the do or die moment. Once these words leave my lips, there can be no going back, no changing my mind or running away from my fate or searching for another way out of this mess. The moment I walk through that door, my life is over— surrendered as payment to guarantee the survival of others.

Ezra squeezes my waist, and I lay my hand on top of his, squeezing back. Like always, his touch grounds me and serves as a stark reminder of what I'm fighting for.

Of what I'd gladly pay any price in the world to protect.

Leveling my gaze at the Head, I retort, "I came to you with a way to end this war."

Once again, Jaedyn's eyes hold mine for a moment. "Good." She lets out another shuddering sigh. "That's what I was hoping you'd say."

Like the door upstairs on the ground level, the door to the safe room is controlled solely by keypad entry. Deadbolted shut, the entrance is impassable without the code. Or a strong enough explosive.

Or someone who can tear through metal with their mind.

Fortunately, we don't need to resort to the two latter options—I'm too drained for anything more taxing than walking, and an explosive would be more likely to cave in the passage than to actually break into the room, not that we have any on hand to find out.

But we do have the code, which Jaedyn inputs after casting one final apprehensive glance in my direction, that single look exposing her indecision as to whether she should trust me. In that split-second when our eyes were locked, I could see the doubt so clearly in her gaze, the swirling depths of her eyes alight with the question of if I really am here to help them end this war like I claimed.

Regardless, she enters the code, and when the keypad registers the final digit, the buzzing of a motor fills the passage, the sound vibrating through the floor into my feet. Beyond the hum, I hear the click of tumblers shifting and the whirring crunch of gears turning as the deadbolts sealing the entrance slide free.

Gripping the handle, Jaedyn pulls the door open, then steps over the lip into the darkness beyond. We follow behind her one at a time—Duke first, then Jenner, who he helps over the threshold, trailed by Quinn, Ezra, and finally me. We proceed single file into a narrow corridor, which continues for a few steps before feeding into a larger, more spacious compartment lit by the familiar glow of blue emergency lights.

As we shuffle into the safe room, I realize it's less of a room and more of a fully equipped bunker with hallways branching off from the main area, likely leading to sleeping quarters and other living spaces built to help wait out whatever event would usher its eventual occupants down here.

Occupants like Nolan, who rises from a chair as we enter, eyes pitched wide in disbelief.

He looks different than when I last saw him, as if he's aged ten years over the span of only a handful of days. His ashy blond hair is sweat-slicked back off his forehead, his beard longer, like overgrown weeds on his face. Scorch marks riddle his clothes—his fingers and cheeks smeared black with ash— but, physically, he otherwise appears uninjured. Mentally, I can't say the same, noting the alarming disconnect behind those pale, unblinking eyes.

A few other figures turn as we enter the room, and I immediately recognize them as the other Heads of PHOENIX. Of the eight I stood before less than a week ago, only five are here, including Nolan. One of them, a man with red hair—whose left arm and the left side of his face are covered in superficial burns—gapes at me from where he sits slumped in a chair.

"Is that—" he chokes out, while the elderly Head looks around at the others in dismay.

The last Head—a man not much younger than Nolan— inches as far back into the room as he can get, gawking at me but saying nothing.

"Rodrick—" Jaedyn begins, but an explosion of unhinged laughter drowns her out.

"So, they were right," Nolan rasps, staring at me. "You really are back from the dead."

He takes a step closer, those almost colorless eyes narrowing, assessing first my face then the way my chest heaves as I lean into Ezra for much-needed support. Without him, I'm not sure I'd be able to stay upright, my body worn out, stripped of any lingering energy.

Nolan's attention lifts back to my face, and he flashes an unnerving smile. "Though, from the looks of it, you might not be far off."

Behind him, the other Heads look confused, and their bewildered expressions remind me of the rumors Duke told us about earlier. About how Nolan claimed I attacked him and escaped from the bunker where I was being held as PHOENIX's prisoner. Although Nolan had said he'd rescued me from the State because of my father, that was a lie—an excuse to get me back in his grasp. The truth was, all he desired was my power. To use me and then discard me once I'd given him what he wanted.

Clearly, the Heads had believed these lies, too.

Running a hand through his bedraggled hair, Nolan scans our group, sneering at Ezra and Jenner on my right—undoubtedly irked to see them still alive—before his gaze passes me by, catching on Quinn. Understanding pulls the edges of his lips taut.

"I suppose I have you to thank for sparing their lives?" He clicks his tongue. "How disappointing. Although, I suppose there's a lesson to be learned in all this as to who we allow into our ranks moving forward. After all, how much loyalty can we really expect from someone who used to be the State's dog?"

Quinn bristles beside me, his expression mutinous, his shoulders trembling under the force of his rage.

It's only now, with us positioned side by side before Nolan, that I realize how much we have in common. Unlike Ezra and Jenner, who escaped the toxic clutches of the State sooner than either of us, we weren't just victims of oppression and fear like so many others in the Heart.

We were tools used to inflict them.

But we both broke free of the shackles that bound us, and like me, Quinn isn't anyone's pawn anymore. Or dog.

Least of all the State's.

The hair stands up on the back of my neck, my fury rising at Nolan's insult. A snarl rips from my throat as I jerk free of Ezra's hold, my fingers curling, reaching for my power—the monster inside me hungry for blood.

"Wynter, don't," Quinn says as I put myself between him and Nolan, his panicked breath shaking me free of my rage.

Nolan's brow furrows as he peers back and forth between us. "Last I saw you two together, he was about to kill you. And you as well," he adds with a dismissive wave at Ezra and Jenner. His eyes flick to Quinn, curiosity written in the grooves of his weathered face. "You were always so adamant that she's a monster. I'm interested to know what changed your mind."

Low mutterings erupt now among the other Heads, but Nolan either doesn't care or is too lost in the moment to notice.

My pulse flutters under my skin. Does this mean Nolan hasn't figured out that Quinn was a double agent placed in PHOENIX by Bilken? That the man who helped him orchestrate this attack—who he once considered a friend—was actually the one behind our escape?

Would it even matter at this point if he did?

I consider the repercussions that might arise if Nolan determined the true scope of how—and why—I survived that day. Would Bilken's perceived betrayal affect his willingness to make a new deal with our attackers? Surely, Nolan still wants an end to this war. Even if I plan on making damn sure he never gets the power he lusts for, he must still value his life. He must want to live.

At least, enough to make the call.

"What *changed*," Quinn seethes through clenched teeth, and my already erratic heart rate ratchets higher as I anticipate his answer, "was knowing I was working for another version of the State." He spits each word, feeding Nolan a story in the same vein as the one he gave me when he saved our lives in the field outside the farmhouse.

While it's not a lie by any stretch, it's not the whole truth. Quinn might be guided by his morals, but I doubt he would've ever helped me to begin with if there wasn't something worthwhile awaiting him at the end of that aid.

Still, half-truth or not, Quinn's outrage is explosive as he continues. "I wasn't going to sit by and help you murder thousands of innocent people—"

"Murder?" Nolan balks, his cheeks ruddy as his own anger flares. "I'm trying to *save* this country!"

"You can cut the act," Ezra growls. "We know all about the deal you made with the people attacking us."

"Deal?" The elderly Head reels back, squinting at Nolan. "What deal?"

For the first time, the cowering Head at the back of the room finally speaks up. "Rodrick, what is he talking about?"

"Yes, Rodrick," Jaedyn croons, crossing her arms. "Tell us. What *is* he talking about?"

"I don't—" Nolan begins, but I cut him off.

"Don't try to deny it. I *saw* it," I say, pausing to let the meaning of my words penetrate. "You betrayed us all, admit it. Tell them how you arranged this attack so you could seize power."

Nolan's lips peel back, exposing his teeth. "I used a terrible, *unavoidable* situation to our advantage. But that's not exactly a secret. Don't you remember, Wynter? You were there. You were the one who told us the details of the attack." There's a note of accusation to his tone that suggests I am to blame for how things have turned out. While there's truth to that—while I might be guilty of igniting this war—that doesn't negate the fact that he is responsible for letting it escalate this far.

Hell, as much as he influenced the situation, I can't even blame Bilken for this. He might have handed Nolan the gun by introducing him to our attackers, but Nolan was the one who pulled the trigger. He, and he alone, shoulders that blame.

"Cut the shit," Jenner barks, his voice surprisingly strong given his weakened condition. "That's not what she's talking about and you know it." Taking a limping step forward, he looks around at the other Heads now, meeting each of their startled gazes in turn. "Nolan already knew the attack was coming because he's the one who arranged it. He then used Wynter's vision—a vision that was only triggered at all because of his actions—to coerce you into agreeing to this coup."

"But it hasn't exactly gone to plan, has it?" Quinn asks, his tone derisive.

Nolan's upper lip quivers with contempt, his nostrils flaring. "Everything I have done has been for the betterment of our society—"

"If you really believe that, you're delusional," Ezra scoffs.

Sweat beads the Head's upper lip, and his right eye twitches as he glances around the room, as if searching for a target to lock onto. Silence falls among the remaining Heads, who all stare at Nolan like he's lost his mind.

"What does it matter how we got to this point?" Saliva flies from his lips as he turns in place, a greasy tendril of hair falling into his face. "All that matters is that the State is crumbling before our eyes—"

"People are *dyin'*, damn it!" Duke shouts, making me jump. His muscles pulse as he glares down at Nolan, his large frame towering over the older man, even with the space between them.

Nolan scoffs. "Sometimes, sacrifices must be made to pave the way for a better tomorrow."

A stunned breath escapes me. "You really are just like him," I whisper.

All eyes swing in my direction.

"Like who?" Nolan asks, his tone mocking.

"Richter," I bite back through clenched teeth.

I remember thinking it once before—when Nolan said I would be doing the people of our country a great service by helping him. The Head had tried so hard to make his plan seem noble, like he really was acting on behalf of the people. But now, with failure on his doorstep, I see just how little they mean to him. He'd sacrifice an entire city of innocents if it helped him take the power he believes he deserves.

I blow out a furious breath through my nose. From the stunned looks on the other Heads' faces, I can only assume Nolan never voiced these particular viewpoints before to anyone other than me. If he had, they would realize what I already know—what I can see them all now beginning to realize.

Nolan doesn't deserve to lead. Not PHOENIX. Not whatever the State becomes after this war. Given his actions, he's lucky I'm not ending his life the same way I ended Dr. Richter's.

"Richter's dead, by the way," I say, my tone blunt but the words sharp enough to cut. "In case you were wondering."

Nolan's expression hardens. "Is that a threat?"

A fresh surge of fatigue creeps through my body. I shake my head, more than ready to be done with this conversation. "I don't need to threaten you because, without me, you're all already dead."

The red-haired Head visibly stiffens. "What are you saying?"

I swallow, my mouth and throat painfully dry.

No turning back.

"As we speak, there are an unknown number of soldiers in the city posing as Enforcers, and soon, the bombings will continue, regardless of your calls for a ceasefire. Once that happens, they won't stop. Not until..." I trail off, the rising lump in my throat blocking the words.

"Not until what?" Jaedyn asks, trepidation rife in her voice.

I glance at her, then at each of the Heads, before turning the full force of my gaze back on Nolan. "Not until they know I'm dead. You see, that was the deal Nolan made with these people. Power in exchange for the DSD...and my life."

The silence that follows this revelation is strained, and the Heads wear matching scandalized expressions that reassure me as to how little they actually knew about Nolan's plans. While their confusion before when Ezra mentioned the deal Nolan made would've been enough to convince me of this, their shock at this moment confirms it. It tells me PHOENIX hasn't been completely corrupted, like I feared it had. That my father's legacy wasn't destroyed, just tainted.

Tainted but redeemable.

Jenner snorts, his disgust apparent, even though every word

that breaches his lips is labored. "Why are you all acting so shocked? Like you didn't agree to just sit by and watch as the Heart was attacked?"

"We believed the attack was futile," Jaedyn murmurs, her eyes downcast on the floor, "not that—"

"It was a power play by the very person you all chose to be your leader?" Quinn mocks.

Nolan's complexion is gray now, and I glimpse a level of panic in his wandering eyes as he tries to figure out how he can retake control of the situation. His manic mannerisms remind me of Richter when we returned to the DSD to find Rai, that mask of brilliance slipping, revealing the madness under the surface. Like Richter, Nolan's mask has slipped and I can see the real man underneath, exposed now in his desperation.

"Proof or no peace," I mutter, just loudly enough for everyone to hear. "That was what they said to you."

Nolan's gaze snaps to mine, his remaining composure unraveling at these words. As he crosses the room, storming toward me with murderous intent, Quinn roughly shoves me behind him. At the same moment, Ezra steps forward, pulling me protectively back against his chest.

Duke lunges forward, shoving Nolan, who thrusts a finger toward me, spitting, "Stop acting like this isn't your fault! This war is happening because of *you*. Because of what you've done!"

My chest squeezes. "I know." More than anyone, I know what I'm responsible for. What my existence has caused. I live with the guilt of it every day. "And that's why I'm here trying to fix it. To give them an alternative to this destruction. To *end* this."

Nolan stills, and a momentary hope flickers behind his blue eyes. "End this, how? They want proof of your *death*. Are you willing to die to put an end to this conflict?"

I always thought, once I reached this moment, I'd hesitate to answer this question. That part of me would be so overcome with fear, I would need some final push to make me say it. To agree to do what needs to be done, even though there was never a doubt in my mind that I would make this sacrifice willingly.

But now, as Nolan's words hang in the air between us, I feel only a calm acceptance. An eagerness, even, to finally shift the weight of this burden off my shoulders.

"If I'm given certain assurances, yes."

The four lesser Heads exchange furtive glances, while Nolan just laughs, the sound biting and callous.

"*Foolish* girl." He grimaces, and whatever hope I thought I saw in his hooded gaze is swallowed by the bleak darkness of defeat. "There is no end to this. Even if we give them what they want, it won't be enough. It's over. We aren't safe. Not down here. Not anywhere." The color drains from his face as he stumbles backward, his eyes glazing over as his fingers reach for the edge of the nearest chair. "We're all going to die."

Ezra's arms tense around me. "Why do you say that?" His breath beats hot and fast against the back of my neck, his heart pounding so violently I can feel it through my jacket.

Nolan just shakes his head. "Because it wouldn't be enough for me, and it sure as shit isn't enough for them. They had already agreed to decimate the State, to help install PHOENIX as the new ruling power. But now…" He clamps his teeth onto his lower lip before crying out, "They don't trust me! Don't you see? To these people…everyone in this city is a threat. And the only way to ensure a threat is eradicated is through total annihilation. Extermination," he adds, muttering that last word under his breath.

Tears spring into my eyes. After all this, after everything we've been through, that can't be the only outcome. Death can't be the only option.

Otherwise, what am I fighting for?

"They aren't you," I breathe.

Nolan raises his head, fixing me with lifeless eyes. "Are you so sure about that? Would you bet *their* lives on it?" He gestures to Ezra, then to Jenner and Quinn, his expression smug.

"No," I counter, and I step free of Ezra's arms once again, finding strength in my resolve. "But I'm willing to bet mine."

A low hiss escapes through Nolan's clenched teeth, and there's a deranged glint in his eyes that unnerves me. "Have you not listened to a word I just told you? It won't be enough—"

"It will." *It has to be.* "I can see the future, remember? I'll know." *And if they go back on their deal, I'll kill them.* "I just need you to contact whoever you made your deal with and make a new agreement. My death in exchange for peace."

For a long moment, Nolan just gapes at me, and though no one else in the room dares to speak, I can sense the gravity of their unspoken thoughts in the encompassing silence. Finally, Nolan clears his throat.

"Why would you do that?" he asks, his voice hoarse.

Two faces flash through my head—not just reminders of why I *should* do this but the reasons why I will without doubt or regret. Why would I sacrifice myself, Nolan wonders?

For friendship, I muse, glancing over my shoulder at Jenner, who gifts me with that lopsided smile. The smile that made me know what it felt like to be unconditionally accepted.

For love. My eyes drift to Ezra's and linger there, taking in every detail of his face and imprinting them on my mind alongside the memories we've made together. Memories which are so few but more precious than anything else I possess in this world.

When I look back at Nolan, a third face fills my thoughts. As it manifests, a smile tugs at my mouth, calming the waves of fear, doubt, and unease rising up and beating against the walls of my heart.

"Because I have something I want to protect," I assert, "and because…I want to follow my father's example."

I've been called many things over the last year. Monster. The State's weapon. Richter's angel of death. But if I am anything, I am my father's daughter. My father, who tried so hard to defend what he cherished. Who only wanted to preserve a piece of the world—a kinder world—he once knew for his child.

Just like I want to guarantee a life after all this for Ezra and Jenner.

Nolan blinks at me, as if he can't fathom a scenario where someone else's life is worth the surrender of his own. And, for a brief moment, I pity him until I remind myself that monsters like Richter and Nolan—people who would intentionally cause such carnage—are undeserving of pity. Like Richter, Nolan deserves what's coming to him. But unlike the man who tormented me for years, I want Nolan to live.

To watch as the world moves on and becomes better without his influence.

Jaedyn steps toward me, drawing my focus from Nolan, her gaze skeptical despite her confident tone. "You said you wanted certain assurances," she says, and the other three Heads watch us closely, hanging onto every word. "What are they?"

I lick my lips, weighing my thoughts before I voice them. The Heart can never go back to what it was before. Even if the State did manage to stay in power after this conflict, the death toll would only rise once they catch and punish all those who ran to PHOENIX for aid. The battle beyond these walls might end but the war would continue for those who remain in the Heart. The oppression and terror that afflicts their everyday lives would only worsen.

That leaves two alternatives: seeing our city razed to the ground…

Or PHOENIX.

While the rebellion alone isn't a threat to the State—as proven by the swarm of Enforcers outside—the people assaulting the Heart have the means and the will to ensure the State is removed. Without me, the State is at a huge disadvantage. Even with every Enforcer at its disposal, it can't wage a war against the whole world. Its days are numbered.

But so are PHOENIX'S without peace and support.

At one point, despite what's occurring right now, our attackers were in favor of PHOENIX seizing power. Even if they don't trust Nolan, there's time to make them support PHOENIX again. To work together to put a stop to this madness.

Only days ago, I saw PHOENIX as the lesser of two evils, but it doesn't have to be that way. Without Nolan, it can once again be what my father created.

It just needs someone else at its helm.

Nolan once said to me that power can always be taken away. Time to put that theory into action.

"We can't have peace as long as the State is in power," I say carefully, "and I know our attackers feel that way, too. But"—I observe the faces around me—"we can't have peace with Nolan leading either."

"What are you suggesting?" the Head standing at the back of the room asks.

A pang in my forehead makes me wince, but I shake it off, ignoring the way the room seems to spin under the glow of the emergency lights overhead.

I swallow, trying to steady my voice. "Rodrick Nolan is to be stripped of his title—"

When Nolan begins to protest, Ezra steps forward, pulling out the pistol he wrenched away from the now dead enemy soldier upstairs. "Shut up and listen," he snaps, aiming the barrel at the older man.

My eyes shift to Ezra's face, then to his finger, which hovers over the trigger. He's more calm and steady than I've ever seen him, but there's a resignation in his gaze that breaks my weary heart.

That makes me realize he's finally accepted how this situation will end.

Swallowing again, I glance at Jaedyn, who nods for me to continue.

Drawing in a deep breath, I repeat, "Nolan is to be stripped of his title and is to have no involvement in what you choose to build in the State's place once this is over. I don't care who takes charge, but it needs to be someone who actually has the people's best interests at heart, not their own." I spit that last part, scowling at Nolan.

Jaedyn considers me for a moment. "Anything else?"

"My friends—" My voice catches, obscured by the tears in my throat when Rai's face appears in my thoughts, followed by Alivia Laramie's.

Say it, my conscience chides me. *This is your last chance to save them.*

Glancing first at Ezra, then at Jenner and Duke, I whisper, "They've only ever tried to do what they thought was right, to protect those who couldn't protect themselves." I lock eyes with Quinn next, who nods, his obsidian eyes aglow with an emotion I never thought I'd see from him.

Respect.

"I won't let them be punished for my actions," I declare, facing the Heads once more, "and they deserve a say in what the Heart becomes next. I won't agree to anything or do anything until I know for sure they'll be safe."

The elderly Head huffs out a breath. "Any other demands?" he drawls.

I narrow my eyes at him. "Be better. Be better than what came before us."

Scowling at the old man, Jaedyn steps toward me, extending her hand. "Your requests are perfectly within reason. If you help us, I will *personally* see to it that it's done."

Behind her, the red-haired Head pushes up from his chair. "I think we can all agree it's time for a clean slate." He looks to the last Head, who nods in agreement.

As I reach out to take Jaedyn's hand, Nolan lets loose a demented, bone-chilling cackle. "Jaedyn, you don't need to make concessions for this traitorous child." He spits the word *traitorous* like it's left a sour taste in his mouth. "She's the reason this war is happening. If she's so convinced her plan will work, let's just hand her over and be done with it."

Ezra moves so quickly I barely register the movement, his

lips peeling back in a snarl as he pushes the muzzle of the gun between Nolan's eyes. "You will *not* touch her," he growls. "This is *her* choice, not yours." He laughs once, the sound bitter. "You should be thanking her for saving your worthless life, you arrogant shit."

Flop sweat glistens across Nolan's brow, but I don't tell Ezra to lower his weapon. Instead, I say in a bored monotone, "Need I remind you, I have slaughtered entire armies. If you think you can make me go without giving me what I'm asking for first, then try." Nolan's eyes flash to mine, and I shrug. "But don't for a second think I won't let you die to get what I want. All of you," I add, peering at the other Heads.

As much as I desire a peaceful end to this war—a world in which Ezra and Jenner can thrive—I am more than ready to let everyone and everything burn if there's a chance they won't be safe once I'm gone.

My time is running out. I can feel it. But I won't hand myself over without these assurances, and without the deal, we're all dead anyway.

All I can hope for now is that the Heads don't call my bluff.

Jaedyn blanches at the unfeeling threat in my voice, and the column of her throat shifts when she audibly swallows.

Good, I think. *Now, they know I'm serious.*

Jerking her head, Jaedyn says in a rush, "That won't be necessary. We agree to your terms." Then, glaring at Nolan, she barks, "You got us into this mess, Rodrick. Now, you're going to get us out." Closing the distance between them, she thrusts a communicator into his hand. "Call them. Broker the deal."

Nolan's expression turns stony. "And if they don't agree?" he asks. "What then?"

With the mask of the monster firmly in place, I smile. "If they don't, tell them I'll kill them all."

TWENTY-SIX

I LEAN OVER THE METAL basin in the washroom, choking back the urge to throw up. It's been twenty minutes since Nolan vanished into one of the sleeping quarters to make his call—accompanied by Duke and Jaedyn, who were intent on keeping a close eye on him to ensure he wouldn't betray us. Every second since then has been like a knife slowly sinking between my ribs, the blade tip piercing through muscle and tissue until the lung it punctures fills with blood, suffocating my breaths from within.

The pressure I've sensed building over the last few days is everywhere now, clawing at the underside of my skin, and the vibration of my power as it slips further beyond my control is a constant taunting hum in my ear. I feel the current like an ever-present itch at the roots of my hair, and my fingers tingle with the urge to rip the strands from my scalp if it will make the sensation stop.

I retch, but nothing comes up, my stomach empty in a painful way, as if something is eating me from within. My inability to ease the gnawing ache only drives me that much closer to the brink of madness.

Assuming I'm not already there.

Cupping some cold water into my mouth, I lift my gaze to my reflection, recoiling from what I find staring back at me in the small square mirror above the sink. My skin has a mottled, grayish hue, and the whites of my eyes are bloodshot, the harsh red veins converging at the edge of my irises, which bleed black, blotting out the green and blue.

"There's still time," I whisper, repeating Rai's words, willing them to be true. Since that dream, I've been heeding what she said, even though, deep down, I know it wasn't really her speaking to me but a figment of my imagination created in my grief to console me. To give me a shred of hope to hang onto.

All this time, I've been chasing a ghost, and now, so close to the end, that manufactured hope feels so far away, like it might slip through my fingers if I'm not careful.

Still, real or not, I cling to those words, repeating them again and again. I repeat them until my voice is hoarse and tears streak from my eyes, burning my cheeks.

I repeat them until I believe them.

A sudden knock makes me jump, and I startle, choking on the half-spoken word in my mouth. Wiping my face dry with my hands, I turn from my reflection and fling the door open to find Ezra waiting at the threshold.

His expression is solemn. "Nolan's made the call," he says. He doesn't elaborate more than that.

Like me, Ezra couldn't bring himself to be present when Nolan contacted the people attacking the Heart. Perhaps he feared he wouldn't be able to restrain himself and didn't want to jeopardize the outcome of the call. Or maybe listening in on that conversation would've made what's coming far too real.

Too immediate.

Too inescapable.

Swiping my wet palms on my jacket, I exit the washroom behind Ezra, following him back into the main area of the bunker where the Heads all look nervously at each other, as if fearing this moment will spell out our doom. They all remain seated except Jaedyn, who stands with Duke off to one side of the arrangement of chairs, shooting him the odd worried glance. On the other side of the room, I spot Jenner and Quinn, who linger at the periphery of the space, using the wall behind them for support.

Concern swells in my gut as I observe them, my fear like spoiled milk, turning my stomach. They're both pale, *too* pale, and while Jenner's arm is now tied up in a makeshift sling— his chest bandaged and the belt tourniquet gone—his shirt is soaked through with an alarming amount of blood. Who knows how much he's lost by this point.

My chest tightens as I take in their faces again. All this standing and waiting around can't be good for either of them. They need help. *Real* help.

Help they won't get down here in this bunker.

Help they'll only get if I succeed.

Nolan clears his throat, and after a split second of hesitation, I meet his gaze, acknowledging him for the first time since re-entering the room. He looms, frowning, at the front of the space, like an instructor about to deliver a lesson—the communicator clenched tightly in his right hand. Behind him, I can just make out the outline of the locked bulkhead door in the shadows of the hallway we came in by.

My thoughts drift, wondering if the flames have penetrated

the passage by now and if we'll still be safe in here once they reach the safe room entrance.

Shaking that fear from my head, I focus on Nolan's lined face, the skin wizened beyond its years, making him look at least a decade older than he actually is.

"Well?" I ask, breathless.

With a disparaging sniff, Nolan raises his chin just enough to glare down his nose at me. "They've agreed to the ceasefire, providing our evidence is legitimate."

I cock an eyebrow. Whether those words are his or the enemy's, one thing is clear.

He doesn't think I'll go through with this.

"They said to deliver the proof to Central Station—"

"The proof?" Ezra's voice is a threatening growl, and I grab his forearm when he takes a step forward. "She's a *person!*"

Nolan scoffs but doesn't spare Ezra a glance, trapping only me in the heat of his stare. His pale eyes burn with indignation. "If they saw her that way, we wouldn't be in this situation—"

"When?" I interrupt, tightening my grasp on Ezra's arm. He trembles, rigid beneath my touch.

One corner of Nolan's lips—the skin dried and flaking—hooks upward, part smile and part sneer, raising goosebumps all over my body. There's something about the detached way he looks at me, like he no longer cares how this conflict plays out.

Like he doesn't want this plan to succeed.

Maybe he doesn't, I consider. With everything he's been working toward for years ripped away and no prospect of power to look forward to, what does he stand to gain from a peaceful resolution?

His life, my conscience retorts, but I'm beginning to think maybe that alone isn't enough.

But if it isn't, then why make the call?

Nolan's quivering upper lip catches my eye, and it occurs to me that I might have it all wrong. He isn't looking at me with such fervent hatred because he *doesn't* want this to work; he's looking at me that way because he *does*. He's just convinced himself that failure is inevitable and our impending demise is futile. And for that—for the dire outcome, the *only* outcome, he sees before us—he blames me.

The weapon whose mere existence foiled his plans.

"Two hours," he grinds out, pulling me out of my thoughts.

"So soon?" Jenner asks, his tone panicked.

I meet his gaze across the room, then quickly avert my eyes to the floor. It was already hard enough to look at him knowing he's hurt because of me, but the dejection on his face now makes it unbearable. I'd rather never look at him again than see him stare at me that way.

As if determined to test the limits of my heartache, Ezra mutters under his breath, "That doesn't give us much time."

I'm not sure whether he's referring to how long it will take to get to the agreed location or if he means for us to savor these final moments together. Knowing just how soon we'll have to say goodbye to each other makes me not want to ask.

I draw in a deep breath, then let it out, repeating the process twice to steady the tremor I sense at the edge of my voice. Once I'm certain I won't break, I look back at Nolan. "Did they make any new conditions?"

Arching a wiry brow, he chokes out a low, scornful laugh. "Well, the fact you're alive after I told them you were dead has made them…reasonably wary. They don't understand why you would—"

Why I would surrender myself to die…

"They don't need to understand," I snap, cutting him off. *No one does.* "They just need to agree to our terms."

"And they have," Nolan counters. "Or rather, they will," he amends.

I stiffen at the vague threat in his words.

"What do you mean, 'they will'?" Ezra asks. The suspicion in his tone mirrors the dread and uncertainty twisting my thoughts into every worst case scenario I can imagine.

"They *will*," Nolan repeats after a moment, that eerie half-sneer half-smile returning, "so long as when you arrive, you're still breathing."

This revelation takes me aback, and I gape at him, confused. "I thought they wanted me dead."

"They do." His fatalistic expression hardens into the cold, calculating leader of PHOENIX I met in the bunker outside the Heart. The man I recognize now, not as a savior as he professed to be, but as a monster.

Like me.

In this moment, with our facades shed, I see the man behind the mask more clearly than ever.

"But they want to be the ones to do it," he explains. "To be sure the danger you pose is eradicated for good."

The danger. It takes everything in me not to laugh. If only they knew what I was protecting them from by choosing to hand myself over like this. By *choosing* to die instead of waiting for this disease to end everything the way fate intends.

I don't bother enlightening Nolan to the truth—to the real danger he's oblivious to. In his eyes, and in the eyes of everyone else here, except for Ezra and Jenner, and possibly Quinn now, I would still be a monster. The harbinger of their deaths or, at the very least, a life-threatening hazard. Nothing I say at this point will change that. Not after everything I've done. Not after all the suffering I've caused.

So, instead, I just say, "If those are their conditions, so be it."

Regardless of the road I take to get there, all paths lead me to the same end.

Shaking his head, Nolan rubs a hand over his mouth, his nails scratching at his scraggly facial hair. "This is all going to blow up in your face," he warns. "You're going to die for nothing."

There's a cruel undertone to this premonition that makes my body go rigid, like he's said these words, or some variation of them, to someone before. The frustration and disdain in his gaze when he looks at me strikes a familiar chord, and it makes me wonder if the person in question, the one who received this warning, was my father.

I can envision it—Nolan reprimanding him, telling him his eventual death would be meaningless if he abandoned their cause. That if he wasn't part of PHOENIX then he was against it.

That his betrayal made them no different than enemies.

My teeth clamp down on the tip of my tongue as I recall how Nolan knew my father would be executed and did nothing to stop it. And as a fresh wave of hate rushes through me, I realize I don't just want him to be stripped of his title and role in whatever new world PHOENIX makes. What I want is for him to feel just as helpless as my father must've felt that day, bloody and beaten on the floor of our home.

I want him to feel just as powerless.

My lips harden into a scowl. "Then I guess it's a good thing you won't be there to watch it."

Terror ignites behind Nolan's eyes, and he takes an involuntary step back, the fear wafting off him so potent I can practically smell it. The sudden tension permeating the silence is thick, and I can feel the others watching me closely, anticipating what I'll do next. Wondering if I'll act on the obvious threat behind my words.

I stare at Nolan without blinking, letting him stew a while longer in the uncertainty of this moment. Letting him debate if I'd actually kill him.

I would, it occurs to me as I scan his face, noting the droplets of sweat beading along his hairline. But I won't. Not because he doesn't deserve it, but because enough people have already died because of me and my soul can't take anymore. I'm done.

I don't want to be the reason anyone else has to die.

When I turn from Nolan, he lets out a small gasp, as if I was forcibly holding his gaze in mine and that connection is broken now that I've looked away. Quiet, distressed breaths escape him, but I ignore them, focusing on Jaedyn.

"Does this bunker have a secure room that can be locked from the outside?" I ask.

I can sense an unspoken question on the tip of her tongue as she glances between me and Nolan. Her furrowed brow smooths out a moment later as understanding dawns in her gaze.

"There's a storage room filled with nonperishables just down that hallway"—she points over my shoulder to the corridor leading past the washroom. "I only had a quick look inside a few minutes ago, but it should be fit for purpose. Duke?"

She casts an expectant glance at the brooding hulk of a man standing close beside her, who snaps to attention with a jerk of his head.

"On it," he barks before crossing to Nolan. "Come on, old man," he growls, grabbing his arm. "Let's put you someplace where you won't go around causin' any more trouble for anyone."

Nolan curses under his breath, his eyes flashing to mine as he fights against the larger man's grip. "You need me!" he shouts. "Without me, *everything* will fall apart!"

This time, I don't bother suppressing my laugh. "Richter said the same thing to me just before I killed him."

I take a slow step forward, relishing the way Nolan flinches back when the space between us shrinks. Duke's grasp on his arm holds him steady, and on his other side, Ezra appears, wielding his gun like a whip. There's nowhere for Nolan to go. Nowhere for him to escape to this time.

You're helpless now. Just like you deserve.

"Move," Ezra growls, pressing the pistol's muzzle into the older man's side.

Grimacing, Nolan does as commanded.

"Wait," I breathe when they've only taken two steps.

Ezra and Duke both pause, the latter holding Nolan in place by the nape of the neck. Ezra's eyes cut to mine, and I nod toward their captive's trembling fist.

"You won't be needing this," I murmur, reaching forward and tugging the communicator free of his fingers.

Now, you're not just helpless. You're also alone.

As Duke and Ezra lead Nolan out of the room, I hand the communicator to Jaedyn, who comes to stand beside me, her expression sullen.

"I'm ashamed I didn't challenge him sooner," she laments with a sigh.

I shake my head. "The past doesn't matter." Although it haunts me, it can't be changed. Only one thing can. "Only the future," I whisper.

"And what is it you see when you look at ours?" Jaedyn asks.

For so long, I've wondered if it was even possible to change the future—to alter course on our preordained paths. Has anything I've done to prevent the terrible fate I've seen awaiting us made any difference? Or was every act of perceived rebellion on my part already planned by some greater power? In trying to change the future, did I inadvertently cause it?

These are the questions I've been running from since I first found out about my disease.

Questions I now need the answers to.

Drawing in a calming breath, I slide my eyes shut and slip into that state of deep focus I've been to many times before. It's harder to reach now without my collar, and my head pounds with the effort, but I push through my discomfort.

My hands shake at my sides as I search inside myself, reaching for that mental thread that will draw a line between me and the future I'm now desperate to see. When I find that thread, I latch onto it without hesitation.

A shiver of apprehension runs through me as the image takes shape behind my closed eyes. My heart sinks when the destruction that plagues my every waking thought rises in front of me like a wave, although the vision isn't as clear this time, the scene almost translucent.

That ember of hope I've been holding onto so tightly bursts into a flame as another image appears behind the first, sharpening as the desolation I've grown so accustomed to gradually fades. The image isn't fully opaque, the picture quivering, like this possible future might vanish if I so much as breathe wrong, but the details are clear enough for me to make out a different version of the Heart—not untouched by war, the scars still visible in the details around us, but *healed* from it.

The people walking the streets smile and nod to each other, no longer afraid of untoward attention or proximity, and children run and laugh freely among them, a sight I don't think I've ever witnessed except for that one glimpse of Ezra's childhood. Bright colors bring life to the cold grays of the buildings in the form of expressive clothing and flowers, and a beautiful melody floods the air instead of the strict, enforced silence I've always known.

A piano, I realize, and a tear slides down my cheek at the unbidden memory of my father.

I scan my changed surroundings with interest, faltering when I suddenly find myself before the East Gate, the wall enclosing the Heart looming over me. As I look up, I notice the wall is intact, but the gate stands open without an Enforcer in sight. No guards. No closed metal doors.

The gate is just open, granting passage to anyone who wants to leave.

Clamping a hand over my mouth, I stifle a cry, an intense relief filling me until it feels like my body might explode. This vision… It means there's still a chance. A chance for the Heart to thrive. A chance for a new world where the city is no longer a cage and fear is no longer a prison. A future where, after so long, the sacrifices of the people I love will be realized. A world where we will finally have—

"Peace," I gasp, my eyes wrenching open. A thick line of blood trickles from my nose to my lips, and a headache beats against the inside of my skull, but despite the nagging pain, I smile.

Because after everything we've endured, if that future I saw just now is what awaits at the end of this war...

It will all have been worth it.

I meet Jaedyn's stunned gaze, and she exhales sharply, as if releasing a breath she was holding. "That's reassuring. It means your plan will work."

I nod, reaching for something to hold myself upright when the room starts spinning. My fingers find the back of an unoccupied chair.

"Any idea how I can get there?" I rasp, wiping the blood from my nose on the sleeve of my jacket. "I don't think going back the way we came is an option."

"Probably not," she agrees. "Even if the fire wasn't an issue, there are still the Enforcers outside to contend with."

I nod again, swallowing the acidic burn of bile as it sweeps up my throat. At this point, I'm not sure I could overpower even one soldier let alone the dozens, possibly hundreds, waiting in the plaza above us.

"*But,*" Jaedyn adds, and I shoot her an expectant glance, "there's a passage that leads from the back of this bunker and feeds out into the tunnels, which you can take to get there. I haven't seen it myself, but Rodrick told us about it when he was leading us down here. We were planning on getting out that way."

I snort. "So much for them being unusable."

"Unusable?" she echoes.

I shrug, brushing the sweaty hair back off my face. "It's just something Ezra told me Bilken said." When she raises a brow for me to elaborate, I sigh. "According to Bilken, the State believes the tunnels were filled with toxic gas and that's why they never thought to monitor the system for PHOENIX. But clearly that was a lie, otherwise why build an escape route leading into them that would be used by the State's leading officials? People they wouldn't want to die."

The Head scoffs. "Because, sometimes, lies are easier than the truth. Especially when you can benefit from them."

Like how the State benefited from PHOENIX's reputation as a danger to our society.

If what Jaedyn is insinuating is true, then the State didn't just know the tunnels were perfectly usable… It *wanted* to keep people away from them. But why? So, citizens wouldn't seek out PHOENIX for themselves?

Or so they wouldn't start asking questions, like why the State hadn't eliminated the threat?

"If there's one thing governments thrive on, it's bullshit. Those at the top of the hierarchy will always spout lies to their underlings to keep them from asking questions or poking their noses where they don't belong." Jaedyn crosses her arms with a huff. "The State has always loved its rules, but if there's one thing I've learned over the years, it's that rules are created for everyone *except* the people in power."

I nod. Bilken's office and his collection of hypocrisy were proof enough of that—of the laws disregarded by the very people who helped to create them.

Mulling over that thought for a moment, I glance at the other Heads seated behind us, the three men huddled together in quiet discussion.

"I hope you'll do things differently." Although the words are soft so only Jaedyn can hear them, there's an edge to my voice—an unspoken warning that, if they don't, any peace I saw will be forfeit.

Jaedyn cocks her head slightly, drawing my gaze. "Everyone thinks you're a monster, that you brought this hell into our lives,"—she peers at me as if she's trying to see behind the guise this war has forced me to don—"and while that may be true, do you know what I see when I look at you?"

Silence. I go still, all nausea and light-headedness forgotten.

I don't want to know, I try to say, but I can't find the words.

When I don't answer, she says, "A scared little girl." There's a note of uncertainty in her tone, and the pitch when she speaks is uneven, like someone fighting back a strong surge of emotion.

Like someone who thinks what's happening to me is wrong… even when it's the only option.

She steps closer now, lowering her voice to a whisper. "Can you really follow through with this knowing the cost?"

The cost?

What is one life worth when weighed against millions?

What is *my* life worth when weighed against the people I love?

"It's overdue," I breathe, then clear my throat, eager to change the subject. "What will you do about Nolan?"

Her eyes shift in the direction of the storage room. "For now, we'll keep him confined." Then, nodding to herself, she says with more force, "But once things have calmed down, he'll need to answer for his crimes. A trial, I think. Like the way things used to be done."

A smile lifts the edges of my lips, and for a second, I hear my father in Jaedyn's words. The way he used to talk about the old world and what life was like before the State. The way his recollections held a glimmer of hope.

Like we could someday return to that place.

She is exactly what PHOENIX needs.

For the first time, that peace I saw really feels possible.

There's only one thing left to do.

"I should be going."

Jaedyn's gaze snaps back to mine, and she frowns. "I could accompany you—"

"No. We have no idea what they'll have planned for me. Besides…" I swallow, the words thick in my throat. "I need to do this alone, and *you* need to survive. I'm counting on you to honor our agreement."

Her frown deepens, but she acquiesces, nodding. Then, looking me up and down once, she offers me her hand again. "Goodbye, Wynter."

Pressing my palm against hers, I grip tightly. "Good luck."

As our hands slide apart, my vision goes bleary. It's time to go talk to the others—the one thing in this world I'm not ready to do. My chest tightens when I think of Jenner, as I picture his face when I utter that final, tearful farewell.

By comparison, surrendering myself to be executed sounds easy.

Still, it needs to be done, and so I draw in a breath—mentally ready but emotionally unprepared to go say my goodbyes—only to turn and find Jenner and Quinn standing behind me. I didn't even hear them approach, and a surprised squeak escapes me as I glance between them.

Although physically they look like a strong wind might blow them both over, their eyes are bright and determined, their faces set in matching glowers.

"Jenner—" I begin, but Quinn cuts me off.

"We were eavesdropping," he says in a blunt monotone.

Jenner shoots the ex-Enforcer an appalled look. "No, we weren't."

"We *were*," Quinn says again, rolling his eyes.

Misery softens the hard edges of Jenner's frown, and for a moment, he just stares at me, a sense of pleading behind those blue eyes. Finally, he admits, "We heard you say you were leaving."

The ex-Enforcer scoffs, and before I can respond, he adds, "What he *means* to say is we're coming with you."

"What?" I blurt out. Panic rockets through me as I envision the two of them topside again, caught in the chaos outside in their current conditions. "You can't. It's too dangerous—"

"And everything else we've done hasn't been?" Quinn retorts.

My lips press into a line. "This is different," I hiss.

"No," Jenner mutters gently. "It's not."

"I…" My heart hammers against the inside of my throat. I need to say something. *Anything* to convince them I should do this without them. Ignoring the danger, I don't want them to see it.

I don't want Jenner to watch as I die.

"Don't try to talk us out of it, Wyn." Jenner's expression is pained, as if the concept of me leaving without him is a betrayal he can't bear to put into words. "We've come with you this far, haven't we?"

"He's right."

I whip around at the growl of a third voice behind me, a voice I would know anywhere. Jaedyn is gone—I glimpse her walking away to meet Duke, who lingers at the edge of the room—and in her place, Ezra stands a few feet away, staring at me, as if he can see into my battered soul.

When I meet his gaze, a tear slips down my cheek, but I can't find the strength to lift my arm and brush this tangible evidence of my fear and heartache from my skin. Closing the distance between us, Ezra takes my face in his hands, like he has so many times, and wipes the wetness away with his fingers.

"We go together…remember?" he breathes.

Once again, I glimpse that bleak resignation behind the familiar warmth of his eyes. I wanted to part with Jenner and Quinn here—to spare them from what comes next in my journey—but Ezra never had that option. Like his mother warned me, he has a role to play yet. A role only *he* can step into.

"No one else can do it but him."

Her words haunt me, and more than ever before, I feel the truth to them in my bones. Regardless of my intentions to hand myself over, to let the enemy handle the threat as they see fit, I fear we won't make it that far. And even if we do—

"This disease likes to protect itself."

A shudder rips through my body. What's stopping me from losing the last of my flimsy control and massacring everyone who lifts a finger to harm me, even if I agreed to it? What if Alivia was right, and surrendering alone won't be sufficient to prevent the destruction I'm destined to cause? I might've seen a different path in the Heart's future, but that's all that image was: a possibility. A glimmer of light at the end of the tunnel.

It wouldn't take much for the darkness of death to extinguish that glimmer and swallow us whole.

That's why Ezra needs to come with me—so he can do what he's destined to do before that prospect of peace I witnessed is jeopardized. If the plan goes to hell and no one else can kill me, he needs to do it himself, like he promised. Even if it means killing me before I surrender to avoid further bloodshed… So long as they *see* it…

So long as the enemy *knows* that I'm dead…

That might be enough.

I had hoped it wouldn't come to this, but I realize now that as much as I wish I could spare Ezra from this task, I can't. Even I don't have that power. Still, my chest aches at the thought of what this might do to him. Of the trauma I'm thrusting upon him by asking him to pull that trigger.

"His fate has always been tied to yours."

Ezra might've made me a promise, but I made a promise, too, even if I never said the words out loud. A promise to myself. A promise to his mother, her dying words a painful blemish on my memory. If I'm going to save his life and put an end to this war for good…

This is the only way.

A sob catches in my throat, and I exhale a soft whimper. Then, looking him in the eye, I whisper, "Together."

TWENTY-SEVEN

THE PASSAGE AT THE BACK of the bunker feeds into the tunnels, just like Jaedyn said, and after a quick goodbye to Duke—who opts to stay behind with the Heads and help them once it's safe to resurface—we set off, ready to meet my fate.

Water soaks into my boots as I trudge through the murky run-off flooding the tunnel floor, our forward progression lagging, slowed by injury and illness. Still, I push ahead through my exhaustion, and as we follow the curve of the path in the general direction of Central Station, I'm struck by a dizzying sense of déjà vu, just like I was in the weeks before I got my memories back.

This moment… This is just like when I returned to the DSD, except, there's no promise of a cure awaiting me at the end.

Still, there is one glaring difference to that night that brings me comfort now, even if all I see at the end of this road is darkness.

Unlike then, I'm not alone this time.

My pulse trips as I glance ahead at Jenner and Quinn, then over at Ezra, who stays close beside me, crushing my hand in his grip, a weighted silence saturating the damp air between us. No one has spoken since we left the bunker over an hour ago, even though there's still so much to say.

"Tell my son I love him."

Alivia's words trouble my thoughts, stirring all too familiar feelings of guilt.

Feelings I never seem to escape.

I urge myself to relay her message to Ezra, but how? How exactly do you tell someone you spoke with their dead mother? I can't imagine there is an easy or right way to do it. All that matters is that I do. He deserves to know—to hear her final words.

To be given the chance to finally put his unresolved feelings about her illness and death to rest.

"Ezra," I force out, slowing my steps.

My fingers tighten around his, and he pauses mid-stride, looking back at me, his expression worried.

"I..." A growl of frustration rumbles deep in my chest, leaching into my voice. "This is going to sound insane."

Ezra offers me a small consoling smile. "More insane than seeing the future?"

A melancholy laugh parts my lips. "Probably."

Although his tone and gaze are teasing, there's a heart-wrenching sadness behind both that grab me by the throat and squeeze. I try to swallow, to free myself of the suffocating sensation, but my mouth and tongue are dry and every breath feels like broken glass in my airway.

When I don't say anything more, the corners of Ezra's mouth twitch, dragging down into a telltale frown that betrays the panic undoubtedly rising to the front of his thoughts. I see it flashing behind his hazel eyes when he steps closer to me.

"Wynter, what is it?"

Say it, my conscience chides.

"A few days ago," I blurt out, wincing at the harsh croak of my words. Clearing my throat, I start again. "A few days ago, back at the safe house, I had a vision of you as a child. Your brother and Rai were there, too. And…" I hesitate, steeling myself. "Your mother."

His brow, which was furrowed, now raises in question. "What were we doing?"

"Playing, but—"

"That's strange." His eyes drift away from mine, narrowing. "I don't remember my mother ever watching us play."

For a moment, he stares blankly over my shoulder, as if searching for the memory. Unable to find it, he looks back at me, intently now, and I can hear each beat of my heart in my ears. I know what he's thinking—that it wasn't safe to play out in the open the way he, his brother, and Rai did as children. That they wouldn't have done it with parental or *any* watchful eyes in sight—not considering the way we were all raised to understand the potential consequences of drawing unnecessary attention to ourselves.

Thinking back on that vision, I recall their stifled laughter and the way Rai tried to hold in her cries, like they were aware that what they were doing was dangerous. Even as young children, they knew—just as I learned early on—it was better to be neither seen nor heard.

"Wynter," Ezra presses, and goosebumps wash over my skin at the gentle prodding way he says my name.

I let out a choked breath. "That's because she wasn't there," I confess, shuddering under the weight of each word. "Not the way you were."

His expression contorts, vacillating between shock and trepidation. "What are you saying?"

My palm is slick against his, my grasp faltering. I curl my fingers tighter.

"She was there the same way I was. We spoke."

Ezra blanches, and a surprised sound escapes him that makes me feel sick to my stomach.

"That's…not possible," he stammers.

"We are the epitome of what shouldn't be possible, and yet, here we both are."

As his mother's voice stirs in my memory, I recall the sharpness of her face in my vision. How alive she had seemed to me. How real.

And, more than ever, I'm certain it wasn't a dream.

"We were both looking at the same moment," I murmur, repeating Alivia's explanation. "Me, from the future, and your mother—"

"From the past," Ezra finishes, the realization stretching across his pale face. Then something else occurs to him and he gasps, the words that follow almost inaudible. "She was still alive."

He averts his gaze for a moment again, digesting this information, before abruptly snapping his eyes back to mine. There's something different about the way he looks at me now, with suspicion burning behind his stare.

And when he next speaks, his tone is harder than it was a moment before.

"What else did she say, Wynter?"

This time, there's a coldness to the way he utters my name— spoken not without love but like that love is encased in a thin layer of frost, the warmth underneath barely perceptible.

"She…" Sweat prickles the back of my neck as the nerves writhing in my stomach twist my insides in knots. *Damn it, Wynter, just speak.* "She explained why she told you to find me."

Ezra's eyes narrow again, his gaze now accusatory. "That's why, isn't it? Why you made me promise that I'd—" Voice catching, he wrenches his hand free of mine, and running it over his face, he takes a step back. His expression under his palm is aghast.

My heart breaks at the sudden distance between us, and without thinking, I reach out to take his hand again, needing his touch to ground me like I need air to breathe.

"It's the only way," I manage through tears, clutching his fingers, pulling them away from his face. "No one else will be able to do it—"

"Why?" he growls, shaking me off. "If you're so eager to die, I'm sure there's a firing squad waiting for you at Central Station."

I resist the inclination to flinch, hearing the quiet venom in his tone for what it is. Pain. His words might be cruel but so is what I'm asking of him. He's the one who will live with the repercussions of our words and actions, not me. I have an escape from that heartache.

Even if it's an escape I don't want.

"I don't *want* to die," I whisper, fighting to keep my voice steady. "But I don't want you and Jenner to either."

His jaw trembles, and a tear breaks through the hard exterior he's pushed into place until the stone facade cracks completely. He grimaces, trying to force the tears back, but they just keep coming.

Rising onto my toes, I press my forehead to his. "If I have to choose…every time, I will choose you."

As I erase the remaining distance between us, I taste the salt of his grief on my tongue. At first, he doesn't kiss me back, his body stiff and unyielding to mine. But, gradually, his lips part as I knew they would, giving into me the same way I always find myself giving into him. His free hand curls around my waist, his fingertips slipping under the hem of my jacket, grazing the skin at my lower back. I shiver at his caress, which is both reluctant and desperate—his hand pulling me closer but not close enough.

When we break apart, he cups my face in his hands and leans back just enough to look me in the eye. "I won't talk you out of this…will I."

It isn't a question but a statement of cold realization, which robs me of the warmth his touch stirred within me only seconds before.

"'Two brothers,'" I breathe, holding his tear-soaked gaze. "'One, the creator of a terrible weapon. The other…destined to destroy it.' That's what your mother said." My fingers circle his wrists as I let my own tears fall. "The truth is…this disease won't let anyone else pull that trigger. It *has* to be you."

"Because my mother *said* so?" He spits the words, vehemently shaking his head. "Just because that's how she interpreted what she saw doesn't make her word law—"

"Because I love you!" I cry.

As these words leave my lips, I realize this is the first time I've said them, *really* said them, out loud to the one person who deserves to hear them most. The proclamation is long overdue, and I hate myself for saying it like this—for throwing such beautiful words around as nothing more than an angry riposte.

Chest heaving, I force myself to continue. To *make* him see why there's no other way. My tone holds a pleading edge. "Every time I come close to hurting you, I *always* snap out of it."

Bilken's office when I became consumed by the flashback of my father and us playing the piano together.

Earlier today when I lost control and snapped, killing however many Enforcers.

Both times, I came close to hurting Ezra. Or worse.

And both times, I got my senses back before I could.

The only two times I *did* hurt Ezra—first, when I choked him shortly after PHOENIX extracted me and then, when Richter pulled at my strings and made me lash out via the remote for my collar—I was in a subdued state of manipulated control. My powers weren't awake and wild, in need of taming. Not like they are now.

With the collar, the monster was asleep, but now, it's awake, and the only person it will answer to isn't me.

It's him.

"My power… It won't stop you," I whisper, more certain than ever as the hum of pressure building under my skin seems to calm for a moment, reinforcing this line of thought. Maybe this disease doesn't actually want the release it's been leading me toward all this time. Maybe what it actually wants is an end.

Maybe what the monster really desires is peace.

"You were right," Ezra mutters, lowering his hands from my face. "This does sound insane."

A joyless smile finds its way onto my lips. "Maybe. But since you made me that promise, I've seen the possibility of a different future. A world where the Heart can have peace. The image was weak, almost like fate hadn't decided its course yet.

But I saw it, Ezra. It can happen."

"You aren't making this any easier," he grits through clenched teeth, his arms shaking under the lingering touch of my fingers.

"It's not meant to be easy." I lift a hand to wipe away his tears, trailing my thumb across his wet lower lip. "But that doesn't change the fact that you still need to do it."

I drop my hand, and for a long moment, we just stare at each other, neither one daring to speak a word. When I can't bear the silence any longer—or the uncertainty of whether or not he'll fulfill his promise—I clear my throat, ready to play the only card I have left.

"Your mother," I begin, and Ezra's eyes blow wide, the hazel depths terror-stricken. "I was with her in her final moments, and do you know what she asked me to do?"

I note his small intake of breath and the way his chest ceases movement in anticipation and dread of what I might say. He gapes at me, but I don't waver under the intensity of his gaze.

"She begged me to save you. To die to ensure you would live." A sacrifice I was ready to make before she even asked it of me. "So, if you can't do this for me, because *I* asked you to do it, then do it for her. Do it because it was her dying wish to see her remaining son live."

"Wynter," Jenner calls suddenly, and I turn my head toward the uneasy sound of his voice, peering down the length of the tunnel to where he and Quinn watch us from a respectful distance away. Even in the thick cover of shadow, I can see the discomfort on each of their faces—can see the way their eyes flick from me to Ezra, as if the tension between us is a tangible thing they can see.

Maybe it is, I consider, pursing my lips.

Maybe they can see it as clearly as I can feel it pushing me and Ezra apart.

When I meet Jenner's gaze, he nods toward the left side of the tunnel where a ladder stands a foot away from the curved wall, leading up into a circular opening in the ceiling.

"We're here," he says, and those two words are like lead in my gut.

I risk a glance at Ezra, but he doesn't return it, his eyes downcast on the floor, ringed with tears. Gulping down the lump in my throat, I brush past him and continue through the shallow covering of turbid water to where Jenner and Quinn wait up ahead, pausing beside the ladder. I'm not sure if they overheard our conversation or if I care one way or the other. What I can't stand is the pitying looks on their faces.

"Is the station far from wherever this leads out?" I ask, eager to direct their focus elsewhere.

"Not exactly," Quinn mutters. When I arch a questioning brow at him, he points at the ceiling. "It's directly above us."

My eyes dart to the unlit hole above as the air expels from my lungs in a nearly silent "Oh."

Everything that's transpired since my placement exam—both the good and the bad—has been leading me to this, to the culmination of my existence. It's strange to finally be here after so long, and at the same time, it feels like this moment has come too quickly, like my death—however prepared I am for it—has snuck up behind me without warning. I haven't had enough time, not only with Ezra and Jenner but with myself. With the *real* me, freed from the constraints of our society.

I haven't had enough time to live.

Shaking my head of those thoughts, I breathe out through

my nose to steady my nerves and place a hand on the closest ladder rung, the metal rusty and flaking beneath my grip. My fingers tremble, but I tighten my hold. Then, placing one hand over the other, I climb.

I don't look back, but I hear the clink of each step as the others follow, trailing me into the claustrophobic darkness of the maw-like opening. My panting breaths reverberate around me, and I can't help imagining they belong not to me but to some great beast, like the ones from the stories my father used to read to me when I was young. I feel the heat of every exhalation reflected back on my face as if I'm trapped in its mouth, about to be swallowed whole.

Desperate for fresh air, I hasten my movements, but the ladder doesn't go as high as I expect and my head soon collides with the underside of a manhole cover at the end of the vertical tunnel. Profanities unfurl on my tongue, but I swallow them and direct that anger at the metal, pushing against it with all my strength. Thankfully, it lifts without much hassle. My fingers curl around the lip of the cover, finding leverage, and I shove it out of the way, reveling in the brush of cooler air on my face.

I scramble out of the tunnel onto one of the station's platforms but remain on my hands and knees as I work a little too hard to catch my breath. My lungs feel like they're on fire and my head is swimming with a disorienting vertigo that blurs my surroundings. Or what I can see of them in the minimal glow of Quinn's flashlight.

"Wynter?"

I glance up at the sound of my name, but it takes me longer than I would like to register Jenner standing over me. He plants a tentative hand on my back.

"Are you okay?" he breathes.

With a grunt, I nod and push up to my feet, then look over my shoulder, scanning the shadows for the others. I spot Quinn first—also struggling to climb to his feet—then Ezra shortly after, his light hair drawing my gaze as he emerges from the hole in the floor.

Once all four of us are upright on the platform, I ask, "How long do we have?"

When Quinn checks his communicator, a frown immediately forms on his lips. "Fifteen minutes, give or take."

This revelation sombers us, and we head for the lobby without another word.

Just like when we were last in Central Station, there isn't another soul in sight. The fluorescent bulbs overhead, which had worked intermittently when we passed through here before, don't even buzz this time, trapping us in a shroud of darkness broken only by the beam of Quinn's flashlight. He guides the way, shining the light in a straight path, and the trash and abandoned possessions littering the floor get caught up in its glow, all coated now in a fine dusting of ash. There's a permanence to seeing them like this that unsettles me. Perhaps because I know, if my plan goes wrong, life will never return to this place.

When we reach the turnstiles, I fumble over the barrier without the rush of excitement I experienced only days ago at the train terminal in Zone 7. The others seem to share my lack of enthusiasm, their movements hurried but reluctant, as if they're the ones walking to their deaths and not me. I try not to dwell too much on that thought—on what awaits me outside this station—but I can sense the clock ticking down over my head like a physical presence I can't shake. Each passing second weighs me down.

Our steps are gunshot loud in the silence as we proceed toward the stairs leading back aboveground, and with every inch of the lobby we cross, my heart beats faster, pummeling into my ribs. When we finally ascend, emerging into the gentle light of the breaking dawn, I go still, pausing beside Quinn, who clicks off his flashlight.

The immediate area outside the station is still dark, but the pink light creeping across the sky has drastically softened the shadows, revealing enough of the plaza for us to make out the contingent on the other side. A clear path stands between us and them, as if some greater power has shifted the rubble and buried corpses aside.

Once again, I'm struck by an overwhelming sense of déjà vu. I suppose, like my many returns to the DSD and our repeated trek through Central Station tonight, this is just another example of fate guiding my steps and turning the wheel that is my life full circle. After inflicting so much pain on this world, it's fitting my final moments would look like this. That my death would be witnessed and initiated by an army just like the ones I helped to slaughter.

It really is a firing squad, like Ezra said. I suppress a bitter laugh at the thought.

A delegation of at least one hundred soldiers lines the opposite edge of the city square, their commanding officer—possibly even the same person Nolan spoke to earlier—standing at the front of the congregation, his face a pale smear in the distance. I'm not surprised by the show of force. If anything, I expected it.

"That must be the welcoming party," Quinn grumbles.

Jenner snorts from somewhere on Quinn's other side, but the sound, while derisive, lacks humor. When he speaks, I can hear his voice waver. "They don't look very welcoming to me."

Sucking in a breath, I turn to the left, aware of Ezra standing a few steps behind me on my right. As much as I want to, I can't bring myself to look at him. Not yet.

Instead, I focus on Jenner and Quinn. "Before I go, I'd like a moment to speak with each of you alone…if that's okay."

Jenner's eyes drop to the ground at my words, the vibrant blue depths glistening with unshed tears. Quinn, on the other hand, looks unfazed—his expression pinched into a disgruntled frown that I've come to learn is his normal face.

And yet, I spot an unexpected tenderness from the ex-Enforcer when, after a glance back at Jenner, he sighs and gestures with a leading tilt of his head that he'll speak with me first. It might not seem like much of a sacrifice, but he's bought Jenner the delay of a few precious moments. Moments before he'll have to finally acknowledge the reality of the situation…

And say goodbye.

Quinn and I move away from the others until we're out of earshot, pausing beside a message board several feet away, on the left side of the station entrance. His obsidian eyes watch me closely, but he doesn't force the conversation, instead giving me time to find the right words.

"Once it's done, call Jaedyn," I say, keeping my voice as low as possible. "Let her and the other Heads know it's finished and put them in contact with their commanding officer over there, if you're able to." Quinn listens intently as I repeat the frequency band Jaedyn told me just before we departed the bunker, then he follows my gaze when I jerk my chin in the direction of the distant figure standing front and center at the opposite edge of the plaza. "Whatever you do, don't let *them*"—I nod again toward the enemy army—"see you or Jenner as a threat. Especially Jenner."

Terror floods my chest at the thought of how he might respond once this is over. I've seen it—seen how he reacts when emotion gets in the way of sense. But I've also seen him show remarkable strength when everyone around him is falling apart. I have no way of knowing which way the scale will tip—if the pain of loss will outweigh his resilience. So, the only option is to make sure someone is watching his back once I'm gone. Someone objective to my death who won't let him try anything stupid.

Never one to waste words, Quinn nods, his expression as sullen as ever. "I can do that."

"Quinn—" I grab his arm, and for the first time, genuine surprise fills his eyes. When he looks at my hand, I loosen my grip and instead wipe my sweaty palm on my pant leg. "I-I don't really know how to thank you. I know you don't like me and I understand why, but I'm still grateful you helped us get this far. Without you, we wouldn't even be here at all. And…" A broken breath jumps from my throat, and I stifle a sob. "You saved Jenner's life. If I could repay you for that, I would—"

"Don't worry about it," he interrupts, and this time, I'm the one gaping at him, lost for words. Frown deepening, he shakes his head. "Besides, after this, I think we're the ones who will owe *you* a debt. You're doing the right thing, by the way."

A startled laugh rips from my throat. "Are you just saying that so you can finally be rid of me?"

His eyes, always hard like chips of onyx, do something I didn't think them capable of. They soften. To my ongoing surprise, the ex-Enforcer, who once hit me over the head with a rifle, cracks a smile.

"Maybe."

The disdain I was always so certain Quinn feels for me seems to dissolve with this single word, leaving us with a mutual respect and something almost resembling friendship. As that realization sinks in, I suddenly find that everything that's happened between us, the lies and deceit... They no longer matter.

All that matters is this moment.

"Hey," Quinn says, placing a steady hand on my shoulder. "I'll keep an eye on them for you. I'll make sure they come out of this okay."

"Thank you," I breathe, and wiping away a tear, I peer over my shoulder at Jenner, who watches me with bloodshot eyes.

With one final appreciative nod at Quinn, I inch back toward the stairs, ignoring the way my heart seems to cave in on itself. Although Jenner's only a short distance away—in the very spot I stood in nearly three years ago, the day of my placement exam—the effort it takes to cross over to him is immense, every step more draining than the last. I'm exhausted in both my body and my soul, and with each passing moment, I feel more ready than ever to do what I came here to do if only to find the freedom of relief at the end of it.

"Why does it seem like I'm always begging you not to leave?" he asks when I reach him, the words strangled and raw in his throat.

"I wish I didn't have to," I whisper.

He gnaws on his lower lip for a moment, avoiding my gaze. "First, Rai. Now, you," he rasps as a tear curves over his cheekbone. "I won't be able to bear it."

Reaching out, I grab his hands and tug on them, urging him to look at me. "You underestimate yourself. You're the strongest person I know, Jenner. If anyone can make it through this, it's you."

His face scrunches into a grimace as more tears follow the first, their trails colliding at the point of his chin.

"Listen to me," I plead, and releasing his hands, I grab him by the sides of his face. "They're going to need someone like you, so I need you to keep fighting, okay? To make this place better than how I left it." My arms snake around his shoulders, pulling him in for a hug that I wish could last forever. "You're the only person I'd trust with the job."

When my hand combs through his thick hair, he nods, pressing his face into my shoulder.

"I wish—" he begins, but I cut him off, hugging him tighter. "I know."

There's a lot I wish. There's a lot I would've done differently in my life, but not this. Never this. If given the chance to go back and do everything over, I would make this sacrifice time and again without hesitation. There isn't a timeline or world that could exist where I wouldn't put his life or Ezra's above my own.

Where I wouldn't gladly die if it meant they could live.

When we pull apart, Jenner offers me a barely-there smile, even though all I see in his eyes is pain. I cup his cheek in the palm of my hand, hoping to leave him with some sense of lasting comfort, just as he's always comforted me. My lips turn upward, mirroring his, but it feels wrong to look at him this way and say the words that still need to be said.

By the time they breach the silence between us, my smile is long gone. As is his.

"Goodbye, Jenner," I murmur.

He leans into my touch, never once breaking my gaze. Not even when I pull away.

"Goodbye, Wynter."

My tears stream freely and without effort as I turn my back toward him and cross the pavement to the only person remaining in our group who I haven't spoken to yet. Ezra stares me down with furious eyes and is already shaking his head before I can even open my mouth.

"I won't say goodbye," he growls. "Maybe, if we make them *see* that you're not a threat, we can—"

"Your mother told me to tell you she loves you." At his startled expression, I step closer, lingering beside him just long enough to say one more thing. "Remember your promise," I whisper.

Before he can respond, I continue into the plaza, my gaze fixed on the blurring line of soldiers ahead. As I walk, the surrounding shadows lighten, the sky overhead filling with the soft glow of morning. Unlike earlier, the city is silent now, as if the entire Heart—or at least Zone 1—was abandoned in the time we spent underground getting here. I glance left and right, assessing the buildings on each side of the square, and just like in my vision, there isn't a single light to be seen or any signs of even the slightest movement or life.

If I don't look straight ahead or back, it's easy to imagine I'm the only one left. That I really am the sole survivor at the end of a world I am responsible for destroying.

A strange sensation takes root at that thought, and I stumble, falling carelessly to one knee. My torn palms slam into the asphalt, but I barely notice the ache in my hands, the terror and resurfacing pain spreading through me seizing my undivided attention.

I've experienced this kind of pain before, but there's something different about this time—something truly terrifying about how fast that violent, familiar heat rushes through me, like liquid fire in my veins.

Blood drips from my nose onto the backs of my hands and spatters the ash-covered ground, and time seems to slow as the crimson collides with the stone, each splash echoing back in my ears. Behind me, I hear someone calling my name, but the dull ringing in my head is drowning them out.

My arms shake beneath me as I push myself upright, but I manage only a single step before staggering again. Around me, the buildings stretch into disfigured streaks, and the rippling waves of static distorting my vision wash the world in tones of sepia until all I see are varying shades of muted brown.

It takes me a moment to realize the brown I'm seeing is actually dirt, the wind whipping the small particles up around me in a frenzy.

No, not the wind, I correct myself, lurching forward one more graceless step. Me.

I'm the one doing this.

The impairing fog is just like what I always saw in my vision, the city and destruction just discernible through the thick haze. But that's where the similarities end. The fear, the hysteria bubbling under my skin—those are stronger than they ever were when I was just a spectator to this moment.

Considering how many times I've seen this, I thought I would be more prepared. Less afraid. But I'm not. Any and all bravado I felt before slips away.

Muffled shouts reach me, and the pressure building in my chest reacts through the pain, my powers locking onto the soldiers at the far edge of the plaza, who are indistinct smudges of black in the distance. By now, they've all realized something is wrong. And, like so many before them, they're going to make the same mistake that left thousands of others dead.

Stop, I try to say when they reach for their guns, and as that word fills my thoughts, it occurs to me this might be the escalating moment—the trigger that sends my unstable powers into meltdown.

I never saw what caused my world-ending outburst, and I never stopped to consider what the vision wasn't showing me, too focused on the details it always repeated. On the elements I hoped I *could* control.

Now, I just want to laugh at my idiocy. Every aspect of my visions really have been self-fulfilling, like I feared. After all, I was the one who pushed for the deal that led us here into the arms of aggressors, just as it was the bullet meant for me that injured Jenner and left him bloody, like he was in my nightmare. Everything I've done to change the future and steer us from this course has only cemented our path.

When the world ends, it will be entirely my fault.

And yet, through the suffocating weight of my guilt, doubt grabs at me, pulling me back up for air. If these visions are self-fulfilling, then what about that glimpse of peace I saw?

How can I make that our new future?

The answer comes to me so quickly, it knocks the breath from my lungs. The options I saw were destruction or peace, there was no middle ground. Destruction is simple—my natural tendency. But peace?

For that, I need to die.

"Ezra." His name is a whimper on my lips, and slowing, I turn back toward the station, searching for him through the growing storm of debris. The ground rumbles beneath my feet, and my fingers tremble at my sides as the howling wind grows more wrathful. I don't see him, but I know he'll come. I've seen this moment enough times to be sure of that.

Still, despite that certainty, something breaks inside me when I catch sight of his face, his features the picture of clarity against the obscured backdrop of the city. I see him more clearly than I've ever seen him, and a tear slides down my cheek as he races forward, closing what feels like an insurmountable distance between us.

For so long, I've seen Ezra as two different people—the Ezra I know and the Ezra from my vision. But now, as he shouts out my name, a terrified distress in his voice, they are one and the same. And in his hand, he holds the gun from my vision.

Ready to end this just as fate intended.

A wet heat seeps from my ears, and as the pain in my head intensifies, I know this is it. For good, this time. No collar could fix me now, even if I had one.

The end is finally here.

"I'm afraid!" I admit without thought, my rising panic pushing me over the edge into madness. It's a cliff I've been stranded on for a while, and now, there's nowhere to go but down.

Down into the tides below where I will surely drown.

Ezra falters, and as his pupils blow wide, I can imagine all too easily what he's seeing. The blood streaming from my nose and ears. The black, soulless eyes of a monster. I have completed my transformation just like he has become the stranger from my vision. Now, we will step into the roles we were destined to play, offering two different paths for the future.

And I know which path I want to win.

"I don't want to kill anyone else," I cry, even as the ground quakes beneath my feet. Straining my jaw, I try to push back the power pouring out of my body, but I can't grab onto it, feeling it slip through my fingers like wisps of smoke. "I don't want to do this," I scream, hoping to goad Ezra into action or that fate will hear me and spare me from this terrible burden. Then, a choked sob escapes, and a truth I don't mean to utter spills out. "I don't want to die!"

Ezra gapes at me, horror spreading across his face like spilled ink, and I instantly wish I could unsay those words—that I could withdraw them from his memory just like I would erase all recollections of me if I could. Anything to make this easier on him, which is the opposite of what this confession will do. If anything, it'll only make this harder. Even if I meant those words with every fiber of my being as much as when I told him I love him, even if they're the truth, I would still take them back in a heartbeat. Because he needs to see this through. He *needs* to secure a future for this world. For him and for Jenner and Quinn.

And for that to happen, he needs to pull that trigger.

A bullet whizzes above my head, stirring the monster's impulsive rage, and I know if I don't end this quickly, that vengeful, savage power inside me will destroy everything, including the peace we've been fighting so hard for.

Focusing the pressure seeking a release from my body into the dirt whirlwind around me, I build it up to act as a shield between us, hoping to buy a few additional moments. Then, finding a thread of sanity to hold onto, I push back my retaliatory reflexes and shout, "You have to do it now before it's too late!" But Ezra doesn't move a muscle, not even when I scream *"Kill me!"* at the top of my lungs.

Running out of time and strength, I stumble forward, desperation guiding my steps, and drop to my knees in the dirt before Ezra. His lower lip quivers when I grab the hand holding the pistol destined to end my life, and raising it, I press the cold metal of the barrel against the middle of my forehead.

"Please," I breathe, and when I close my eyes, tears slide through, scalding the cuts and scrapes on my cheeks. "Please," I repeat, wrapping my fingers around his. "I don't want anyone else to die."

"But it's okay if you do?" Ezra asks. His voice is strained but the words are as loud as if he had shouted them to my overstimulated senses.

My lips part on a shaky breath, and I peer up at him through tear-soaked lashes. "If it means you live…then yes."

"That's the thing…" Shaking his head, he takes a step back. As the distance between us grows, the chilled metal of his gun slides away from my forehead. "I don't want to live without you. I won't."

The pain in those words is a noose around my neck, tightening around my windpipe and ripping the very air from my lungs. I stare at him, eyes burning but unable to blink. Unable to move.

Unable to breathe.

"I'm sorry, Wynter."

When he finally says it—the three words that have haunted me almost my entire life—the realization that comes with it is devastating. A tear cuts a line in the ash on his cheek, and shaking his head again, he slackens his fingers. The pistol falls from his grip to the ground.

Just as I always knew it would.

For a while, I've wondered what this part of the vision was trying to tell me—if Ezra really wouldn't carry out his promise or if these words would only come after he had. Once I saw the possibility of a future with peace, I hoped the outcome would be the latter, but now, disbelief stings me as it occurs to me just how wrong I was. Ezra might not want to lose me, but I also know he isn't that selfish. He can't really be willing to sacrifice the whole world just to avoid doing this…can he?

Doesn't he grasp that, even if he refuses to kill me, I'm still going to die?

"What are you—" I gasp, but he's speaking again before I can get the words fully out.

"I can't do it," he confesses, the tears coming fast now. "I know I promised, but I can't. I *won't*. Screw what my mother said!" he shouts into the howling wind. "Screw *fate*! I'd rather die with you than pull that trigger."

As this admission leaves his lips, I'm assaulted by that image I saw of him years ago—of that nightmare where I watched as he was reduced to ash, his remains blown away by the wind as if he never existed at all. If that's what awaits, then what was the point of every atrocity I committed and every choice I made to protect him? He'd be depriving those sacrifices of meaning…

And robbing the world of a chance to exist and thrive long after I'm dead.

"You have to," I beg. "If you don't—"

"No one else has to die." He looks half-crazed, the words tumbling out of his mouth in a rush. "There's another way. You just need to believe it."

Believe it?

I can taste the swarming dirt on my tongue, and the throbbing in my head only grows more brutal, distorting his face as he moves closer, sinking to the ground before me.

"You're capable of control. I've seen it," he says.

"With my collar!" I protest, letting out a deranged cry of pain as the agony in my head threatens to gouge my eyes out of their sockets.

His hands shoot out to steady me, gripping my shoulders. "You saved us from those soldiers," he counters. "And you did it without my brother's leash."

I blink at him through the tears obscuring my vision. He said soldiers, not Enforcers, and I realize he isn't talking about the moments after the explosion when I lost control and murdered almost everyone in the magistrates building. He's talking about the blockade with my mother, when I saved our group from certain execution by the task force sent to track me down.

He's right. I did control it then. Just as I called on my power to look into the future when prompted by Jaedyn. It was difficult, harder than any other time I used my power, but I did it using my own strength, without the borrowed control of the collar.

I did it without Dr. Richter.

"So, if you can't stop it..." Ezra looks up, his eyes trailing the swirling vortex around us. "Redirect it," he urges. "Contain that power."

"Where?" I press, my tone frantic and shredded. "There's

nowhere to contain it to—"

"Here," he murmurs, taking my hand and pressing it over his racing heart. He then knocks me gently under the chin, forcing me to meet his gaze, before placing his other palm against my chest in the same place mine rests against his. My pulse beats like moth wings under his touch. "Contain it *here*. Find your control and think of us. Only us."

Think of us.

My eyes widen. "If I do that—" Everyone will live except for him. No…except for *us*. But then, my death was always inevitable. It was his that wasn't, and I never wanted a scenario where everyone else would survive this except the one person I wanted to save.

"I know."

His left hand never moves from on top of mine, his palm hot against my skin, his fingers squeezing, offering reassurance… and making it clear what he's chosen.

For over two years, every decision I made was with Ezra and Jenner in mind. I only wanted to shield them—to spare them from the monster inside me and a terrible future no one, not even Richter, deserved. But, the thing is, they never asked me to protect them, and I never once stopped to consider what they wanted. If they even *wanted* to be saved or if I was just too afraid to let them go. To see history repeat itself, the way it did with my father and Rai.

Ezra's eyes scan my face, pausing to take in every detail. I can see it now, the acceptance in his gaze. He's made his choice just as I've made mine. I won't be able to talk him out of it.

Even if I wish I could.

"But…I only wanted to save you."

A sympathetic smile tugs at his cheeks, and when he speaks, I hear the heartache in his words…as well as the haunting truth behind them. "That makes two of us."

"Ezra, please—"

The full extent of my power slams against the invisible wall of my resistance, and I feel a crack form in that barrier—in the last remaining defense between life and all-consuming death. Any moment now, it could break.

I reach for the discarded gun on the ground, but he grabs my hand before I can touch it.

"No," he says firmly, and this time, it's his tone that holds the pleading edge. Shaking his head again, he pulls me close until I can feel his breaths against my cheeks.

"All I've wanted the last two years and five months," he begins, his voice thready, "was for us to be together again. This way…we can."

He looks down at our hands, nudging my chest with his palm, and as he pulls me close, my mind reels back over every time he uttered that word.

"Together…" I echo. How many times have we said this? How many times have we sworn it to each other—sworn not to leave the other behind?

A vow that outweighs the promise he's broken.

His hand combs through my hair, brushing the sweaty strands away from my face, and as I stare at him, taking in his features for the last time, I realize his tears have stopped. His expression is resolved, the love in his hazel eyes undeterred.

"Always," he swears.

Time seems to slow as a memory drifts to the forefront of my thoughts, and suddenly, I'm back at the blockade in Zone 3, just after parting ways with my mother. The words Ezra spoke then come rushing back, setting every hair on my body on end.

"*...you and I both know I'll always be here for you, Wynter. Even—*"

"Even at the end," I breathe.

"Forever," Ezra says.

His lips brush mine for a moment that's far too short, draining me of the last of my resistance. Both against him and against this disease.

And as the pressure rises inside me, I do as he asked.

I focus on us.

For years, I've wondered if the future could be changed, and I've carried the burden of that task, but maybe it was never only up to me.

The promise of a future was only possible once Ezra made his decision. Not to kill me as I asked but to *join* me.

As the dust thickens and the world fades to black, I consider that maybe Ezra's real role in our star-crossed paths wasn't to subdue the monster. It was to love it.

Maybe, all along, that was the real cure.

EPILOGUE

JENNER

THE AIR BURNS MY NOSTRILS, reeking of smoke and a musky, sweet odor that turns my stomach. Even now, weeks after the conflict has ended, the scent of burning flesh still lingers. It's a smell I don't think I'll ever get used to. A smell I can only hope will fade as the memory of what happened here fades along with it.

The dirt crunches in protest beneath my feet, the earth outside the city's walls a tangle of dehydrated weeds and other struggling plant life born from many long years of neglect. Perhaps, one day soon, with the gates of the Heart now open, life will thrive out here again. After everything we've been through, I have to believe it will.

Otherwise, what was the point of all this?

I carry on, taking the same path I've walked every day the last two months. The sun is setting, beginning its steady decline toward the distant horizon behind the darkening silhouette of the city. As it sinks, the rays stretch across the dried grass, and the glowing orange light against the yellowing vegetation makes the world around me look as if it's on fire.

My feet falter as I'm reminded of a night not that long ago

when we tore through these very same fields to save Rai. I recall the pounding of my heart against my ribcage and the painful hitching of my breaths, which only grew worse with each frantic step we took toward the Heart. Our progression was hurried and desperate but determined despite the potential threat before us. We knew what we were running into, and we embraced the unknown outcome regardless.

In that moment, nothing else mattered except saving our friend.

A lump rises in my throat as a gravelly, humorless chuckle escapes through the seam of my lips. I never thought I would miss those days—the days where I looked death straight in the eye and laughed without hesitation or fear. But I do. They held pain and true, immeasurable grief, and yet…

I miss them more than anything.

A spasm shoots through my right arm and I wince, trying to clench my hand to ease my discomfort, but my fingers don't move beyond a twitch. To my frustration, my arm sways limp at my side, the nerve damage in my shoulder rendering the entire limb useless—just as it's been since the day I was shot. The wound might've healed, but the lack of mobility and the ever-present ache I'm left with are inescapable reminders that nothing I did was ever going to matter. I could have jumped in front of a thousand bullets and, at the end…it still wouldn't have made any damn difference.

My feet slow to an unsteady halt, the dirt kicking up in a small hazy cloud around the toe of my boots. Although I'm no stranger to this place, every trip here feels like the first one all over again, my grief now just as ardent as it was in the beginning, the pain in my heart never easing. I keep hoping this is all only a dream and that, any second now, I'll wake up to a different reality where that day—the day that changed everything for this city, for the world, for *me*—ended differently. Where we managed to find an alternative to the decision that gave us this tenuous peace.

I remember those final moments as if they only happened yesterday. The violent dome of swirling dust that formed over the center of Zone 1. What we all saw once that dust finally settled.

The uncertainty that hung in the murky air while I waited to see if the war was over.

In the hours that followed, a covenant was made between the remaining Heads of PHOENIX and our attackers. The discussions didn't last long; they all agreed, with the threat at the source of the conflict eliminated, there was no further need for bloodshed.

In the end, our reformed enemy got what they came for.

And so, the people who were once our assailants became our allies, honoring the initial arrangement made with Nolan. An arrangement he had no hand in this time. There was only one unresolved matter to settle: the residual presence of the State in the Heart, which both sides wanted to see abolished.

Over the next few days, our attackers turned allies worked with PHOENIX to liberate the city before withdrawing their troops and parting with the promise of amity between us. With the proviso, of course, that we nourish this peace and do nothing to jeopardize it. That we be better.

Just like Wynter wanted.

But although the Heart is now at peace, there were sacrifices that came with our newfound freedom that I struggle to reconcile. Our world feels so different now. *My* world feels different.

And each morning, I wake up wishing this wasn't real.

Lowering my tear-streaked eyes to the ground, I sink into a squat and flatten the palm of my good arm against the sun-warmed surface of the erect stone slab jutting out of the earth. I'm at least a mile away from the Heart, and yet, the acrid smell that still plagues the city seems to have tagged along with me today, trailing my steps like an unwanted companion. The odor shrouds my body like a suffocating blanket, accosting every one of my senses. But the worst part isn't the odor—it's the memories that smell triggers within me.

Memories I fear I'll one day forget.

Scrubbing my hand over my face, I close my eyes and drag in a slow, calming breath. With my eyes squeezed shut, I can see her so clearly. How long will that last? How long before I can't remember the details of her face any longer?

How long before she's nothing more than a distant memory I can't recollect?

Swallowing my rising nausea, I force my attention to the heat of the rays on my face and the orange-tinged darkness beneath my lids. The solitary silence is peaceful, and as the seconds tick by, I try to forget where I am, as I often do when I come out here. Instead, I pretend I'm someplace else. In another time. Another life.

In a world where the people I love are still here.

But, eventually, my eyes have to open again, and when they do, I'm reminded, as I always am, that the past will always be out of reach. It can't be changed, no matter how many times I dream otherwise. The events that led to this moment are written, etched into the timeline of history.

Just like her name in the graffitied tombstone before me.

Anger rocks me, and my lips peel back into a grimace at the sight of the untidy word scrawled into the smooth gray surface above her name. Because of the State's greed, many knew who she was, her notoriety like a phantom presence. At first, knowledge of her was limited to those directly involved in this war, but over time, especially since the conflict ended, normal civilians living here who knew little of the State's outside actions heard of her, too. And, in turn, began to shift their blame. They grew to view her as the State had wanted her to be seen—as a weapon of their war. She became the villain, the one they viewed as culpable for the losses we suffered and the destruction we're still working to rebuild, all the while ignoring what else she was responsible for.

The reality that it was because of her they survived.

Scowling, I pluck a sharp rock from the ground and scratch the slur out with the jagged edge until the letters are illegible. Then, I scratch new words beside it. Ones that speak the truth of her actions that day regardless of what she did all the days before it.

Wynter knew what people thought of her, and she wore that label despite the burden it carried because she believed it as much as they did, maybe more. But she was never a monster—not the way Richter was—even if she was forced to do monstrous things. In the end, she proved that.

Dropping the rock, I admire my handiwork through tears, brushing away the resulting sandy residue with my fingertips. Even if no one else agrees with these words, even if I'm the only one who knows the truth of what almost happened that day, *I'll* always know.

And I'll carry that truth with me like a promise carved into my heart.

Wiping my palm on my pant leg, I push to my feet and direct my gaze to the grave marker standing to the right of Wynter's. Whenever I think of Rai, my mind instinctively pictures her on that bed in Richter's lab, a living doll he kept for his own sick amusement. I can barely stomach the thought of what that asshole did to her—what he *took* from her, not only in life but in death. Every day, I'm grateful he suffered. That he got exactly what he deserved.

But the satisfaction of his death is never enough to ease the festering sickness of regret inside me, and I often find myself dwelling on all the missed opportunities—the moments I could have told Rai how much she meant to me. That she didn't just draw me out of my own self-destruction after my family died, but that she *was* my family. The one I went to for advice.

Advice I could desperately use right now.

The thud of boots on dead earth resounds in my ears, and out of habit, I reach for the gun at my waist. Whipping around, I brandish it with my good arm, although my grip falters a little, the weapon awkward in my left hand.

"Calm down," Quinn grunts, raising his arms in mock surrender. "It's only me."

Exhaling a ragged breath, I holster my pistol. I'm not sure why I'm so on edge. We finally have the peace we fought for, and since the war ended, I haven't had to use my gun once. I shouldn't feel the need to even carry it anymore, let alone direct it at every sound.

Then again, maybe the fact that I do is proof the paranoia and fear instilled by the State will never go away. For some of us, we'll carry these scars forever.

As I rub my hand across my face to erase the evidence of my mourning, I clear my throat, forcing my voice to be steady. "What is it?" I ask. "Everything okay?"

"Jaedyn's looking for you," he says, but I can tell by the look on his face there's something else he wants to say.

"What?" I press.

He hesitates for a moment before taking a cautious step toward me, his dark eyes flicking between my face and the graves. "Was it worth it?"

I stare at him blankly, slightly raising my brow.

Discomfort stretches across his face. "Losing the people closest to you," he clarifies. "Was it a justifiable cost for this?"

I follow his gaze to the Heart, envisioning the ways our society has changed since Jaedyn and the other Heads took over. Several high-ranking officials were captured when the allied forces swept through the city, and the Enforcers who didn't surrender were killed. Those who did yield were put in Detention alongside Nolan to undergo a trial and determine if they can be safely reintegrated into society since many were only following orders. But that process will take time, and there's always the risk the State's brainwashing may be irreversible.

As for the city itself, PHOENIX has been slowly shifting the rubble outside the walls and rebuilding the areas the bombs hit the hardest. There are plans to restructure the wealth system and citizens have been told they'll have a say in what jobs they do moving forward, although nothing has been reorganized as of yet. Like everything else, it will require time for the roots of change to take hold, but once they do and the ripples of that change are felt, this city should function the way it did before the State seized control thirty years ago. Instead of creating something new, we're returning the Heart to what it was always supposed to be.

To what it was before tyranny crushed it.

With the mental picture of that potential future taking shape, I ask myself the same question Quinn posed only a moment ago.

Was it worth it?

"Losing them won't be for nothing," I vow.

Quinn scoffs. "Are you sure about that? The city is in shambles. We're divided, no one trusts each other. This peace you lost everything for is so fragile the smallest mistake might break it. I know you're an eternal optimist but, surely, even *you* can see we're in over our heads."

There's an unreserved fury in his voice that fails to mask his fear. I don't blame him for feeling this way.

Those are two emotions I know all too well.

Quinn and I, along with a few others like Duke, have been providing support to the Heads through this uncertain period of change, which has meant that a lot of burdens have straddled our shoulders. Oftentimes, that weight is unbearable, but we struggle through it because we have to. Because we're *choosing* to survive, and survival means finding the strength to continue.

"It's okay to be afraid," I murmur, and Quinn bristles at my words as if I've admonished him. "What we have right now might be broken, but change doesn't happen overnight. It will take time, but we have that time now, thanks to them. What they did…"

I look over my shoulder at Wynter's tombstone, then at the one on its left. For so long, I've avoided looking at that grave— at reading the name inscribed on the stone surface. I suppose part of me hoped that if I never read it, I could pretend this wasn't real.

That I could somehow convince myself that my best friend, my *brother*, is still here.

But now, as I finally face Ezra's grave, I don't feel the pain or sorrow I expect. Only comfort in knowing that, at the end, they were together…as they were meant to be.

My thoughts drift back to that day, and I relive the apprehension of staggering forward through the settling dust and clumsily sliding down the side of the crater that formed where the plaza in front of Central Station once stood. I relive the agony of finding my two friends on the ground, hand in hand—their bodies embraced, limbs tangled, like two halves of a whole rejoined. Grief had consumed me as the realization of what I was looking at sunk in, but past the pain tearing my heart to shreds, I noticed the matching looks on their faces.

The gentle smiles that made me hope they both finally found some small measure of peace.

A fresh tear slips down my cheek, and as I wipe it away, I whisper, "We wouldn't have a future at all if it wasn't for them."

Quinn is silent for a moment, and when he next speaks, the anger and disdain are both gone from his voice. "So, what's the plan?"

The plan…

I glance up at the darkening sky—at the stars peeking through the fading light—and for the first time in what seems like forever, my loneliness stings just a tiny bit less. I feel the ghost-like presence of my friends beside me, and when I imagine their encouragement, the answer comes easily, as if I've known it all along. As if we were always meant to end here, like this.

"We take it one day at a time and do whatever we can to create a world they would be proud of."

Quinn cocks a dubious eyebrow, crossing his arms. "Just like that, huh?" he asks skeptically.

Drawing in a trembling breath, I turn my gaze to the Heart, which, although fractured, will heal with time. The last of the diminishing daylight glows around it like a halo, giving me hope.

And before it all, in the distance, I swear I see Wynter. She looks at me with that shy smile I loved from the first time I saw it and has one hand outstretched, urging me forward.

As I take a step, lured by her beckoning, I recite the words I carved into her tombstone, and through my pain, they give me courage. The courage to keep fighting for the future she gave herself to protect.

SHE SAVED US ALL

"Yup." A smile tugs at one corner of my lips. "Just like that."

THE END

DEAR READER,

Thank you for reading *Subject Zero*! This series has been a huge part of my life for many years now, and it's bittersweet finally seeing it end. I hope you enjoyed every moment as much as I did.

To keep up with the latest news about my work, sign up for my newsletter at **www.bookishden.com**.

For more information about the *Project W.A.R.* series and for an interactive version of the map found at the beginning of this book, please visit **www.maphipps.com/projectwar**.

I love to chat with readers, so feel free to get in touch! You can contact me through my websites or through any of my social media accounts. Or you can join my fan group on Facebook—just search for **The Bookish Den**. We'd love to have you!

Lastly, if you enjoyed this book, please consider leaving a review on your retailer of choice, BookBub, and/or Goodreads. Reviews help authors, like myself, gain exposure, so we can keep sharing our stories with the world.

Thanks again for reading *Subject Zero*. I hope you'll continue to enjoy my work!

ACKNOWLEDGMENTS

I don't even know where to begin with these acknowledgments. A huge thank you, first off, to the readers who have been waiting a very long time for this book. I know this series has gone through many incarnations over the years, and I can only hope the final part of Wynter's story has been worth the wait. And if you're a new-to-me reader, thank you for your support! I sincerely hope you loved this series as much as I loved writing it.

As always, a huge thank you to my brilliant cover designer, Nathalia Suellen, for another gorgeous cover. I don't know how, but every cover is more beautiful than the last!

To my amazing beta readers, Rebecca Milhoan, Lindsey Pogue, and Alisha Wood, you guys are the best! Thank you for putting up with my insanity and for just being wonderful people. I cherish you and feel so lucky to count you among my friends.

I definitely can't conclude any acknowledgments without mentioning Martina McAtee. I literally don't know where I'd be without you. Thank you for always talking me off a ledge and for just being there whenever I need you. You are my literary rock.

Finally, to my husband, Daniel, and my beautiful daughter, Aria. Thank you both for always supporting me and for being the best people I know. I'm so lucky to be sharing this crazy life with you.

ABOUT M.A. PHIPPS

M. A. PHIPPS is an American-born British author, who resides near the ocean in picturesque Cornwall with her husband, daughter, and their Jack Russell, Milo. A lover of the written word, it has always been her dream to become a published author, and it is her hope to expand into multiple genres of fiction.

Subject Zero is her third novel.

Visit her online at **www.maphipps.com** or **www.bookishden.com**.

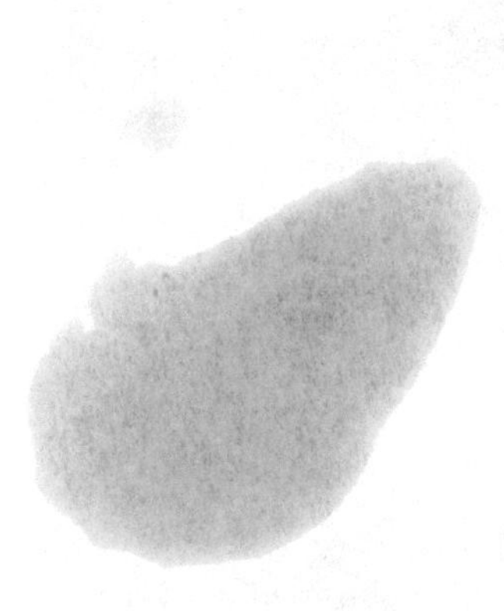

www.ingramcontent.com/pod-product-compliance
Lightning Source LLC
Chambersburg PA
CBHW060726190726
48285CB00001B/85